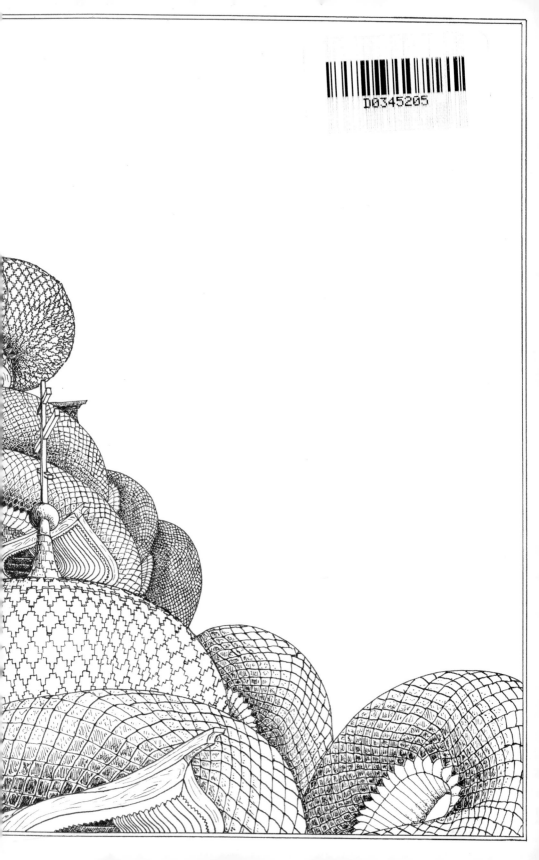

THE GREAT GLASS SEA

Also by Josh Weil

The New Valley: Novellas

THE GREAT GLASS SEA

a novel

Josh Weil

Grove Press
New York

ISBN 978-0-8021-2215-5
eISBN 978-0-8021-9286-8

Grove Press
an imprint of Grove/Atlantic, Inc.
154 West 14th Street
New York, NY 10011

Distributed by Publishers Group West

www.groveatlantic.com

14 15 16 17   10 9 8 7 6 5 4 3 2

for my brother

Always the island had been out there, so far out over so much choppy water, far beyond the last gray wave, the groaning ice when there was ice, the fog when there was fog, so distant in the middle of such a huge lake that, for their first nine years, Nizhi—that church made of those tens of thousands of wooden pegs, each one as small as a little boy's finger bones; those woodshingled domes like tops upended to spin their points on the floor of the sky; the priests' black robes snapping in the wind, their beards blowing with the clouds, their droning ceaseless as the shore-slap waves—might have been just another fairy tale that Dyadya Avya told.

And then one day when the lake ice had broken and geese had come again, two brothers, twins, stole a little boat and rowed together out towards Nizhi . . .

"Into the lake," Dima said.

"To hunt the Chudo-Yudo," Yarik said.

"Until they found it."

"And killed it."

They were ten years old—Dmitry Lvovich Zhuvov and Yaroslav Lvovich Zhuvov—and they had never been this far out in the lake, this lost, this on their own. Around them the water was wide as a second sky, darkening beneath the one above, the rowboat a moonsliver winking on the waves. In it, they sat side by side, hands buried in the pockets of their coats, leaning slightly into each other with each sway of the skiff.

"Or maybe it came up," Dima said, "and crushed the boat."

"And they drowned," Yarik said.

"Or," Dima said, "it ate them."

They grinned, the same grin at the same time, as if one's cheeks tugged the other's lips.

"Or," Yarik started.

And Dima finished, "They died."

They went quiet.

The low slap of lakewater knocking the metal hull. The small sharp calls of jaegers: black specs swirling against a frostbitten sky. But no wood blades clacking at the rowboat's side. No worn handles creaking in the locks. Hours ago, they had lost the oars.

Now they were losing last light. Their boat had drifted so far into Lake Otseva's center that they could no longer make out the shore. But there was the island. All their lives it had been somewhere beyond the edge of sight, and now they watched it: far gray glimpse growing darker, as if the roots of its unknown woods were drawing night up from the earth. It humped blackly out of the distant water, unreachable as a whale's back. And beyond it stretched the lake. And all around: the lake. And beneath them the rocking of its waves.

At their feet the tools they'd taken scraped back and forth against the skiff floor: axe, hatchet, cleaver, pick. Each one freshly sharpened. In the bow, behind their backs, a brush hook's moon-bright blade swayed against the sky. Beneath it, a cloud of netting. And, nestled there to keep from breaking, wrapped in wool blankets to warm the life in them: two dozen eggs, a gestating nestful of yolky souls. Out of the stern, the fishing rod jutted, its line lipped by the waves—tugged and slacked, tugged and slacked—going down down down into the black belly of the lake where its huge hook hung, gripping in its barb the red fist of a fresh goose heart.

Way out over the water, far beyond the island, the edge of the lake met the end of the world and there the sky was a thin red line drawn by a bead of blood. Then it was just a line. Then the line was gone, and there was just the darkness of the earth meeting the darkness of the sky and the boys rose unsteadily on the unsteady boat and crouched atop the netting, unfolding the blankets from the eggs. Dima unscrewed the tops from the canning jars. Yarik cracked the shells against their rims. One by one he slid in each yolk on its slick of albumen. One by one Dima closed the tops again. When they had all the eggs in all the jars, they tied threads around the glass necks. Each thread they tied to an oarlock or a hole punched through the gunwale or a ring at the prow, the two brothers crawling around the boat, reaching over its edge, letting go the jars. At the ends of their strings they floated, the glass gleaming, the eggs like a lakeful of eyes.

"How many heads do you think it has?" Dima said.

It had become more night than dusk, and there was no moon, no way to see the fishing line. But they watched the rod.

"At least six," Yarik said.

"Probably twelve," Dima said.

Yarik told him, "Twenty-four."

Dima said, "I want the axe."

Reaching down, he found it, and—arms thin as the handle, shoulders straining—lifted. Beside him, in Yarik's small boy's hands, their old uncle's pistol seemed huge. They sat huddled together, cold and silent and knowing the other was scared: the line would snap tight; the boat would jerk; the weight would suck down the stern; the water would wolf their feet; the thing's two dozen heads would roar up around the boat, one set of jaws mouthing blood and metal, the other twenty-three agape, their tongues, their teeth.

"What if it doesn't come?" Dima said.

That was when the rod bent. They watched it arc, watched the arc deepen until the rod was almost doubled on itself, shaking.

3

"It's going to," Dima whispered, and Yarik said, "break," and Dima said, "come loose," and then the stern dropped so fast that for a moment there was just the strain of all the air cupped within the boat against all the water trying to suck it down, the sound of something splitting, tearing . . . and then the boat jerked back up, its stern lifting off the surface, knocking the boys forward, noses to knees, and when they looked up the rod was gone.

Stumbling to his feet, Dima stood scanning the water for a hint of the rod streaking away. Or hurtling back at them.

The boatwall boomed.

He jerked, ripped a hand off the axe, flailed for the gunwale. Behind Dima: his brother laughing. Even in the dark, he could see the panic on Yarik's face, the unnerved giddiness in his eyes as he banged the metal barrel on the boat-side again.

"*Trusishka*," Yarik called him. He tried to make clucking noises as he bobbed his head, but he was laughing too hard; only sputtering came out.

The laughter passed from Yarik to Dima as these things always passed, as if the placentas that had once fed them were still conjoined, and Dima climbed onto the rowboat seat, shakily stood, threw back his face, and crowed a laughter-rippled rooster's call: *"Kukareku!"*

Yarik climbed beside him, crowed out his own: *"Kukareku!"*

On the thin metal bench, they stood side by side, beating their chests, calling into the night.

From the night, a call came back to them: some rooster of Nizhi crowing its reply. Such a long sound! So drawn out and furious! They counted it—*raz, dva, tri* . . . *fifteen, sixteen, seventeen*—longer even than Dyadya Avya's old crower, longer than they could push their own breath when they emptied their lungs in a wild burst of crowing back. How the rooster bellowed his challenge again at them! How they threw their crowing, boys and bird, across the black surface of the lake!

Until their crows turned to shouts, their shouts back to laughter, the laughter to breathing, the breathing quieting. They stood there,

4

rocking. Above them, the stars filled the sky like sand filling a bucket of water until it seemed wholly comprised of grains of light. Below, Otseva's surface filled with their reflection. All around the boat, the floating jars gleamed: a drifting constellation, waterborne.

"What if it comes back?" Yarik said.

And they passed between them the knowledge that that was why they had come out. For it to come back. So they could kill it. They stood thinking of their father, and how he must have tried, and they passed between them the truth that he had failed, and that they would fail, too, and they wondered again, silently, the thoughts they had wondered aloud in the night in their beds at Dyadya Avya's—where in them lived their souls? And had they grown side by side, same to same, in their mother's womb as well? And if one was swallowed up, or died, or simply left, would the other go, too?—and then they climbed down off the seat and went around the boat again, Dima with his axe, Yarik with the cleaver, cutting all the strings.

One by one, the jars floated away. The gleams separated from each other. The darkness between the boys and the boat widened and widened and then swallowed any sign of the jars at all.

"Out to see Nizhi," Dima tried. And after a moment: "Into the lake." And then: "Where they sank, and the water swallowed them up, and they drowned." Dima grinned, waited to feel his brother grin.

But his brother was clambering for one side of the boat, and Dima was scrambling to the other to keep from tipping, and into the darkness that somewhere hid the island Yarik was shouting, "Help! Help!"

Dima reached for him and drew him down again, beside him on the bench, whispered it would be OK, they were together. On the island, Yarik's shouting had stirred some dog of Nizhi. It barked, so far out its sound was quiet as a creaking in the dark, and the sky drifted above the drifting boat, and the cold came on, slow and steady, as if the creaking was its footsteps creeping across the night towards the boys, and they leaned into each other, shivering.

When Dima climbed off the bench, Yarik followed. They slid together along the bottom of the boat until they lay stretched out, boots to bow, out of the wind, side by side, rocking. In the sky, the stars flickered, flickered, as if each distant dog bark caused the night to blink.

In unison, the brothers unzipped their jackets. They slipped their arms out of the sleeves. They paired each strip of zipper with its mate on the other's jacket, worked at the pulls along the teeth until they were zipped in, facing each other, their jackets become one jacket that encased them both. Inside, they slid their fingers into each other's pits. Against his hands, Dima could feel his brother's heartbeat. Or was it his brother's hands beating beneath Dima's arms? Or was it his own heart pulsing? The wind rushed by above.

He might not have woken if it wasn't for Yarik's struggling. Over them, the searchlight washed across the boat, sparked off the empty oarlocks, was gone again.

Yarik tore the zipper open, shoved loose, sat up. Dima stayed lying where he was. He watched the light find his brother.

"Look!" Yarik called down at him.

Instead he shut his eyes.

"Allo!" Yarik shouted. "Allo!"

Dima listened to the night swallow the shout, to the water shushing beneath Yarik's banging scramble for the bow, his brother's frantic *passed by, unseen, missed*—until the gunshot silenced everything. Its blast filled the boat fast as if the bottom had been blown out, water rushing around Dima's ears. Through it, he heard another boom, another. Eyes squeezed tight, he counted the shots—*four, five, six*— waiting for the seventh that would mean the gun was empty. It never came. Instead, there was his brother saying his name, asking him to sit up, telling him to look.

But when Dima rose, he kept his eyes shut. He would have stayed in the hull if, without his brother, it hadn't been so cold. He climbed by feel onto the bench, leaned against Yarik. When the light hit his brother's face, Dima opened his eyes. Bright as a full moon, the searchlight came, sweeping the lake, them, the lake. Until it held, blasting. Dima shut his eyes again. Through the water, he could feel the ship coming, the shuddering of its engine, the small boat beginning to shake.

The Lit Side of the Earth

Sometimes, climbing up the steps of the autobus on his way to work, Dima would pass Yarik climbing down and feel, for a moment, his brother's palm on the back of his neck, still warm from Yarik's coat pocket. Or punching in at the entrance to the Oranzheria he would spot his brother in the crowd shuffling out: Yarik would nod to him, too tired to speak; he would nod back. Sometimes, twelve hours later, Dima would hear his brother, returned for his next shift, calling to him: *Good morning, little brother!* And he would call back: *Good night, big brother!* Born a mere eight minutes apart, it was how they'd called each other since they were kids, and the whole tram ride home he would play it over and over in his head—*good morning,* bratishka; *good night,* bratan; *good morning,* bratishka; *good night . . .* —trying to keep the voice just right, to hold the image of Yarik's eyes.

And, though weekends were an idea discarded long ago, sometimes on Unity Day, or Defender of the Fatherland Day, or any of the half-handful that he got off, Dmitry Lvovich Zhuvov would go to his brother's home. He would take a tram across town, shortcut through the playground, skirt the small lake puddled at the building's entrance, climb the concrete steps inside the dimlit stairwell, knock on the apartment door, and step into his brother's hug and kiss the cheek of his brother's wife and eat with the children some sweet thing she had made, and they would gather—his little nephew leaping up and down on the couch, his infant niece nursing at his sister-in-law's breast—while the two brothers, lying hidden behind the coffee table, raised hands: a mitten bear, a glove of a rooster, simple socks making a pair of horses to pull the sleighs in the tales the brothers told. Then Dima would turn his cheek on the rug and, watching so close he could feel the breath behind his brother's whinny or roar, try to catch a glimpse of Yarik as he used to be.

Sometimes Dima would almost feel that Yarik still was as he'd once been. Helping hang an icon for his brother's wife, Dima would straddle Yarik's shoulders, whoop and flail as his brother, roaring, tried to stand beneath the weight, bellowing until they both collapsed into a laughing heap. Clearing away the dead lilacs that lined Yarik's street, they'd taken turns with the bow saw, one brother urging the other on with hollered bursts of folk songs, each banging out the beat with the flat of his hands on the sawer's back. It was the way they'd always worked together, and, later, pouring a drink, Dima would stare across the table—Yarik's hands full with his daughter's diapers, ears with his son's babble, face flush from shouting over it to his wife—and tell himself, *I am seeing him, here, right now,* and know it wasn't true. Always, then, Dima would think of the lake and the rowboat and the blanket of stars. His eyes would ache. His lips would shiver. He would cover them with his fist.

They had the same big fists, were the same high height, had grown the same thick bones. Heads round as ball-peen hammers, hair black as raven wings, eyes like the gray of that bird's breast feathers stirred with the blue of its sky. Their father used to call them his two tsareviches, claim they had flown to him as crows, morphed into infants before his eyes, would one day turn back into birds and fly away again. Instead, with each year, they only turned a little more into themselves: Yarik's shoulders a little wider, his forehead a little higher, the skin around his eyes a little more cragged; Dima's eyes seemed to grow more blue, his face to lengthen, a mole marking his cheek. Still, until a couple years ago, strangers had struggled to tell them apart. Now it was easy: one was brown as their farmer uncle after a summer in the fields, the other pale as his wraith-white skin in winter.

The first year Dima worked at the Oranzheria, it had scared him—watching his face turn wan and wrinkled—each shift beneath the mirrors' thin light leaching his color a little more until he was as pallid as any other night worker high on the surface of that great glass sea. Vast hectares of panels stretching across an endless scaffolding of steel, it spread northward from the lakeshore, creeping over the land like a glacier in reverse: the largest greenhouse in the world. On the news they talked of its unceasing expansion, of the whole country's future in ever brighter bloom, of a Russia risen again on the wings of her space mirrors.

Kosmicheskie zerkala. An idea born during Brezhnev (*Oh for a satellite to reflect the sun into our Siberian night! Oh to snatch day from the earth's bright side, expel our long darkness from this northcold land!*) and designed under Andropov (*These giant dragonflies! Their steely abdomens the size of submarines! Their solar module wings!*), built in Gorbachev's last years, scrapped by Ivashko, reborn with the oligarchs and launched in the last decade of the past century, rocketed through the exosphere on the arching backs of freshly molted entrepreneurs. It was a man from Moscow who built the first (the people of the city shook their heads, took it for just what this new breed of billionaire did when it got drunk), and it was his corporation that quieted their laughter to whispers (*he was going to launch it for science, for Russia, for Petroplavilsk, for free*), and finally to awestruck silence the day the Space Regatta Consortium put the first one up: belly to belly with the world, it slid the planetary curve, in its wake a gleaming disk of Kevlar, big as Red Square, reflecting the sunlight down. But it was the Ministry of Energy that paid for the Consortium to send up another, and another, and the next, and the one after that.

9

Soon there were five floating in the night sky above Petroplavilsk. Petrovskaya Plavilnya, Peter's Foundry. Once the city had clanged and glowed with the workyards of the tsars—monstrous anchors forged for Baltic men-of-war, Great Catherine's cannons rolled out to disembody Turks—but for many years it had manufactured little but melancholia. A place of concrete buildings, busted piers, skeletons of trees beneath streetcar wires scratched into sky, graveyards gray with snow, the absurdity of crocuses, of even the color purple, of old people standing in their underwear on the shore of the still-frozen lake beneath the cries of gulls, the birds' solitary drifting and sudden frenzied flocking like the days of the work-hungry men, their job-starved wives.

That was how it was after perestroika. That was how it was until the mirrors came. Until the oligarch proposed to make an experiment of the city, the first place on earth illumined by the sun for every hour of every day of all the seasons of the year. He would take the most depressed, torpid town in Russia and grow its productivity as if beneath a heat lamp, sprout a work rate unparalleled in the world; it would be a hothouse of output, a field of ceaseless yield. No long months of winter brooding, darkness drawn over Petroplavilsk like goose down. No twilight melancholy, no dreaminess of dusk. No midnight urge to lie on dewy grass between the trolley lines inhaling summer's scent. No evening-ushered crime spike. No streetlamps. No car headlights. No night.

The first *zerkalo kosmosa* lit only the center of the city. It painted gleam on the bronze pates of scowling heroes, flared pilfered sunlight off the memorial cannons and stacks of iron shot. The people of Petroplavilsk gathered at the light's circumference, their backs bathed in blackness, their faces aglow. Some crept to the edge, their hands held as if to dip their fingers in the light, faint shadows blooming beneath their bodies, their edges sharpening to noonlike, until they found themselves bathed whole in the caromed sun. In those first nights of that first mirror the city's heart thumped to the sounds of celebrations. Parents brought their children. Sons carried in their dying mothers. No one slept. They would lie in bed looking through their windows at the glow, or shut their curtains and lie there thinking of it.

The second zerkalo lit the rest of the city. The third, the sprawl of concrete apartments to the west. The fourth, the eastern same. The fifth one lit the dockyards and a swath of the sea-sized lake.

Fishing boats trawled through daylight and mirror-light, the droning of their engines incessant as the waves, their crews pulling twelve-hour shifts, clambering aboard in midday brightness, alighting onto docks in a midnight like a low-watt noon. Along the Kosha River the old ironworks roared through the semblance of sunset, the factories on the Solovinka thudding into sunrise, their rumble unrelieved by the passage of days, weeks, months. Sleep was freed from nature's hours. Breakfast was what happened before work. Stores never closed. On once-empty shelves new goods appeared: prewashed greens, low-fat avocados. On the way home from work women bought machines for cleansing tableware, shaving tools that ran off batteries; their husbands picked up suppers cooked by strangers' hands.

In the last hour of nature's light, as the planet rolled away from the sun, the zerkala rose off the eastern horizon, their refracted glow red as the sky in the west. People called it *voskhod zerkala*. Mirror rise. From then to dawn the satellites drifted overhead, a sliding swatch of stars, their mirrors ever angling to cant the sun's light down on the same circle of earth. And as the first zerkala followed their path over the world's western edge, the bank of mirrors behind them took up the task, and then the zerkala behind them, and behind them, all through the hours that once were night.

No longer. Dusk to dawn the city was eerie with a luminescence like a storm-smothered day with shadows sharp as noon. The planners had hoped a people used to the north's white nights might adapt with ease, that it would feel little different from summer's solstice: the long wait for dusk, the anxiousness that built by the hour until at last the sliver of night would drop and puncture it, pressure whooshing out like the long day's sigh. Except beneath the zerkala there was no puncture, no release. Not even summer's few hours of dark. And in the fall, the cold days drew behind them no blanket of night. Winter never grew its black coat. And what was there for spring to shed? From what would it wake?

Outside the spot of erased night, small villages slept on in their enduring dark. Beyond them lay the woods. Vast lands of larch and fir, aspens and birch. All fall, while their canopies turned the colors of the sunsets, while night yawned wide above their shedding leaves, while branch tips hardened against the coming cold, each tree beyond the zerkala's reach must have wondered at the way, inside that circle of light, the others stayed green. Their leaves still on their branches. Where, when winter hit, they rotted.

In spring, the stretching days woke those who'd slumbered, dormant, beneath nature's blanketing dark, to an eerie sight: beneath the zerkala light all their brethren stood dead or dying, stuck in winter-broken bodies, not a single bud. Even the evergreens had succumbed: the tops all winterburned, the bottoms sprouting suckers, their shapes forever changed.

In villages, gardens ground to a halt, field crops grew confused. Barley forgot to form seed heads. Pea shoots paused preflowering. Where tubers had been sown the soil waited. A few farmers tried to hang on, to pasture milk cows on clover that didn't bloom, to grow the few things that seemed able to withstand the constant light: plots of cucumbers and onions, a few patches of strawberries. While all throughout the city the people watched their old trees swapped for ones grown in the Consortium's great greenhouse. Park gardeners planted beds with Consortium-cultivated flowers. Seeds developed in the laboratories of the oligarch went on sale.

Though even the researchers who had found the light-sensing gene, who'd flicked off the molecular switch, couldn't ease the panic that coursed through the mice, tree frogs, bats. Voles were hunted as if with spotlights. Housecats grew fat on their kills. New prey presented itself to dogs. Out beside the soon-doomed woods fields became feasting grounds for foxes, falcons, their hunting an unimpeded bliss.

But why were the snowy owls booming their mating calls, displaying their wings, when their spring fledglings were barely out of their nests? Why, so long after spring had gone, were the warblers and wagtails stirred to sing so often and so loud? The geese watched the time for flying south come near, still waiting for flight feathers to grow. Deer didn't mate. Bears browsed lazily as in midsummer, oblivious to their approaching sleep. And when the cold arrived, did they hear their stomachs groan? Did a shiver run up the flanks of the wolves beneath their summer fur? First snows came, and how strange to see the silhouettes of arctic foxes that had forgotten to turn white, to watch them try to creep upon hares equally unable to hide. And how frenzied the white world seemed then, teeming with ermines and polecats and minks, the panic of their dark shapes.

All that was before the rumors of a dozen more mirrors going up, the confirmation on the news, the oligarch's oaths to turn the tsar's foundry into the country's garden, Petroplavilsk into Rossiyasad, before the Oranzheria. The mammoth solarium collared the city, a necklace of unceasing gleam. From underneath, it was a second sky of glass. Over fields sewn year-round with engineered seeds, the sunlight streamed down, yanked up sprouts at twice the speed: rapeseed, sunflowers, barley, rye. In air so humid it fogged their throats, workers picked enormous soy pods, cucumbers engorged with warmth and light, harvested ceaselessly, whether the rest of the land lay in bloom or under snow.

By the time the rumored new mirrors were seen one night—a constellation of seventeen fresh stars rising in the sky beside the five expected ones—the Oranzheria was big as the lake, its clear walls encasing the city, its vast roof flat and wide as Otseva's surface of winter ice. And it was growing. Through mirror-light and sunlight, in unceasing shifts, twelve hours at a time, twelve thousand laborers swarmed beneath it, over it, at its fringes, every day. A quarter of all the workforce of the city. The first time new hires rode the buses out they crowded at the windows, eyes widening, cheekbones knocking glass. Four stories up, the edge of the Oranzheria cut across the old sky like a second horizon. When the shift switch aligned with sunset, the strip of glass went roseatted, as if dusk had cracked open to show the nearing workers a sliver of some more colorful world. As they passed

13

beneath, it reddened above them, deepened . . . and then began to brighten again as the rising mirrors' light replaced the last of the sun's.

In those first years atop the Oranzheria, back when Dima and Yarik still worked beside each other on the same shift, the same crew, there was something about being so high up, so close to the sky, that spurred the brothers' dreams. Laying lines of adhesive along strips of steel where the glass panes would be laid down, bent over their silicone guns, they eased the ache in their necks with talk of their uncle's old chicken coop, of how many hens it would hold, how many Russian geese, American turkeys, laughed so hard at their own attempts at warbling that their gasket lines wriggled in parallel gaffes. One brother on each end of a half-culvert, they debated the merits of wheat and barley, rye and flax, wound up lost in memories of crickets leaping in the communal fields, openmouthed boys chasing the bugs as if to catch them on their tongues. Fitting the trough into the long line of a rain canal, they talked of how they would one day do it again, of how this time the whole harvest would be theirs, the fields theirs, the farm.

The last time they'd worked together was more than six months ago. And that day they had not even been working, not when the drumming began, heavy as sudden rain, on the top of Dima's hard hat. Yarik stopped, stared. Watching him, Dima started to rise from his crouch. The drumming ceased. In its place: the weight of a hand pressed down.

"Why get up?" Dima stayed squatted beneath the foreman's sarcasm. "I wouldn't want to disturb such an engrossing conversation." The fingers drummed again. "Maybe, you want me to bring you some tea?"

Turning his head beneath the patter, Dima looked past the foreman's legs, across the high glass plain, to the yawning hole a ladder hatch had sprung. It huffed with the heat of the world below, thick and shaking as jet engine breath. And with it, climbing up out of the hatch: a man in a silvery suit. Others were already up, clustered there, four pairs of sunglasses watching Dima back.

The only one not wearing shades was the man coming out of the hatch. He rose into the stillness of the standing others, only their suits moving in the wind, his own beginning to whiffle as he made the surface in a movement fluid as the rippling of his sleeves, no pause even as he stepped out of the hatch onto the glass, eyes sweeping the scene, stride already taking him through the group, towards the foreman, the brothers.

Then he was there, between them, looking down at the glass around his boots. They were boots dyed the blue of Lake Otseva on a deep-skied day, made of squamous skin that might have been peeled off some creature of that inland sea, toes like two serpents' heads, heels heavy as hooves. The man's slacks rippled, his jacket snapped. From his neck, two strings hung, weighted by metal nibs, their leather the blue of his boots, the same color—Dima squinted up—that seemed to tinge his eyes. Except, as Dima looked at them, they grew more gray. Around them, the man's long hair was swept straight back, nearly to his shoulders, bleached blond as his mustache, his golden goatee. His face was tanned, soft, something about the combination so unnatural it made Dima want to look away. But the eyes that he had thought were gray, he saw now—stranger still—had begun to shimmer with a hint of gold.

The man's gaze flicked back to the glass below his boots, between the brothers. There the surface was streaked with yellow scrawl. It was bad enough that they were pausing more and more in the movements they were paid to make, bad enough their chatter had caught the ears and slowed the actions of the workers nearby, but to have been bent over their grease pencils, lost in a moment of no work at all, in dreaming up the layout of the milking parlor they'd reconstruct from their uncle's abandoned barn, right at the moment when the man had come through the hatch, the man who paid the men who paid the men who paid their foreman, who paid them, the man who said to them now, "What's this?"

On Dima's hard hat, the foreman's fingers beat their tattoo.

Yarik was already rising from his crouch, standing up into the spill of his own apology, when the man gave him a look that cut him quiet.

15

"Are you some cowboy?" the man said. Silence. He turned to them both. "A couple Cossacks?"

"They're just—"

"No." The man shot the foreman a smile that shut him up. "I'll guess." He contemplated the grease-pencil scribblings. "A blueprint?" He raised his eyebrows, scanned their faces. "For new sector expansion? A brainstorm of improvements to our equipment?" With a silver-tipped toe he poked at Dima's drawing of herringbone stalls. "These are the snow dispersal chutes?" Traced the lines Dima had drawn to show how cows could be arranged. "These are slides to more efficiently direct the shovel-loads? To prevent the spillage onto the crops?" His boot sole hovered over the milking parlor. He planted it, traced with his other toe the lines Yarik had drawn—arrows showing better access to the udders in a retrofitted tie-stall barn—the metal tip scraping against the glass, the gesture twisting the man into a strangely dainty pose. "Here," he insisted, "you're trying to solve our problems with ventilation when ice builds up." He made a little circle with his toe. The foreman looked away, as if his boss had donned a tutu. Stepping from holding corral to chutes with quiet exclamations of surprise and pleasure—"I see. Very clever. Top-notch work."—he seemed a small child making his way through a hopscotch game.

Until he stopped. Crouching between the brothers, he reached out, placed a hand over the foreman's drumming fingers. The patter quit.

Dima could feel the weight of both men's hands, then the lightening as the foreman's withdrew, then the other's redoubled, pressing down again. That close, he could see the soft red corners of the man's eyes, the gleam in them. "Look at all these fuckers." The man spoke low, as if just for Dima's ears, his gaze roving the other laborers who had shifted their work close to better hear, the men in suits stepping nearer to see, the foreman trying to look like he wasn't straining to listen, too. "Prairie dogging fuckers," the man said. He threw a grin to each of the brothers, two quick tosses made to force a catch. Yarik was still standing, but he crouched down as if to scoop it up, and the three were level, low, close.

16

"Fucking fish-fooders," the man said, and laughed. "Come on, you cowboys. Tell me. Am I right? About the snow chute? The ventilation? You were recontextualizing the whole Oranzheria, yes? Inventors," the man declared. "Our own Korolev! Our own Sikorsky!"

Dima was already nodding, about to tell the man what he wanted to hear, when Yarik said, instead, "We weren't inventing anything."

"OK," the man said.

"We were only thinking."

"About?"

"Tourism."

The man beamed. "Loop me in, cowboy," he said. "Give me the helicopter view."

Dima could not imagine how his brother did it: looked straight into those eyes and laid out a lie as intricate as any of Dyadya Avya's tales. Some sunsets, Yarik said, he and Dima were overcome by the way the wide glass surface broke lightning into a thousand reflections crackling across the panes; how, staring down, you could fit yourself into a V of geese flying above; when mist rolled over the Oranzheria it was as if the cloudbanks they had dreamed of walking on as children were suddenly made real.

"All this," Yarik said, "and nobody but us to see it. And we see it all for free. But"—he paused—"if there were viewing platforms . . ." Pointing to the stalls as if they were windows through which visitors would watch the magic shows of hail, he said, "Here's the route they could take. Here, a tram that would ride ten meters up along the underside of the glass." And by the time he was laying out a vision for buses to bring out the people of Petroplavilsk, the man had stopped following the drawings. He was looking only at Yarik's face.

Watching, Dima thought he heard a humming sound. Low and quiet. There, then gone. Only when he saw his brother's eyes flick to the man, did he realize where the noise was coming from. Yarik stopped talking. The man stopped the sound. Yarik began again. The sound, again: louder, heavier. The man opened his mouth, let the noise expand into a low, wavering, mournful vowel, round and long and nearly sung.

The foreman stepped back. The suits who had started forward stopped. Their boss stayed crouched, looking back and forth between the brothers, grinning. Nobody moved, nobody spoke. Yarik cleared his throat, looked at the scribbles on the glass, once more began to talk of the money that could be made. And it was only then, when the blue-booted man sat back on his haunches, lifted his face to the sky, and let out the groaning moan like something boiled in his belly, a bellow fit for an animal twice his size, that Dima realized what it was: a moo. A cow's moo. The man was mooing.

The next day, the brothers arrived at work to find their foreman come to send one of them home. Not fired, the man said, just rescheduled. Separated. Which one would switch from the natural-lit shift to the mirror-lit, who would get on the bus and return in a dozen hours just as the other was getting done, he left to them to decide. Dima stood there, silent. So Yarik chose the daytime (*If I'm only home when the kids are up I'll never screw my wife*) and the new crew (*Dima, who'll keep an eye on Mama during the day?*) assigned to ground-level jobs. They were to work on different planes—Dima high up laying the glass, Yarik below in the stanchion crew—at opposite times. And life would split in two: the time of them together, the time of them apart.

All their years till then, work had been just another way the world had paired them. As children, they'd milked the collective's cows in tandem, four small hands squeezing four synchronous streams. As teens, they spent each weekend of every Potato Month, bused out to the fields with all the other schoolkids, not caring how many hours they raked tubers from the finger-cracking dust so long as they were doing it together. Which was why, when all their former classmates scrambled after occupation placements that promised promotion, privilege, the brothers simply chose the first slot they could fill side by side: the floor of a factory where they passed their days shouting to each other above the din, pouring molten metal into casts of tractor doors, fitting windows into cabs, each pane held between them like a glimpse of the thing that had invisibly bound them since birth.

Now, watching his brother turn away to find his new crew, Dima could feel it crack. Right then—with his new foreman, then his foreman's manager, then whoever he hoped might listen—he began to try to get his shift aligned again with Yarik's. But there was a manager for every manager, each tied to the orders of another above, and above seemed set against him for reasons he could not glean, until it felt as if he'd fallen back two decades into the old state system and, six weeks of bureaucracy later, he did what anyone in The Past Life would have done.

Gennady Shopsin, in the apartment below, was an assistant to the manager of the office of scheduling for the sixty-first sector of the North-North-East Branch, but ever since he'd heard a rumor of promotion he'd been intent on securing an apartment adjoining his to renovate into a place more suitable for the associate manager that he'd soon be. Standing in the hallway last Unity Day, Dima and he had made an agreement: the day his mother died Dima would sell the assistant manager their home—a two-bedroom flat the state's collapse had left her, assigned long ago to their long-gone family of four, now down to her and him—so long as, every day until then, Gennady would schedule Dima for whatever overtime could be had, even if it meant mirror-light and natural-light, eighteen hours on the glass, so long as it would let his shift overlap a little with his brother's.

For over half a year now, that had been the best that he'd been able to do: Yarik below the glass, himself above. If they were in the same sector they might manage to take their quarter-hour rest together. Lying on a cool patch of sod not yet ripped up, hard hats over their faces, voices muffled, they'd fill each other in on the last month of their lives. Yarik would ask after their mother. Dima, after his niece and nephew. But mostly they talked about what their lives had become, what had become of the world they lived in—the Oranzheria and the zerkala and work—about the time they would cut loose from it all, strike out together, live someday on the farm.

Long ago, for one near-orphaned year—their father drowned, their mother lost to grief—they had. Slept nights alongside nesting hens in straw against one wall of the one room of their uncle Avya's peasant

19

house, woke mornings to the scent of fresh-laid eggs, the crackle of kindling catching, Dyadya Avya huffing the stove into heat, smiling at them through the smoke. All around the *izba* where Avery Leonidovich Zhuvov had lived there had stretched the *kolkhoz's* vast collective versts, but, to them, that year that they turned ten, that their uncle took them into his care, the real farm had been the half-hectare the state allowed their *dyadya* to harvest as his own. He'd hoed up every inch of soil around the livestock lean-to, meager plots squeezed between the privy and the chicken coop. All day, while their uncle worked the kolkhoz's wide fields, his nephews labored in his: what they grew in that small space, they knew, was all there'd be to eat. Most evenings they made it themselves—a bowl of boiled potatoes, soupy with grease; a torn chunk of hard bread dipped in milk to make it chewable—brought it out to the place where their father's body lay. He was buried in the farthest corner of the plot their uncle claimed, far from the well, no fence, just heavy field rocks piled over his grave to keep the hog from digging him up. They would climb the mound, sit on a stone, and, crunching into an onion or cracking a chicken bone, watch the gloaming deepen over the fields, feel the sweat dry on their skin, wait for their uncle to come home. And at night they curled together in their beds of hay, hens warning them from nests, Avya's old wolfhound, Ivan, stretched out beside him on the floor next to the stove, a bottle balanced on their dyadya's belly, his voice like a snoring in his thick throat as—*once upon a time*—he would begin another of his tales.

And a decade after he had died, buried beneath his own pile of rocks beside his own brother, a dozen years gone by since the farm where their uncle and father lay was sold, on the rare breaks—one a month, at most two—when Yarik and Dima might still manage to take their tea together, they would lie side by side upon the churned dirt beneath that glass sky, and talk again of what they'd promised long ago. "Soon," Dima would say into the steam of his tea; or, "In six months . . . ," the heat wetting his face; or, on one spring afternoon, "By June we'll bring the money out there."

It was always summer beneath the glass, but at the unfinished edge, where bare girders reached towards a forest in retreat, the April air still augured snow.

Yarik pressed his warm cup to his chin, rolled the Styrofoam against his stubble. "Maybe, bratishka."

"By June," Dima said, "I'll have my half."

Over the rim, Yarik raised his eyebrows.

"We'll bring it all out to the farm, go into Stepan Fyodorovich's house, empty our rucksacks all over his table."

"The old *kulak* will have a heart attack."

"Then we'll take all the money and put it back in our rucksacks."

Yarik grinned. "And bury the body in the woods."

Dima raised his cup. "To heart attacks."

They tapped Styrofoam rims. Yarik squeezed his to make it squeak.

But Dima was already listening to a woods whispering at the edge of a hayfield, the *shrushing* of footsteps that took him farther in, the wind in the canopy deep in that forest where white birch trunks dropped down like beams of sunlight around the place where he and his brother had long ago buried themselves beneath the leaves. "Baba Yaga's," he said, his look lost in the tea. "You think it's still there?"

Once it might have been a hunting cottage, long collapsed, or perhaps an eremitic chapel reverberating with the mumbles of some wild-eyed recluse. When they first found it there seemed a small steeple engulfed by the caved-in roof, a bulbous dome subsided into rot, a door decayed as if to invite them in. And in they burrowed, hauling at rocks, digging a tunnel, two small boys with bruised arms and faces blackened but inside a hideaway opening up, just big enough for them. Through it tree trunks grew, their bark rough as rooster legs, their roots spread out like talons. Baba Yaga's, they'd called it, lying in the soil-scented dark, trying to remember that part of Pushkin's epic tale, the windowless witch hut perched atop hen's feet. Whispering into the blackness inside, they added their own scenes that wrote out Ruslan and Lyudmila, starred themsevles instead, told them to each other beneath a forest floor abloom with mushrooms. Hundreds of

21

them grew on the mound above—purple wood blewits and golden chanterelles, ox tongues stiff and red, milk-caps and pheasants backs and puff balls huge and white—spread bright as a quilt beneath the trees. Each time the boys left they picked it apart, filled their baskets. And each time they returned to it regrown.

"You think," Dima said now, his words made visible in the steam, "we could still find it?"

Beneath the sound of hammering from above, his brother breathed out a sudden, small laugh. "My God," Yarik said, as if he hadn't thought of it in years. "All those mushrooms!"

"Hundreds!" Dima said.

"Thousands!"

"We could be picking them right now."

Reaching over—"And what?"—Yarik plucked the top of Dima's ear. "Slave in the kitchen? Instead of taking it easy like this?"

Dima ducked his head away, his face brightened, as if his brother's fingers had flicked a switch. "Your *kids* would be slaving in the kitchen," he said. "We'd be telling them stories."

"The last time I got home early enough to tell Timosha a bedtime story . . ." Yarik's smile slipped. "I can't even remember."

"Soon," Dima told him, "we'll tell them stories every night."

"In the summer we'll be too beat."

"But in the winter," Dima said, "after the harvest, there'll be nothing to do but sit by the stove."

"And starve," Yarik said.

"And eat soup."

"Without meat."

"With mushrooms," Dima said.

"I *do* love mushroom soup."

"We'll have it all summer."

"And in the fall?"

"In the fall, Mama will bake them in sour cream."

"And in the winter?"

"We'll have the ones she pickles."

"And in the spring?"

"By the spring I'll kill you if you say another word about mushrooms."

"By the spring," Yarik said, "we won't be speaking to each other."

"We won't *need* to." Dima took another sip of his tea. "We'll just wake up, together, without trying, like we used to. The smell of the chickens, the stove. I'll make the fire. You'll take Polina from her crib. Timofei will crawl into the straw, get us eggs. And we'll eat them, all of us around Dyadya Avya's old table, before we go out to the field. That's how it'll be in spring."

Yarik had tipped his cup and was staring up into the empty bottom. The Styrofoam filtered the light and softened it on his face, and about his mouth there was the hint of a distant happiness Dima knew meant he was thinking of something else.

"These days," Yarik said, "I usually wake up to Zina snoring." His eyes slid to Dima. "You know, I go to sleep with my nose against the back of her head? I love the smell of her hair. Ever since our first time, you know what she's smelled like to me? Crushed weeds. I know, I know, but I love it." The hint was gone; the happiness was there. "When we . . ." Yarik's smile widened. "I like to bury my face in her armpits. Like this," he said, and flopping over, launched himself against Dima's side, pushing at Dima's clenched arm with the top of his head, and Dima, spilling his tea, clamping his arm tight to his side, squirmed away until they were both sprawled out, Yarik stretched on his belly, Dima half-collapsed onto his back, their laughter for a moment swallowing all the din of the Oranzheria. Amid sounds of men and machines that swept back over Dima's quieting, he propped himself up on his elbows, watched Yarik still chuckling into the dirt. He could still feel the tug at his ear, the sweaty head nuzzling his chest, the thing in him only his brother could brighten still filling his face with its glow.

Wiping his hands on his pants, he found his overturned cup, sat chewing the edge, smiling through the sound of his teeth on the Styrofoam, until they had both gone quiet again. Always, with five minutes left, they would stop talking and silently exchange their hard hats, each brother using the other's to shade his face for a few stolen moments of sleep.

That day Dima said, "You know what your hair smells like? Birch. Like a birch switch run under the hot water in the baths."

Yarik lay with his face turned down to the soil. And when he turned to look up, his neck bent at a crazy angle, he was grinning again. "You know, bratishka," he said, "we really need to find you a wife."

Once, before the end of the world they'd grown up in, before the beginning of the one growing around them now, in The Past Life, on summer evenings after work, they had gone down to the lake together every day. There, amid the shore-swarm crowds, they'd launched each other from their shoulders. Whoops and laughter and one brother stirring beneath the curved soles of the other's feet, three quick taps on Dima's ankles, the same returned on Yarik's head, the rush of water dropping away, of them rising together out of the lake.

In winter, they would join the others in a line a hundred wide, everyone side by side on skates, snow shovels in their hands, and, chanting *raz! dva! tri!*, in one cheering communal rush plow clear a smooth square of ice. All those whooping voices! All that thunderous scraping! Winter birds blasted up into the sky: a swirl of caws and wingflutter above the crowd of skaters as each began their swooping glides below. Someone always brought a boom box. Big brassy marches, orchestral strings, the wail of fiddles and the balalaika's trill and a hundred voices singing *Ya shagayu, shagayu*—I am walking, walking—in a hundred synchronized puffs of breath.

Every evening, those same clouds filled the air around the statue of Peter the Great where poets, high on the plinth, clinging to the tsar's bronze side, sang out their verse. Every weekend, the bread factory filled with even warmer steam, each apartment complex coming together to bake in the industrial ovens. Once a month each building's kooperativ gathered to stitch rips and darn holes on the machines of a textile plant. And every time the Cultural-Educational Organization arranged a reading on the National Theater stage—actors reciting

Akhmadulina, Tvardovsky, reading stories by Krylov and Gogol—the grand auditorium rang with the rhythmic booms of an entire city's hands: *clap! clap! clap!*

Free Time, economists had called it, and once had recognized its role in people's lives (*new and substantial developments in self-education,* the director of the Institut Ekonomiki I Organizatsii Promyshlennogo Proizvodstva had written, *improvements in levels of culture*); once, it had even been the goal: *It is intended,* he had proclaimed, *based on the steady increase of labor productivity and reduction in labor time, to make a transition to an even shorter workweek. . . .* Thirty-five hours, economists predicted. Thirty, they dared to dream. But no one, not even the director of the Institute Ekonomiki, foretold the zero-hour workweek that came.

Gorbachev, glasnost, perestroika, years of depression, devaluation, the decommissioning of the tractor factory, degeneration of Petro-plavilsk, a time of worry and hunger, poverty and despair. For most. For Dima, those had been his favorite years. Workless, he and Yarik would wait together beside the Kosha River, at a bend in the road where traffic slowed, flapping their arms at farm trucks, jogging after tractor wagons, lying back in the coolness between cucumber crates, the river running beside them all the way out to the old kolkhoz. The kulak who had bought it up in the days of reprivitization had fired his fieldhands, let the fields go fallow, and, cutting the last of his losses, counting on a day when the worth of his land might remake his fortune again, shut down the farm. Out there, there had been nothing but the sound of the truck or tractor leaving, the thrum of crickets, sometimes their uncle's old Yurlov Crower belting out his call, the long cry turned lonesome with all the bird's brood gone. Someone had found Dyadya Avya's old milch cow half-wild in the woods. Someone slew the swine. One by one the feral chickens were gathered up out of fields themselves gone wild. Cowbane and Gypsyweed and Rattle and Yarrow: the brothers still sometimes found a hen hunkered in the scrub. The only gun they had was Dyadya Avya's old revolver, and neither could bring himself to use it, so they lured birds with rotted seed, set their uncle's rusted traps, sat along the riverbanks angling for fish, cooked them over open fires, slept beneath the open sky.

And if the day darkened, if the evening threatened rain, they went to the woods, hurried beneath wind-rattled branches, the rush of rain-drops battering leaves, until, in the twilight between white birch trees they caught a burst of color and, crouching low, on hands and knees, crawled in. By then their older eyes had recognized the remains of a bench, a broken ladle, half a metal basin filled with rocks, and they knew it was nothing more than some forgotten bathhouse farmworkers must once have used. But still, the old *banya*'s seclusion stirred their dreams, its darkness let them loose, and, lying there amid the scents of soil and each other, they would swear to one day make them real. Then they would go quiet, listening to the rain drum at the earth above, or two trees knocking at each other somewhere in the night, or sometimes the *wo-hoo, woho-uhwo-ho* of a Ural owl calling to its mate, before their breathing would fall in synch, the den filled with a sound steady as a single chest breathing peacefully in sleep.

Now, Dima could barely make out his brother beneath the glass. It had been weeks since he'd seen Yarik, and he was working overtime with a pane-laying team when he caught a glimpse of him through the steel frame just before a sheet of glass was settled in. Through the pane the scene below was blurred soft, but he knew that tall, thin shape, the way that hard hat hung forward on that long neck, how Yarik's legs bowed when he was carrying something heavy, that voice—he was sure he heard it—reedy barking, quick yelp of a laugh. Kneeling, he rapped with his knuckles. The glass hardly made a noise against his gloves. He smacked at it with the flat side of his ratchet. Across the pane from him, a worker tightening a bracket down glanced over without slowing the cranking of his elbows. The crane had laid the glass a little off its frame, and, like a man drinking water from a creek, Dima dropped his face close to the gap. "Yarik!" he shouted through it. If his brother heard him, he didn't show it. "Yarik!" The backhoe rumbled alive, its shovel crashing into the bricks. Dima slid to his belly, his face turned so the cheekbones bruised against the surface.

Down there, they were taking the top off an old farm building. "Sizing" the Consortium called it: everything that was in the Oranzheria's way smashed or sawed or toppled low enough to build the glass panes over it. Later, the razing crews would finish the job. After, the extraction crews would clear the rubble from the fields. Then the tractors would come. Here, at the edge of the advance of the glass, two wrecking machines twice the size of bulldozers rolled slowly past it all, a heavy chain—the links thick as a forearm—stretched between at five meters height. It lopped off whatever it hit—silos, chimneys, canopies of ancient trees—like a trimmer on a hedge.

Over the noise, Dima bellowed his brother's name again. And there at last: Yarik looking up. The crack between the bracket and the pane was just wide enough for Dima to fit his fingers through. He shoved them down to the knuckles, waggled them.

His brother lifted a hand in a wave, started back to work.

"Come here!" Dima shouted, his fingers beckoning.

But only the workers around his brother looked: the tops of their hats, their faces glancing up, the tops of their hats again. He watched Yarik's yellow hard hat, waiting for the moment when it must tilt back, too, waiting to glimpse once more the small blue spots of his brother's eyes.

The Golden Phoenix

"You have to stop doing that," Yarik said.

They were playing *Zmei*, the five of them stretched out in a line held hand to hand to hand: Yarik's five-year-old, Timofei, followed by Yarik's wife, Zinaida, then Yarik, then Dima, and their old mother, Galina Yegorovna, tugged along as the last swishing joint of the serpent's tail. It was Dima who suggested the game ("Oh," he'd told the pouting boy, "I'm pretty sure even Timofei—maybe *especially* Timofei —couldn't manage to shake loose *my* grip!") and, as they zagged and whipped around the apartment complex playground, he squeezed Yarik's hand a little tighter. Three links of hands ahead Timofei was all loopy laughter, jerking the line sharply as he could.

"Squeeze, Yarik," Dima said.

"You have to stop it."

"I'm just saying hello."

As Timofei wound them around the spring-mounted animals—the bear, the hedgehog, the goose with the broken bill—Dima loosed his

28

grip on his brother's hand just enough to clasp his fingers farther up and grip again.

"It's distracting," Yarik told him.

"You don't want—"

"I *do*, Dima. That's *why* it's distracting."

The boy led them through the cut-out fuselage of a rocket ship, all climbing bars and rusted fins, Dima stooping as he pulled their mother behind. "You aren't even trying," he told his brother.

"Bratishka—"

"Mama can grip better than you."

"You'll lose your job."

The line whipped; Yarik's hand jerked loose.

"So?" Dima said.

In front, Timofei whooped, "Break! Break! Dyadya Dima's the Chudo-Yudo!" Behind Dima, still clinging to his hand, their old mother blew exasperation through her lips, leaned over, spat.

Yarik stood, still holding Zinaida's fingers in his, separated from Dima by a black tractor tire half-buried in the dirt.

"So?" Yarik said. "So, I'll lose *my* job."

From the city center the booming began, the kettle drums and bass drums and snares, the tromping soldiers' boots. It was May ninth, Victory Day. Soon the guns would fire—still celebrating the surrender of the Germans so long ago—and they had come back early from the parade, before the cannon could scare the baby into a fit. Galina Yegorovna hadn't understood why they'd had to leave; she had gotten dressed in her old uniform—green jacket pinching the loose skin of her arms, buttons unbuttonable around her belly, gold epaulettes frayed as old rug tassles, hammer and sickle pin aslant, the *kosinka* with which she always covered the massive bun of her white hair replaced today by an army cap—and she wanted to stay to see the salutes.

"What will the Party think?" she'd hissed at Dima as they had left.

"The Party's dead, Mama."

"Oh!" She'd thrust her wrinkled papery palm against his lips.

"Mama," he'd said, "you don't want to make Polya cry on her birthday, do you?"

And, on cue, his mother's eyes had begun to tear up instead.

Polina Yaroslavovna Zhuvova had turned one year old two weeks ago, but now that International Workers' Day had been de-recognized by the Consortium, deemed tied to the worst backward ways of the past, Victory Day was the closest to her birthday that Yarik could get time off. Zinaida had made a cranberry pie. Their mother had brought blini. Dima had worked the last hour of his twelve, climbed down from the Oranzheria as the zerkala sank out of sight, boarded the bus just as the new sun rose to warm the back of his neck. But there had been no Yarik to pass him on the stairs. And Dima, forsaking sleep between his shifts, had taken a different bus, the opposite direction, all the way out to Dyadya Avya's abandoned izba, where he had shrushed alone through the leaves to their mushroom warren, gathering milk-caps and morels for the blintzes he and his mother would bring. While he was out there, he'd gone to the old kulak who now owned the land and gotten the baby's gift.

There it sat beside the sandbox: a pine green tarp cinched into the shape of a sack. The sack was jerking. They'd left the baby beside it, swaddled in blankets, while they'd played their game. Now Polya began to cry. Each boom of the drums ramped up her squall. Yarik stepped over the tractor tire and past Dima and jogged to her, Zinaida hurrying after, Timofei trudging behind, glaring at the baby's wailing face, rolling his eyes. Dima's mother still held his hand, her whole face gripped with eagerness, her eyes darting from street to square for a sight of the parade.

"It's this way, Mama." Dima turned her gently.

By the time they reached the sandbox, the guns had started in the distance and Polya was screaming as if the volleys had been fired at her. Beside her, the sack was in convulsions. Yarik cradled his daughter, his too-aged face bent nose to nose with her red and screaming one.

"The booms are for you," he was saying. "For your birthday!"

"No they're not," Timofei said.

"Timosha!" Zinaida scolded.

"Boom boom boom," Yarik said into the baby's belly.

"They're for the heroes of Mother Russia," Timofei said.

Galina Yegorovna's face lit up: "The martyrs!"

"See?" Timofei said.

"Boom boom boom," went Yarik.

"It's not for Polya, is it Dyadya Dima?" Looking up at Dima, Timofei's striken face was a picture of the sound the baby was making.

Dima could not remember what that face had looked like when it was as small and scrunched as Polya's was now, but he had never forgotten the look on Yarik's face—those hospital fluorescents flickering in that wet gaze—the first time his brother had laid eyes on his newborn son. It had been how Yarik used to look at him. Remembering that, he almost told the five-year-old, *Yes. A whole parade just for your sister. A whole streetful of soldiers just for her.*

"Boom, boom, boom," went Yarik, looking into his daughter's eyes just the way, before her, he had looked into his son's.

Dima reached down and scrunched the small boy's hair in his fingers. "No," he said. "Of course not, Timofei. It has nothing to do with her at all."

His words were followed by such a silence that he thought, for a moment, somehow the baby had understood. Yarik had quit his booming. Polya had quit her screaming. The air was drawing its breath in preparation for the next blasts. Dima glanced from his brother to his brother's wife, expecting their reproval. But they were looking at the sack. Polya, too, her face unclenched, her eyes gone wide. Out of an airhole Dima had cut, a small head jutted: two tiny eyes, hard as cherry pits, staring back. Above them, its skull was crowned by a fin of flesh, bloodred and ragged as an ear chewed in a fight. Below its chin hung a flap like the part gnawed off. Its curved beak was smooth and pale as ivory.

Timofei reached for the thing; the sack sucked it back in.

In the distance, the cannons thudded.

31

"A rooster?" Yarik said.

"Not just any rooster," Dima said.

"This is your gift?" Yarik's face was spreading with a grin.

Dima grinned back. "It's a Golden—"

"For Polya?" Zinaida cut in. "For a one-year-old?"

Around the baby all the other gifts were piled in a mound: tiny ones wrapped and sealed as carefully as candy bars, huge ones the size of samovars, ones with bows so big they hid the thing they'd been tied to, each one in bloom with a bright white card taped on—*Polya, Polya, Polya, Polya*. Beneath Dima's hand he could feel his brother's other child look up at him. Timofei's thin hair was soft as the breast of a bird. Through it Dima could feel bone, skull, heat, pulse.

To his sister-in-law, Dima lied, "Of course it's not for the baby." To his nephew he said, "It's for you."

Pulse, pulse went the boy's head.

"Really?" Timofei breathed.

"Yarik . . ." Zinaida prompted.

"Really," Dima said.

And Timofei's head was gone, the whole boy hurled forward, as if thrown at the bag by the expellation of his whoop.

"Don't touch it," Zinaida said at the same time Yarik said, "Careful with it."

"How can he not touch it," she said to her husband, "if you're telling him touch it."

"I only said—"

"He's touching it."

"Timosha!"

But the boy was on his knees, hand already through the hole, arm buried up to his shoulder, fingers grasping for the panicked, squawking, sack-trapped body inside.

"Yarik!" Zinaida shouted, and, as if Yarik's free arm had been waiting for the starting gun of his wife's voice, he lunged forward, baby in his other arm, his fist snagging his son's pants' waist, hauling him away from the roiling bag of bird. Beaming, Timofei held his own fist up into the air. In it: a hunk of golden feathers.

"My God!" Zinaida said. "He's bleeding."

But he was not. The small streaks of blood on his wrist and knuckles were from the quill tips of the feathers that had been torn out.

Yarik passed the baby to his wife and with his two big hands pried open his son's own. A few sticky feathers dropped in clumps; the others fluttered off: bright gold flakes. In Zinaida's arms, the baby reached out, tried to catch one in its tiny hand. Dima's mother echoed its grasp with her own old fingers.

"Why would you do that?" Yarik said to the boy, but Zinaida, holding the baby, looked at Dima as if the words were meant for him.

"It's not a regular rooster," Dima told her.

"It's a *rooster*," she said. "People use those things for fights."

"Not these." Untying the top of the sack, he said, "Let me show you," and brought the bird out. It was as big as Polya, and he gathered it in his arms and held it like a mirror of Zinaida holding the baby. All along its back, from neck to tail, golden feathers shimmered in the late orange light. They draped down its shoulders, over its chest, in dense soft flows, glistening patches of dark blue beneath gleaming like wet rocks behind a waterfall. But all that paled next to its tail: feathers so black they seemed almost purple, so long they swished in the air, unfurling upwards in sweeping arcs, spilling over, cascading down, dropping past Dima's forearms all the way to brush the dirt.

"It's a Golden Phoenix," Dima said.

It tucked in its neck, let out a quiet cluck. The baby, in Zinaida's arms, made a noise so purely happy all of them smiled.

"It's beautiful," Yarik told him.

"It is," Zinaida said.

"Can I touch it?" Timofei asked.

"Gently," Yarik said.

"Be gentle," Zinaida said.

33

"Reach out very slowly," Dima told him, "very smoothly. Good. Good. Like that. Feel how soft—"

The bird's head jerked up and struck down, quick and hard as the needle of a sewing machine: stab, stab, stab.

"Because," Yarik said, "we don't even have any chickens."

The playground petered out at a brightly painted merry-go-round tilted so badly its edge grooved the mud, and the mud from the playground to the street was littered with trash tossed by children, the last mostly melted snowbank black with the leavings of auto exhaust. Dima stood beside it, the Golden Phoenix in his arms.

Beside him, Yarik kicked the snowbank with his boot toe. "And its crowing?" He flipped a hand towards the apartment complex, the playground abandoned now by all but their mother. "The neighbors would kill it."

"He doesn't crow."

"Zinaida would kill *me*."

"I've had him for two days and . . ."

"He put a *hole* in Timosha's hand."

" . . . he hasn't crowed once."

"What's wrong with the thing?"

"Timofei tried to grab his—"

"I mean about the crowing."

Dima smoothed the golden feathers on the bird's long neck. Between the buildings to the west the red sun slipped lower; in the east, the sky was already aglow with the start of mirror-rise. Oktrovskogo Avenue was full of people coming back from the parade: babies in strollers, soldiers with guns, couples holding hands with the earnestness of knowing this was the last full day they'd have together for weeks. More and more of the men let go their girlfriends, or handed the baby to their wives, or swigged the last from a bottle and peeled off from the crowd and gathered at the trolleybus stop where Dima and Yarik stood. Some of them wore old medals; most of them carried hard hats; all of them looked tired. None seemed to notice the bird in Dima's arms.

"You're taking it to work?" Yarik said.

Dima grinned. "Can you imagine?"

"I can imagine *you* doing it." Far down the street, there came the rumble of a tank heading back from the parade. "I guess you have to take Mama home, anyway." Behind them, in the playground, their mother wandered the mud, stooping to gather the feathers Timofei had dropped. "You can leave it with her while you're at the Oranzheria."

Dima yawned as if at the word. The tank was going slow, cars beginning to pile up behind it. Its hatch was shut and on the barrel of its gun the red light of the setting sun glinted. Through its cloud of dust he could just see the first canescent orbs rising. "What would be so bad about it?" he said.

"About what? Getting fired?"

"I mean just not working . . ."

"Everything."

" . . . at the Oranzheria anymore."

"Then you mean not working, period."

"I mean not working like *this*."

"What would you do?"

"I mean *us,* bratan. I mean us living out at . . ."

The tank passed, roaring, covering the rest of his words, then took its roar with it and there was just its dust and the cars and Yarik said, "You better call Mama. The tram will be here and you'll miss it. And then this won't be just some idea, but the real fucking disaster, Dima, that you know it would actually be."

Dima turned and shouted for her—"Mama!"—and when he turned back, Yarik was holding out his hand, knuckles curled and fingers hanging down, as if the rooster was a dog. "I hadn't been out there," Dima said. "Not for a year."

"To Dyadya Avya's?"

One hand cupped over the bird's eyes, Dima's other stroked the top of its head. "This morning, when I went out to get him"—he smiled at the rooster—"to get *you*—the bus took thirty minutes before it got beyond the Oranzheria."

35

Yarik glanced up from the bird.

"But once you're past it?" Dima said. "Once you've finally got out from under the glass? Into the villages, along the Kosha . . ."

"Then it must feel like thirty *years*. Gone backwards."

"No," Dima told him. "Remember how full the village used to be? All the farm trucks on the road? Now there's nobody. Nobody in the fields, nobody fishing in the Kosha. Not even any old people sitting on the benches outside their gates. Everything's changed, Yarik. Even out there."

"God." Yarik reached the rest of the way to the bird's head, cupped his hand over Dima's, gave it a squeeze. "Listen to us. *We* sound like old people."

"Even them." Dima kept his hand still beneath his brother's. "Even the *dedushkas* and babushkas who went out there to retire—seventy, eighty years old—even they're working again."

"And you want to quit?" Yarik slid his hand off Dima's down to the bird's beak, gave it a wiggle. The bird jerked its head, glared. "We'll retire at ninety," Yarik said, trying to force a smile. Dima's face stayed as serious as the bird's. He felt Yarik take his head in his hand, shake it as if he had a beak. "Just hold on another fifty-four years, bratishka," Yarik said. "OK?" And, leaning in, kissed his brother on the temple.

Sometimes it seemed to Dima they had already waited that long. Sometimes it seemed half a century since their uncle had sold the farm, since they had pulled his body from the river, since the day—could it really have been only a decade and a half ago?—that Dyadya Avya had gathered together in the threshing barn all the other farmers from the old kolkhoz. By then it had already been a kooperativ. And the last century had already begun its close. And God—or the people's poverty, or their greed, or a hundred million hearts yearning for freedom—had picked up the world as if it were no weightier than a snow globe, turned it over, and shook. But for all the blizzard of new laws that had swirled down—*On the Peasant Farm, On Development of Agrarian Reform, On Realization of the Constitutional Rights of Citizens Concerning*

Land—the scene itself, the izba, the fields and barns, though now turned upside down, stayed pretty much the same: the managers remained the managers, the brigade bosses still bossed the brigades, the *nomenklatura* became the oligarchy, the ones who once had worked the black market became the ones who saw how it could work once it was brought into the light. The kolkhozy splintered, their shards divvied up by free market laws: here a farmer got a few hectares of land, there another received the seed; one a milking parlor, another the cows; somewhere a tractor, elsewhere its plow. There had been nothing for them to do but salvage some semblance of the collectives they'd had before: cooperatives owned piecemeal, and without the backing of the state. They had failed. The cooperatives incorporated, the farmers suddenly shareholders in farms too big to work themselves. Then came the men who all along had pulled the strings of state-run collectives, who in The Past Life had scraped salaries off the backs of the *kolkhozniki,* had fattened off the old corruption, men who now saw how much they stood to gain from impoverished farmers with no clue how much they stood to lose.

It was a man who had never set foot in the fields who saw it first; a man from Moscow who moved so fast that by the time one farmer knew the oligarch had bought a neighbor's share he had sold his share as well; a billionaire who spent so furiously he held 51 percent of nearly 100 percent of the farms that surrounded the city by the time the decade crumbled into collapse; a man who, when all the money nearly everyone else had saved lost nearly all its value overnight, had his in foreign markets, in Swiss banks, and most of all in land.

In Moscow they called him The She Bear. Businessmen said it out of envy, politicians out of respect, cartoonists with their pens: jaws gaping, claws raised, guarding cubs in bibs that read ZERKALA or ORANZHERIA, LAND or LAKE or LIGHT. In Petroplavilsk the people called him The Baron, spoke of how he had turned all the city, all the land around it, into his personal estate, how someday he would own the rest of Karelia, too: an entire vast region of vast Russia ruled over by him. By Borya, as his mother had called him. His friends still called him Baz.

But his name was Boris Romanovich Bazarov, and, when they said it, the farmers from whom he'd taken the land let their spit fly.

Dyadya Avya hadn't even bothered with the name at all: he just spat. His had been the last kooperativ still holding out—no money for pesticides or feed corn or food for families, just Bazarov, having already bought off a third of the old kolkhozniki, offering the only way for the rest to eat. *I don't care if I have to make borscht out of my nephews*—their uncle had shoved a finger at Yarik and Dima for all to see—*I wouldn't sell to that*—in place of the man's name, he hawked up phlegm and gobbed it at the ground—*wouldn't sell him the hole under my shithouse.* But one farmer mumbled, *Your nephews won't feed all of us,* and another called out, *You'll sell when you've got nothing to eat but the shit* and Avya, beating his fist on the side of the barn, shouted them all down. *Did I say we shouldn't sell?* he bellowed. *Sell! We have to sell! But we don't have to sell to that*—he hawked another, spat a smaller stream. The shouts went up: *Then to who?* Avya shouted back: *To one of us!* Laughter, snorts, jeers. *If you've got that kind of money,* one said, *you must be storing it up your ass.* Another heckled, *No wonder he won't sell his shithouse.* And Avya roared over the laughing, *Not to me, you fools! And sure as hell not to any of you!* But men clamped under fear don't have it in them to laugh long, and by the time his shout was done it rang out over an already quieting barn. The farmers shifted in their boots, their eyes serious. *To who?* they asked again. And the brothers' uncle had to look away when he said the name: *Kartashkin.*

Stepan Fyodorovich Kartashkin was hated almost as much as the billionaire. A district manager in the kolkhozy days, he had been one of the string pullers, the top-scrapers, a skimmer of profit and black market trader who had managed in those first lawless days of the early nineties to make for himself what in a small village had been a small fortune. Everyone knew he had gotten it at the expense of all the others and everyone resented him for it, but he was the son of the son of a villager; he gave more than anyone to the cripples at church gates; he came to the cultural house for every dance; he had been a farmer, was still a farmer; was, at least, one of them.

We all pool our shares, Avery Leonidovich explained, *land and everything, and sell it to Kartashkin.*

They shook their heads: even Stepan Fyodorovich didn't have enough to match what the billionaire was offering.

So we sell for less, Avya told them.

More head shaking, more grumbling, more questioning of why, why take a loss, *What would we get for it in return?*

It stays in the village, Avya said. *It stays out of the hands of that*—he hawked again, but couldn't mouth more than a dribble.

And what, one of the farmers asked, *is to keep Kartashkin from turning around and selling it all to The Baron for a profit?*

That, Avery Leonidovich told them, *is what we get for it. We put it in the contract. It has to stay a farm.*

The billionaire—

And, their uncle rode over the objections, *it can't be sold to anyone but one of us. Or of our kin. We put it in the contract.*

Which was how the old kolkhoz, Avya's izba and outbuildings, and all the hectares around, had become the only swath of land within forty kilometers of Petroplavilsk to stay out of The She Bear's paws. And still within the reach of the brothers' dreams. Now, into the hollow of Yarik's neck, Dima whispered what he'd been wanting to say all afternoon: "Bratan, I have it."

Yarik's fingers quit shaking his head, let go.

"My half," Dima said. "I have it *now.*"

Somewhere down the street one of the parade stragglers dropped a bottle. Yarik looked towards the crash, watched the half-smashed bottle roll. Reaching in his jacket pocket, he drew out a pack of cigarettes, tapped it and shook one out, and reached in the same pocket and brought out a matchbook and lit it. "Half of what?" Yarik said, exhaling. "Of what we thought the land was worth four years ago?"

"Just this winter—" Dima started.

"Or even six months ago? Because, bratets"—with his free hand, Yarik picked a fleck of tobacco from his lip—"anything you've saved with this goddamn deflation has gone down in value and"—he spat—"everything out there"—he swept his hand at the skyline of the city—"has gained in it. Before we do anything, we have to have enough between us so we can go to Kartashkin while we're still working, and find out his price, and meet it, and be able to keep up with . . ." He trailed off, drew on the cigarette, held it out to Dima.

If it hadn't been for the small strip of white shivering at the tip of his fingers Dima wouldn't have been able to tell that his brother's hand was shaking. He left the cigarette there to show it, said, "How far are you?"

Yarik finally looked at him.

"How far," Dima said, "from your half?"

The bottle had stopped rolling. "We said we'd try." Yarik brought his hand back. "We didn't say we'd have it by *now*. We didn't set a date that you—"

"I saw Kartashkin."

Yarik held the cigarette a centimeter from his mouth.

"When I was out at Dyadya Avya's," Dima told him. "Guess what he charged me for the rooster?"

Yarik moved his hand to his lips, drew in.

"Nothing," Dima said.

Through the smoke, Yarik looked at him.

"He gave the bird to me for free. He's buttering everybody up. I talked to some of the others. He's offering to give them a cut of whatever he makes from the sale of the farm. He's going to sell, Yarik. He's going to find a way to get out of the contract, and he's going to sell."

Yarik shook his head. "Not yet." He tossed the cigarette down at his feet. "Not until the old kulak knows exactly how high he can go."

"What if one of the others—"

"He'll wait, Dima. So long as the Oranzheria is still being built, he'll wait. He'll wait to see how much the Consortium is willing to bid."

In Dima's arms, one of the rooster's legs worked free, jutted out, scrambling at the air. "But the contract—"

"You said it yourself. He'll find a way. Or more likely their lawyers will. Some clause, some bribe. One of the old kolkhozniki who used to farm with Dyadya Avya, one of their kids . . ."

"That's why," Dima said, "we have to go to him *now*."

Again, the pack of cigarettes; again, the two quick smacks against Yarik's palm. "You don't think someone else already has?" One of the rooster's talons snagged in his brother's shirt, yanked the fabric. Yarik clenched the fresh cigarette in his mouth and with his free hands reached to work the bird's claw loose. "But he won't sell to them. Just like he won't sell to us." He freed the rooster's foot and held it for Dima to take. "Not till the Oranzheria is at his goddamn door. Then he'll sell. And that, bratets, is when we'll know how much is half of what we need."

Dima squeezed the knotty foot in his hand. "But the Oranzheria won't go that far." The day was as dim as it would get, the mirrorglow not yet enough to lift his brother's face out of the almost-dusk. "It can't just keep going," Dima said.

Yarik drew in, a red flare at the end of his cigarette. "Of course not."

"It's too far."

"I know that."

"It—"

"*You* know that. Because we work there." Yarik smiled just enough to let the smoke leak out. "But the old kulak doesn't. He won't know it till the work on the Oranzheria stops. Till it stops growing. Till it's done."

"And then . . ."

"Then we'll go to him." Yarik drew again on the cigarette. "And that is why it can't be now, bratets, why we have to keep at it until the minute the last pane of glass is laid on the last hectare of the Oranzheria. So that we have enough, so that our halves—*your* half—keeps growing with the value of the land, so that we can go that day, that *exact* day, and bring it to him, bring him more than the others in the village have, before the others in the village know."

Pressed against the skin of his arm, Dima could feel the Golden Phoenix's warmth, the softness of its feathers, its small heart working. "How long do you think it will be?"

Yarik shrugged. He took the cigarette from his mouth, looked at the half-spent stub. "Longer than it takes me to go through one of these."

"Bratan . . ."

"I don't know, maybe in five hundred packs? Maybe a thousand?" Yarik tried to make his mouth smile.

"Bratan," Dima said again, and his brother looked away, up the street, as if he already knew what Dima was going to say. "How much have you been—"

"There's the tram."

"Yarik, how much have you been able to save?" Dima watched the back of his brother's turned head. "When it comes time . . ."

"You don't have a wife," Yarik said. "You don't have kids."

Above the tram, the contactors stuck up like two antennae, feelers that worked their way along the web of wires woven over the street. They hit a switch, clattered, came on.

With his free hand, Dima reached over, into his brother's shirt pocket, drew out the pack. He nudged its top open with his thumb and, beneath the rooster's ruffled neck, worked his fingers after a cigarette.

Yarik leaned close to light it. "What was it like? Out in the village?"

"Out there," Dima told him, "the mirrors' beams still haven't reached."

"You were there at night?"

"Out there"—Dima drew in, let the smoke out—"the roosters crow."

Over his last word, the tram's brakes began their long slow squeal. The Golden Phoenix struggled. Dima pressed the bird against his chest.

"I'll have it," Yarik said. "By the time we need it, I'll have it." Then he turned and shouted back towards the playground,"Mama! Mama, the trolleybus!"

And Dima turned, too, and joined him in calling for her.

She was on her knees in a patch of new growing grass, the tiny bright green blades thin as hairs, a few last golden feathers scattered around her, shining more dully now in the semblance of sunlight the zerkala threw down. Above the trolley stop the wires had begun to hum.

From all the way across the water he can hear the chattering of the birds. Their wind-prick calls coming through the slap of the waves, the smack of the oars, borne on the wind that gusts over Nizhi, across the lake, to them. What wind! What blast of it! He can see the whipping grasses, the stands of bent-necked spruces shaking like the manes of huddled horses, the churches alive with a flock of storm petrels gathered in the leeward, clinging to lintels carved centuries ago, to wooden shingles set in place by long-dead monks, small birds taking shelter behind the dozens of delicate onion domes, half a thousand dark whifflings waiting out the wind.

Looking over their shoulders, their red scarves flapping, the brothers watch it come. It grabs the lake and shakes, makes sails of their jackets, shoves their rowboat back. They hack faster, thrash their oars against it. The wind holds them in place.

And while they row the sun sinks, and the birds rise to spread across a sky gone red, and the wind comes on. The boat drives backwards against their struggling. They grip the handles harder, heave the paddles splash by splash, brother matching brother, one keeping pace with the other who rocks faster to keep pace with him until their backs burst into flame, their grunts to shouts, their fingers burning, their palms rubbed raw . . . And the oar jerks loose from Yarik's hands. Just leaps free. How the boy lunges for it! How his fingers rake the air!

And Dima can see it: the pale sliver of wet wood rising and dipping on a wind-chopped wave, winking as it slips away. He can see the back of his brother's head, so still and stiff against the seething lake, can see such mortification in that frozen neck, knows the way his brother's eyes will look when Yarik has hidden the shame and fear, tried to pack it deep in his pupils, to keep it somehow from his twin. But Dima feels it, feels it like the splintery handle of the oar still

43

gripped in his rubbed-raw palm. And then his fingers are free. Cold air kissing the torn skin.

One, two, three, four . . .

In his dream, he reaches down into the jars and soothes his blisters with the yolks of the eggs.

. . . five, six . . .

And with his dripping hands reaches up again and holds his brother's. And soothes them.

. . . seven . . .

"*Kukareku!*" the boys shout.

. . . vosyem . . .

Such a long call! So drawn out and furious!

. . . devyat . . .

Wavery as a hurdy-gurdy's wail! Listen: a *kolyosnaya lira* keening!

. . . desyat . . .

Hear the whooping of the crowd!

Dima woke to a sound in his throat like a bow striking a fiddle string, some strand of joy reverberating in his chest. Music. For a moment, he thought it came from out on the street—how many years had it been since he'd seen musicians play?—and then the chorus burst in, breaking with static, and he knew his mother had finally found her folk songs on the radio. That morning, after working his twelve-hour shift, he'd returned home to find her still dressed in her Red Army uniform, her cap replaced by a flowered scarf, turning the dials, confounded by the absence of her favorite evening show. Now, from the kitchen, he could hear her accompany it with clapping.

He lay on his cot, his eyes still shut, coming back into the world as slowly as he could. Outside his bedroom, the song wound down. The radio crackled with heavy gongs: the clock bells in the country's capital keeping everyone on track. *One, two, three . . .* Each peal shook the daylight against his eyelids. He knew he should go back to sleep—in a couple hours he'd wolf a bowl of soup, catch the tram, get back on the glass, maybe pass Yarik returning from work—but he was watching windows in the distance: the lights of the cultural house pulsing, a celebration shaking the *dom kultura*'s walls. When he'd gone out to get the rooster, he hadn't had time to travel farther down the road. Now, he was seeing it as it used to be: crammed with trucks and tractors, the fields to each side flickering with flashlight beams of farmers coming, the bonfire lighting all the faces of the kolkhozniki that swarmed the yard, clambered through the doorway into the hall. On his breastbone, he could feel their boot clomps, the beat of the double bass, and he kept his eyes closed, his breath quiet, tried not to leak out any of the air inside.

In the hall, it was thick with cigarette smoke, the waft of wet wool, alive with thuds of mud-matted boots as the crowd surged onto the dance floor, laughter in their eyes, vodka in their cheeks, whoops and cries and the guitar's sudden strumming, the plucking of the gusli, the fiddler bending to his bow. Hands on hips and waists, boots banging down, the crowd began to dance. *Barinyas* and *troikas*, *kamarinskayas* and *khorovods*. The brothers wading in. Dima with his high-kneed stomps, Yarik's horse-in-harness prancing. Until the musicians broke, the crowd cleared, the clapping began: the Cossack competition. Always, if the twins were there, they danced it. And if they danced it, they won.

At the bandleader's call, the floor full of dancers would go still: crouched low, hovering on haunches, one leg stretched straight, the other bent beneath. The rules were simple: everyone at the same low squat, the same single kick per beat, the beats quickening, the legs tiring, the dancers collapsing until only one remained. There came the balalaika trill. The singer's voice: long vowel swooping up and up. And the first beat would boom from the band, the second drowned beneath the crash of half a hundred heels hitting the floor as one, another hundred hands coming together in the rhythm-keeping clapping of the crowd. Everyone had their strategies: barefooters hitched heavy skirts high up their thighs; boot wearers padded their heels with hay; collaborators circled up, held shoulders for balance; singles crossed their arms, or pumped them, or flapped at the air as if hoping for lift.

But Dima and Yarik would simply face each other, grip each other's hands and, leaning back, lash their right legs out, their left, kicks so synchronized the muscles of one seemed to move the other's, locked eyes blinking simultaneously at sweat, grins tighter and tighter until their jaws bulged, their thighs shook, the floor around them shook, the shaking floor emptier and emptier, and then just them, the thunderous clapping, the frenzied music, the brothers holding on.

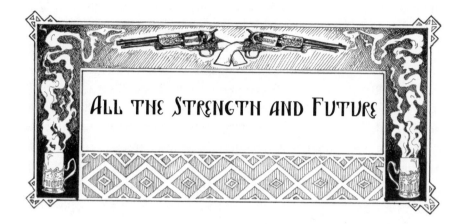

ALL THE STRENGTH AND FUTURE

Yarik sat by himself behind the dark windows in the backseat of the sedan. In his lap, one hand lay palm up, holding the mint the driver had made him take, the red and white cellophaned swirl shaking like a pinwheel on the edge of starting to turn. His other hand held tight to the rim of his hard hat, upturned on the seat beside him and shaking, too. He was still wearing his work gloves. When the foreman had called him over, told him to brush off his coveralled ass, shoved him towards the car—some new model of some non-Russian make, all gleaming black and glinting chrome—he had been too surprised to do anything but walk. When the driver had stepped out of the car to open the rear door, Yarik had waited for whoever was inside to climb out. But the backseat was empty. *Gospodin . . .* the driver said. Yarik couldn't recall another time in his life when he'd been called "sir." Ducking in, he had clanked his hard hat on the car's roof, and by the time he'd yanked the hat off and shoved it down on the seat beside him, the driver was sitting in front, turned to face him, a smirk barely hidden in his eyes. The man held out a small silver box. *For the ride,* he said and flipped open the top. Inside: a dozen candies in shiny foils—rubies, sapphires, small squares of gold. The pinwheel mint was the only one with a wrapper clear enough to see through. Too late, he realized his fingers were still bulky with gloves. The driver, smirk slipping over his entire face, fished the mint out for him, held it until Yarik turned up his palm.

Now, on the car radio, the long knells of the Kremlin's bell tower rang out. Three o'clock, Moscow time. His son would be with the neighbor they paid for after-kindergarten care, his baby crawling the rugs of the old woman's apartment. His wife would be at work. His brother would be asleep. By now, Yarik would have been pushing through the toughest time of the day, out with his crew at the Oran- zheria's far edge, trying not to count the hours till the transport bus would carry him back along this road. The car sped on, passing heavy trucks and little Ladas that drove onto the shoulder to let them have their way. In every field he passed, the monstrous sprinklers slowly rolled, their long metal backs arched from one high wheel to the next, linked together for kilometers, darkening the earth with their artificial rain. Above, collection gutters ran like veins through the clear skin of the glass, tubes dropping to storage tanks, workers lining the irriga- tion ditches, manning the distribution valves, directing the flow of the canals. All paused when they saw the car. He saw the faces of the workers follow him and knew that he had felt that look before, felt it coming from his own face; he had simply never known till now what it felt like directed towards him.

It felt like he was someone else. As if, for a moment behind that tinted glass, he had become the man his mother had hoped her boy would grow to be. When he'd been born—he knew because she told him—she had brought him to her breast before Dima had followed into the world. Sometimes he wondered if his brother had come first would she have chosen Dima instead? Set Dima aside for success? Checked his schoolwork first? Insisted he learn to drink black tea while still too small for such bitterness, showed him how to suck it through a sugar cube, told her six-year-old son it would help him stay awake to study? Would she have brought Dima instead of Yarik to social evenings at the army base? Introduced Dima to the men who could pull strings, who she flirted with, cajoled, tried to ensure they'd tug just a little in just the right place for him?

By the time Yarik had turned nine, she'd found that place: his school-boy fascination with Gagarin, Tsiolkovsky, Korolyov's dream of men on Mars, the Mir space station orbiting above. He would be an engineer. And all her years as a secretary on the Petroplavilsk base, what favors she could nurse from her boss, what little she could save for bribes, had gone to opening a slot for him. One slot for one boy. All the pull she could put together would have never been enough for two. It was the way The Past Life worked, and all his earliest years he had worked towards it: memorized the multiplication charts their mother made him, learned his constellations—*Ursa Major, Hydra*—off a plastic place mat she gave him for his birthday, accompanied her to speeches by men who she said mattered. While their father, who had never understood ambition, took his other son to the park to hear the poets read; while their father, who was proof of what happened when a man had no will to rise, lay on his boat beside Dima beneath the stars, telling tales of the great bear, the sea serpent that swallowed the sun; their father, who suddenly, one day, was gone.

And then their mother, too. So subsumed by grief she had been taken away to a place where others could help her overcome her helpless-ness. And alone with Dima out at Dyadya Avya's, month after month in only their old uncle's care, what track had there been for Yarik to run on but whatever rail would keep him alongside his brother? What future was there to work towards but the end of the next day? And when, after that parentless year, the state gave them their mother back, when the three of them returned to the apartment on Avtovskaya Street, where was the woman who'd once wished for a bigger flat, a better life, who'd been so driven to drive her firstborn? Gone as her good secretary's job, as her once-black hair, as her faith in him. Back then, he could feel the hollowness inside him where his mother's hope had been scooped out: every connection she'd made, broken; every path she'd pushed him towards, closed; her hand too weak to pull him anywhere, let alone up. At night, back in their old room, he would leave his cot, crawl in with Dima, the two of them too used to sleeping together in the hay of their uncle's izba to fall asleep apart. Curled into the curve of his brother, he'd stare across the room at the wall: behind there, he knew, their mother slept in a bed still sagged with the weight of her dead husband, knew she'd returned from the sanitarium stripped of the thing that had stirred her dreams of a bigger life for him, just as he'd known he had to let go of those dreams, too.

A slapping sound—the rubber strips that curtained the exit to keep the warm air in—and they were out of the Oranzheria: glass roof giving way to girders that became open sky, the earth preparation crews, and then the clearing crews, and then the logging crews, until the car was past everything but the receding din. Then that was gone, too. In the quiet, the car felt even bigger, the seat beside him emptier. Outside, the road was lined with tall pines, their needles new to the mirror-light, stands of birches still unaware of the pandemic winter would bring. He watched them flash by, nothing on either side but walls of woods. Until, up ahead, he saw the sign: THE DACHAS.

They weren't really dachas, of course—no one had time to putter in cottage gardens on the weekend anymore; no one had weekends—but once the sign had pointed to a hundred summer cabins, each with its own flowering lilacs and vegetable plots, a village like dozens of others that used to surround the city, this last one still called by what it had once been, as if the people of Petroplavilsk wished to deny what it had become. A ghetto. Yarik had never seen it, but he'd heard about it from his wife: the flophouses, the fleas, the homemade vodka stills, the dogs she'd seen roasting over fire pits, the giant billboards mounted on the walls and tilted down to show those kept inside unremitting images—*vareniki* billowing steam, cucumbers gleaming with oil, personal computers and women's glossy lips and men in suits smoking cigarettes. She said giant TV screens ceaselessly displayed the outside world—Moscow nightclubs, resorts on the Black Sea—surrounded the village with advertisements and, every now and then, a video of someone's mother making a plea, a father breaking down in tears. *I wouldn't last a week in there,* Yarik had heard others say, *I'd want a job within an hour,* or *work with a smile the rest of my life,* or *kill myself,* or *come out cured,* or they simply praised the way the city, guided by the Consortium, had kept such unproductive influences out of sight.

But not Zinaida. Not his gentle-hearted wife. It was part of what he loved about his Zinusha: her certainty that she could do something to help. Once a month she went with a busload of women from her church, brought cans of food, bags of clothes, got off the bus and stayed outside, withstanding the scolding of their friends (*enabling shiftlessness, encouraging sloth*), the sneers of guards (*Why don't you go in and give them the rest of what your husbands work for!*), while the gates opened (a guard drove the bus inside) and closed again and from behind them there rose the hoots and bellows, the whistles and whoops and jubilating clamor of those who had no work, who refused the work there was.

After each trip out there his wife came home and cried. It was un-Christian, she would sob into his shoulder, that they should be rounded up and kept inside those walls and made, each minute of every day, to face their decision not to work. As if it was their fault. Surely, she would say, they were too sick, or feebleminded, or emotionally scarred to make that choice; surely, such souls deserved pity, instead. He would nod, his lips against her hair, and think of how in the old system they would have simply been made to work, driven at hard labor beneath a harder hand. He didn't know which way was worse.

But, passing by the turnoff to The Dachas, peering out at the tops of the billboards, their bright colors splashed above the dark pines, he knew this: his Zinusha was wrong. It *was* a choice. It always had been. To roll over in bed and go back to sleep, to stay out drinking one hour more, to steal that first sun-warmed strawberry from some roadside field, to eat half a bowl of kasha and put the rest away for lunch, to scrape it onto the plates of your kids, to get up and leave for work before your wife could notice you'd had no breakfast at all, to accept the way things were, to fight to change them for those around you, to slip quietly to the side—it all led back to some decision. *Who is to say which is the right one?* In the rearview mirror, the driver's eyes flicked to Yarik. He wondered if he'd spoken it out loud. Of course, he thought, people said which was right all the time, people in power. And some listened to them, and some didn't, and that was a choice, too. Watching the last glimpses of the billboards through the trees, he felt for the crank on the door, found a button, instead. The window slid open a crack. The rush of air whooshing by the car, the dwindling sounds of the homeless shelter, some loudspeakered lamenting voice. Probably one of the videos of the fathers, Yarik thought. And it struck him then that if his own father had lived he never would have been on a video like that. It would have been his mother on the screen. She would have been the one making the visits, taking the bags of clothes out on the bus like Zina. Because his father would have been inside. That was the choice his father would have made.

Then the last of The Dachas was buried beneath the rush of air, the hum of the asphalt beneath the tires, the pines whipping by. Yarik slid his window up, took off his gloves, stuffed them inside his hard hat. He turned it over, flat on the brim so it wouldn't roll. He put the mint in his pocket and felt the pack of cigarettes and sat there, smelling the clean car, wanting to pull the Troikas out and smoke. Because now that they had passed The Dachas there was no question where he was being taken, or to whom.

Once a northern palace built for the tsar, for royal hunts of bear and wolf and wild boar, it had become a camp for the apparatchiki in the Party, a private place where Stalin went to mull his purges, where Kosygin recuperated from the failure of his heart, where only army generals and directors of the GRU, politburo secretaries and the occasional chest-starred Hero of the State, were allowed through gates still topped with twisted spikes, still attached to the two stone pillars that had always lined the drive. But the brass hammer that had replaced the double-headed eagle once mounted on the leftward pillar was now gone, the brass sickle that had matched it on the right removed.

In their place: a rough-hewn crossbar made of cracked, grayed wood. And in its center, staring out at the road: a bleached-white skull. It had the eye sockets and muzzle of what Yarik thought to be a cow, but from its head sprung horns too huge, more like elephant tusks. Above them, centered over frontal bone, sat three iron letters: БРБ. *Boris Romanovich Bazarov.* The gates slid open. Yarik looked behind as he passed through in the hope they might not swing closed. And, watching them shut, he noticed, for the first time, the base of the pillars: below each post the marble had been carved into the talons of a giant eagle's foot.

That was when he wished Dima was with him. He would have liked to see his brother's face. Their uncle's whispers: fowl feet beneath a witch's house. Pushkin's lines: lanterns made of tree-spiked skulls. He would have liked to hear Dima tell the story of *this*. For a moment he wished he could see it through his brother's eyes, that his own first thought wouldn't be, instead, *how foolish.*

But it *was* foolish. Gold domes like a boy's trophies shelved in the sky; the topiary like a toy model of the Petrodvorets Palace grounds; the marble statues of Rus warriors in chain mail, of high-headdressed Indians brandishing spears, Greek maidens replaced by reclining squaws; the filigreed horse sleigh sitting at the end of the drive, the fact that someone had shot arrows into its sides.

And yet there was something about it all that made Yarik reach for the candy in his pocket, work at the wrapper with his hands; something that, when the driver stopped before the wide stone steps, made Yarik shove the mint into his mouth just to keep his jaw unclenched; something that, when the driver got out and opened Yarik's door, made Yarik grind the mint up in his teeth. It was the foolishness itself that made it worse: the man who'd brought him here knew what he'd think, what men a million times more important would think, knew it—and shrugged. If it made Yarik smile, good. If it made others laugh, so be it. If it made the visitors who the billionaire had brought here swallow sharp chunks of unchewed candies at the crack of the front doors opening, that was probably the point.

"Mr. Bazarov," the driver said, motioning with his hand to the top of the steps.

Instead, a woman stood in the doorway. She'd gathered her blond hair in a white kerchief rimmed with the red needlework for which the region was famed, wrapped herself in a similar Karelian shawl, and when she turned and led him in he could see, following, how it was cut to slip down her arms and leave her shoulders bare, how her cool blue dress barely reached to her thighs, how her heels were dyed to match the needlework, how she walked in them in a way that made her long braid swish, that made him have to turn his head away.

The parquetried floor and velvet drapes, panels of mirrors and painted ceiling and all the glass chandeliers: none of it compared to what hung from the walls. There were enough weapons along one side to have given pause to a Tartar horde—long swords, rapiers, battle-axes, bludgeons—while along the other enough tomahawks and arrows and eagle-feathered lances to pull a cavalry regiment up short.

The clacking of the woman's heels stopped so suddenly he almost ran into her. She took a swift step aside, as if she'd been blundered into before, then took another step to the closed door, knocked, spoke to the wood—something in English—stepped aside again, pushed the door open for him to go in.

The billionaire was standing in the middle of the room. Not behind a desk, or with hands on a chair, or near any furniture at all, but just standing there. He looked Yarik straight in the eyes. "What do you want?" he said.

Behind Yarik, the woman, or some automatic thing, shut the door.

"Excuse me?" Yarik said.

"I asked you, what do you want?"

Yarik tried not to look away. The bits of mint he'd mashed into the depressions of his molars had hardened and stuck; his teeth felt glued together. The billionaire watched him, motionless. He was dressed in another shiny metallic suit, another leather string tie. This time the tie was orange. So were the boots. They were cowboy boots, Yarik realized, made from the kind of scaly leather he'd seen used on women's handbags. Something about that gave him the strength to get his teeth unsealed; they came apart with a pop.

As if the sound was a latch coming loose in the billionaire's cheeks, the man's face sprung a grin. He whistled, a piercing, high-pitched noise that came through his teeth and lifted his eyebrows and brightened his eyes, and died fast as it had come, leaving the man grinning even wider. "Look at you jump," he said. "You *are* nervous. You better sit down."

"Sir—" Yarik started.

"Sit down," the man said. "I'm just joking, sit down."

Yarik didn't know if the man meant he was joking about the sitting, or about what had come before. With one hand, he hitched the hard hat up where he held it against his side.

"Sit!" The man shot the word through his smile, finished it off with a smack on the back of the couch.

It was a leather couch, plush and deep, and it was the only seat in the room. The room was an office—a big-windowed, beige-carpeted, airy, vast office—but in the whole office the only other piece of furniture was the desk. Behind the desk: no chair. On the desk: a computer, a phone, a lamp, three glass picture frames on clear glass stands with their black felt backs turned to him. Beneath the lamp, in the center of the desk: a pair of wooden hands carved out of burl-whirled Karelian birch. In the hands: two guns. They were antiquated, long-barreled, cylinder-loaded pistols with ivory handles and brass trigger guards and heavy-looking muzzles, and taking in the scenes of galloping horses scratched into the gold plate over their chambers, Yarik wondered if they had ever even been fired, and then if the billionaire had been the one to fire them, and at what, at whom. He had not touched a gun in more than a decade, since the day that Dyadya Avya—drunk, said the kulak who'd bought their uncle's land; sober, Yarik knew—waded out into the Kosha with his old army pistol in his hand, the day the brothers had splashed in after him, shouting for their dyadya out in the current, the day that Yarik had grabbed the gun too late.

He looked away. In one of the corners, a huge wood-burning oven made of blue and white china stretched from floor to ceiling. In another:

a sea green orb of translucent plastic. One wall was completely covered by a painting Yarik remembered from some high school textbook: a field of heavy horses thundering forward at full charge, on their backs Rus knights in plated mail and glaring helmets, lances lowered, swords drawn. Across the room, on the opposite wall, another painting just as huge: grassy plain, hot blue sky, white teeth gritted beneath wide brimmed hats, bandannas unfurled like flags, a cavalry coming on in a dust-billowing stampede. Between the two, there was the desk, the couch.

Yarik sat down on it. Tall as he was, it sucked him in. He sank so low that he felt like he was in his first day of first form, six years old and sitting at his tiny desk before the teacher's full-size one, until he realized he wasn't that low at all; the man's desk was just that tall. The billionaire went behind it now. He lay his forearms on top. He smacked his hands down flat. The revolvers in their wood hands shook. "So," the billionaire said, "show me what you've got."

Yarik sat with his hard hat in his lap. "Sir—"

"Baz," the man said.

"Sir, it was—"

"Bazarov."

"Yes, sir."

"Boris Romanovich Bazarov."

"Yes, sir, I know."

"So why don't you call me Baz?"

"Baz?" Yarik said.

"Baz," the man said. "Baz, Baz." He grinned, waited.

For a second, Yarik dug with his tongue at one of the candy-jammed grooves in his teeth. Then he said, "Baz—"

"Yes?"

"I only wanted to say . . ."

The oligarch nodded. "I'm listening."

"It was *your* driver who brought me here."

Bazarov nodded again. "And?"

Through the closed door, Yarik could hear high heels clacking towards the room, louder and louder on the hardwood floor.

"You were thinking," Bazarov said, as he stood up, "about viewing platforms." He came around to the front of the desk. "A tramline going"—with his index finger, he made a squiggly sign in the air between them—"along the underside of the glass." He was facing Yarik, his back to the desk, and without looking away he reached behind him, pushed back the gun stand, put his hands on the desktop, and, with one quick shove, popped himself up. He sat there, legs dangling. He opened his hands, turned his palms upward, held them hovering above his knees. "And?"

Yarik could still feel the way his words had dried up in his throat that day on the top of the glass when the man had begun to moo. He could still hear the sound, see the gleam in the billionaire's eye, the look on the man's face that said *got you!* and *how much fun!* at the same time.

"You were thinking," Bazarov said again. "You were telling me your thoughts. And I interrupted you. Rudely and even, perhaps, even a little ridiculously, I admit, a little bit of foolishness, I interrupted you, I'm sorry. I apologize. You were thinking." He motioned for Yarik to resume his thoughts.

Yarik could feel the gloves he'd shoved in his coverall pockets bulging against his hips. "We were just thinking."

"*You* were thinking."

"My brother and I were just—"

"*You* were just."

"Sir?"

"Baz."

"Baz?"

"Did I bring your brother here? If I wanted to know what your brother was thinking, I would have sent two cars."

Yarik tried to imagine Dima there, next to him, the two of them getting through this the way they had always gotten through everything together, but he could only see his brother entranced by the paintings, or still stuck in the memory of passing The Dachas, and he knew he would have had to do all the talking on his own anyway. It struck him then that this man, this Bazarov, this *Baz*, must drive by The Dachas every day. And must dismiss them the way he had brushed aside Dima, as if he, too, could be stored away behind the blur of dark pines. Yarik could see *that*—his brother like their father that way, capable of making a choice that would land him living in there—and it chilled him. He leaned forward as best he could in the couch. He tried to straighten his back. He said, "But it was my brother's idea."

Bazarov let his hands fall to his knees.

"We were thinking of it together," Yarik told him.

The man looked down and, one after the other, flipped the picture frames around so their photographs were turned to Yarik.

"He loves working on the Oranzheria," Yarik told the man, "as much as I do."

They were photographs of Bazarov: falling through the sky in parachuter's gear, his dark shades reflecting the sun; underwater, eyes goggled above his goatee, feeding a chunk of meat into the gaping maw of a shark; astride the mound of a blood-maned boar in a blinding field of snow, one hand gripping the beast's upper teeth, opening its mouth, the other lifting one of the long-barreled pistols above the steam of Bazarov's own breath.

"He's better at laying out dreams," Yarik went on. "We were just dreaming about it, is really what we were doing."

Bazarov left his pictures where they were, slid himself off the desk.

"About what it might be like for others," Yarik said, "others from town, or from St. Petersburg, tours that could come up from the Volga into the lake." As he talked he turned his head to follow the billionaire. The man was walking around the couch, towards the door through which Yarik had come. "It could be a whole added stream of revenue," Yarik said to his back. "We were thinking that right now the Oranzheria is stuck in the area where it's built. It has to ship the products grown under it out to the rest of Russia. But this would bring the rest of Russia to it."

Bazarov had opened the door and let the woman in. No: the same blond braid, and shawl, and dress, but a different woman wheeling a small cart. On it, two glasses rattled, empty. Between them: a silver teapot. The woman left the cart in front of Yarik, left the room again. Shutting the door behind her, Bazarov came back carrying an electric kettle in one hand. In the other, he held the cord.

"You aren't really interested in this tourism stuff, are you," Yarik said.

Bazarov set the kettle down on the top of his desk, turned. He was still holding the plug from the chord. "I'm interested in what goes on in here," he said and, reaching out, touched the plug's prongs to Yarik's forehead. He held it there. Outside the door, the receding clacks of high heels echoed. Slowly, the sound was replaced by a low shushing. It grew louder, louder, until it was a rolling burble.

Yarik watched the man make the noise with his lips. Then the lips split into that grin again, and the noise stopped, and the man laughed. He drew back the plug and reached under the desk and stuck it in a socket in the floor. Flicking the kettle on, he turned, stepped to the green plastic ball, rolled it back, and sat on it. The cart between them, he lifted the teapot and carefully poured the dark, strong tea into one glass, then the other. He filled each a third of the way. Behind him the electric kettle was already beginning to boil. He waited for the boil to roll, for it to click off. "Yaroslav Lvovich Zhuvov," he said, filling one of the glasses the rest of the way up. "Yaroslav Lvovich." He paused with the kettle over the second glass, looked at Yarik. "Do you mind if I call you Yaroslav Lvovich?"

Yarik shook his head. They sat, Yarik on the couch, Bazarov on his inflated ball, both holding their glasses of tea by the rims.

The billionaire blew on the surface, smiled. "Yaroslav Lvovich," he said. "Son of Lev Leonidovich Zhuvov, fisherman. Of Galina Yegorovna Zhuvova, secretary, seamstress, Party member, mother, of course. Grew up in an apartment complex on Avtovskaya Street, went to the Secondary School Number Eight, lives now in the Varkayusa Apartments near Ilyinsky Square. With a wife who works in a ticket window at the railway station, a boy about to start first form in the Number Seventeen school downtown, a girl who goes to day care at an old woman's apartment on the floor above. A good father, a good husband.

A real son of Petroplavilsk. So how," he spoke through the steam coming off the top of his glass, "did you come to live for a year out in the boonies with your uncle?"

Yarik could feel his fingers burning. "How do you know all that?"

Bazarov made his face look almost affronted. Hurt, even. He sat back a little on his ball. The rubber squeaked. "I was born on the Volga, in a small town to the east of Nizhni Novgorod. I remember watching the sunsets with my father, the light on the river, the silhouettes of the domes. He was a soldier. I rarely saw him. My mother? She was"—he acknowledged the coincidence with a pursing of his mouth—"also a seamstress. We lived on Gryiboedova Street, in a home that we shared with three other families. My first kiss was with one of the daughters of one of the families, an event brought about by our arguing over a cigarette we had found." He rocked a little on the ball, smiled. "I had two sisters," he went on. "They died in a fire." He made his smile into not-a-smile. "Unrelated," he said, "to the incident with the cigarette. I went to school at Lobachevsky University. I did my service in Afghanistan, the last year that we were there. I got a wife, got a kid, got divorced—they're all in Moscow—got rich, wound up here." He leaned forward again, the ball sighing under him. "There," he said. "Now we're having a heart-to-heart."

Yarik held his hand over the top of his tea, felt the steam wet and warm on his palm. "Our father died," he said.

"I'm sorry," Bazarov said.

Yarik shrugged. "We were nine."

"And your mother?"

"We stayed with our uncle while she was recovering."

"Your uncle must have been a real Russian muzhik," Bazarov said, "right in the line of the good peasants of old. All the strength and future of Russia lies in the hands of the muzhik." His smile widened, his voice deepened. "It is they," he said, as if reciting, "who will start the new epoch, show us our real Russian language, our true laws." He gave a little bounce, sat there beaming. "Turgenev?" he prompted. "*Ottsy i deti*? No?"

Yes, Yarik thought, his uncle had been a real muzhik: he had loved his land. And lasted less than a year after the half-hectare he'd lived on all his life had been sold. Yarik could see him out in the river, floating on his back, his bare white belly huge with held breath, the gun glinting as he pressed it to his chest. Yarik could feel his reaching arm, the sting in his palm, the bruise in his fingers, the heat. He put his tea down. "Mr. Bazarov . . ." he said.

"Baz."

". . . why did you bring me here?"

The man's smile spread itself into a grin. "Yaroslav Lvovich," he said, "why did you come here?"

"Because you asked me."

"But *what* did I ask you?"

Yarik wanted to shove the grin away. He kept his hands flattened to the curve of the hard hat in his lap. He said, "What do you want?"

Bazarov laughed. A short happy yip of a laugh that made Yarik grip the hard hat tighter. "Yes!" Bazarov said. "Yes, exactly. *What do you want?*" Reaching out with one hand, he pushed the tea cart away, rolled the ball beneath him a little closer, sat with his knees almost brushing Yarik's. When he spoke again the mirth was gone from his voice. "Yaroslav Lvovich," he said, "what do you want?"

The longer Yarik looked at the man's eyes, the more their color seemed to change, the closer it seemed to come to the color of his own. He leaned back a little. "From you?" His back pressing into the couch. "You mean what do I want from you?"

Bazarov's face stayed where it was. "I mean"—his eyes held— "from life."

There was nowhere farther for Yarik to lean. So he sat with his shoulders pressed against the couch's back, looking down at his hands on the hard hat in his lap, and, for a moment, he could almost smell the scent of Dima's hair when he would set his brother's hat over his face, his wife's sweat when they made love, his son's morning breath when the boy kissed him good-bye before work, the life shared between his daughter and her mother and himself that almost overcame him

61

when he bent to blow on his baby's belly button, and when he looked up from his hard hat again, he said, "Time."

Bazarov sat back.

"Time to be a good father," Yarik said. "A good husband. A good son. A good brother."

"A good choice," Bazarov said. "And how do you plan on getting this time?"

Yarik looked at him straight. "I don't know."

"Through work." The billionaire got up and reached behind him to the desk. "Work equals time," he said. "Time gone, but also gained. An exchange you pay up front. So that eventually, with a little luck"— out of a birch-carved hand, he lifted one of the long-barreled, heavy-looking guns—"you make enough so you can pay others to pay out in the exchange for you." Sitting back on the ball, he held the old pistol between him and Yarik. "So that, with a little luck, you have time to lounge about, paying your own employees their hourly wage while you drive them out to your home and share with them a little heart-to-heart over tea."

Yarik watched the revolver where it dangled from the man's hand. "Then I guess what I'm missing must be the luck."

Lifting the gun, the billionaire pressed the barrel to his temple. "That," he said, "is why I keep this around." His smile was so wide it wrinkled his skin against the metal. "A Colt Walker. 1847. From Texas. Cost me half a million U.S. dollars. That one"—he tilted his head, the gun barrel tilting with it, at the revolver's twin, still on the desk—"cost me the other half." With his free hand, he reached up and gave the cylinder a spin. "They remind me how much of it is luck." The chamber clicked around, and clicked, and was still. Bazarov waited, as if what happened next was up to Yarik. He raised his eyebrows.

"Don't," Yarik said.

The eyebrows rose farther. Pulling the barrel away from his temple, Bazarov held the gun out to Yarik, instead. "You want to try?" But before Yarik could answer, the man was reaching with his other hand for Yarik's lap. He lifted the hard hat off. "Maybe," he said, "I'll even let you wear this." He held the hat for a moment. "No?" Then, turning it over, put it on his own head. It was too small for him. He grinned. "Good choice," he said and rapped the tip of the Colt's long barrel against the hard plastic atop his head. "Because you don't need a gun to tell you your luck has changed." He took the hat off again, reached over, put it on Yarik. "Now that you're a foreman."

The same woman who led him in led him out. This time, he didn't even try to look away from the sway of her braid. At the car, the same close-shorn driver got out to help him in. He waved the man off, tugged open the back door himself. Before they left, the driver turned around and offered him the box of candies again. This time he took one wrapped in gold.

On the way back, he noticed that the forest around the mansion had been logged. Old pines clear-cut and, in their place, new ones planted. He wondered if this new woods was Bazarov's preparation for the day when mirrors would reach here, too. And when they passed The Dachas, the place seemed different to him—the trees less dark, billboards less garish, even the sounds simply background noises of any busy store—and he felt so far away from the kind of people who were in there. Turning from the window, he lay his head back on the headrest. He pulled his gloves out of his pockets. He put them over his face and shut his eyes.

It had begun long ago, his brother slipping away from him. Sometime in the years when they were young and living off what they could scavenge out at the old kolkhoz, when the country was still scavenging, too, picking the bones of its dead empire to feed the dreams of Western wealth perestroika had begot, its people ever more desperate as there was ever less of it to have, sometime in the first years of the new century when the onetime citizens of the old superpower chose for their next president an oil oligarch who shouted over the swelling orchestration of his ads: *I am Kirill Andreievich Slatkin, and I will run Russia like I run my business!* Watching the chained-down TV in the corner of a blini shop in town, Yarik had wondered just what that

63

meant—*Unfetter the free market! Shed the last vestiges of old socialist ways!*—until the new president turned his promises into laws: gone was the winter hardship supplement; gone, the assurance of a job; doctors turned away the sick; pensioners opened their checks from the state, squinted at the minuscule amount, used all they had left to buy some padding for their shoes, a better cane, returned to work. And just two years after she had retired—her pension just enough to live on, her apartment assured—Yarik's mother left for the textile plant again. Two years: in this new land, that was too long ago to measure. Such was the speed of life in the new Russia.

While, inside their buried den, Yarik had lain beside his brother, Dima still flipping through the same old fables, and turned to science fiction instead, books by inventors as much as authors, stories about *how*, *why*, ideas with practical use in the actual world, the one of work and responsibility and caring for their mother that, halfway through their twenties now, Yarik insisted they had to face, had to choose to set aside their wandering days, turn back together to the city at the edge of the lake.

There, the man they'd called The She Bear, The Baron, was building ships. Fishing vessels the size of the factory trawlers that plied the northern seas. No one had known why he would need ones so huge, only that he was paying men to build them. Fishermen eyed the better wage, grounded their old wood drifters, went to work on the docks. Yarik had watched them go, seen the lake grow empty of boats, gone instead back to their father's old gillnetter, retooled its motor, patched its hull.

Each day, before dawn, in the years when dawn had still been a lifting of the dark, he and Dima would load the skiff with bait, push off the beach, row out. All day they fished among their father's memory, leaning over gunwales he'd carved, hauling in nets he'd repaired. And, in the evening, heading back to shore while Dima cleaned the catch, the day just good enough to keep them until the next, the next day promising the same, Yarik could feel his brother's contentment, his own peace.

Maybe it would have stayed that way if Bazarov had never launched his mirrors. By the time the fifth was drifting through the sky, the fishing industry, paused by all the shipbuilding, had boomed again.

In the unending light, algae spread across the surface of Otseva, tadpoles flourished, fry multiplied, carp swelled to twice their size, sturgeon lived as if in everlasting spring, their roe harvested easily as berries from a bush—but all of it slipping out of the brothers' reach. Seeking waters cool and dark the fish swam down, down too deep for the tackle of their small smack. But not for the oligarch's leviathan trawlers, his sea-size seiners, their fog lights crowding the lake, their nets smothering it.

Above the boat, the sides of giant ships slid by like cliffs, their nets claiming ever greater swaths, the lake shrinking around the brothers, their catches, too. But the more Yarik worried, the more Dima swore all they had to do was shrink their needs as well: new clothes given up for secondhand ones, movie theaters forgone for evenings of reading aloud, shots of vodka savored instead of swigged, meat made luxury, sometimes a whole meal skipped.

His brother hardly seemed to notice, though Dima must have seen how it hit Yarik: the way the older twin spat back onto his plate the chicken bones he'd cracked for marrow; the evenings he stood outside the theater's exit door, ear pressed to metal, eyes shut tight, trying to imagine the sight; the hours at home, back from the boat, that he spent slumped before the television, flipping through channel after channel of news.

All the stories of all those men in Moscow: one who made a killing on fish flown overnight from Asia, another who ran a mountain range of pastures efficiently as factories, shepherds to meatpackers, management rocketing overhead on shuttles launched into the exosphere by yet another who, in The Past Life, had been a low-level apparatchik, a failed actor, a farmboy, heir not to fortune but to a state of mind, the same that once drove the Soviets to try reversing their rivers' flow, to drill in search of the center of the earth, the sort of wonders that the USSR had failed to realize, that only the Russia which replaced it—oligarchs bred beneath the clamp of communism let loose upon loot-fueled dreams—could make come true.

Even in those early days there had been an entire TV channel devoted to Petroplavilsk: the Consortium, the space mirrors, the great glass sea. News stories about another satellite sent up. Progress reports on the Oranzheria's increasing reach. Documentaries on the ecosystem chain that led from Lake Otseva's blooming algae to its bigger yields of fish, the scientific feats that reached into plants' cells and found the genes that felt sunlight, knew to blossom, bear fruit beneath a longer or a shorter night. Sometimes, after watching a story on some new flower the Consortium was planting in the parks, Yarik would shut the TV off, wander outside, crouch down, touch a petal. Sometimes, on the boat, laying out nets in what once would have been dark, he would gaze up at the zerkala, eyes watering at their light, and hear again the television's voice: *spectrums* and *non-special-case geosynchronous orbit* and *a thousand kilometers up in the sky*.

And lying in his bed in the room he had still shared with his brother, listening to the night sounds on the street that in his childhood had been the sounds of day, he would wonder how the billionaire had done it, what The Baron had been in the life before—A brigade manager on some factory floor? A beetle-browed student? An aspiring engineer?—who Boris Bazarov had been as a boy. Behind the wall, his mother coughed in her sleep. His twin tossed in the cot they used to share. Dima's unsettled breath, the creaking of the springs. Yarik had known that if he got up and lay beside his brother the tossing would stop, the breathing would calm. From the apartment upstairs: a tinkling of water; the rush of it flowing down through the pipes. Sometimes he could feel time trickling between him and his brother. Eroding, gullying. Until the gulf between them seemed wide as the space between their beds. His own breathing would ruffle. He would sit up. And, rising, pad to his brother's cot, climb in.

There were nights, too, when he didn't, when he never even climbed into his own, nights when he left Dima at the docks and, claiming some chore that needed doing, went behind the clanging yards to an old shipping container where a woman or two sat on the ledge, inside the open loading door, swinging legs in zerkala light. There were nights when he went out to clubs, stood against the wall until some dance-slicked girl came up to him; others when he went to the dom kultura without his brother, danced with girls out there, instead.

Sitting in the back of the billionaire's car, watching the tree-splintered light flicker over his shut eyelids, listening to the tires' ceaseless hush, he knew Dima would have said it had been his need for a wife that had carved the gulley between them, his son that eroded one shore, his daughter the other, their work on the Oranzheria, day after day, rising like a flood.

When he'd first told his brother about the jobs—how much the Consortium would pay, how fast they'd be snatched up, the fact that he was going to apply—Dima had listened silently, gathering the mooring rope hand over hand, watching it coil at his feet. Until Yarik reached over and stopped him.

"Bratets," he said, "I have to. We have to move out."

"Where?" Dima asked.

"To our own apartment."

"Why would we need our own apartment?"

This was September. Zinaida had been living with them since July. Yarik waited for Dima to understand, listened to the waves slap at the hull, the sharp cries of the gulls, said at last, "She's pregnant." His brother turned away. The faint thuds felt through the boat. The deck swept by the shadows of the birds. When Dima finally spoke it was only about fishing: how he couldn't continue by himself. Yarik had reached up, then, buried his hand in Dima's hair. Half of Yarik had wanted to grip hard with his fist—nothing about a nephew, an Uncle Dima, the fact that Yarik would soon be a dad?—and half of him had needed more than ever then to hold his brother in a hug. But Yarik had only given Dima's head a little shake. "Why would you need to fish," he'd said, "when you'll be working on the Oranzheria with me."

He could feel right through Dima the same rocking that he could feel below his own feet—the wake of the steel ships that plowed by in endless embarkation and return, to and from the new built dock, The Baron's fisheries—and suddenly he hadn't wanted to let go. He let his fingers knead his brother's head.

Dima shut his eyes. "What will we do with Papa's boat?"

"Sell it," Yarik said.

And then Dima's hair was gone from his hand and his brother was lowering himself unsteadily to the deck. At Yarik's feet, Dima lay down, his back on the boards. Yarik stood above, watching him. Then he crossed to the engine house. "I need to get an apartment," he said, before ducking his head inside. From in there he shouted, "And you need to buy a baby gift." He cut the motor, ducked back out. "A really big one." He came back, crouched down in front of Dima, held his gaze. "A hundred hectares big." Lying down beside his brother, he had lain it out: how much more quickly they could buy the land, live on it there together, with wives, children . . .

"A dog," Dima had said.

"Named Ivan."

"The Second."

"The Terrible."

"No," Dima had told him, smiling at last, "that will be your baby."

Out there, in the becalmed boat in the middle of the lake, beneath the sky that would have long ago been night, they had lain quietly side by side, the boat rocking their bodies together and away, together and away.

"Yarik," Dima had said, "do you remember?"

Yes, he thought in the stillness of the car's smooth speed, he did. All these years later. That night, all those years ago. But this—this leather seat, this road unfurling beneath him—was now. And his brother was wrong. What had risen between them wasn't anything more than simply time, the steady drip of years, the way life was. Lifting the gloves off his face, he went to shove them in his jacket pocket, felt the cellophane-wrapped cigarette pack, and drew the Troikas out. He could still see the steadiness of Bazarov's hand, the pistol motionless, as if soldered to the side of the man's head. Where, he wondered, had

Dyadya Avya's old gun gone? Had Dima taken it from the izba after the farmhouse was sold, buried it with all the other remnants in their uncle's trunk? Yarik shook free a cigarette. Soon, he would go look. In their mother's apartment, in the chest she kept in her room. And if he found the pistol he would bring it home, hide it somewhere safe. No one would know. He stuck the smoke between his lips. Until—he lit a match—the day he'd mount it on his desk.

What Else Is There for the Devil to Eat?

That evening, in the strange light of the switch, they met each other as they had met each other every evening for years, Dima in the shuffle getting off the bus ("Good morning, bratan"), Yarik in the line to get on ("Good evening, bratishka"). Except this time Yarik's neck looked a little less bent, his face less caked with dust, his eyes more alive. Instead of a quick cupping of his hand on Dima's neck, he held it there till Dima stopped.

"I'm going to be a foreman," Yarik said, and, right in front of all the other hard hats, pulled Dima into a hug.

The line of men getting on and off flowed around them, jostling as if to break them apart, sweep them away to bus and work, but when they loosed their grip it was only to lean back far enough to see each other's face.

Yarik gave him a shake. "Bratishka, it's good news."

He did look happier than Dima had seen him all year, his smile so wide Dima could smell the cigarette smoke. Dima felt a sudden thickness in his lungs, told himself it was the smoke and, smiling back,

70

began to ask how the job had come about, but his brother was already on to what it could mean—for them, their future. . . .

"Maybe now," Dima cut in, "you can get me on your crew?"

Someone's shoulder shoved past, seemed to knock Yarik back a little, his neck stiffening, his eyes suddenly a little more serious. Though no less bright. "Maybe now," Yarik said, "I can really start to save." On Dima's nape, his brother's hand gave one more squeeze. Behind Yarik the last of the stragglers climbed through the bus's doors. He broke away—the air on Dima's neck somehow more heavy than the hand had been—and started after them. "Maybe now," he called back, "by the time we're ready I'll be ready, too." Then the doors were closing and Yarik was jamming himself between them: his shoulder, his elbow, gone.

Out at the far eastern edge of the Oranzheria, the support crew had built the scaffolding across the Kosha River, and that night Dima worked a half-dozen meters above the water. Above him, small broken clouds mottled the sky. Behind the clouds the zerkala were albescent creatures in a murky sea, and, on the glass, the workmen wore head-lamps strapped around their hard hats, their small yellow cones of light sliding from job to job, a thousand of them drifting like some current-borne school spawned by the mirrors above. Now and again, the zerkala would find a clearing in the clouds; their beams would pour down; the men would all shut off their lamps: a thousand candles blown out in one roving breath. Then, for a while, Dima could see the river below—its gleaming ripples rolling slowly towards the distant lake, the splash of fish, of night birds after them—before the clouds would close together again: a hundred sky-hung lanterns snuffed out.

He flicked on his headlamp. The glass showed him his own face back. He was preparing the brackets for the panes and he tried to focus on the adhesive strip that he was laying down, but in the reflection he kept seeing his brother's face, the way Yarik's eyes looked when concentrating on a task, the way his jaw jerked with frustration at himself. When the silicone ran out, Dima held the gun in the air, the old cylinder still in it, and sat there, leaning over his reflection, pressing

71

his lips tighter, turning down the edges of his mouth, leaking a little more weariness into his eyes, until he had it right.

"Ey!" the foreman called to him. The panes shook under approaching boots. Dima reached out, put his palm over the reflection. "I'm sorry," he said, looking up.

But when the zerkala cast down their light again, he could not stop gazing at the world they showed below. On the near bank, he could see what had once been a farm. The inside of an izba poked through its collapsed roof like the skeleton of a sun-shrunk corpse: the white of a woodstove, a mattress with its horsehair springing out, a kitchen cupboard spilling shards of china and glass. He saw a row of stumps where a windbreak must once have stood. The stone foundation was all that was left of what had been a barn. The last intact building, a chicken coop, he watched collapse: a bulldozer smashing through one corner, the wood crashing into its own cloud of dust.

Dima watched the earthmover shove the wreckage into a mound so high it almost touched the glass. There, just below the faint reflection of his face, were rugs that had once lined a wall, small white feathers clinging to torn patches of screen, fork tines glinting, the bowl of a tobacco pipe. Where its dark stem disappeared among the remains of soil and memory, Dima could make out the white of the teeth still clenching its tip.

His slow crawl stopped. In his headlamp's beam: a dead man's clench-jawed grimace. Dima bent his face down closer—his own eyes forming in the fog of the glass, the outline of his own tight jaw—until he could see the old dog's teeth again, yellowed and stained with spots of brown, feel the receding gums, smell the breath, warm and gamy as meat left in the sun.

"What are you doing to that dog?" Dyadya Avya called across the floor from where he lay.

"Brushing his teeth," the boys said.

In the flickering lamplight the brothers' eyes passed laughter back and forth between them. Earlier that night, when Dima had gone to dump his bones into the dog's bowl, he had found a chunk of ivory lying there with its rotted root. Yarik had suggested they brush old Ivan's teeth. Dima had come back from the water basin with the toothbrush Dyadya Avya used.

"Oh," their uncle said, his shoulders shrugging against the boards, as if he had been brushing Ivan's teeth since the dog was a pup. His neck was canted back so that his thick red throat was arched and his felt cap was crushed, and his red face was upside down, staring at them. He said, "I thought you were trying to get him to smoke my pipe." He belched. "My pipe," he said again, and his eyes grew watery in the lamplight. Then he lifted his head on his neck and took a swig from the bottle and rested the bottle back on his chest. There was his upside-down red face again. But the eyes were shut."Don't let Ivan smoke my pipe," he said. "It's all I have left of your father." The lamplight drew two wet lines from the corners of his eyes down to his temples where they disappeared in the dark felt of his hat.

The dog panted, slow and even. Yarik had stopped brushing. Dima, still holding Ivan's lips away from his gums, could feel on his fingers the hot air of the dog's insides.

"He loved his pipe, didn't he?" Dyadya Avya said. And, when the boys didn't answer, he answered himself: "He did." Another swig from the bottle, another sigh. Then the man's eyes snapped open. "I know what your mother says. I know she says he did it to himself. No." His felt hat rubbed back and forth on the floor. "No, my children, don't think it. It's not true!" The old dog's ears swiveled towards the shout. "It was"—Dyadya Avya's voice guttered—"the Chudo-Yudo." His upturned eyes looked from brother to brother. "That snake! That beast! That devil!" He tried to turn the bottle's mouth to his without lifting his head and the vodka spilled around his lips and he shook his face, violently, coughing. "I warned him," he said. "I told him he was tempting the devil. 'No', he said, 'the Chudo-Yudo stays in the river.' Ha! Where does he go when he grabs the girl from the bank? When he swallows the horse whole and cannot move? Where does the current take him as he rests? The lake! The lake, I told him. Into the lake! But still, there he was, every winter, sitting out there, cutting a hole in the ice just big enough for the Chudo-Yudo's head to fit through. Up!" The man's whole body jerked. "And grabs him!" He jerked again, once, like the last flop of a fish on a dock.

Dima, nine years old, his fingers on the teeth of the dog, jerked with him.

"In winter," Dyadya Avya said. "I told him, 'In winter what else is there for the devil snake to eat? Lyova,' I said, 'what are you doing out there? Every day? Alone? You don't even bring home enough fish for supper! Why don't you just work? Why don't you come join the road crews with me? Where you're supposed to be. We would clear the streets of Petroplavilsk together. Proscribed hours, state wage. Lyova, your family is hungry! Your wife is angry! Your sons . . .'" His words dribbled away. He quieted. He looked at them. "Oh, that beast!" he said. "Oh, that fucking beast." He was crying.

Dima let go of the dog. The dog went straight to the sobbing man. It stood over him, licking at his face. "The teeth," Dyadya Avya said, from the darkness beneath the thick hanging shag of the dog, "the teeth."

"But, Dyadya," Dima said, "I saw . . ."

And, because he couldn't finish, Yarik said for him, "We saw them pull Papa from the ice."

And, still, a quarter century later, Dima could see the dark blur of the body beneath the ice, feel his father's frozen eyes staring up at him. Still, crouched on his hands on knees, looking down through the glass at the half-buried pipe—no, not teeth: just a few dried kernels of old feed corn spilled—he could hear Dyadya Avya's reply: "Oh, my children, the Chudo-Yudo does not eat the body. It swallows the soul."

On his first break that night, he climbed off the Oranzheria and walked down to the river's edge to drink his tea. Small things fled his footsteps, shaking the reeds. The sounds of their splashes, the rustling of cattails and canary grass, were smothered by the rumbling of the earthmovers, the groan of shovels clawing rock, men bellowing back and forth through it all.

He shut his eyes, lowered his face till he could feel the tea's warmth on his lids, the waft of it filling his nostrils, and wished it was the scent of his brother's hair instead. Foreman! He thought of what Yarik had said, how now he'd be ready with the money by the time the Oranzheria was done. But how long would that be? And what if they were wrong? If the expansion was never meant to stop? Opening his eyes, he watched an egret sail between the glass sky and the surface of the river, skimming low, its plumes pearly in the mirror-light, its reflection slipping through the shaky reflections of the artificial moons. Was it possible that the Oranzheria would simply go on like this forever? A sea of glass that never stopped growing, creeping outward over the land with a hunger that could not be sated? Was it possible that this was what the new way meant? Yesterday, his brother a laborer. Today, his brother a foreman. Someday, his brother a manager. Years from now. When they were old and life was almost gone. And he would get off the bus, gray-haired, and greet his gray-haired brother and his brother would cup his neck and tell him, *Bratishka, I have good news.*

Far off over the river, the egret rose towards the sky until its wings brushed the glass, then dipped again, skimming the water, and flew on, and tried again. Sipping his tea, Dima watched it—its sudden rise, the shock and flutter, swooping down in frantic flight and panicked rise again—until the last flicker of white disappeared into the small space between the distant river and the distant glass.

Across the water, on the other bank, a woman stood staring at the same far-off place. In each hand she held a large wood-slatted crate; her shoulders, beneath her shawl, showed how heavy each was. Between the slats, white shapes stirred. Each crate must have held half a dozen chickens. He watched the stillness of her standing there, the boxed panic of the birds, dark hair loosed from beneath her kosinka, black strands hanging around her face. She was still looking upriver to where the egret had gone.

"What happened?" their mother had said, so long ago, wringing the washrag out, a stream of hot water drumming at the bones of his bent neck, trickling down his spine.

75

He had been seven, steaming beneath her hands, his hands still stinging, the whole of him still shivering. "We were trying . . ." The words knocked at his teeth.

And Yarik, crowded into the corner of the tiny bathroom, the fleece of his coat still gravelly with frozen snow, the melt dripping around his boots, finished for him: "We were trying to catch enough."

"Fish?" their mother said. Beneath the warm rag she swabbed through his hair, Dima nodded. "Enough for what?"

The brothers glanced at each other. Earlier that night when they had slipped out of bed, they had not even discussed it, had simply known between them what they would do. Their father had been gone all day, would be all night. Gone with their uncle to the dom kultura, gone into the bellowing and boot stomping, the spilled drink and the dancing and the fights, the smoke-and-song-filled night.

The night before, their mother had forbade their father to go. Then she had pleaded with him—*At least come home to fish tomorrow, to bring something for dinner so we won't starve*—and, after he had gone anyway, the two boys had crept out of their room, past their mother still crying in the kitchen, to the hallway closet where their father's tackle waited and out into the quiet that was back then the middle of the night. All the way to the lake's edge they encountered no one. Beneath the moon, only faint hints of tracks: the long lines where men had slid their winter fishing shacks out on their skids. At the end of each trail, a dark hut hunkered among the others, black and still.

Inside their father's, they lit the lamp, crammed in between the scrap-wood walls, Dima hugging the heavy spool of fishing wire to his chest, Yarik doing the same with the bucket of bait. Between them, a stool perched beside the hole. A lapping blackness in the lamplit ice. They listened to the water the way they might have to the noises of some animal from the safety outside the bars of its cage. Around them, outside the hut, the blind wind felt along the walls, found the window hole, whistled in. Through the opening they could see the distant cranes splintering the dock lights through their black bones. They took turns watching, one standing at the window with his gloves over his face

76

against the sting of the wind, the other sitting at the edge of the hole, gripping the wood handles of the wire spool, the line dropping straight down into the dark water. . . . Which was where Dima was when the ice burst open beneath him.

What broke it? What caused the crack? What came crashing through? Or was it simply the ice crashing down, the stool swallowed, the ground gone, the water there, the cold clamping onto him sudden and strong as jaws snapped shut. It cut his skin like a thousand teeth, chewed through his muscles till it hit bone. If something brushed against his body, he could not feel it. If something eyed him as it sank back down into the black, his shut eyes would not have seen it. If Yarik had not found his parka with his hands, had not lay flung out over what solid ice was left and held on and hauled back and got him out, he would not have had anything at all to tell.

As it was, his mother did not believe him, didn't want to hear it at all. She lay the steaming cloth over his face and worked her finger softly at the skin around his eyes, and called to Yarik to get out of his clothes, too, to climb in beside his brother, and as she ran more hot water in the bath, she sang them a lullaby over its rumble the way she used to when they had been too small to make up songs, or stories, on their own.

The night has come
And with her brought the darkness
Mama has gone
And behind her closed the shutters
Sleep, sleep.

Now, at the river's side, Dima held his cooled tea to his lips. Across the water, the woman was trudging away up the bank. Everything about her seemed tired: the way her hair hung, the slope of her shoulders beneath her shawl. Dima watched each slow step—her crates of birds knocking at her knees, all wilding whiteness inside—then he drained his cup and climbed back up the bank on his side and onto the glass and went back to work.

Or would have, if his foreman hadn't stopped him. "Zhuvov," the man shouted, and began a long stream of beratement over the heads of the rest of the crew as, bent over the brackets, they tried not to look at the one being rebuked. When the tirade ended, the foreman was pointing eastward with his stiff hand, towards the place where the Oranzheria ceased and the uncut woods began.

Walking there, across the floor of new-laid glass, Dima could see her beneath his feet: the dark shawl, the panicked hens. She had come to the back of a flatbed truck and was heaving the crates onto its wood, handing them off to a man who stacked them with all the others already brought.

So many times had he opened the door to his mother's knock and seen her hunched like that, dragged down by plastic bags stretched heavy with other people's clothes. So many times had he heard her breath gusting in the stairwell, found her halfway up the stairs, newly home from work, struggling with the weight of the tailoring she'd begun taking illegally on the side.

Neck bent, peering down, Dima made his way slowly towards his new sector, looking through the glass around his boots at all that the woman below was leaving: the dried mud patterned with the hoofprints of cows, the flower beds of wet black soil still waiting for first green shoots, the doghouse with its chain stretched to its empty end.

The bag full of bread ends stacked into a semblance of a loaf. The window boxes and the bright red begonias that their mother planted in them each spring. The way she beamed when she unloaded from her shopping sack a bloody slab of beef. Matching wristwatches, the first they'd ever owned. A new pipe for their father. A gold-plated chain hidden close to the skin beneath her blouse. So she could feel it when she went out—to work, to Party meetings, to other apartments where, in secret, she fit other people for her handsewn clothes—gone more and more from home.

Down below there was the house, the wood shingles curling, chimney still blowing smoke. He walked over it, watching its gray billowing against the glass below his boots, the way it spread and crawled along the clear ceiling, searching for a way out, hunting a crack through which to gain release.

Until he came to it: the end of the glass. What thin smoke had made it there curled up around the lip of the last pane, wafted into the air in front of Dima, and disappeared. Here, the cranes rose up between the girders, swung clear panels. The men steadied them, settled them into slots, secured them, went on to lay the next. He could see his new crew working a half-minute walk away. The new foreman. Not Yarik. He'd known it wouldn't be, not tonight, not ever. The muscles of his neck were weary, as if he'd already worked all twelve hours of his shift, too tired to keep holding his head up, and he walked on, along the girders, boot before boot, until he was past the crew. If his new foreman called to him, he didn't hear it; if other workers motioned *turn back*, he didn't see. He was watching the fields below, the slow slipping away of their grass, the stone wall coming and going, the cattle pond muddied from their last gathering, its surface aswarm with insect clouds, until that was past, too, and there was just the woods. There, the girders stopped. The Oranzheria ended. A forest of birches stretching away beneath the open sky.

It was a sky cleared of clouds, filled only by the drifting zerkala now. Their glow lit the white birch bark, drew the shapes of the trees out of the darkness between. A forest full of bright branches forking into the shards of canopy twigs like a vast field of lightning frozen, the bolts reversed from ground to sky. A breeze stirred them. He could see on the closest ones the first green leaves unfurling from their buds. How long had it been since they had first felt the zerkala's touch? Was it beneath spring sun or the mirrors' semblance that those buds stirred to life inside the bark? And did they struggle so at their casings because they knew this was the one chance they had, that there would not be another season again? In the wan light their color was stripped from them, but he could feel it in his chest: the new green of the new leaves sprouting. Reaching behind him, he lowered himself and hung his feet off the girder's edge and sat and watched.

79

ONCE UPON
A TIME

Once upon a time there was a man who rode the buses of the city every day, all day. Each morning, the sun would find him by a window, would warm his face, spread down his neck, flickering with the speed of all the things slipping by outside. Then stilled. The doors' sigh. Their folding open. *Good morning, bratan,* the man would say. *Good morning, bratishka,* said the one stepping on. Together, they rode out of the city, towards the glass, one turning a hard hat slowly in his hands, the other with hands laid empty in his lap, sitting together until the bus hissed still, and the older brother lifted his hat and rose into the current of others flowing out and the younger lifted his hand and watched him go, and stayed.

The bus filled again with the weary quietness of other men, their few words to each other, and, alone in his silence, he would sit and watch the river slip by. On its surface, the sun painted the shadows of the girders, vast plaid markings cast by the huge panes blanketing its banks. Beneath, they passed hectares of fresh-turned earth, of cut brown stalks, of cornsilk gleaming like spiderwebs in first light, bright green wheat shoots beside ripe golden fields, the dust boiling behind the threshers, rolling in clouds against the glass.

And then they were out from under it, and, bursting past the windows as if at the break of a tidal wave, there came the rush of concrete, bleak buildings rising around tram tracks slick with sun, the wires strung above, the morning sky. He pressed his cheekbone to the shaking window, cold on his skin, watched the city pass.

All the lampshades gone from all the streetlamps, and, bolted in their place, loudspeakers shouting advertisements at passersby. Fairgrounds reborn into a life devoid of leisure, repurposed as a site for dealerships, sparkling cars beneath streamers bright as those that once flapped over the merry-go-round. New Ladas and Zaporozhtsy driven out through the gate where coachmen on their horse-drawn sleighs once offered rides. Between the granite pillars of the old art museum, the used hardware market spilled down the steps, the clatter of the kiosks filling the square. The sports stadium had been converted into a multilevel parking lot. The university into an outdoor market. People thronged the streets, swarmed the maze of tin-roofed shacks sprung up on lawns where students used to lounge, the crowd achurn with an air of panic at all there was to do.

Sometimes, after he had sat for hours watching what the world had become—the shaking of the tram tracks in his face, their clacking buried in the bones of his spine, the city blurring before his eyes—he would feel the driver's glare. The ticket collector would wade through the crowd towards him. A woman in a suit jacket might lean over and ask his name; a man covered in concrete dust might shake his shoulder, ask where he worked. A few times he had even seen policemen gathered around a dark figure down some sidestreet; once, he had watched them carrying a bearded, rag-wrapped, wild-eyed man away; occasionally, they would be waiting at a bus stop, or getting on through one of the doors, and he would rise and slip through the crowd and get off through the other.

Sometimes, then, he would go to see the lake. He would pass beneath the giant statue on its pedestal, the long dead tsar's long bronze finger pointing down at the city, as if to put it in its place. He would hear in the whispering of the aspen leaves the voices of the poets who so long ago had climbed the plinth and stood with an arm around the ruler's waist, a hand gripping his bronze sword's hilt, and read: sometimes their own words, sometimes others'—Batyushkov, Bryusov, Tsvetayeva—but always to a gathering crowd, always him among them, a small boy come down after school to meet his father, who always brought his boat in early to stand beside his son and listen.

Now, he would go down to the shore. He would stand by the cold metal railing, lean against the cold cut stone. No one passed. No one climbed out of the icy waves and stood in their underwear, warming in the sun on the dark rocks. There were only the old pleasure boats, the day sailers and fishing skiffs, decaying in piles of broken glass and rusting motors, splintered masts hung with rotted rope. Beyond them, the shipping yards clanged and boomed, the high cranes moaning their way from tanker to dock. When he would walk back to the trolley stop he would pass beneath the statue again: the Consortium's tulips at its base, their bright redness horded beneath the green of the buds, the wind shaking them as if to spill it.

Sometimes he got off at a movie house and stood on the sidewalk before a marquee that hadn't changed in years. Reflected in the dark glass of the empty ticket booth: a stream of people flowing around him, giving him berth, faces lifting only long enough to scowl.

Sometimes he climbed the cracked stone steps of the once-grand Russian Theater, slipped between the grooved columns crowned with gilded dancers, crawled through a broken window into the dark. Where he would lie down in an aisle, look up at hints of chandeliers lost in the blackness, listen to the echoed wind of his breath. Once, he took the tram out to a different park, different statue: Marx and Engels, their bronze hands caught in the excitement of their conversation, their metal eyes catching each other's thoughts. And standing before them he felt them catch in his eyes, too. Then turned and went back to the bus stop and got on the next tram, his chest tight with the churning ache of his own small insurrection.

But, always, at the end of the Oranzheria shift, he would meet his brother beneath the glass to take the bus back home again. Yarik wore a foreman's windbreaker now, the Consortium's logo above his chest, and when he talked of work there was a heaviness in his voice, as if even his sounds sagged with the weight of new responsibilities, and he seemed, if anything, more tired than before. Watching Yarik rearrange the bills in his wallet, sorting them small to large, all facing the same way—as he always had, now simply with more to arrange—Dima would press his shoulder against his brother's, in case Yarik needed a place to lean, a cradle for his head, a few minutes of sleep. Beneath his brother's weight, Dima would try to absorb the jolts of the road, to take the juddering of the bus into himself. And on these lengthening days of spring into summer, he would wake his brother at their stop and walk with him to Yarik's building door; they would climb together up the stairs; he would take his brother's hard hat from him, his rucksack, his coat on the days—rare, and then rarer—that they would go inside the apartment together.

There lay Timofei, stretched out before the black-and-white TV, its fuzzy screen silhouetting the boy's static-feathered hair as he turned to see who had come in. "Dyadya Dima!" he would shout, and scramble up, kicking his sister's toys out of the way, charging into his uncle's swooping arms. And Dima, lifting his nephew up, would bare his teeth and roll his eyes and bury his face in the boy's belly, slobbering and snorting, smacking his lips, chewing at the small fingers, the toes. Through Timofei's squealing he would bellow, "A fork! I need a fork! Somebody bring me a fork!" And Zinaida would come from the kitchen with the baby on her hip, unsling Polina, hold her out. "Take this instead," she would say, and, "I see we're feeding the riffraff tonight." Kissing Dima once on each cheek, she would scrunch her lips and bemoan the fact of his growing beard. He would tell her that she had too kind a mouth to hold such a shape, that her cheeks were warm and greasy from the stove, smelled like fried oil and fish. "I like it," he would say, and she would leave him with the baby and over her shoulder tell her husband, "You better grab your brother, Yarik. He's getting ready to eat my cheeks."

"A fork!" Dima would cry.

In his arms, Polina would gnaw, slobbering, on his neck. With Timofei clinging to a leg, he would lurch over to the coatrack that, long ago, their father had carved—the legs whittled into fish tails, the stem swirled like a narwhal horn—and, struggling one-handed to hang up his and Yarik's coats, would glimpse, again, the earliest memory he and his brother shared (each twin's little legs wrapped around their father's waist as, holding them in his arms, building the muscles of his thighs, he groaned and roared across the living room, lunging back and forth before the open bathroom door where their mother stood, her face half-made, trying to do her lipstick through her laughs). Always, then, draping his coat over the back of his brother's, adding his scarf to a rack already swaddled in the family's own, Dima's throat would fill with such a surge of happiness that all he could do was stand there, gone still, trying not to swallow.

But sometimes, in these daybloom weeks, the northern half of the world tilting ever closer to the sun, some evenings when the air was balmy with the scent of lilac blossoms, Yarik would scoop his children up or wrap his arms around his wife and suggest they all go on vacation. Then, Dima would keep his jacket on, toss his brother's back to him, help Zinaida into her sweater's sleeves, wrap a scarf around his nephew, niece, and with them all pile back out the door into the hallway, the smells of supper spilling out with them, the family bringing their plates into the stairwell, up four thumping, clattering flights, until they reached the doorway to the roof. Up there, they would spread out a towel stamped with a picture of palm fronds around the spire of the railway station far south in Sochi, adjust the squeaking backs of the rusty beach chairs till they lay flat. Zinaida called them chaise lounges. Timofei called the towel his chaise carpet. Dima, beside his brother, sharing a chair, the plastic strips sagging beneath their weight, would watch the sky for each new zerkalo, each new flash of reflected glow seeming to warm his face a little more.

Those times he could even understand how Zinaida liked the mirrors. The way night used to seem a black breach in the path of the sun, the zerkala now drawing day's clear track through, as if their small bit of earth had been blessed with a new kind of light. She talked of a day when there would be so many mirrors they would seem simply a return of the sun, no difference at all between day and night, all that light warming their patch of the world, as if all Petroplavilsk was beneath a ceiling of glass. Winters without snow, lilacs in December. She spoke of their chosen city, their favored lives. And lying there, listening to her, his own dream—all of them out on Dyadya Avya's, farming as a family together, suppers around one big table, nights huddled together around a stove, all day spent in the fields with his brother—seemed so simple.

On colder days, on evenings when clouds pushed the world back towards winter, they would take their plates to the big couch opposite the old rug that hung above the TV, squeeze all four together, watching *Vremya* or *Gorodok* while Polina toddled and tripped around their feet. Sometimes, he would take the children to the couch alone, watch them while Yarik went with Zinaida into their bedroom to spread out bills and papers on the mattress, to confer on matters of family and home.

Then, Dima would hold Polina in his lap, gather Timofei to his side, tell them stories his own uncle had told him: Emelya the Fool standing over the water hole punched through the ice, the hoary pike fish in his fists gasping through its flapping mouth, *Let me go and I will grant you any wish;* the way Baba Yaga would cut off a dead man's hand, creep into homes, wave the severed palm over sleeping souls so they would never wake; how, to punish her, the townsfolk knotted her long hair to a horse's tail and sent it—whirling, kicking, galloping—across a stony field until there was nothing left of her but her thumping head. He would tell them about the aged, lonely peasant couple who yearned so for a child that the old husband carved a piece of apple wood into a baby's shape and the old woman wrapped it in her shawl and they named it Teryosha and rocked it and sang to it until one night they heard it gurgle, stared as it begin to stir.

Close your pretty eyes, Teryosha
Sleep, my baby child!
All the fishes and the thrushes,
All the hares and foxes wild,
Have gone good-bye in the forest.
Sleep, my baby child.

And when they were asleep, his words would slip into a quiet humming, and he would sit beneath the weight of their lolled heads and hear inside his own the one tale he never told: how one day, long, long ago, the Chudo-Yudo emerged from its lair and, arching its long back, leapt out of the water and into the sky. For a moment, all its heads were silhouetted against the heavens, its flailing body flickering in the light. Then it opened its jaws and swallowed the sun. In the sudden darkness there was only the sound of its body splashing back down into the lake. *That was the day*, Dyadya Avya would tell them, *that all the land became a world without light.* In the dawn it was as dark as noon and noon was as dark as night. And in this lightless land there lived an old couple who had two sons. One was clever and hardworking as an ox. The other was a simpleton. His name was Ivan, his surname Popolyov, but everyone called him Ivanushka the Fool. For twenty whole years he did nothing but lie at the foot of the stove, buried in the warm ashes his family shoveled out. Until, one day, he arose. He shook himself, shed a pile of ashes a meter high. Stomping over them, he called out, *Make me a mace for I am going to kill that Chudo-Yudo snake!*

Sometimes, Dima would have heard his uncle's voice tell the whole tale, all the way through to the end, before the bedroom door would open and his brother would come out. Sometimes, Yarik would come out earlier and save him from hearing it. Then, his brother would help him ease out from under the sleeping children and they would go, the two of them together, into the dim hall and fill steaming glasses from the samovar and take a moment—short, and as time went on, shorter still—to simply be there with each other, doing nothing, thinking nothing, just standing by each other's side, and Dima would know that he had done the right thing, that whatever would happen now, whatever might come next, it would be worth it just for this.

Weeks ago, when Dima had quit his job, had simply refused to return to work, to even stand, he had not understood that he was leaving, had only wanted to sit, watching the light of the newly risen sun slip slowly down the white birch trunks, had sat like that for hours, through the foreman's fury, the urgent tugs from fellow workers', until his brother had come. Crouched beside him, Yarik had whispered *What's going on?* And when Dima hadn't answered, he had slid his hands beneath Dima's arms, and, gently as he could, dragged him away.

That morning, standing alone outside his home on Avtovskaya Street, listening to the receding sibilation of the trolly taking his brother back to work, Dima had gazed up at the apartment he'd lived in almost all his life. In his childhood it had been a gray building, paint peeling down to concrete. Now, all eight stories were freshly blue. But it felt grayer. No grass greened the mud, no buds on the trees, just the dull orange dirt-filled flower pots provided by the Consortium's Landscape Replacement Crew, one on each balcony, their gene-altered bulbs waiting to bloom. Years ago, each railing would have fluttered with laundry, each square slab alive with fowl. Now they were all empty. Even Dima's. Even though he'd left the rooster out when he'd gone to work.

That got his legs going, got him upstairs. Inside, the apartment was freezing, the glass balcony doors folded open, a wind blowing in. "Good evening, lyubimy," he heard his mother chirp, but when he turned to correct her, as he did every morning, she wasn't even looking at him.

Atop the television, the rooster stood staring at them both, undeniable desperation in its eyes. He'd covered the defunct TV with a tablecloth to keep his mother from trying to turn its knobs, and beneath the bird the lace was smeared with scat. At his first step, the rooster

87

leapt, stumble-landed, took off at a run. Its long tail trailed behind it. Across the room it went, beating its wings so hard Dima felt the wind, no closer to flying than a strange pathetic hop before the weight of its trailing plumage brought it down again.

Still, it took him most of a minute and all the energy he had left to corner the thing. He almost gave in, just stomped down on its tail feather train, but the idea of the six-foot plumes ripping out stopped him. Instead, he peeled one of the blankets from around his mother, advanced with it spread before him.

On the tiny square of balcony, he dumped the Golden Phoenix out. "Stay," he told it, as if it were a dog.

Stepping back inside, he said, "Mama, you have to keep the doors closed, OK?"

But she was focused back on her sewing, bent again over the machine. Beneath the table, he could see her foot poking out from the folds of the blanket, working the pump. He crossed the room and, resting his sockfoot on top of her slipper, pressed her treadling still.

She looked up.

"What are you mending?" he asked her.

"Your shirt."

He took the free sleeve in his hand.

"It was full of holes," his mother said.

The cuff had been sewn shut. She was halfway through sealing up the other one. On the couch behind her, the rest of his shirts were piled. He could see their collars had been stitched closed, patches sewn over their buttonholes, turtlenecks turned to traps for an unsuspecting head.

He gave her back the sleeve, lifted his foot off hers.

The chattering of the needle again.

Flopping onto the couch, into the pile of ruined shirts, he watched her. Beyond her, the door to her room was open. At the foot of the bed, he could see his uncle's old chest, the wood sides his father had whittled with wingspread shapes of geese in flight. He made a mental note to get a padlock before she dragged out Dyadya Avya's last belongings and went to work on them. To work. It hit him then—tomorrow he wouldn't go—hit him too hard for a mind so tired; he couldn't think about it; he wanted only to be already asleep.

"Mama," he said, his lids lowering, "have you been doing this all night?"

"I made you *shchi* for supper."

"It's breakfast," he told her.

But she only bent forward, bit off the thread, and, smiling, proud, held up the shirt for him to see.

He shut his eyes.

So soft, the dry skin of her palm when she pressed it to his cheek. So soft, her voice: "It's been a long day."

"A long night," he corrected her. "You should sleep while I'm gone, Mama, so when you're up I can be here and . . ." His hands searched the pile of clothes, lifted some random part, dropped it again.

When he opened his eyes, she was looking out at the rooster, the sun-blasted concrete, the railing thinned to brittle by the brightness.

"It's still light," she told him, as if just discovering it.

"It's always light," he said.

The wrinkles on her brow seemed to deepen, the skin to shrivel a little more around her mouth. And meeting her confused gaze, her eyes milky and filmed as the mirror-faded moon, it was all he could do not to turn away.

They sat at the small table in the kitchen, hunched over their bowls, the two of them and the empty chair at the third place his mother always set. The room was filled with the warmth of the steam and the smell of boiled cabbage. He slurped spoonfuls with his eyes shut, the morning brightness bleeding through his lids, and wondered if this was the last bowl of supper fare he'd have to eat for breakfast. By feel, he tore off a hunk of bread, soaked it in the shchi, and chewed it (but what worse would they have to eat now?) and ripped away another piece (how would he bring home even this?), all the while aware of the empty space beside him (what would Yarik say if he was sitting there?). Squeezing his fist around the bread, Dima tried to feel the fingers of a hand squeezing back. Instead, for the first time since he'd sat down on the glass, he felt the full weight of what he'd done.

"Poor thing," his mother said.

He opened his eyes. From beneath her flowered head scarf a few strands of white hair floated, backlit by the window, aglow with morning. For a moment, he thought something was fluttering against the glass behind her—some bird trying to get in—and then he realized the wing-clatter was coming from the balcony behind him.

His mother beamed. "A mute rooster."

Wiping a wedge of bread around the inside of his bowl, he told her, "He's not mute."

But her smile only grew. "A cock," she said, "that can't crow." And, sinking back against her chair, the old woman let out a hoot.

It was the wild unloosed laughter of a child. He tried not to look at her. Turning to the bowl she'd set out for her other son, he reached across the table for another helping. But there was the ache beneath his arm where Yarik had grasped him that morning, the rawness from being dragged across the glass, and he snapped, "Mama, can't you understand that there's no sunrise?"

In the window's slant of morning light, that seemed to only make her laugh harder.

"There's no break," he told her, grasping his brother's bowl, "between the night and the day, not enough, nothing but the zerkala, the Oranzheria, the goddamn—"

The hurled soup bowl, the smashed window glass: they seemed to disappear at the same exact time, nothing left behind but the sound of the crash.

A breeze prickled the hairs of Dima's arms, shook the dish towel on its hook. He closed his hands around the back of the chair. He didn't remember having stood up. But in his eyes he could feel the same desperate thing he'd seen in the rooster's. Quietly, he pushed his chair in. He went to his mother. He knelt down, and kissed her cheek, and whispered a plea that she might stop crying.

Later, after he had gotten her to brush her teeth and put on her nightgown, after he had watched her shuffle to the couch, after he had bunched himself into the cushions beside her, silently handing her shirt after shirt, after she had sewn closed cuff after cuff until finally falling asleep over the machine, and after he had carried her into her bedroom and lowered her to her bed and shut the door, he went back to the couch and picked up one of the shirts and began to break the stitches she had put in.

Her sewing scissors were in the spools of threads in the wooden sewing box she'd had since he'd been born. They were shaped like one of the great herons of the lake, and he used its sharp beak to pry beneath a thread, cut it, pry beneath the next. Its handles were wings plated in gold. Years ago, most of his lifetime ago, sometime in the months after they had found his father, after his mother had stopped going to work, after she had refused to leave the house, and then the bed, after her hair had become streaked with white and crinkly as an old man's, after they had gone—he and his brother—to live with their uncle, sometime in those months Dyadya Avya had told them about the scissors.

"Once upon a time," he had begun, the way he always began, "there was a woman who had the most beautiful hair." He was lying on his back on the worn wood floor beside the warm woodstove, a bottle resting on his belly below his bare chest sheened with sweat. "Even when she was a girl, strangers would ask to touch it. Her mother used to wake her long before dawn, long before the others in the house were up. She would burn half an hour of kerosene brushing her daughter's hair by lantern light. She wouldn't let anyone else near it. Not even the girl's aunt was alowed to braid it for her. So much her parents spent on oils! On scents! Her father never touched her. Not a kiss on the cheek. Not a hug. Except when he would come behind her and lift her hair in his hands and admire the weight of what he called her dowry.

"When she grew older, of course, everyone wanted to touch it. To touch her. She had lovers. It was very wavy." He lifted a hand, eeled it

91

over the floor, as if riding the swells of the lake. "It was very black," he said. "Black as this." He looked at the iron stove door and drank from the bottle and shook his head violently. "No," he said. "Blacker. Black as . . ." He looked at the two boys. His eyes widened, his face smiled. "Black as yours," he said. "But by then, it was long. So long that when she held her skirt to her knees to wade across the creek, the tip of her hair would get wet. So long that in a strong wind it became a great flowing tail. When she tied it up beneath a kosinka it was so huge on her head that she looked like a Turk! But she almost never wore it up.

"Because, you see, she was ugly. At least she *felt* ugly. Because *others* made her feel ugly. Her lovers?" He looked at the boys. "How old are you?"

"Nine," they said.

"Nine!" their uncle bellowed. "When I was nine what was there to think about but humping? Humping and humping. Are you humping yet?"

"No," they said.

His sigh seemed too heavy to rise off his lips. "Her lovers . . ." He shrugged his shoulders against the floor, said, "Nine!," needed another swig of the bottle to go on. "They would ask her to spread it out. If it was humping from the back. If it was from the front, and she was lying below them, they would lift it with their hands, her hair, and cover her with it. She told me this. She told me she preferred to be on top. So she could cover her face with her hair herself. Poor girl!" He drank again.

"Until your father. Your father gave her that." He made to point at them with the hand that was steadying the bottle on his belly and caught the bottle and instead flapped in their direction with his other hand. Dima was holding the scissors. Yarik had asked about them. They were the one thing she had tried to take with her, the one thing that had been pried from her hands, the one thing that, in all the weeks since their father had been found, had brought her tears.

"He gave her them," their uncle continued, "one night about nine months before you were born. Yup." He belched. "Just before the act. They were naked. He lay down on the bed. He said, 'Stand over me.' She

92

stood. She flung her hair over her head, down over her face, a curtain of it so long it almost touched his thing. Maybe it did. All right, it barely brushed his thing. She was about to sit, when he brought the scissors out, when he held them up to her, when he told her, 'Cut your hair.'"

Sitting on the couch with the heron-shaped scissors in his hand, Dima knew that his uncle must have told them the rest—how long it took with the tiny scissors, how they'd gazed into each other's eyes each excruciating second of the wait—must have ended his story with the way his father had called her his beauty, the way he'd said, "Now, marry me," but he was seeing it, again, the way Dima had seen it in the hot dry air in the house that smelled of liquor and old man sweat and his brother's skin and the smoke of burning beech wood, seeing again the way she cut her hair in small strips, bit by bit, the lamplight slowly slipping in, flicker by flicker, where her black curtain had kept it out, the impossibly long strands falling onto his father's chest, belly, thighs, until he was blanketed with them. How their oils must have shone! How soft they must have felt dropping to his skin! How warm and heavy before she was done.

By the time the door to his mother's room opened again and she came out, the knob rattling in her hand, Dima had reopened only half of the sleeves. She was still in her nightgown, and the old yellow fabric was so thin he could see through it the shape of her, no longer a woman's shape, but just an old person's, with skin hanging heavier in places than it might have on an old man. Her mouth in the past years had shriveled inwards, as if her lips now found more comfort in their closeness to each other than to anything of the outside world. Her eyes were as blue as ever. Her thinned hair was wrapped in a white bun beneath her kosinka, as he had always known it, and her breathing the low whistling wheeze it had become, and the confusion in her face put a sadness on his as it had done now for years.

"I must have slept late," she said. She was looking out the window, a tremoring hand shielding her eyes from the morning's light. "But I feel like I haven't slept at all."

93

"You haven't," he told her.

And when she came and sat at the machine and reached for one of the shirts he had unsown, he gave her the scissors instead. They shook with the unsteadiness of her hand. "We're opening these up," he told her, giving her one of the sleeves. But she just sat there, the cloth in one hand, the scissors in the other, both shaking.

"Aren't you going to work?" she said.

"Yes."

That day, he tore down the light-bleeding curtains from the windows, the winter-heavy rugs from the walls, and nailed the *kovry* up where the curtains had been. He hung an especially long one over the glass doors to the balcony, the rooster standing on its railing perch watching him make it and all the world outside disappear. Inside, it was so dark he had to stumble to the foyer to find the flashlight. In its yellow beam he hunted in his mother's sewing box for her larger shears, went to her bedroom and dug through his uncle's carved chest, found Avya's old felt vest and hat, but could not do it. Instead, he cut the dead man's heavy felt boots into strips. He took the apartment door off its hinges and nailed the strips all around its edges and put it back up. All the while his mother kept asking what he was doing, and when he was done he shut the flashlight off again. In the blackness he went to her. He felt with his hands until he touched her and then he knelt behind her chair and put his arms around her and could feel beneath his forearms the insubstantiality of her breasts. He kissed her where her kosinka covered her temple.

"Go to sleep, Mama," he said.

Sometimes he could see in the confusion and sadness and fear in her eyes a glimpse of what had happened to her when he and Yarik were boys. Sometimes he felt the same tightness twist through his chest. Though then, at least, it had happened fast, weeks instead of years: by the time the men had come to carry her out of the apartment and down the stairs and to the sanitarium she had refused to leave her bed for almost a month. He and Yarik had sat beside her on the mattress, one son's fingers trying to smooth her brow, the other with his hands buried in her stiffened hair. But her shoulders had refused to ease, her face to soften. Her eyes had stayed open, found her children, held them hard, as if gripped by her hands. What had she been trying to make them understand? That she loved them? That they would be all right? That she would be?

Sometimes, now, he wished that he could tell her the same. Sometimes he thought what was happening to her now was worse. Then, at least, they had had hope that there was something they could do to help bring her back. Visit her, the doctors had said. Bring her things that will remind her of her life before. And each Sunday, squeezed beside their uncle on the bench seat of the old Ural the kolkhoz loaned him, they had ridden in the loud quiet of tires rumbling on the Kosha road, holding in their laps the gifts they'd brought: craft projects from school, photographs from field trips with their Pioneer Group, wax paper wrapped around river fish they'd caught and kippered the way she liked. Rounding a bend there it would suddenly be, the compound, those high ivied walls that hid the gardens, its high stone towers, wrought iron lampposts standing sentry, the ancient oaks spreading their heavy canopies over the entrance road. Their uncle stopped the truck. In their chests, the gravel kept on crumbling. He left them at the cloister's gates, went to wander on his own among the gardens, scared of the inside of that place in a way they had never seen him scared before, and together they had gone up the wide stone steps to the big double doors and raised their hands—two small fists side by side, pale against black paint—to knock.

Inside, a nurse led them through the rotunda, down a green-walled hall, past the open double doors that leaked a ceaseless clattering of work—the cavernous chamber where patients sat all day at long rows of sewing machines, doctors pacing between them scribbling notes—past the patients' rooms, doors sanded down to try to hide the scratches, heavy brass racks bolted to the floor, some holding men's shoes, some women's, one their mother's.

Always, before they entered, Dima would open his hand. He would feel his brother's fingers slip in between his own. He would hold on as they went in together. In their other hands they would hold the gifts they hoped might help to make her better. They would put them on the blanket beside her body.

"Mama," they would say, "how are you feeling today?" And wait for her to turn to them and show them the answer in her eyes.

Always the same. Except for the day they brought her the book.

In Dima's memory it seemed like a story Dyadya Avya might have told: how he and Yarik had almost drowned or froze or died some other way that night out on the lake; how the state had threatened to take them out of their uncle's care; how their uncle had cried about it, and then laughed about it, and then, as always, turned it into a tale; how in his telling it had turned into a fable worthy of a book; how with his help they had turned it into a real one, each scrawling the words beneath the pictures the other drew, bound it with a leather shoelace stitched though its binding like the suture of a wound; how they had brought her this story of what they'd done—*Once upon a time* and *out to see Nizhi* and *lost their oars* and *almost drowned*—how she had pulled them to her, worry crowding out everything else in her eyes; how the next visit she had spoken first, asked over and over if they were all right; how she had made them promise to never do something like that again; how that had been the beginning of the months that brought her home; how he wished there was something he could bring her now to do the same; how he knew there was not. He could still feel the pressure of her hand on his cheek, his other cheek pressed to her breast, his own hand holding his brother's, his gaze locked on the part of the window he could see—those thin birches gathered just outside the garden wall, all those still white trunks beneath the shimmering leaves.

When he woke, he did not know what time it was. Somewhere near: his mother's slow breathing. He stirred and felt her with his feet. She had curled into a ball at that far part of the couch. Lifting his legs off her, he shuffled, arms before his face, towards what he thought was the balcony door. His fingers brushed the hanging rug. He raised it.

Out there, the sun was an orange bulge of fire breaking over the city in the distance. Then it rose and he realized he had slept all day, and all night, and it was dawn again. He looked at the rooster outside in the red light. The rooster stared back. Through the glass he thought he heard it cluck.

When he turned back to the room, the light was streaming around his shape. His mother, in it, blinking.

"Good morning, Lyubimy," she said.

"Good morning, Mama," he replied.

That day he rolled the rugs up and held them rolled with screwed C-clamps. He went to meet his brother on the bus, and passed the day on the trams, and that evening, home, he took a pair of socks out of his mother's hands and threw them at the pile of all the others on which she'd sewn shut the tops. From a closet bin he scooped a handful of chicken feed, dumped it into an old dog bowl, brought it out to the rooster. When he was small, he'd ruined his uncle's straight razor scratching the word *Ivan* into the tin side of the same bowl that swallowed the bird's head now. Watching it eat, he pointed at the eastward glow of the mirrors coming. "That's not the sun," he said. And when the first blinked on over the city, he said it again, "That's not the sun." He said it for each one that showed itself, until half a dozen filled the lower edge of the sky. Then he reached down and yanked the rooster's head out of its bowl and made it look. "What's the matter with you, Ivan?" he said. The rooster kicked out its talons. He lifted it by the neck. "Why don't you crow for each of them?" he demanded of it. "Why don't you crow all the time?" When he and Yarik were kids out in the country the cocks had kept them up all night. Was it simply because this one was alone, no others around to goad him with their calls? Or did it think it was some fable bird, its feathers too bright for ordinary life? The rooster's eye swiveled at him. "Why you?" It tried to gouge his knuckle with its beak. "Who says *you* get to need the sun?" Its legs lashed out. Now that he had gotten it mad, he realized, he could not put it down.

Pushing the glass doors open, he headed for his mother's room, the bird held out at arm's length, its long black tail dragging on the floor.

In the old carved chest he found his uncle's felt farmer's hat, dropped it over the rooster's head, clamped it with a fist around the feathered neck. With his other hand he unstrung the leather laces from his boot.

Back out on the balcony, he set the hooded rooster on the concrete floor, scrambled inside, shut the doors. Through the panes, he watched its fury. It got in three quick steps before it hit the wall. Stumbling, it turned and ran full speed into the railing. It stood, kicked out its talons as viciously as a dazed and blinkered rooster could, turned again and ran smack into the glass. Dima knelt down, eye to hood. Behind the bird, the sky was full of mirrors, growing bright.

One day, he got off the bus at the used electronics market in the University Square, wended his way from booth to booth until he found a merchant of old CDs who had the one he wanted. That night, he put it on: peeper frogs chirping at first dark. He set it to repeat and let it play.

Another day, he got off the bus at the Oranzheria, hiked to its edge where the loggers were felling trees, spent an hour searching through the wreckage that they'd left. Home, he knelt beside his mattress, distributing the fresh-cut branches, a forest floor spread beneath his bed frame.

Each evening he ate supper across from his mother, helped her to bed. He fed the rooster, tied on its hood of felt. Stepping inside, he shut the glass doors, unclamped the rug, let it unroll, breathed in the green pine scent, fell asleep to the memory of a world long gone.

And each morning he loosened the laces around Ivan's neck, took off the hood, and listened to the Golden Phoenix crow.

For a while, then, the passengers on the trolleybuses he rode couldn't help but stare at him. Not in the way he was used to—the tight-faced glances of disgust at his indolence, the red-eyed glowers of men coming off eighteen-hour shifts that he'd once worked—but with a new keenness, a wondering, as if recognizing in him something their bodies remembered but their minds had lost, their faces growing easeful with the watching—sometimes a wistfulness in their eyes, sometimes a yearning, a smile, the creep of jealousy—until they turned away, embarrassed that any of the other passengers should see. And he? He sat and watched the city pass, the white footbridges arcing over the Solovinka, their thin wood guardrails woven like lace, the grass on the riverbank green as something grown for a children's storybook. At noon the huge dome of the Alexandro-Nevsky Church shone golden in the midday heat, the market around it filling the air with sun-loosed scents of onions, carrots, cabbage. If he caught the number twelve at Griboyedova Boulevard at 11:55 it would pass by the belltowers just as they began to ring. The tulips around the statue of Peter the Great had bloomed and gone and been replaced by rusty marigolds. In the quiet of the late day before it turned to evening, when the heat had passed its zenith and was slipping slowly towards the cool of night, he would make his way around the statue, cutting blooms. Nobody was ever there to notice. Though on the bus they gazed at him as he brought the orange flowers to the Oranzheria, a gift for his brother's wife. Even the other workers could not look away when he rose, his face lit with the sight of Yarik climbing on.

Where We All Sleep

The marigold in his brother's lapel had lost its luster, its petals curled brown at the tips, but seeing the bloom in the dim entrance to the apartment they'd once shared lit Dima's face full as if from a fresh-picked bunch. Still, he would have crushed it in a hug if his nephew, clinging to Yarik's leg, hadn't been in the way, if his brother hadn't been already hugging a silver samovar big as the boy—a gift, Dima knew, from Zinaida's parents five years ago today.

"It's for Mama," Yarik told him.

Zinaida undid the baby from her sling. "Who has time anymore to sit around a samovar?"

How long had it been since Yarik had invited him up to his home? These days his brother spoke instead of scarce seconds alone with Zinaida, the precise number of pork chops she'd bought, the baby being sick, said *tomorrow* and *next time*, looked away.

Now, Yarik set the samovar down, scooped up his son instead. "Hi, Mama," he said.

Their mother, hunched over her sewing machine, looked up and beamed. "How was work?" she asked him.

"Mama"— Yarik's smile only brought out the sadness in his eyes— "where do you think I work?"

Freshly shaven, he was in a suit—their father's? uncle's?—its shoulders sagging, sleeves too short; he'd cut the pants' cuffs, turned them down so they reached his shoes.

Zinaida's dress fit her like she'd had it tailored to every part of her shape. Dima rarely thought of her as an attractive woman, and it surprised him each time he realized she was. She had on heels so high they changed the muscles of her legs, an eel skin purse, earrings dangling.

"It's our anniversary," she told their mother.

"Oh?" The old woman's hand fluttered up to her kerchief, smoothed it over her hair. "Which factory?"

"No," Zinaida started.

But their mother was already holding her hands out to Yarik. "This one," she said, "I've always known would one day be a *nomenklaturshchik*!"

Stepping in front of Yarik, Zinaida took his mother's hands for him. She glanced back at her husband, her wink failing to cover her concern. "Me, too," she said. "To me, he's always been a big man."

Yarik's half-laugh came out barely a hum. "Yeah," he said. "Direktor of the Zinaida Industries."

But their mother had already retrieved her hands, was hunched over her machine again, the needle hammering. Dima watched her shaky fingers feed it the waistband on a pair of his underwear. When he glanced back at Zinaida, her tweezed brows were raised at him.

"OK," his sister-in-law said, "you don't want me to find you a girl from work. You've made that clear. But Dima . . ." She flicked an amused glance at the pile of underwear.

"It's Mama," Yarik said. "She's afraid of being left out of all the fun we'd have on double dates."

101

And, feeling his brother's grin take hold on his own face, Dima almost stepped to their mother, swept her up, waltzed her to Yarik who, he knew, would do the same to his laughing wife, but when he turned his own grin towards Zinaida he saw only concern creeping into her face. She had begun to lower the baby to the ground, to let Polina wander; now she paused, the girl's legs dangling. Dima watched her eyes sweep the room. She lifted the baby back up.

It was true: he had bartered away the vacuum. It had been one of the first things to go. True: on the wallpaper the ghosts of pictures hung, nails through dark rectangles where the light hadn't reached before. He hadn't noticed till then how overpowering the smell of cabbage soup was, how cobwebs covered the furniture legs, how dusty the moldings. But she wasn't looking at the moldings. He watched her take in the piles of clothes his mother had stitched shut, the other piles of ones he'd snipped back open, the windows browed with rolled rugs, the broken one he'd covered over with a trash bag and tape. The plastic rattled and breathed. Behind the balcony door, the rooster paced, huffed-up and staring back at them. It stopped. Then leapt at the glass, whacked with its beak, beat its wings, scrabbled with its taloned feet, and Zinaida jerked so violently she nearly dropped the baby.

"It's just for two hours," Yarik told her.

"Oh, Dmitry Lvovich . . ." Around her eyes, the skin bunched with concern.

"It'll be fine," Yarik said.

"We forgot the toys," she told Dima, as if apologizing to him for something else.

"It'll be fine," Dima said.

"No," she told him. "I wouldn't leave you with them for two hours with no—"

"Zinusha," Yarik said, "what do you want me to do? Take Dima to dinner instead?"

How embarrassing to stand there feeling his heart leap like that, feeling hope balloon in his chest like one of the toys they had left behind, something that would squeal when pressed and collapse. He was

102

sure they could see it on his face. Just as, before, at Yarik's mention of a double date, they must have seen how much he hated the thought of some woman squeezed beside him at one of the few suppers he and his brother still shared. He knew he should be happy for Yarik on his anniversary, for Zinaida, and he told himself he was, he was—but he had never understood it, the chase everyone else seemed compelled to make, the way everyone seemed to need to dilute their love. Lust, he could imagine—Yarik's trips to the dockyard women, his nights with the dance club girls, the way something in the urge seemed stirred by newness—but love? Why the drive to spread it ever thinner? To go from a mother, a father, a brother, to a wife. To a child, another, a mistress. No, he could not understand how in the end it could make anyone more happy than they'd been when they began.

After his brother and sister-in-law had left, Dima stood with the baby squirming against his chest. Behind him, Timofei stood swiveling his head between the couch with his grandmother and the balcony door, the chatter of the sewing machine and the wing-thwapping, claw-scratching of the bird.

"What's it doing?" the boy asked.

Outside, the rooster's feathers whipped about, its comb flapping, its beak and talons sparks on the glass.

"Trying to get in," Dima said.

"Why?"

He considered. On the one hand, he knew it was time for its supper —simple as that. On the other, he had a sudden urge to tell the boy it was because the bird hated children, hated that it was Timofei who'd stayed while his father had gone, hated even that he was here at all.

"Because," Dima compromised, "it wants to eat you."

The boy's face seemed to slowly squish, as if pressed by invisible palms. He squinted hard at the bird. "I will eat *you*," he said.

Looking at Timofei, it seemed to Dima he just might try. With his free hand, Dima reached out and slowly swiveled the boy's head back towards his grandmother.

"What's *she* doing?" Timofei said.

"Sewing my underwear."

The needle whirred, her foot pedaled.

"She's good at it," Timofei said.

Dima nodded. "She's had a lot of practice."

"Can I?" the boy asked.

"I don't know," Dima said. His mother was bent to her task as if the machine was a steering wheel and the couch a car, going fast, and without brakes, and she was driving it. "Why don't you ask her?"

Which was how Dima ended up spending the next half-hour walking in circles, bouncing Polina on his shoulders, swinging her between his legs, while, seated behind the sewing machine, his mother pumped the treadle, her hands darting in to touch the fingers of his nephew, who stood beside her guiding Dima's underwear into the needle's flash. They had gone through the pile and started over, this time sewing up the leg holes, and the sky outside had finally passed into its long half-light when the bouncing and the swinging and crawling stopped working and Polina began to bawl.

Galina Yegorovna's foot froze. The needle stopped. Beside her, Timofei stared at the wailing child.

"Oh, shit," the boy said.

His grandmother raised her eyebrows.

"Watch your language," Dima told him.

"Well," the boy said, "she won't stop crying, now. Not for a hour. She never does."

"Oh, shit," Dima said.

Timofei let the half-stitched underwear hang off the machine's thread. "Now what are we going to do?" He grabbed another pair from the pile, punched his small fist through the remaining open hole.

Polina, pressed against Dima's chest, redoubled her squalling, as if her brother had punched her, instead.

"Maybe," Dima offered the boy, "you can hold the baby?"

Instead, his mother pushed herself up from the couch, came around the table with arms held out. Her face seemed to slip back two dozen years. "Lyubimaya," she asked, eyes shining, "what happened?"

Handing Polina to her, Dima stood back, as if his presence might spoil the effect his mother would have, as if he expected the child's malaise to dissipate like fog burned off by its grandmother's warmth. Instead, the girl's red-faced roaring only climbed another notch above endurable.

Over its screams he called to his nephew. "Maybe you can help me feed the rooster? Timofei, do you want—" The boy's head shook vehemently back and forth. "I thought," Dima said, "that you were going to eat him?"

But Timofei had gone utterly still. In his eyes there seemed true terror.

Dima glanced at the balcony door. The bird had calmed: its dim shape stood still. Shrugging, Dima crossed the room towards it, stepped out onto the balcony, shut the door behind him. The bird scuttled to a corner against the bars. For a moment Dima dropped his face into his hand. *Why did you say that?* he thought. He's just a kid. Through his fingers he could see the rooster's mirror-lit eyes. They glared at him over its beak. Bending down, Dima snatched the bowl, carried it back inside. Filling it with feed, he could feel the movement of his mother rocking the baby in the kitchen, the frozen stillness of his nephew watching. A memory: a hog, all chewed ears and sharp tusks and slabbering teeth and him, no older than Timofei, the animal four times his weight. He carried the bowl back out and, watching the Golden Phoenix attack its supper, remembered how terrified he'd been, the beast's grunting, Dyadya Avya pouring out the slops. His own uncle. Dima felt like hiding. Inside, the baby's wailing guttered out. Scrape, scrape, scrape went the rooster's beak, digging for the last grains in the metal bowl. Dima unfolded the hood.

Stepping back through the door, he stopped so short he nearly let the blinkered rooster in. Timofei had shoved the sewing machine back

105

against the sofa, the end tables against the walls. In the middle of the room, the boy had tipped both armchairs against each other, back to back, an inverted V. In their long shadow Dima's nephew crouched, all but hands and knees hidden by one large sofa cushion. The other two had been set on their ends to make walls. Carefully, Timofei lowered the last cushion to rest on the edges of the others: a roof. The boy looked up and, seeing Dima, beamed.

"Is that your house?" Dima said.

The boy shook his head.

"Whose house is it?"

"It isn't a house," Timofei told him. "It's a barn."

At his calves, Dima could feel the rooster pushing. Its wings rustled. He shivered. Then, stepping in, slid the door shut behind him. "Whose?" he said.

"Ours."

Crossing the room, Dima crouched next to his nephew, rested a hand on the boy's small head. "You and me?" Dima said. The boy nodded. Dima worked his fingers through the softness of hair. "What about your papa?" he asked.

"Him, too," Timofei said. "All of us."

His nephew had never been to Dyadya Avya's, probably never even seen a picture. And, still, Dima couldn't swallow. "Where . . ." He squeezed a cough inside his throat, tried again. "Where do *we* sleep?"

Timofei turned and pointed behind him: the two armchairs tilted into the peak of a roof. "That's the house."

Of course: the boy would know farms from picture books. Not the two-room izbas—one for large livestock, the other for hens and humans—but little white houses, big red barns, silos like in America. Still, watching his nephew's eyes, the small face close, Dima told him it was a very nice house. "We'll all be very cozy."

"Except the baby," Timofei said.

"Polina?"

"The baby sleeps there." The boy's small finger jabbed downward at the roof of the barn.

"With the horses?"

"And the cows."

"And the pigs?"

"Yeah," Timofei said, "and all their shit!"

They laughed, a quiet, shared laughter kept inside the world the boy had made for them there on the rug.

It was not much later, but long enough that they had turned the samover into a silo, built fences from old schoolbooks stood spine-up, comandeered Dima's mother's two-wheeled shopping basket for a cart, filled it with hay-colored yarn; long enough that the winkered rooster they'd put in it had worked itself into a frenzy, that Polina, pulling the cart, had gone from giggling to a tired quiet crawling, her harness of yarn gone slack, her brother standing over her shouting *Kha! Kha!*, his small hand flailing as if he held a whip; late enough the baby had just begun to cry when Zinaida walked in.

A few minutes after Yarik had followed her, Dima stood with his brother in the middle of the wrecked room, their mother in the kitchen heating up the shchi, Zina in the bathroom with her children. The door was closed, but Dima could hear her vehement whispering to Timofei, the slosh of the washrag as she scrubbed Polina's skin.

Dima said, "I didn't know the marker was permanent."

"Oh come on. After you'd covered her body with it? What were you doing?"

"Me?"

"Yes, Dima. While my son was blackening my daughter with splotches of permanent ink, what were you doing?"

Seeing it again—his niece on her back, his nephew crouched over her, the pen squeaking on her skin as she giggled and squealed—he struggled to suppress a smile. "I was holding her down."

"This isn't funny, Dima."

"Bratets . . ."

"This is crazy."

107

"Timofei was teaching her how to moo." Dima watched his brother's face mirror his own. They stood there, trying not to grin. From the bathroom came the rumble of Zinaida adding water to the tub. From the kitchen, the clanks of their mother at the stove. The older brother reached out and stilled the younger's fingers beneath his own.

"Dima . . ."

Dima tried to keep his hands as motionless as possible, to make them a good resting place for his brother's. "She'll be OK," he told Yarik.

"I know," Yarik said. "I'm not worried about her." It didn't matter: his brother lifted his hands off, anyway. "Why are you doing this?"

Dima lifted his gaze to Yarik's; his brother's eyes were more resolute than his hands. "I don't know."

"You must," Yarik said. "Because you're the one who quit your job. Who rides around on buses all day. Who refuses to work . . ." He reached to his throat, pulled at the knot in his tie. "They talk about you," he said. "At work. On the bus. At Zinaida's work. They talk about you, but you're the one who makes them talk. You're the one who threw away your job, who refuses to stop this, to just do the same thing we all know we have to do. You must know what this is doing to you and still . . ."

"I'm OK," Dima said. "You don't have to worry so—"

"This fucking thing." Yarik yanked the tie loose, dragged it through his collar. "Do you even see yourself, Dima? Do you see anything around you?" Slowly, he wrapped the tie around all four fingers of his other hand. "Forget the looks they give me when I get off the bus. Forget the way Zina looks at me when I bring you home. Can you imagine the things the other kids say to Timofei at school? His uncle a tramp? A throwback? Their parents: 'You don't want to wind up like *that*.'" He came to the end of the tie. "You must know. You must, and still you choose . . ." And he stood there, holding it tight, a bright bandage around his fingers. "I *do* worry. Bratishka, I worry about you."

"Bratan," Dima told him, "nothing's going to happen. I haven't done anything. We were just playing." He took a step towards the tilted-together armchairs. "Look, this is a barn." He crouched down.

In there, a row of four empty glass jars glinted. "We even put in milk cans." Still squatting, he turned to the couch cushion house. "This is where we sleep." Patting the rug in time to each name, he said, "You, Zinaida, Timofei, his Dyadya Dima. He wanted to sleep between his mama and his uncle. You, he wanted over here"— he patted the rug— "on the other side of me. But I told him you'd want to sleep beside your wife."

"Is that what this is about?"

"This"— Dima rose, stepped across the rug—"is the cart. This is the hay."

"This is about Dyadya Avya's?"

"Here is the rooster." Dima bent down and untied the bird, and when he stood again he was holding it to his chest. "If you take off his hood he even crows."

Yarik looked away. His eyes seemed to land on everything in the room except his brother. In the opening to the kitchen, their mother stood staring into a pot, gone still but for a few white wisps of hair fluttering in the steam.

"And Mama?" Yarik said. "Where is she supposed to sleep?" He turned back to Dima. "Or did you forget her? Did you think she'd just stay here? Go on living like this? Or not? Because, like this, how long can it be before she . . ." He shook his head. Around his fist the tie was so tight it cut the color from his fingers.

All his life, Dima had seen it: the way their mother weighed on Yarik, her expectations, his shame at failing them, resentment at the fact that he still had to love her, at the ease with which Dima did.

"You were supposed to take care of her," Yarik said.

Long ago Dima had learned to let it alone, stay silent. He buried his own fingers in the soft belly of the bird.

Yarik sighed. Slowly, he began to unwrap the silk. "Zina and me," he said, "while we were at dinner, we decided . . . we want . . ." Before his hand was free, he was already reaching for his pocket. "I only have a few hundred on me, but—"

"No," Dima told him.

"We can afford, each month—"

"No. I am taking care of her, Yarik. Look at her." She was tasting the broth, a spoon to her lips, her eyes shut. "You think she needs something other than soup, her sewing, her son—her *sons*—to be happy?"

Yarik stood with the unwrapped tie hanging in a low sag between his hands. "You think she is?"

"I think," Dima said, "she'll sleep on top of the stove like Dyadya Avya did." He smiled. "Keep your money, bratets. Take whatever you were going to give us and save it for your son. The barn, the izba . . ." He motioned with the rooster towards each, the long tailfeathers swaying. "When we go out there, Timofei won't have to make believe. We'll play the games Dyadya Avya used to play with us. Dump a bucket of potatoes onto the table. Tell him and Polya whoever peels the most gets a sip of vodka. Do you remember him lying there drinking while we peeled? How he'd tell us a story? The way we used to get slower and slower as we got closer and closer to the last potato, how we'd wait, with that last peel hanging, not wanting his fable to end?"

"You make a fable of *it*," Yarik said.

"You remember it."

"You tell it how Dyadya Avya would have told it."

"But you remember it."

"Yeah. Because it's a memory. And memories of that long ago *are* fables, Dima. It was before the zerkala, the Oranzheria. Before I married Zina. Before Timosha and Polya. Before I was a foreman. Look at this." He held his hands forward, the red silk shining between them. "Zina picked it out. Not one of Papa's from thirty years ago, but one she—one *we*—picked out together. Maybe all Mama needs is soup, Dima, but I like that I can take my wife out on our anniversary. For barbecue. Have you ever eaten American barbecue? Do you remember when there was no meat in the stores? Do you remember how even when we were working at the factory, the only meat we got was gray and sour and all gristle? Do you remember, in this fairy-tale childhood of ours, what we would eat every night at Dyadya Avya's?"

"Potatoes."

"*A potato.*"

"And cucumbers."

"I still eat potatoes, Dima, but now I have them with meat. *Beef-shteks, cherbureki.* And I take them out of the freezer and put them in the toaster. In a *toaster,* Dima. Potatoes. Shredded into patties and precooked and crispy. And I love them." He leaned towards Dima, low as if he would rest his forehead against Dima's own. But he stopped, his face so close Dima could see the lines creased around his eyes. "Almost as much," Yarik said, "as I love you. Even your fairy-tale ideas."

Dima shifted the rooster in his arms, spoke with his lips moving against the hood, his eyes on his brother: "You didn't think it was a fairy tale when you said we should sell the boat, sign up for jobs on the Oranzheria."

Yarik straightened, began to gather his tie. "That was a long time ago."

Dima lifted his cheek off the felt. "Don't you still want it?"

"Of course." Yarik stood there bunching his tie into the palm of a hand. "We were talking about what we *had.* Back then. Not what we *will* have. Someday." He was staring at the silk, the red seeming to grow more red as it filled his hand. "Bratishka," he said, "when I shut my eyes at night, when I finally go to sleep, do you think it's about toasted potatoes that I dream?"

There was the mewl of a knob turning, the rasp of the bathroom door against the floorboards. Zinaida came out holding the baby. Polina was wrapped in a towel, her forehead smeared gray.

"Bring me a cushion," she said to Timofei and the boy passed behind Dima and lifted the roof off the home and carried it to his mother who, laying the baby on it, ordered him to clean up the rest. Wending around the brothers, the child broke down the house, replaced the cushions, pushed apart the barn, gathered up the straw. And despite the ruination around him; despite the fact that Zinaida, zipping a jumper shut over the baby's body, refused to look at him once; despite the way Yarik restrung the red silk over his neck as he prepared to

111

leave; despite all that, when their mother came out of the kitchen with her oven mitt on and a look on her face that Dima knew meant she thought they had all just come in, that in a moment she would ask *How was work?*, he could not help but imagine that the words out of her mouth would be *How was school?* instead, that the soap-and-iron-scented steam was pipe smoke wisping from the bathroom, that their father was in there shaving, that their mother was not old, that her hair had never been struck white, that it was only he and Yarik left alone before supper in the home that was theirs again.

A Flame in the Blood

That night, and the next morning, and in the days that followed, his brother's *Why?* refused to leave his mind. *Why are you doing this?* There was a time when they would not have had to ask that of each other about anything. Now, on the tram, shouldering some exhausted worker's lolling head, Dima could not quit thinking of Yarik's twelve-hour shifts. Reaching out to help up a woman his mother's age too work-weary to climb the few bus steps, he could not keep from seeing how old his brother's eyes had grown in a mere month. Could not help but ask it back: *Why?* Was it possible they had changed so much? That one day they would come to understand each other as little as their parents had? He remembered his father on the couch with his books in his lap and his pipe wagging while he spoke—*I am working, I'm working on myself*—remembered his mother standing there, shaking her head, as if she'd lost the ability to communicate with him through speech. Was it possible that they had started out like he and Yarik, that the tracks they had run on side by side had somewhere down the line simply hit a switch that sent them slowly separating?

More and more now, he got off the tram at a tall column topped with a small bronze model of the great tsar's ship, its prow pointing west towards the lands young Pyotr had explored, a symbol of the spirit that had once filled the law school and the science labs and the steps that rose beneath the stern steel letters—UNIVERSITET—that overlooked the square. University Market, where now electronics and appliances were bought and sold. Each time Dima pushed his way through the throngs, into the Universitetski Rynok, he was surprised to find some hawker hadn't scrambled up the plinth, wrenched off the ship, shouted down a price. But the brass sails remained unfurled above the maze of kiosks, the used goods stalls where Dima sometimes sold small things—a kitchen scale, a curling iron—brought from home.

Though these days he came with nothing, climbed the stone steps, pushed through the groaning doors. Inside, sales goods had usurped the classrooms, electric stoves gathered in place of scholars, sound systems rattling the remains of blackboard chalk. In the lecture halls where students once studied Akhmadulina, Yevtushenko, TVs shouted each other down. Dima would walk past it all to a stairwell at the far end of the first floor, where, behind the door, all the cacophony faded away. His footsteps tamped the noise further into quiet. In the basement, the building's heating and cooling machines murmured, the clacks of his shoes muffled by a floor so thick with coats of paint it felt soft beneath his soles.

As far as he could tell, the door he'd found down there was the only unlocked way in. But if anyone else used it, there was no sign. He would shut it behind him and savor for a second the utter dark. Then he would reach to the wall, slide his fingers until they hit the switch. The fluorescent tubes hummed, flashed on. A few more flickered. Until a long row of bookshelves showed. At the dim edges of the light, more dark stacks stretched out. He walked down them, flicking the switches, each row shuddering into light, as if they were the night tracks of some great railway station and, as he passed, engines rolled in, flooding each platform with their beams—Karamzin, Leskov, Pushkin, Merezhkovsky—until he stopped at whichever one he chose to board.

Hours later Dima would emerge, mind still buried in some book, hurrying back through the market to catch the next tram to the lake. With the windows open, he could smell Otseva as the tram drew close: a scent like rain hitting soil, wet feathers in silt. No one else got off there. Down at the lakeshore he would lean alone against the railing, the iron warm from the sun, and watch the small shapes of the massive ships drifting in the distance among their invisible nets. Farther down the shore, at the harbor, the cranes clanged, swung their bony arms around the sky. But here, where he stood, the water was empty of all but birds: a flock of black jaegers afloat on a breeze, below them seagulls bobbing white on the waves.

When he and Yarik were boys the calls of children would have chorused with the caws of birds, swimmers bobbing between the smacks and sailboats, the small skiffs moored near the shore where, each early light, fishermen would gather to row out.

In summer, Dima and Yarik would go down there with their father. Dawn would have already cracked the dark, the distant edge of the lake rimmed with a swelling strip of red as if the night sky was a lid lifted by some unseen hand. The low-flung light would find them all there on the littoral—the men and their boats, the spools of nets and the upslanted oars—all casting long shadows onto the gravelly beach behind them, where the boys would help their father haul the heavy bait boxes, the coolers of ice, his clanking wood-carver's case. And on mornings when Dyadya Avya had spent the night, stayed up drinking vodka and smoking pipes, slept over on the couch, he would come down with his only family, sit in the sand sharpening filleting knives, the two boys crouched near, fingering a net for tears, and tell them his tales of Nizhi. He had been there, once. Their father, too. *When I was not much older than you. Your papa was not much younger. We were both in the Young Pioneers.*

They had gone out as a troop, the boys and girls crowding the deck, their blue pants fluttering, blue skirts held down against the spray, around each neck a Pioneer scarf, blood-red and snapping in the wind. The schoolmarms and Komsomol minders who led them out had arranged with the monks for a tour of the churches enclosed by the wood walls of the *pogost*, but their uncle and father had hidden on the ferry, slipped out after the rest, escaped to see the world beyond the gates instead: the wind-whipped pines and vast stands of reeds and the life the monks lived on that island so far out in the middle of that sea-sized lake.

Out there, Avya said, *they still make fishing nets from rope rolled out of bark. They use a drawknife to skin green aspen trees, soak sheaves of the long strips in the bog water beneath boards weighted down by stones. And when it's dry it's soft and golden as a young girl's hair and they roll it between their hands.* He would set down his knife and sharpening stone, place his palms on his knees, and show them. He told of looms that looked medieval, of the intricate cloths the weavers turned out, the crosses and icons the monks carved into everything from soup ladles to cowbells. There were plows fashioned of ropes and planks, blades made in the island's forge. *They curved downward,* he said, *long as your arm, like teeth pulled from a Chudo-Yudo's mouth. And do you know what pulled them through the earth?*

Working at the tangles of the nets, their fingers red in the red of the sun, the boys guessed mules, oxen, even goats.

Men, their uncle said. *A monk behind pushing at the handles, another in front, hauling a rope around his waist, and both of them chanting while they worked.*

He spoke of men singing as they threshed the flaxseed; of others rolling themselves across cut fields, frocked bodies smashing stalks back into soil, a dozen monks turning over and over among the shadows of the clouds. *One's sole work was to ring the bells. He'd climb the bell tower, wrap himself in the ropes: around his forehead, looped over his chest, attached to each elbow, ten strings tied to his ten fingers. When he played them the sound was like a dozen men each ringing a dozen bells. But it was the sight of him you never forgot: strung up in ropes, his whole body flailing, his mouth hanging open, his face twisted by bliss.*

Like this, their father said, and, gathering his fists full of the net, threw his head back, dropped his jaw, and spasmed so wildly his boys leapt back, laughing against their laughing uncle's lap.

On those long summer days they spent every hour of light out on their father's boat. He had named it Once upon a Time, the words—ZHILI-BYLI—carved in its stern like the name of any other fishing smack, but in its gunwales, in the door to the catch well, in all the places their father had carved, it was unlike anything else on the lake. Sunrise to sunset they worked surrounded by scenes he'd chiseled. The gurdy's thick shadow slipping away from fur-hatted Ivan Popolyov lifting the lid off a pot: inside, the snowball half-turned into a maiden, blushing pink with early sun. Midmorning blasting the transom bright where, on either side of the motor, a water pail danced on legs. Around the corner of the wheelhouse, another Ivan gaped at them, his face gone golden in late light. And, lit by the moon, he was on top of the structure, too, in kaftan and boots, straddling a carved branch beside a carved nest while a carved owl taught him the language of birds.

Once school started up again, their father went out alone, returned while the other fishermen were still at work, sunlight still full, his hold still half-empty, in time to meet one son waiting on the strand for him. Their mother kept Yarik home to study, but Dima was always there: together, they would walk up the shore to stand, father and son, in the last hour before sunset, listening to the poets atop the statue of the tsar.

Now, an hour before the mirrors rose, Dima would leave the lakeshore and walk back through the park, and pass beneath the giant pointing arm of Peter the Great and to the bus that would take him out to the Oranzheria to meet his brother.

One day he stopped at the statue, instead. It was raining and the wind blew in off the lake, streaking at a slant against the tsar's bronze back. In the lee of the plinth the low step leading up to it was the one dry place. He had left the railing early, his face raw from rain, his shirt wet, and so he let himself sit for a while, leaned his back against the base, watched the trees shake.

Even in weather like this they used to gather. Not many, but always some, always a few hunched into their raincoats, sharing umbrellas, listening to whichever poet had managed to scramble up the slippery plinth, to stand at its top getting soaked, an arm around the tsar's waist, and shout his verse through the racket of the rain. Always his father was there to hear.

Now, the square was almost empty. Under the aspen trees, among the dandelion puffs heavy with sog, two old people sat in their hats and raincoats atop two upturned plastic drums, manning the receptacle collection site—one ruble per plastic bottle, two for cans of tin—a makeshift recycling center run by what was left of the Communist Party in Petroplavilsk. On the opposite side, around the bus stop, a few small shapes huddled. Nearer, beneath a tree at the edge of the square, a trashman in his orange poncho, his broom over his shoulders, waited out the rain.

It had quit, and there was just the dripping from the leaves, from the tsar's stiff arm above, by the time it came to Dima: of course no listeners were there; for a long time now there had been no speaker atop the statue for them to hear. He craned his neck. Up there: the toe of Peter's boot, the bottom of his coat, the underside of his outstretched hand, the gray and rolling clouds. From the cobblestones there came a shrushing sound, slosh of water. Silence. The shrushing again.

It wasn't easy climbing up. He got his shoe tips on the stone ledge, but from there bronze swooped out in a grip-denying slope, and he had to stretch to reach the hold above it, haul himself with shaking arms and scrabbling legs until he could grab the great tsar's toe.

Standing foot to foot with the statue, one arm clamped around its wet cold waist, Dima looked down at a square unexpectedly far below. The rustling of the leaves seemed louder now that his own clothes were flapping in the same gusts. The shrushing on the cobblestones had stopped. Instead, there was the silence of the trashman looking up at him. In his hand the man held the push broom straight up, its bristles dark and sopping, its wide head facing Dima like the pan of a photographer's flash. Over at the bus stop, the commuters had turned to watch him, too. Looking at their faces beneath their black umbrellas, Dima could feel the hairs prickling all down his neck. He tried to think of how he would begin a poem if he were a poet. He coughed. The trees rustled. He tried to think of what he might have inside him to say. His face felt feverish. At the bus stop a man began to shake his umbrella out. Dima watched another turn away, look down the street.

A flame is in my blood, he thought. The statue's waist felt like it was trying to slip loose from his fingers. He imagined saying *A flame is in my blood*, and thought his throat was so dry the words would stick, and when he finally said them—"A flame is in my blood!"—he was trying so hard to get the words past his teeth they came out twice as loud as he'd intended.

The old Party members' wet hats swiveled towards him, white beards in the brim-shadows. They shifted on their red plastic buckets.

A flame is in my blood, he thought, and thought blood, bone, burning, throat, dry, life, *burning the bones dry* . . . "Burning the bones dry of life!"

The noise of the bus covered his voice, and he shouted the last word—*that's not too bad*, he thought—and then was glad for the bus's interruption so he could stop and think. He watched the people get on, one person get off—a young, thin woman with black hair all buzzed but for her bangs, dressed in the yellow vest of a bus-fare collector—and when it pulled away again there were just the ones who'd been there before, two waiting for a different number tram—they'd turned their backs to him—and the fare collector woman already shifting her glance away. He looked down at the trash sweeper. The man swung the broom-head back to the ground.

"I sing . . ." Dima tried.

The shrushing of the broom, the slosh of the water it pushed over the stones, the shrushing again.

"I sing . . ."

The man flicked his eyes up at Dima and Dima tried to catch his glance, but the man yanked it away again.

"I am singing of . . ."

As the man moved off, his orange back hid the broom, his poncho swishing to the sound, so that it seemed the shrushing came from the man himself. Beneath the sound, Dima could hear his own words lingering; he wished the man would walk faster, or shove harder, or do whatever he had to do to cover them up.

Sliding down, he sat at the tsar's feet, his own feet dangling against the plinth, still far from the ground, the metal folds of Pyotr's coat crowding his head so he had to hunch. He sat there, imagining what his father would have thought; he would have walked away, too. Or tried to climb up and get him down. And, thinking of his father, it came to him: *A flame is in my blood, burning dry life to the bone.* The first time he'd heard it, he had been sitting on his father's shoulders. *I do not sing of stone, now, I sing of wood.* Was it Akhmatova? Pasternak? He tried to hear the rest—*It is light and . . .* something . . . *made of . . .* Something about a fisherman, an oak . . . *hammer them . . . hammer them . . . hammer them in . . .* —he couldn't do it.

When the sun came out again he was still sitting there. He shut his eyes, watched the redness it made of his inner lids, felt its faint warmth on his face. Surely he could remember something he had read in the old library. . . . But there was only the sudden booming of his father's voice, the bellowed tune to Glinka's opera, the dom kultura fires flickering, the steam of all the villagers packed inside to see their fellow farmers perform that year's rendition of Pushkin's epic poem, as they did each year, and everywhere, in cultural houses across the land, in rural schoolyards and city auditoriums and the theaters of the capital, places where once, in a time long past, the entire country would seem to pause from life, different days, at different hours, but all gone still, grown men and women mouthing the few stanzas they'd learned as children, children learning them anew, all brought to silence as they listened to the beloved verse . . .

> *By a distant sea a green oak stands;*
> *to the oak a chain of gold is tied;*
> *and at the chain's end night and day*

a learned cat walks round and round.
Rightwards he goes, and sings a song;
leftwards, he tells a fairy tale.

"... What magic here! What magic ... magic here ..." But that was all he could remember. He sat listening to the whispering of the trees, the clang and boom of the faraway docks. A bus came, went. It wasn't until its rumble had faded again that he realized it had taken with it the shrushing sound.

He opened his eyes. The sweeper was still down there, his broom motionless now, his eyes already on Dima's. The man took one hand from his broom. With it, he made a scooping gesture, palm to his chest, fingers curling, a motion that might have meant *come down, come down* or might have meant *more, more* or whatever it meant that the two old Communists now stood up from their bucket stools and hobbled closer, that the fare collector who had taken off her rain boots to stand barefoot in a puddle, cigarette between her lips, only now broke her stillness to light it.

That Switch, Dima rode the tram out to meet his brother, but when they got off at Yarik's apartment complex, instead of waiting in the hope he'd be invited up Dima hugged his brother there on the street. Then he got back on another tram and took it to the Universitetski Rynok. That night, in the old stacks of the abandoned library, he found what he was looking for. And the next day, at the same time, he climbed the statue of the tsar with a copy of *Ruslan and Lyudmila* in the rucksack on his back.

There, below him: the park sweeper, leaning on his broom handle, looking up. To either side other trashmen stood, one with a huge plastic bag, another with a poker, scraping quietly at the cobblestones with its sharp tip. With them, gathered on the cobblestones around the statue: a woman in a business suit wolfing pirozhki with greasy hands, a man beside her holding an empty dolly at an angle, as if about to drag it away. The last time Dima had seen even such a small scattering of people standing around the square so still was so long ago the three old folks who'd turned over their red plastic buckets in the grass wouldn't have yet been old. They had brought bags of bottles with them, were sorting the plastic from the glass, the small sharp sounds skipping like rocks across the surface of the wind in the leaves. Over on the street, a trolleybus pulled up. Dima glanced to see the same thin woman stepping out of the doors again—black hair catching the breeze, fare collector's bag swinging as she hit the sidewalk and saw him and quickened her pace, as if she thought he'd already begun.

He had forgotten, before, that Pushkin had opened his epic with a dedication. Now he started it over again, from the true beginning. "For you," his voice broke through the breeze, "tsaritsas of my soul, my beauties, for your sake have I these golden leisure hours . . ."

A few last clanks of the old Communists sorting their bottles. Scrape of metal on stone: the man with the truck dolly lowering its lip. The trashman with his poker stilled. For a moment the stillness of them down there, of their eyes on him, stoppered his memory. He could recall the next words—*devoted to writing down this fable whispered*—but not what came after, and he was about to give up, to slide his rucksack around his shoulder, unzip it, draw out the book he had been studying on the buses all day, when the fare collector drew the cigarette from her mouth and stepped to the statue. She was not long out of her teens, too young to remember the poets before. But she held out the cigarette for him to take. Her fingernails were painted black, and keeping his eyes on them, he took the smoke, sucked in, started to straighten up. Her fingers snapped. She beckoned with them. Thinking she meant him to lean close, he glanced at her eyes. No, she just wanted the cigarette back. Something about that made him smile, and when he'd given it to her he pulled himself straight, waist-to-waist with the statue again, and spoke on—of the feline raconteur, the ancient oak, a world of fables redolent of long ago Russia, the Rus of old. . . .

> I was once there; I drank of mead
> I saw the green oak by the sea;

I sat beneath it, while the cat,
that learned cat, told me his tales . . .

He went as far as he had memorized—the wedding feast; the gusli's wavering announcement of the bard; the newlywed knight Ruslan, eyes only for his Lyudmila, too full of lust even to swallow; his sullen rivals, onetime suitors of the bride—went all the way into the bedchamber, until (*But lo!*) thunder rips the air (*a flash!*), the lamp goes out: the eerie voice, the black figure, the bride disappeared (*groping, trembling, Ruslan's hand seizes on emptiness . . .*). By the time he stopped, a handful of others waiting for the tram had wandered over, let their trams pass by; a shopkeeper across the street stood just outside his door, as if fighting the pull to abandon his job; a vendor in stained apron and steam-wet mustache had done just that, left his *pelmyeni* cart untended to come close enough to hear. In the quiet after Dima's words, they all looked up. And panicked: in these ever longer days of early summer, the zerkala could rise nearly unnoticed, bleach dots speckling a sheet of still-bright sky. The business-suit woman clacked off in her heels, madly wiping fingers needed for her phone. The fare-collection girl put her shoes back on—she'd been sitting on the stones, black toenails in the sun—and got up. There came the clatter of the old Communists returned to their bottles and cans. The trash sweepers went back to work.

But the next day most of them were there again. And the shopkeeper, too, his shop door shut. Above it, in the second-story windows, the third-story, the fourth, men in ties and women in skirts stood, fingers parting blinds, foreheads pressed to glass, peering out at the gathered crowd. The Communist Party members had moved their whole collection center—buckets and folding table and stacks of crates—close enough the old people could hear. There were a gaggle of them now. The trash sweepers and litter pickers, sidewalk washers and railing painters—their orange vests bright as buoys floating among all the rest—made way for a long line of little children brought by their schoolteacher to hear the revered old epic told, mingled with the men on the repaving crew who shut down their steamrollers and silenced their jackhammers and stood, hard hats pressed to hips by arms still sheened with sweat, listening.

To the old tsar's plea to the gathered knights: find his stolen daughter, earn the hand in marriage Ruslan had forfeited by failing to safeguard his wife. To the descriptions of dust boiling up behind the racing chargers ridden by the reinvigorated suitors, to the names—Farlaf, Rogdai, the Khazar khan Ratmir—that all but the schoolchildren had heard so many times so long ago. To the shame of disgraced Ruslan stumbling half-dead with hopelessness upon a light, a cave, a hermetic mage waiting inside. When Dima voiced the old recluse's revelation—that it was the necromancer Chernomor who'd stolen the bride away—it seemed the crowd leaned in as if to touch the fable as much as hear it. And when he reached the end of what he knew, and his last words settled over the people gathered in the square, he felt it, too: the calls for more, the scattered clapping, a shouted guess at the next line, a sense that this, this thing he'd started, was not his to stop.

The next day, the crowd had swelled to twice the size. A thin drizzle pattered off umbrellas and hat brims, briefcases and newspapers held over heads, so many gathered there that what should have been soft murmuring turned to a rumble that threatened to drown Dima out. He shouted over it, picking up where he'd left off, reciting what he'd memorized that day—(Ruslan: "*Why came you to this wilderness?*" The hermit: "*Long ago I lived in Finland . . .*")—shouting out the old Finn's own tale, watching the faces in the crowd as they strained to hear him.

Alone, I shepherded the flocks to graze
In vales untouched by any other human's eye.

A man in thick glasses beaded with rain, standing openmouthed, missing front teeth, his tie loosed around a neck red with razor nicks.

There, reclined in pastures,
I rested beside woods and streams,

carefree, even as I worked,
a poor man of simple pleasure.

A woman in a lunch counter's aproned uniform, holding a food tray above her head, her hands encased in clear plastic, her eyes shut, her face slack.

But, alas, such a satiating life of silence
Wasn't to be mine for long.

The woman opened her eyes, the man shut his mouth, others tipped their umbrellas back. *Why?* their faces seemed to ask, *Why was that life no longer his? How could he lose it? Who stole from him those carefree days?* Dima could feel them looking at him for the answer, but, even as he recited the rest of the tale, it seemed to him they were asking for more than he could give them with the poet's words. All the hours he'd ridden around the city, bent over the book, memorizing verse, it had knocked beneath him, incessant as the seams in the tracks: Why *these* words? Why *this* story? This hermit who'd traded away his bucolic youth, this hero who'd lost his soul mate to some dark art he didn't understand. How fast it happened—the loved one stolen, the rules of the world upturned—how hard to bring back anyone once a spell had snatched them. Maybe, he'd thought, it was that Pushkin had written his tale in the thrall of the same ones Dyadya Avya told. Maybe it was that he and Yarik had spent a summer of their own youth beneath the epic's spell. All he knew was that the way the hermit found peace again in the seclusion of a second life, the fact that, in the end, the searcher got his loved one back, shook something in him far deeper than the rattling of the tram.

And different, too, from the faint tapping that touched his chest when he saw the girl. Even though she'd been there every day— unlacing her sneakers, shucking her socks, always barefoot by the time he was done—he'd worried the press of people might have kept her from getting through. But there she was, standing barefoot in the tall grass beneath the poplar trees. The Consortium had planted their own lupines to replace the wild ones that used to bloom, and behind her the trunks of the trees were buried in concentric circles of wet, deep blue. She was letting whatever rain got through the leaves land on her, and her shock of black hair was pasted over her forehead, her mascara smeared to bruises beneath her eyes.

The clang of steel on steel, the crash of boats smashed prow to prow: through the telling of it all, Dima kept glancing at her. She had come with a couple friends—a thin man with a twisted mouth, a fat one with a beard, the two pressed together beneath a detached road sign held horizontal above their heads—and, when Dima reached the words *I ached to see her*, the friends flashed smirks, leaned over, whispered something in her ear. She laughed (O *longed-for meeting!*), they all laughed (O *blessed hour!*), she rolled her eyes.

It caught him like a glimpse of another person's yawn: he felt his own eyes roll and he snapped them straight, shut his lids. What right had he to roll his eyes at Pushkin? What right did she? Why did she come, then? When he looked at her again, she was staring hard at him, and when she saw his eyes on hers, she smiled. It was all he could do not to smile back. She rolled her eyes. He kept his still. She rolled her eyes again, smiled, as if to urge him on. Maybe it was the poem working him, the lines he was shouting out to the crowd—the way the old hermit had himself become a caster of spells—but the thought struck Dima that she came, that they all came, not just to hear the words he said but to see him say them, not just for the poem, but for the permission it gave them to spend time doing nothing but watch him.

> *Dreams aglow with new-stoked hope,*
> *senses inflamed with with fresh desire . . .*

When he let his glance slip to her again, she was still gazing at him. Between her smile she stuck out her tongue.

The lightning had flashed, the thunder had boomed, and the mage's story was nearly done by the time Dima returned the following day to find an assemblage grown to fill the square. And he was almost

126

finished recounting for them the rest of the first canto by the time the police showed up.

He saw the movement first, the crowd rippling away from a spot in its center, closing in again behind, the place they cleared coming slowly closer to the front, until he made out the black caps of the police: two of them, pushing through, looking back at him. Through the trees, at the edge of the park, he could see the gray roof of their car, the flashers off, blue and still as the lupines. One of the policemen, bullhorn in his hand, began shouting for the crowd to disperse. The other, carrying a billy club, kept coming, got to the plinth, stood looking up. Between the tsar's feet, Dima sat looking down. On the man's shoulders he could see a *starshina*'s stripes.

"Treasure your love," the sergeant said. He bunched his face into a squint, seemed to think. "And love her?"

Dima glanced at the thinning crowd, one half working their way towards the street, the other half still, watching. Something stung Dima's cheek. He snapped back to the policeman: the seargant, stooping to pick up another pebble, stopped and met Dima's look and said, "Am I right?"

It was the very last line of the first canto, or close enough Dima wasn't going to tell the starshina he was wrong. The man was over forty, heavy necked, small eyed. He stood up. As if to keep the distance between them, Dima got to his feet, too.

"Wrong way," the starshina said. "You want to come down."

Follow the rest of the crowd, the bullhorn was blaring, *out of the square and towards the street.*

Over by the near edge of the trees, the fare collector and her friends shouted back, the road sign held before them like a shield.

The starshina rapped the plinth below Dima's foot with his club. "Get down," he said.

"What am I doing wrong?"

The starshina turned, swept a hand at the crowd. "Because of you nobody's cleaning up the park."

"It's only a half-hour—"

"Nobody cleans up the park, the park gets full of trash. The park gets full of trash, the birds come down."

Cease this disturbance, the bullhorn said.

"Then," the starshina said, "it gets full of shit. Nobody wants a park full of shit. Nobody comes to a shit-filled park."

"Nobody comes anyway," Dima said.

The starshina looked behind him, as if the action proved Dima wrong.

. . . Disperse . . .

"What happens," the starshina went on, "if nobody comes to the park?" He clanked his club against the plinth again. "Crime. Robbery. Muggings. Murders. Rapes. Who knows? All I know"—he flipped the club like a juggler's torch—"is this miserable situation begins with you." He jutted the club at Dima; its tip touched his shin.

"You don't believe that," Dima said.

"Of course not," the starshina told him. "I'm just doing my job."

The blow caught Dima on his ankle, though he didn't know until he had already fallen, his hands scrambling to slow the drop of his body towards the steps, his elbow smacking the plinth where half a second ago his feet had been, and then he was lying half in the flower bed, the orange of the blooms all around him, the starshina in the marigolds, looming over him, his ankle throbbing.

Go back to work, the bullhorn said.

Dima tried to sit up—he could hear the park sweepers shouting, could just make out the fare collector's friends starting to throw things, the girl herself swinging her shoes by their laces, as if about to let loose—then the tip of the club pressed at his chest and his back was flat on the dirt again.

The policeman leaned over him. "That's why," the starshina said. "It's not just the park that goes to shit. It's every place that every one of them works. Now where are you hurt?"

"I don't know."

"You aren't hurt?"

"My ankle."

The starshina nodded. Then he kicked Dima on the side of the knee. Dima grunted, tried to roll. "You're supposed to shout out," the starshina said. "This time shout out." And he kicked Dima in the back. He didn't kick hard enough for it to really hurt, but Dima shouted like it did.

The starshina laughed. "No wonder they like to hear you do the story." Kneeling beside Dima, he whispered, "Don't get up for a while. Don't come back tomorrow. Tomorrow there'll be more than only my partner who needs a show. You come back tomorrow, I guarantee you there'll be guys who aren't just doing their jobs. Guys who do what other guys pay them to do while pretending to do their job. You see what I'm saying?" The starshina didn't wait to hear his answer. "Now yelp," he said, and slammed his billy club down.

That evening, when he got off the tram at his brother's stop, Yarik asked what had happened to his ankle. Dima told him he had fallen off a statue. *What were you doing on a statue?* Yarik said. *Reciting Pushkin,* Dima told him. *To who?* Yarik asked. *The birds?* But Yarik hadn't laughed, not even smiled, just wiped at his forehead with the gloves he'd bunched in his hand, left them over his eyes for second, shook his head. *Whose shoes are those?* he finally said. Dima lifted the shoes hanging from his neck, let them drop back. They knocked lightly against his chest. *One of the birds,* he said. Yarik said nothing to that, but going up the stairs he wouldn't let Dima carry anything; he made Dima lean on him instead. And once they were inside, Zinaida kept the kids clear of their uncle, took off his shoe, sat Dima on the couch while she eased his foot into a basin of water and ice. Later, he sat there, telling tales to Timofei, Polina sleeping on his lap, listening to his brother and his sister-in-law whisper behind the bedroom door, to the hushed sound—pleasing and troubling, both at once—of them saying his name. But only after he'd helped put the kids to bed, kissed Zinaida good night, felt her hold her arms around him a little too long, after he'd hobbled down the steps beside his brother, stood outside the stairwell listening to Yarik climb back up by himself, his footsteps dissipating with each flight until the distant hint of the closing door, only after Dima had hauled himself alone onto the tram for the ride back to his mother's place, only when he felt once more the rail seams knocking at his chest, the question rattling up through him again, did he finally understand.

And the next morning, meeting Yarik at the trolley stop, riding with him out to the Oranzheria, Dima told himself that *that*—the fact he couldn't tell his brother which poem or why without adding to the worry he'd heard in Yarik's voice last night—that was why he would not go back to the statue today. Returning from the Oranzheria on his own, he told himself it was just one more reason to add to all the others why he should not go to the park that afternoon. Though, sneaking into the dim auditorium of the old National Theater, sidling down a row of ragged velvet seats to settle beneath a beam of light leaked through the dilapidated roof, he told himself there was no harm in simply opening the book. And when he'd memorized the start of the next canto, he crept back into the open air and got back on another tram and, holding the shoes against his chest to keep them from swinging with the starts and stops, told himself he would just stay long enough to see if she was there. She'd want them back, hold out her hands; he'd take them off his neck, give them to her, go.

By the time he got there, the statue's square was full. But not with an audience waiting for him. The crowd was in chaos, bodies churning, scrambling, clawing their way over each other, trying to climb trees, tearing away through the grass, their shouting muffled by the noise of the tram until the brakes stopped squealing, the car jerked, the doors folded open to let in the blast of screams, bullhorn barking, swears and high-pitched calls and the sounds of hitting cracking through it all like shots. As he ran closer, he could distinguish wood on wood and wood on stone, the thud the billy clubs made on flesh, the thwack of hitting bone. He could see the old Communists fleeing through the trees, tripping over their canes, toppling to the ground, others already on their backs, holding the plastic buckets before their chests, their faces. Policemen moved among them like they were whacking weeds. A few fought back, hacked with ragged branches, lobbed what stones they could grab. He saw her there, clamped to a policeman's back, her arms around his neck, her legs clenched to his waist, her bare feet flashing, flashing, as the man she rode turned round and round.

That night he was too late to catch Yarik on the bus home, and when he got to his brother's apartment it was Zinaida who answered the door. *He's at your mother's place,* she said, *looking for you.* She had the radio on, tuned to one of the few independent stations. Through her grateful prayers of relief, he listened to its breathy babble, the same that he had heard on the trolleybus he'd taken across town: how the police had overreacted, how the people hadn't been protesters at all, how more would surely show up tomorrow, how it was all started by a man clinging to the statue of the city's founding tsar, a man on a plinth reciting Pushkin (a lunatic, some said; a bum, said others; an agent of the sinking West sent to embarrass a Russia ascendant; a Communist, an anarchist, a poet, a fool). The TV news was off (*They didn't even mention it,* Zinaida said, *as usual*), but in a corner of the room a square screen glowed, brighter even than the television, and in color, too: a new computer where the samovar once sat. Timofei dragged his uncle over to show what his daddy had been watching before he left. The boy reached up and moved a pointer, clicked a button: a video. There was Dima, caught by some long lens, the telephoto making him seem running hard and going nowhere, his beard shaking, his eyes wild, each hand clasped over the toe of a shoe that banged against his chest.

The next day, he made sure to get there early. Already, the park was packed with people. The police sat in their cars, stood at the edges of the woods, rested their hands on their pistols, their billy clubs, did nothing. This time the crowd rippled away from him, made room for him to squeeze through, helped him scramble onto the plinth. He stood there, gazing over them, looking for the trash sweeper, the

pelmyeni vender, the shopkeeper or the women in their suits, the old
Communists, the girl, for some face from sometime earlier that he
might recognize. But there were too many. He had to shut his eyes.
He could feel the shoes swaying on their laces around his neck and
he reached up with one hand and steadied them. Then—"You, who
raise your swords for warfare . . ."—he began.

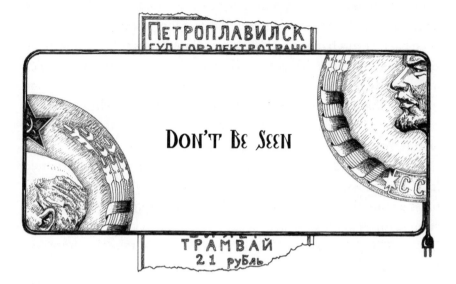

DON'T BE SEEN

This was why he never rode the 119: the tram doors opened, the passengers burst out, Dima barely managed to keep his feet in the jostling, barely managed to shoulder on before the doors folded shut again behind his back. Just as they did, one more man squeezed in, shoved at Dima, grunted as he got caught. The tram jerked forward, engine whining as it picked up speed. Through the gap in the body-jammed door the cold air came sharpened by lakewind and wet with downpour, sent shivers up Dima's soaked neck. This was why he stuck to less crowded trams, ones where he could find a seat, move to a window, watch the outside slip past in peace. The 119 went out to the suburbs where the new megastores—supermarkets, retail outlets, fast-food chains—were being built, and it was so crammed with people so burdened with bags that Dima couldn't even see where she was. Until the next stop, when enough people poured out that he could get up two steps into the aisle and spot her yellow fare collector's vest. Its pockets bulged with tickets and change, and it struck him—as if each coin were a marker for each minute of her shift—that she rode

133

the trams all day, same as him. The crowd shifted with a bend in the tracks. In the bits of space between the passengers' bodies he glimpsed hers: baggy jeans hanging off bony hips; safety pins splicing a broken-zippered sweatshirt; she had a wide peasant's face, heavy brow, thick nose, sturdy mouth, all whittled down to delicate by her near-starved thinness; that shock of black hair flopped over her forehead, the rest of her scalp buzzed so close the skin showed through the stubble. He wondered what she was wearing on her feet.

Her shoes had long ago dried out. He'd knocked the dusty mud from their soles, stuffed them in his rucksack, would have to fight the press around him to get it off his shoulders before she got to him—coming through the crowd, collecting money, checking passes, tearing tickets. When she handed his torn stub back, he'd take the shoes out, give them to her.

But as the tram rocked along he realized it was too packed for her to move. Instead, coins came towards her on a current of passing hands, tickets flowing back like flotsam on a tide going out. He reached in his pocket, felt out a ten-rouble piece, started to pass it forward. His hand jerked, stopped; someone had grabbed his wrist. He swiveled his neck. Behind him, the man who'd gotten stuck in the doors gave a little nod. They were so close his chin touched Dima's shoulder. He was a short man, old, eyes blurry behind greasy glasses, fingers gripping tight as a rubber band doubled on Dima's wrist.

"Allow me," the man said. "Please."

By the time Dima realized what he meant, the old man was already passing forward a twenty-rouble bill.

"I listen to you on the statue," the old man explained, his breath blowing the beardhair on Dima's turned cheek. He smelled like jam.

"Thank you," Dima told him, "but I don't do it for money."

"No, no," the old man said.

"I don't need the money." Turning away, Dima saw the man's bill reach her, saw her glance up to see from where it had come, saw her see him. He lifted his chin a little. She looked away. The gray light leaking through the rain-streaked window had been too weak for him to see the color of her eyes.

"What *do* you need?" It was the man behind him, again. "A new coat? Some warm food?"

"Nothing," Dima said, this time without turning around. He kept his gaze on the girl, waiting for her to lift her eyes again, but she just handed the tickets to someone in the crowd, turned away. The whole time it took for the tickets to come back, he watched her refuse to look at him, and when he finally reached to take them, the old man's arm shot past Dima's face, snagged the tickets.

"A gift," the old man said, handing one to him.

"Thank you."

"No, no. I want to give you a gift." The old man smiled. "Maybe a haircut? A shave?" His teeth were full of poppy seeds.

"I don't need—"

But the tram squealed, the crowd leaned forward in a wave, leaned back, the doors opened, a stream of passengers rushed out, the doors closed, the tram was moving, and the man was saying, "*I* know what you need." His black-speckled smile. "You know what you need?"

"No."

"No?" The smile spread to show Dima the wedges of poppy seeds mashed into the man's gums. "That's because," the man said, "you don't have to stand here with your nose smashed up against your neck."

Dima nodded, as if he knew what that meant, looked back at the girl; she looked away.

"Don't be offended," the man said. "Don't take it the wrong way, my friend." The man leaned in close enough his stubble scratched Dima's neck. "Comrade"—the tram lurched, the man grabbed Dima's shoulder—"Comrade, let me treat you to a bath. A nice hot bath. Who doesn't need a good hot banya on a day like this?"

"A banya?" someone said.

Another, packed close by: "Who's got time for a banya?"

135

"There aren't any," a third said, talk bubbling up around them. "Not anymore."

"Maybe in his apartment."

"His tub."

"Come on," the old man said, taking hold again of Dima's wrist, "this is our stop."

The brakes started their squeal. Dima yanked his wrist free just as the tram jerked, almost fell forward into the person in front who was reaching a hand back to him. In the hand: a piece of paper. A tram ticket.

The doors opened. The cold wet air. "Come on," the old man said again.

The hand shook the ticket at him. Dima glanced around to see who it was meant for, heard the man who was holding it tell him, "She said to give it to you."

A tug at his back: the old man grabbing his coat. Next to him, the people getting off shoved by. She had written something on it. He held it up, squinted at it, sensed behind it, in the distance, that she was looking at him. She was. She shook her head, gave it jerk, as if she wanted him gone, looked away again.

Pvilsk rail yard, car #38, tomorrow, 21.00, don't be seen

By the time he had read it, the doors had shut, the tram was pulling away, there was the clacking of the contactors on the wires as it disappeared down the street.

The iron fence was more rust than paint, the courtyard it guarded all weeds, the same few strains of night-blind scrub spread wild in the stead of photoperiodic flowers, grasses too confused to produce seeds. Over them, a past life's evergreens were exploded with root-sprung branches, strange shapes of trees trying to replace their winter-burned boughs farther up. Between them a path buckled towards the bathhouse door, the black-cracked pink of the flaking stucco walls, the entranceway an arch below a plastic picture of V. I. Lenin—red star and wheat sheaves and hammer and sickle and all—that trailed a long electric cord as if harboring a hope of one day lighting up again.

Passing beneath it, something plucked at Dima's inside, told him *turn around, leave,* but the man was pulling at his arm and by the time Dima had tugged his elbow free they were already in the foyer. As if he'd loosed Dima's arm on purpose, the man slipped behind him, started easing off his coat. From the window of a cramped coat-check booth, an old babushka in a scarlet shawl reached out with heavy arms. Their coats, their wallets: once he'd relinquished those, there seemed nothing left but to climb the steps behind his balding guide, past plastic plants missing half their leaves, walls stuck with pictures that looked ripped off calendars decades out-of-date: photos of factory workers with sleeves rolled up, farmers beaming as if about to sing.

The changing room was packed with men, most old, all either wrapped in towels or nude. They greeted Dima by name, as if guests at a party planned for him. Passing between the benches, he nodded back, silent but for his squishing footsteps. Did he know them? He didn't think so. The man with the poppy seed–flecked teeth set down his bag on the rubber mat, took out two towels, two pairs of flip-flops, two brown bottles of kvass. He popped their caps, handed one to Dima, raised his own. "To chance meetings," he said and tipped his back.

Chance? The word plucked at him the way *leave* had a moment ago. What, he wondered, could this man want with him? What could any of them? Weirder, yet, how could the man have been so right about how much Dima had missed this: the malty sweetness of the kvass, his bare skin prickling in anticipation of the steam. Because the other passengers had been right, too: in the past years, watching the city's bathhouses close one by one, he'd wondered if any would be left, if he'd ever enter a banya again.

The quiet squeaks of their flip-flops on the wet tile floor, the pocket of warmer air between the first door and the second, the way the sounds of all the bathers washed over him with the steam, the heat: Dima could feel his muscles relax their grip on his bones. Outside, the rain beat against the fogged window glass. Inside, a dozen naked men moved through the steam-soft light, filling plastic basins from rumbling taps, scrubbing their skin with soapy sponges, chatting and laughing, their voices mixed with the slosh of water, the murmur of pipes. Dima lifted a basin off a wet bench, splashed some water in. Swirling it around, he asked the man who'd brought him how often they all came.

"We don't," the old man said. "I mean, we can't, not anymore, not regularly." He scrubbed at his basin with some soap. "Only on special occasions," he said, and handed Dima the bar.

Dima glanced at the other men. Some nodded, some just watched him back. "What's the occasion?"

The old man smiled his poppy seed smile. "You." He walked to the other end of the bench, slopped his soapy water over the grated drain. "To congratulate you."

"For what?"

The man passed by, flip-flops squeaking. Filling his basin at the faucets again, he said, "To *welcome* you."

From all around: a rumble of mumbled greetings.

Dima stood with his soaped-up basin in his hands. "Welcome me to what?"

"To the Party."

"The Communist Party?"

"Of course," the man said, and in one heave dumped the entire basin of hot water over his own head. Wiping at his eyes, he blinked them open, smiled. "We're so glad," he said, "to see you following in your mother's footsteps."

"My mother?" In her confusion, might she have made a phone call? Regressed in memory to The Past Life, reestablished some old connection? The man motioned for Dima to dump out his basin, but Dima simply stood there, started, "Why do you say my mother's—"

Grabbing his basin from him, the man splashed it out over the grate, pushed it back at him, all the while nodding, smiling, shaking his head.

"I'm not a Communist," Dima said.

"Of course you are." The man's palm slapped Dima's back as he

138

pushed him towards the faucet. "Why else"—he turned the red lever on—"would you be amassing the proletariat in the square?" The hot water thundered into Dima's basin. "Why else would you be rousing the workers, rousing *us*, against those paid-off thugs of the capitalistic regime?" He reached over, turned on the cold tap, too. "Why else," he said, dipping his hand in Dima's basin, splashing it around, wiggling his fingers in the water before turning the hot tap off, "would we have brought you here?" He yanked the cold lever shut.

"I don't know," Dima told him.

The man's face was a father's amused by some small failure of a child he knows will eventually succeed. He flapped his hands once at Dima: go ahead, get splashing.

Dima reached into the hot water, sloshed it over his front.

"How is your mother?" the man said. "It's been too long since I've seen Comrade Zhuvova."

So, Dima thought, it was this man, and not his mother, who had dug up some connection from the past.

"She was always such a pleasure to have at meetings, Galina Yegorovna. Brought the most delicious cranberry pies, was such a devoted parent."

Dima slopped more hot water at his belly.

"She spoke," the man said, "with such love of you and your brother. Like she spoke of her love for the Party."

"I'm sorry," Dima said, "I just came for the bath," and he upturned the basin over his head. The hot water crashed over him. He wiped his hair away, squeezed out his beard, cleared his eyes with the heel of his palm. There was the old man's shriveled, sagging rear, turned to him. The veiny backs of his knees, the heels of his bright orange flip-flops, the wet-furred back, the crinkled neck, the drooping ears, the black tips of the ear grips of his glasses. He set his red water basin down on the bench, and when he turned back to Dima he held a switch of birch branches in his hand.

"Then why," the old man said, "did you quit your job on the Oranzheria? A good job? A well-paid job? Why would you do that?"

Through the dripping from his hair, Dima watched the man.

"Why would any sensible wage slave, any right-thinking worker dreaming of his place among the bourgeoisie, why would such a man, a man like *you*, do a thing like *that*?" The old man whapped the birch sheaf lightly against Dima's chest. The wet leaves stuck to his skin, then pulled away. "Because," the old man said, "you aren't like that. You aren't such a man. You're your mother's son. Dmitry Lvovich Zhuvov." He held up his fist, rattled the birch switch. "Shall we go into the heat?"

But even as he stood Dima couldn't help wondering if he'd heard wrong, if the man hadn't said *Yaroslav* instead, if whoever had conceived of bringing him here hadn't mixed up the man Dima was with the one his brother had become. Or maybe just the boy their mother had always expected Yarik to be. Of Dima she hadn't ever expected anything. *You are,* she used to tell him in exasperation, *such your father's son.* Their mother's son would have never followed the man towards the stream room. Yarik would have heard *leave* and *turn around* and steered his brother back long before Dima had ever neared the sauna he was stepping into now.

It was a small room already full of men, old men in pointed gray hats woven of nappy wool, guts white and round as the bulging bellies of frogs; a few middle-aged ones marked with tattoos—a spider crawling across a shoulder, a star stamped on a knee—that must have meant something back when they were young and the world was different. Some stood still, arms akimbo, breathing slow; others sat on the wood bench slapping branches at themselves; a few bent over with hands on the worn-smooth rail while their helpmates flogged their backs. All of them were sopping with sweat. Dima squinted at the dimness, the gust of heat on his eyes. The naked men looked back, blinking at their sweat, crammed closer together, slid a little left or right—long row of low parts swinging—to make room.

The man with the poppy seed teeth poured a ladle full of water over the hissing rocks, led Dima up the stairs to stand among the others. He introduced them—Comrade Murin, Comrade Gergiev, Comrade

Agletdinova, Comrade Korotya, Korzhanenko, Nevolin, Comrade, Comrade, Comrade—and put the question to them all: why would a man like Dima quit a job like the job that Dima quit?

The ones beating themselves stopped. The ones being beaten took a moment to breathe. The ones sitting there, sat there. They all seemed to give it some thought.

Finally, one old man two bodies away leaned over, looked at Dima as best as he could, his sweat dripping off his face, and said, "Because you were tired."

The men in between the speaker and Dima nodded like the man had said something profound.

"You were tired," the man went on, "of being a commodity."

The men in between nodded harder. Dima could feel the drops of sweat flung off their chins.

"You were sick and tired," the speaking man said, and another man said "sick!" out of the dark, and the speaker continued, "of your worth as a man . . ."

"As a person!" another said.

"Sick and tired of who you are, what you are worth as a *human*, being resolved . . ."

"Into a *price*," someone said.

". . . into an exchange value."

". . . a rouble."

"A *dollar*."

More sweat flew off nodding faces.

"You were nauseous at it," someone said.

"You were bilious!" another shouted.

"No." The word came out of Dima's mouth so suddenly he wasn't sure he'd said it. Then he said, more quietly, "I think I was just tired."

"Of what?" the poppy seed man said.

"Of bourgeois claptrap," someone called out.

"Of oppression by the overseers," another offered.

"I think," Dima said, "I just wanted time."

They were all quiet.

141

"To do what?" asked the one who'd brought him. For a moment, the man waited for an answer. Then he reached down, cupped his hand around his balls, lifted them, and lowered himself to sit on the wood. With his other hand, he patted the bench beside him. Halfway through Dima's sit, the man's hand shot out. His fingertips snagged Dima's scrotum. Midcrouch, Dima paused. "Careful," the man said. "Hot." And another hand came out of the mass of old men and placed a rag on the bench and the poppy seed man let go of Dima's balls, nodded, said, "OK."

Even through the rag, Dima could feel the burning of the bench. He waited until it had turned to just a warming heat. Then he said, "Nothing. Time to do nothing."

A few questioning grunts.

"Nothing?" someone asked.

Some grunts of dissent.

"Like this," Dima said. "Time to—"

But the poppy seed man had stuck a finger to his lips. Too late. Another old man was already revving up to a shout: "Nothing? To do nothing?"

"Maksim Grigorevich . . ." Dima's guide tried.

"To do nothing is to make . . ."

"Max . . ."

". . . the worker to your right, to your left . . ."

"Max, please."

". . . do more! To want to do nothing is the most dangerous thing, the hope of the bourgeois, the capitalistic dream, to be rich enough to do nothing, to be master of the worker to your right, your left . . ." In the far corner, a man—it must have been the one shouting—had begun to smack the wood before him with his birch-branch switch. "Either an aristocrat," he shouted. Someone else spat: the sizzle of spittle on hot stone. ". . . or a bum!" Another hawk, another sizzle. "Nothing more than an anarchist . . ."

The spitter tried to hawk up more, but either couldn't get enough or missed the stones. The man who'd brought Dima leaned over, whispered, "Comrade Korzhanenko . . ."

"Nothing more than social scum."

". . . believes this is a dangerous class."

"A piece of passively rotting mass," the man shouted, thwacking at the wood, "thrown off by the lowest layer of dead society."

There was the thwack, thwack, thwack of Korzhanenko beating at the wood railing with his switch, then just the man's hard breathing. In the silence a few others timidly whapped at themselves with their branches: the rustle of leaves, the smack of twigs on inner thighs, a few grunts.

The poppy seed man put a hand on Dima's shoulder, gave him a look as if to reassure him all was OK, pushed on his shoulder a little harder. "Bend over," he said. "I'll do your back."

Dima looked at the men beating themselves: some had stood, whacked away at bellies, calves, turned to let their neighbors get a swing at their rears. A roomful of switches slashing and leaves shaking and a dozen pairs of eyes watching him. He bent over his knees.

The old man started easy, a few light slaps along his spine. "I think," the man said over the rustling and thwacks, loud enough the others could hear, "that what Comrade Zhuvova, a clearly learned man, a scholar of Pushkin, what our new comrade means is it takes time to cultivate the mind." He gave Dima a playful whap on the back of the head. "For reading," he said. "For making art."

"For memorizing poetry," someone offered.

"For *reciting* poetry," another said.

"For Pushkin."

"For self-improvement."

"The cultivation of the mind," the poppy seed man said. "After all," he asked the gathering, "what else allows life its pleasure? From what else does a satisfied proletariat come?"

A flurry of rustling and whacking.

"The time?" the man said, as if to Dima. Then, to them all: "The time to pursue one's natural inclinations."

"One's proclivity," someone agreed.

"One's passion in life," another said.

143

"What"—the man leaned down a little, spoke to Dima's bent wet head—"is your inclination?" He smacked at him with the branches, paused again. "What is your passion in life?"

Someone put more water on the stones. The heat rolled through the tiny room. Dima felt it wash across his skin, burn in his nose, steam away the breaths he was trying to take. Even their father had loved to carve, to fish. Their uncle to tell tales. Their mother to see her son succeed. His brother?

The man sat poised with the switch above Dima's back. The others swatted at their neighbors and themselves in silence. After a minute, one of them offered, "Is it poetry?"

"Pushkin?" another suggested.

"Engineering?"

"Carpentry?"

Dima's head felt dizzy. He tried to lower it between his knees.

"Music?"

"Automotive repair?"

He shook his head. Someone called out that he needed air. Someone held a plastic cup of water towards him. The poppy seed man pushed it away. "Your passion!" he said, and smacked Dima's back. "Your proclivity!" He hit him again. "Your inclination!"

But how could he tell them the truth? That he didn't have a *what* but a *who*.

"I guess," Dima said. "Maybe . . ." The poppy seed man stayed his switch. The others leaned in. "Farming?"

A hearty rumbling of approval rose among them. "A man of the soil," they called him, "solid peasant stock," and, slapping him on the back, helped him down the stairs.

Outside the sauna, in the bathing room, they crowded around again. Someone filled his tub with cool water. Another poured it over his head. He sat on the bench, dripping, breathing, not even trying to clear his hair from his eyes. He drank from the cup that was handed to him.

The poppy seed man poured some shampoo into his hand, plopped it on Dima's head, started sudsing his hair.

They were talking about agriculture, about the days of the giant collective farms, about how much wheat was harvested by how many machines, the biggest tractors they'd seen, the days when fieldwork was under open sky instead of ceilings of glass.

"But," Dima interrupted them, "what if you can't?"

"Can't what?" they asked.

"What if someone is kept from it? From being able to pursue that inclination?" His eyes were shut, the suds dripping down his face. "What does that do to someone? What's someone like that supposed to do?"

The poppy seed man's fingers on Dima's scalp went still. "Do?" he said, and they gripped Dima's head. "You *take* it."

Someone else had started on Dima's chest with a bar of soap and whoever it was said, "You rise up. You start—"

And the poppy seed man finished: "A revolution."

Someone lifted Dima's foot. Another's hands were splashing water on him. He could feel all around him their crowded heat.

"Who is keeping you from it?" the man scrubbing his head said.

"Kapitalisti," someone answered, "who have taken over your country."

"And turned it into a bourgeois state."

"To rival even America."

"Even worse! Who took away your time?"

"Your time for your poetry."

"For a garden."

"The banya!"

"For yourself."

"For your nothing."

"For life."

"Who?" the shampooer demanded.

"The Consortium."

"The Oranzheria."

"The corporation."

"How?" the shampooer asked.

"Wages," they said.

"And who put the wage system in place?"

"The bourgeoisie."

"Why?"

"To break the power of the aristocracy," someone to Dima's right called out.

"To stem the power of the monarchy," came from his left.

"To give it to the workers?" the shampooer asked.

The chuckles of the men came low and long as a dozen cannonballs rolling across the tiled floor.

"To gain it *over* the workers," someone said.

"To turn them into commodities."

"To turn time . . ."

"*Their* time."

". . . into a commodity."

"And"—the shampooer withdrew his hands from Dima's head—"once time is a commodity, leisure must be?"

"A loss," someone said.

There was the sound of a water basin being filled.

"Unless . . ." the poppy seed man said.

"Unless . . ." said someone scrubbing at Dima's shoulder with a sponge.

". . . you take their watches from them."

"And put them . . ."

"*You* take their watches."

". . . in the workers' hands."

"In *your* hands."

There was the quiet dripping of water off the bench, the quieter dripping of soapsuds. Someone was carrying a basin, the slap slap at its sides coming closer.

"But," Dima said, pulling his arm away from whoever was scrubbing it, wiping at his eyes, "didn't you already do that?"

And then he couldn't say anything, couldn't hear anything, for the flood of warm water pouring over his head.

While they dressed, the man explained it to him: how, if they could only open the workers' eyes—the limitless jobs the Oranzheria could provide if there was no Consortium to decree when it would stop, the wealth it would bring to everyone if they shared its profits equally, the power simply in the skills they had—they could change the city council, force the oligarch out, socialize the great glass sea. Would Dima have another kvass? He still looked parched. *You can help us,* the man told him, *to make the proletariat see.* Look how they flocked to hear him speak! Surely, oratory was his passion, too. And he must know about Artyom Nebogatov. How he was also a farmer at heart, how when his duty was done he returned to farming again. But in between? He was a Hero of the State! Duty. Surely in any decent man duty must come before even inclination, even passion, before himself. See how he would be honored to lend Dima a hat? It was raining out! It was cold! How could he in good conscience let the Party's newest member go out in nothing but his still damp head, hair wet from water poured by the other members' hands?

Dima nodded where he thought the man would want him to, and drank the kvass, and took the hat. It was an old Soviet officer's hat, replete with polished black brim and bright red star, and he would have laughed at the sight of it if the coat-check woman hadn't handed it over with such solemnity. He put it on. And, escorted by the man who'd brought him in, he walked back through the entrance hall, out the door, under the drizzling rain, and smack into a burst of lightning. No: a camera flash. He looked to his sides: they were assembled all around him, old people spread out to his left and right, each with a red sash strung across the chest, each staring solemn-faced down the crumbled pathway into a camera's lens. He felt the light more than saw it, looked up: the cord had been plugged in, the bulb lit, the V. I. LENIN sign glowing there above his head.

FARMER! POET! LEADER!

The three words sat stalwart in blocky letters upon a ribbon, and beneath the ribbon there was a photograph, and on either side of the photograph a forearm rose, sleeve rolled, fingers in a fist—on the left, it gripped a hammer; on the right, a sickle—and beneath the photograph a caption clamored: *Your Comrade calls you: Join him! Join us! Take our country back!* In smaller print, filling the bottom third of the flyer, there was the heading *Putting the Oranzheria to Work for You,* followed by a bullet-pointed plan for a return to The Past Life. But, for all of that, it would have been nothing without the photograph itself: cropped just wide enough to show an illuminated Lenin near the top, half a chest-bannered old Communist to either side, and, in the center, Dima, shirt damp, dark scraggle beard, a Red Army hat on his head, his mouth open, as if about to speak, his eyes caught in what Yarik knew must have been widened surprise but that would seem to anyone else a fierce, wild gaze staring out from the flyer on the wall.

He stood by the entrance to the new supermarket, staring back. Behind him, the parking lot still smelled of fresh-laid asphalt. Car doors

148

slammed, the wheels of the carts rattled. He wondered if Zinaida had seen the poster. Earlier that afternoon, while he was still at work, she'd met Dima here, swapped charges—his brother taking Timofei, his wife taking their mother. Galina Yegorovna would not have been happy. Each year, every year, she insisted Yarik be the one to take her to her checkup: without his clout, she seemed to think, the doctor would keep her waiting for hours. But a foreman couldn't get someone to cover him as easily as a laborer, and, anyway, they always waited just as long. That was what his mother really wanted: to pin him down beside her so she could talk of the dreams she held for his life, unload her expectations, pat him on the knee. With each touch, his leg would jerk as if knocked by a rubber hammer. Which was why, last night, Zina had come up behind him, laid her cheek against his back. *I'll take her,* his Zinusha had said, and he could feel her smile against his shoulder blade. *After all, I must have some clout too as such a big nomenklaturshchik's wife.*

So she had taken his mother and given his brother the shopping list, told Dima Yarik would meet him in the store after work, would pick up Timofei, bring the money, take the cart through the checkout line.

Now, standing in the early mirror-light, listening to the assibilation of the sliding doors, looking at his brother's picture pasted to the wall, Yarik reached out—the asphalt smell making him feel sick—and tore the flyer down.

Inside, the supermarket seemed big as an entire section of the Oranzheria, wide aisles like field rows, shelves grown too high to see over. He walked between the towering walls of cans and boxes, looking for his brother. Zinaida loved this place. Ever since it opened a couple weeks ago, she wouldn't shop anywhere else. Said it made her feel like Russia had caught up with the rest of the world. He could see why: so many strange products, so many labels he couldn't read, so much to choose from. There must have been fifty kinds of canned fish, an entire aisle just for jars of pickled things. He wondered if Dima, used to tiny corner shops, had managed to find anything. He wondered how long it would take him just to find his brother. Then he heard his son. A small boy's voice shouting three short words: "Farmer, Poet, Leader!"

Dima was in the produce section, standing utterly still, as if afraid to touch even a bag. Around him, everyone mobbed the machines, weighing their picks, punching in numbers, printing out prices, and Yarik could see Dima taking it all in, trying to learn without meeting the stares that were turned back on him. His eyes looked as flash-stunned as on the poster. "Farmer, Poet, Leader!" There was Timofei, sitting in the car-sized cart, crying out the slogan.

Yarik didn't mean to snap so harshly at the boy, didn't mean to stare so hard at the cashier. But he could feel her looking at Dima, as if her gaze was on his own face, and he caught her eyes with a look that lowered hers back to her work. He tried to do the same, worry about nothing but helping Dima unload the cart.

"I'm glad this worked out," his brother said.

"Me, too," Yarik told him. "Thank you."

"I think I got everything."

"Thanks."

"It took me a little—"

"No," Yarik cut him off, "I mean, I appreciate it. Thank you."

In the quiet of the cashier staring awkwardly at her scanner Yarik could feel the confusion and worry coming over his son's face. There were the small sounds of their unloading, then the clamor of Timofei climbing down off the cart. Holding a jar with both hands, he set it carefully on the moving belt. Gooseberry jam: his father's favorite.

On Timofei's face Yarik could see the disquieting desperateness to fix whatever was going wrong. Occasionally, it happened: this glancing at his child and seeing, instead, a small version of himself.

"It's OK," he assured the boy. And to his brother, "It's all right. I'm not mad, I'm not, Dima. I just don't understand."

While they crossed the parking lot, Dima recounted it for him, from *dragged off the bus* to *a real banya* to *Bolsheviks!* "Mama would have fit right in." His grin searched for its twin on Yarik's face. "It was like taking a bath inside her crazy head."

"Except they got pictures," Yarik said.

150

"One picture. Clearly they needed two. Maybe I'm the poet, but everyone knows you're the leader."

"Foreman," Yarik said.

"And we're both farmers. They should have got a picture of you and me—"

"Dima," Yarik cut him off. "This isn't funny."

They took the shortcut to the bus stop, stepping over the curb onto a footpath that crossed the hill where dirt dug from the parking lot had been dumped. The Consortium reclamation grass had grown into tall scrub, and the plastic bags they carried brushed against it, banging at their thighs, handles stretched with weight.

"No one takes them seriously," Dima said. "They're just washed-up old men. They brought speakers to the square today. Played the old marching songs. All these old dedushkas stomping around singing along at the tops of their lungs! Everyone was heckling. They're a joke, Yarik."

"Yeah? You should hear the ones going around at work about you." In Dima's silence, Yarik could hear his crew's laughter. Some were jealous, some bitter, but Yarik knew that hearing about his brother had only made them hate their work a little more. And it wasn't just the laborers; he heard it from the foremen, from his bosses, knew it was talked about even higher up. "Maybe you're not taking it seriously," he said, "but other people are. You're being used, Dima, and you don't even know for what, and *that* makes it dangerous. *That's* why it's serious." At the tram stop, a small crowd was already waiting. Yarik dropped his voice. "Something's going to happen if you keep on like this, something's going to happen to you. Someone's going to see you. Living like this." His shoulders jerked at the weight of the bags. "See you and snap."

Dima shook his head. "Who?"

"Anybody. Some guys just off eighteen hours of work. Some fucking drunk." He glanced at this son, leaned in even closer, till he was almost whispering against his brother's cheek. "Or what about the cops? Any of these people could go to the . . ." He felt the strangeness of how close he was, felt the others at the bus stop sense it, straightened back up. But he kept his voice low. "What then? They come. Asking questions. Where do you think you'll end up?"

"Dyadya," Timofei peered worridly up at his uncle, "where are you going?"

Trying a smile, Dima swung his bags lightly against the one in the boy's hand, let them clunk. "To help bring the groceries home," he said, "so we have something to put in the oven with *you*."

"Dima"—Yarik's stare hadn't softened—"have you ever seen The Dachas? That's how you'll wind up. Or worse."

The bags shushed against Dima's leg, slowly stilling. "What do you want me to do?"

"Worry," Yarik told him. "I want you to worry about me. About Mama. About Timofei. I want you to think what that would do to us. Think, think, Dima, what that would do to me."

Then the bus was there. Packed in with the crowd, they rode in silence. Yarik set the bags down at his feet. They shifted, crackling, pressing against his shins with every jerked stop, falling away again as the bus went on.

"Bratets," Yarik said, after a while, "do you remember the cat?"

Once, when he and Dima were kids, they had found a dead cat outside their mother's apartment. Someone had used a piece of rebar to beat it flat. The iron pole was still there, jammed right through the animal's belly and out in a ragged explosion of spine. The night before, they had heard drunks laughing below the window. Perfectly normal men.

He could see in his brother's eyes that Dima remembered. He could feel his son looking at his uncle's face. Then up at his father's.

"We're next?" the boy asked.

Yarik bunched all the handles of his bags in one fist. Reaching over with his other hand, he grabbed Dima's, too, one by one, until he could lift the whole huge mass away from his brother's legs. The bus braked, shook on its engine, shook the bags.

"That's the worst of it," Yarik said. "I don't know how to protect you, I don't . . ."

The groan of the doors, the shuffling of passengers as Timofei pushed through, the space opening up behind him.

By the time he stepped down onto the street, his son was already running. Towards home? Away from him? "Timofei!" he called. The boy was heading for the playground. "Timofei!" He knew his son could hear him, knew that if Timofei turned to look, he'd stop, come back, knew his son understood that, too. He watched the back of the boy's head, blond hair shaking as he ran. Behind him, the bus moved off. He could feel it inside him, as if the sound were something he had swallowed, more and more muffled as it wound through him, deeper, quieter. That long-ago morning, he hadn't been able to bring himself to pick up the cat, or pull the rod out, or even cover it. That night before, he had heard them out there beneath his window and done nothing.

"Timofei Yaroslavovich!" he shouted, then started to walk, lurching a little with the weight of the bags. He knew the look his brother had given him back on the bus: *Can I come up?* But at the doctor's his wife was waiting for Dima to meet her, to take their mother home. He was growing used to finding reasons to turn his brother away.

Over in the playground, Timofei was climbing the bear, its thick spring shaking beneath him, and Yarik was about to call out again— come back, help carry, it wasn't the time to play—but his son wasn't playing. Hunched over its head, the boy pounded his fists against the paint-worn face, reached into the animal's mouth, and, gripping its upper jaw, wrenched with all the small strength of his arms, all his weight, a yell breaking loose from his thrown-back throat. Beneath him the bear rocked, its mouth gaping, too.

And his son's shouting followed the dying sound of the bus down Yarik's throat, into his belly, deeper. What he had felt from the moment Timofei was born, what a father feels for his first child—the only thing he'd ever felt like that was what had been between Dima and him all those years ago out on the farm. When, he wondered, had he started to feel older than his twin? How had the mere minutes between him

153

and Dima stretched into years? Their father's death? Their mother's collapse? The night they'd stolen the skiff and rowed out onto the lake?

It hadn't been night at all, of course, but morning, March, still dark. Dyadya Avya must have been the one to send out the police, but when they brought the boys off the search boat the two policemen found their uncle asleep on the gravel strand, curled over the groove the rowboat's keel had dug, an empty bottle beside him. One policeman kicked his side. Avya grunted, snorted, slept on. The policemen contemplated the shivering boys, the driverless farm truck, then dragged the passed-out peasant over, hauled him onto the dirt mound in the back, told the twins to get in the cab. Instead, they'd huddled inside the covered truckbed, beneath its flapping canvas, and ridden out of the city holding their sleeping uncle tight.

One policeman had driven the Ural truck, the other following in the yellow Moskvich, past the few lit windows in the old postwar apartments—a family drinking tea, a woman tugging a sweater over a child's head—through the newer section of the city, wood buildings given way to concrete slab that gave way to dark trees whipping by as the truck gained speed, the road rattling them into dawn. Halfway home, they'd passed the sanitarium. First the smell—the sulfur waft of healing waters bathers had flocked to in pre-Soviet times—then the pointed tops of towers, chimneys black against the ashen sky, the rows of windows awake behind their bars, peering back. And on the rush of wind there came the calls: strange and wild as the whoops and chatter of circus animals let loose, sounds both boys knew were the cries of those kept in there with their mother. The tailing cruiser's headlights lit their uncle's ghost-white belly, his shaking jowls, the patch of hair a mist above his chest. Across it, Dima's eyes had looked so scared. That dawn, listening to those sounds, watching Dima go back to staring at the receding sanitarium, Yarik had reached over, touched the rough wool blanket on his brother's back. *Bratishka*, he had said. Little brother. It was the first time he'd used the name. And Dima had turned to him, the look on his face as unfamiliar as the word, so strange that Yarik had known his brother had heard not only

154

what he'd said, but what he'd meant to say: *I'll take care of you*, he'd thought, in the headlights, in the cold. *It will be OK.*

The shopping bags pulled at his finger joints, his elbows, shoulders. The handles dug into his skin. That year, orphaned out at Dyadya Avya's, it was as if he stepped into the role for which their mother, in her hurry to grow him up, had unknowingly been grooming him. What a relief, then, to be so needed for something he was so able to give. A good weight. Back when it had been the only one he had to carry.

Now, it seemed as if the difference between them had somehow grown into a decade, as if he were holding all that time in the handle-straining bags. Out in the playground the bear's back was empty, its spring gone still. Somewhere in the building's stairwell his son was running up the flights. Five stories up, he could see their kitchen window glazed with mirror-light. Soon, his wife would be home, their children hungry.

At Dyadya Avya's table, he and Dima had eaten from the same bowl. In the bath basin, they had scrubbed each other, poured water to wash off soap. Playing rugby in the village, they had blocked for each other, Dima a third arm for Yarik, Yarik an extra shoulder catching the blows meant for his brother. And when they visited their mother, they gripped each other's hand, held tight, went in.

He stood still as the bear, the bags around him motionless, his hands going numb. *I'll take care of you. It will be OK.* For how long now had he been lying to his brother? The excuses for not inviting him up. What he'd left out about becoming a foreman. Everything about Bazarov. A month ago, when Yarik had been taken to see The She Bear. Last week, when Yarik had seen him again.

The billionaire had been standing in nothing but his underwear. Briefs. Maroon. Peering through the window of the car sent to get him, Yarik had wondered if the man matched even his undergarments to his boots. If the briefs would make his eyes look a little red-tinged, too. Or would his irises seem burnt around the edges, picking up the deep tan of Bazarov's bare chest, belly, legs? Or just gray as the lake stretched out behind the nearly naked man.

It was the kind of summer day when the northern world feels the need to remind its people they're never far from winter. Gusts chopped the lake, blew off the water, tore through the trees, shook the driver's suit as he opened Yarik's door. Standing up into it was like stepping into a slap. Yarik squinted past the chain-link fence, the open gate, to the billionaire standing there at the edge of the loading dock. Bazarov. His boss. The night that Yarik had told Zinaida how he'd gotten his promotion, that was what she'd said: *your boss?* And hearing the question in her voice, he'd been unable to keep at bay the ones that had been hounding him. Lying beside each other on the bed, beneath their drying post-celebration sweat, they'd tried to imagine what lay inside The She Bear's mind, what a man like that could possibly want from a man like Yarik. Because—when Zinaida said it it seemed so clear—his boss hadn't handpicked one of his many thousand workers, brought him to a mansion, made him tea, just to impart a bit of good news, indulge a tender heart. Maybe he wanted a local's perspective on Petroplavilsk. Maybe he wanted an infiltrator among the ranks. *A spy,* Zinaida had said, smiling. *Or,* shrugging her small shoulders, *maybe just a friend.* But why, Yarik objected, would he choose me? And, her smile widening, his wife had raised her eyebrows—*maybe more than a friend*—before slipping back beneath the sheets.

Now, his boss was gesturing: bare arms scooping at bare sides, flinging out, almost as if miming the act of treading water. Through the man's wind-whipped hair, Yarik could just see Bazarov was shouting something, something he couldn't quite make out, then nearly did, was on the verge of understanding, had understood just enough to wish he didn't, when the driver spoke up and made it clear: "Take off your clothes."

Yarik stared at the driver. Then at the nearly naked billionaire. Not because he thought there was anything to his wife's joke that night, but because he couldn't help but wonder if the dockworkers would. Bazarov had selected to strip not where the old folks used to sunbathe on the rocks, not at the gravel beach where Yarik used to launch his brother off his back, but smack at the edge of the wharf: cranes loomed above, swung cabled crates, slabs of steel; mammoth ware-houses hunkered beneath their rusting roofs; half-built ships rippled with the movement of their crews; all around the dockworkers milled, shouted to each other, tried not to stare. For a second, Yarik took it all in. Then he handed the driver his gloves, his hard hat, and stripped.

When he reached Bazarov the man was grinning so wide his goatee seemed shrunken. His chest was covered in fine blond curls, the bronzed skin beneath all goose-fleshed. Yarik's own chest hairs felt as if the chill wind was trying to yank them out.

"Cold?" Bazarov asked.

Yarik shook his head.

And, as if picking up the movement, Bazarov began to shake his own. Just a little, a shiver rippled up his neck, and then a little more so that his locks began to tremble, until his entire face was quivering, his ears, his cheeks, his whole body tensed, every muscle flexing, his head vibrating as if hit by a seizure. He stared at Yarik. His lips burst into shaking. The sound he let out was half horse's neigh, half motorboat.

When he stopped, his eyes were wet with held-back laughter. His voice was bright with glee: "You know what you need?"

Yarik started to shake his head, thought better of it.

"A paddle!" Bazarov said. He said it with such a shot of joy that Yarik's body jerked, as if his bare skin was anticipating a smack. But, instead, the man bent down, came up holding what looked to Yarik like a pair of double-headed oars. One of which Bazarov thrust at him.

He had never been in a kayak. Over the pier-side, tied to the dock, there were two of them, long red missiles of boats. Bazarov climbed down, got in, untied his rope, shoved off, all while telling Yarik about stirrups and rudders and steering, and by the time the man raised his paddle above his head, shouting over his shoulder something about holding it in such a way so far apart, Yarik was still trying to figure how to get in.

"What about this rubber thing?" he said.

From the front of his kayak, he heard three thumps—Bazarov tapping the boat's nose, pat, pat, pat—and looked up to see the man already shooting away.

157

For a long time, Yarik followed the figure so distant he could just make out the gold of the man's hair, the white paddle-blades rising and falling far ahead. They looked like seagull wings, the billionaire swift and sure on the surface as the birds in the air. Sometimes it even seemed the man was slaloming, playing with the waves. The same that slapped the side of Yarik's boat, beat at him through the bottom, tried to shove him back. Hacking at them, breathing spray, he fought the wind that tried to grab his boat, spin it around, almost wished it would; he'd keep paddling, back to the dock, the car, climb in, slam the door shut. Instead, he shouted at each cold slosh of water, sometimes at the man up ahead. As far as he could tell, the billionaire never once looked back. Then he was too far away to see even if he had. The paddles were distant flashes of light, Bazarov barely a blur between them. And, for what seemed an even longer time, Yarik followed that. His shoulders burned, his back ached. He wished he'd worn his work gloves. Ahead, the other kayak had become barely a spot of red. He stopped paddling, his breath tearing up his chest, his boat seesawing on the waves. The other boat was gone.

They had been staying far enough into the lake to be out of the algae but in sight of the shore—the distant line shifting from city to suburbs to the ceaseless, glinting strip where the Oranzheria came to Otseva's edge—and he knew he could go on, keep the shore to his left, meet Bazarov eventually; eventually the man would come paddling back. He could almost see his grin, the way the man had mocked him, shivering, on the dock. Nothing of friendship in that act. Even the idea of it seemed as foolish now in the cold wind of the gray day as his wife's insinuation had that night. The waves knocked at the boat like a memory of the man's hand, three small pats. Nothing friendly in that touch. The wind blew lake spray across his back and brought a memory with it: the way Dima, crouched on his shoulders, waiting to dive into the lake, used to signal he was ready to be launched. And Yarik, under water, would echo the count back with his fingers against his brother's feet. Tap, tap, tap. Swaying there on the surface of the lake, his own surface stretched tight from the cold, he wanted those boys back.

But he knew the only way to reclaim someplace for them, to set aside some corner of the world where they could return to, was to go forward. That was what his brother didn't seem to understand; what their uncle had been unable to see; what their father had been unwilling to: when all the world was moving ahead, just holding on was falling behind; striving to stay the same was the same as giving up.

The paddle had torn his hands, and his shoulders felt ready to rip right off, and his teeth were clenched against their chattering, when he finally caught up with the billionaire. They had gone so far for so long that the shore had shed the glass. To Yarik's left the land was a long strip of dark green trees. To his right, Lake Otseva opened up, gray to the horizon. In between, the red kayak floated. Bazarov had stretched out, his feet crossed over the boat's long nose, the paddle resting on his chest like the bar of a bench press.

"You know," Bazarov said, "the last time I went kayaking with someone was with Pavel."

With? Yarik thought. *Went with?* He wanted to shove the man's boat, but he just waited, his kayak bobbing, the ache oscillating in his muscles, the rucked skin on his hands starting to stiffen up. Far out on the lake, one of the oligarch's berg-sized ships droned. From the shore, almost too far away to hear, there came the low wash of wind through firs. And damned if he was going to ask who Pavel was.

"That," the man said, goggles covering his eyes with reflections of sky, "was a long time ago. And also it was on the Black Sea. Have you ever been to the Black Sea?"

"No," Yarik said.

"To the Caspian?"

"I've never been anywhere. Once, to Moscow, when I was—"

"On the Caspian," Bazarov went on, "they have one of these. But theirs is up on dry land."

"One of what?"

Slowly, the rest of his body staying still, Bazarov turned the paddle parallel to him, slid it down into the hole from which he'd drawn his legs, left it sticking up at a low slant. He let go, lay there, blade swaying against the sky.

159

"Have you ever heard," Bazarov said, "of the Caspian Sea Monster?"

Then he rolled off the boat, slipped down the side, and splashed into the lake. Where—his hair floating like a patch of golden algae, his back like the top of a rock, his maroon rear, his legs, his kicking feet—he disappeared. For a moment, the water he'd churned shook Yarik's boat. Then that was gone, too. Carefully, Yarik dipped a blade, drew a little closer to where Bazarov had been. Staring down, he could see browns and greens below, thought he caught a glimpse of something pale moving in the dark. Then: nothing. The depth. The murk. The silhouette of his own reflection. He looked over at the other boat listing lazily on the waves, the paddle knocking, knocking. For the first time since that long-ago night in the stolen rowboat, he felt the enormity of the lake, the power rippling across its surface, the unknowable everything beneath.

Something broke the surface. He heard it like a seabird landing next to his boat, and when he jerked around to look, there was Bazarov, treading, breathing hard. He lifted the goggles; they rested on his forehead like a second pair of gleaming eyes. His own eyes were the color of the lake, quiet, almost contemplative.

"Well, this is it." The man shook his head, flung his wet hair from his face. "Each time I forget what a beast it is. A hundred meters long from head to tail. Stretched out on the bottom like some huge eel."

Yarik leaned over a little to look. A tug on his paddle: Bazarov drawing himself closer to the boat.

"It's down there," the man said.

"Where?"

"Right under us."

"Mr. Bazarov," Yarik started. The man made a face, as if he'd been hurt. "Baz," Yarik said, "what are we talking about?"

And Baz smiled. "Give me your paddle," he said. Hanging an arm over it, he reached up, yanked his goggles off. "Really, you've never heard of it?"

"I don't know what *it* is."

"Then"—Bazarov held out the goggles—"swim down and see."

The Caspian Sea Monster. Somewhere in the far reaches of his mind, he *had* heard of it. But he couldn't see anything. The water was too clouded with particles of plant life rotting away in the lake, too murky with tannins, stirred-up silt, the churning of the waves. He could feel them moving above him, and then he couldn't, and, his hands stinging, his arms aching, his lungs so full of air it fought his strokes, he swam down. Down towards the ever-darkening depths, the water getting colder and colder, and the light from above leaving him until it seemed he was swimming into nothing but black. Had it been a thing out of his old uncle's fairy tales? A creature from the fables his father had carved on his boat? He could almost see his father's mouth, the black mustache, the hole between the open lips, saying the words, could almost hear them.

By the time he saw it through the murk, he was so close a few seconds more and he might have touched its back. That was what he'd thought was the blackness of the water beneath him. That was what had seemed the unseeable bottom of the lake. That was how big it was. His arms stopped moving, his legs stilled, and, for a second, he was suspended there, staring down at what looked like a blue whale's back, so wide he could barely make out where it sloped away at the sides, so long he couldn't see the beginning or end of it at all, only a few places where scales seemed to glint, where the slime that he sensed smothering the rest of it must have been washed away. Then his lungs burst. The last of his air erupted from his mouth, his chest crushed in on itself, and he was kicking, thrashing for the surface, away from whatever was down there. As he flailed upwards, he kept his head bent, his eyes on it, his own voice telling him it wouldn't move, couldn't, wasn't alive . . . But was that a shiver? A ripple? His sight blurred, the goggles pressing into his sockets, and then his breath was gone and his arms were unable to work and the lake water burst into his nose, filled his throat . . .

For a second he didn't know what grabbed him. Then, somewhere in his skull, came the realization they were hands, hands clasped around his chest, arms beneath his own, his own face in the air, a body against him, its breath, Bazarov.

"What did you think," the man said, breathing hard close to Yarik's ear, "that it was going to eat you?"

Yarik flapped his arm, coughed. Bazarov's laugh brought him around as much as anything else. "What the fuck *is* that?" he said, and kicking—"I'm OK"—tried to pull out of the man's grip.

"You sure?"

"What the fuck is it?"

"Not missing any toes?"

"Fuck off."

And Bazarov was laughing again, heaving him up onto one of the boats, hauling himself the rest of the way, and Yarik remembered who he was talking to. He lay flopped over the kayak, belly breathing against the hard plastic, arms clutching the side. "I'm sorry," he said.

There in front of him the billionaire, The She Bear, his boss, treaded water, looking up into his eyes. "You want to know what the fuck it is?"

"I'm sorry," Yarik repeated.

But Bazarov only beamed. "I call it the Serpent of Otseva. The Americans called it—the one they saw in grainy pictures—the Caspian Sea Monster. But what it is is an ekranoplan. Wait." Bazarov gripped Yarik's forearms with his hands. "I know." He held on, still treading with his legs. "I know, Cossack. What the fuck is *that*?"

On the way back, he told him. How, over half a century ago, the bureau for hydrofoil design had built the first: five hundred tons, a hundred meters long, a colossal cross between airplane and ship whose eight head-mounted engines would hurl it forward at such speed its winglike fins would compress the air against the water's surface and give it lift. How, at seven hundred kilometers per hour, twenty meters above the sea, it would rise out of the realm of hydrofoils into one that existed only for it. How, though eventually they'd be built down on the Caspian, the prototype was tested on Otseva first. Then, to keep it from the spying eyes of satellites, sunk. The first creature of its kind, a genius's lifework, and all these years buried in the lake. As if, Bazarov said, he was one day to collapse the entire Oranzheria, let it simply disappear in hundreds of hectares of weeds, woods grown up, a forest hiding the great glass sea.

"You," Bazarov told him, "are the first person I've brought to see it."

They were paddling side by side, the wind now coming from behind, the waves helping them along. And maybe it was his relief at that, maybe just the rhythm they were in, blades lifting and falling in synchronicity, but Yarik glanced at the man beside him and asked, "What about Pavel?"

Bazarov's paddle-blades dipped, rose, dipped again. From the shore there came the distant boom of trees being felled, the first gleam farther up of the Oranzheria's glass. And then: "Stop paddling."

Yarik watched his blade streak by Bazarov's stilled one. The man gave the water one more stroke to bring him back beside. They floated, still slipping forward over the waves, the wind still pushing them.

"Give me your paddle," Bazarov said. And as he took hold of the near blade, he slid Yarik his own. "Hold both." Reaching past his lap into the kayak's hole, he brought out a square of something. Shiny, crinkled plastic. Watching Bazarov unfold it, Yarik realized it was a tarp. And when they'd tied each corner to a pole, and held the poles between them, and opened them up, it became a sail. And their kayaks, sailboats. The wind, a gale. The lake shot by.

Between them, the tarp billowed. Their arms shook. The wave spray blew over their bows and wet their faces and Yarik could feel its sting all over his cheeks, and he squinted into it, let it rush his teeth.

Beside him, Bazarov let out a whoop. Through his whipping hair, his eyes glinted at Yarik. "The Yaroslavoplan!" he shouted.

"The Bazoplan!" Yarik shouted back.

"The Bazoslavoplan!"

And they blew across the lake, the surface a blur, the waves machine-gunning against the bottoms of their boats.

"Pavel," Bazarov shouted, "was always too afraid to do this. Afraid of everything. That picture of the boar? Me and the boar? On my desk? He was even too afraid to take it! A picture! Of a dead boar! The dog handler had to take it. And I had flown him all the way up, brought him on the hunt, hoped to make a hunter of him."

Bazarov's eyes held on him, seemed to take him in, appraise him, and then they left him and the man gazed straight ahead again. "This winter," Bazarov shouted, "we'll go together. Along the northern shore. I have a hunting lodge there. Those woods grow boars the size of bulls. You with one Colt .45, me with the other. None of this big-game rifle bullshit. Cowboy," he shouted, "you haven't lived till you've seen a couple hundred kilos of boar charging at you through the snow and nothing between its tusks and your balls but the barrel of a hundred-and-fifty-year-old pistol."

Bazarov laughed, the sound flung away by the wind, the wind Yarik could feel gusting against the tarp, feel in his throbbing hands, in the way all his skin felt whipped to life. And flying across the lake, the glass now shining on the shore, Otseva stretching out on the side all the way to the horizon, he knew who Pavel was. But it didn't feel to Yarik like Bazarov was trying to turn him into a replacement for a son; it didn't feel like his boss wanted to become some sort of a father. In that moment, Yarik felt, instead, what it might have been like to have had an older brother.

A Time Before the End of Time

Dima landed on the gravel with a quiet crash, crouched, his back against the concrete end of the train station platform, his head hidden just below its upper edge. The world had begun its tilt towards ever shorter nights, but beneath the zerkala the long twilight was stripped of softness, scraped clear. The open rail yard was strewn with shimmers and shadows, a tangle of tracks. Along one, a passenger train came on, its headlight diminished to mere safety signal. Around it, freight rails held long rows of oil tanks and open-topped cars, gravel or coal, whole caravans beneath forestfuls of logs. Among them moved the night-shift workers, crawling the ladders and tracks. Behind Dima, on the platform he'd just jumped off, he could hear the passengers milling. Before him, far in the distance, the thin edge of the Oranzheria was broken, a gap in the glass filled with dark pines: the access line. Between the pines and him, the rail yard's fringe was a strip of stillness, abandoned cars, parts of trains retained for scrap, engines with wheels rusted stiff. Over there, he'd surely draw the eyes of passengers, workers, anyone waiting for him.

Why had she chosen this place? Why not just take the shoes from him while on the tram, stuff them in her bag, the way he'd stuffed them in his rucksack now? He took them out, slung their tied-together laces around his neck, and, staring into the stillness for any sign of her, swore again that tomorrow he would not climb the statue's plinth. He would stay away from the square, stop reciting the poem, go out to the Oranzheria and wait to tell his brother that he didn't have to worry, that it would be OK; he'd tell Yarik everything, all he'd left out earlier that afternoon: the new kind in the crowd, their black button-down shirts, white ties, shaved heads, faces masked by scarves bearing the double-headed eagle of the tsars, or bare and furious with screaming. *My head still rests upon my shoulders!* They had brought copies of the text, shouted along with him. *I still wield my sword with skill!* In their raised fists, he'd seen flashes of metal. *Halt!* Their bellows had shaken the crowd. *Halt!* And he would. Tomorrow. Tonight there was still the girl out there in one of those abandoned cars waiting for him.

Walking across the open, he expected to hear some yard guard's bark, a worker's querying halloo, but when he reached the shadows between the two long lines of train cars, and stopped, there was just the sound of his own footsteps crumbling away into the quiet. Unless—he stiffened—he'd heard the ghost of someone else's disappearing, too. When he began to walk again the shoes clocked at his chest; he held them still, passed boxcars with black cracks between their doors, cattle cars come alive with the sound of scurrying, flatbeds that left him stripped of cover.

By the time he got to the passenger cars, he was seeing her in every window: a stirring in an upper corner where the top bunk would be; a shadow walking through the inside aisle, keeping pace with him—his own reflection flitting from window to window. Until, at a café car, he stopped. From somewhere came the sound of water trickling. Stepping closer, he peered in. Red curtains pulled back, the edges of booths, mirror-light slanting through. In there the air was smoky. He could smell it: cigarettes. He could feel one: a small warm spot on the nape of his neck, hot as a point of sun honed through a magnifying glass, growing hotter. He whipped his head around.

The ember's glow, its sting on his cheek, the hairy knuckles inches from his eyes, the fat face, curly beard, pair of glasses jabbed close—and then the man's hand was on the shoes, the laces yanking Dima's neck, jerking him down, his face mashed into underarm flesh, chest flab pressing his cheek, the slick of the man's sweat, the stench, he couldn't see anything. Clawing for a hold, Dima tried to shove his face free, but the man kept jerking the shoelaces like a choke collar on a dog. Dima coughed, quit trying to grab, rammed a knee upwards instead. The man grunted, loosed his hold long enough for Dima to suck a breath, hear someone else's footsteps on the gravel behind him, and then the shoelaces yanked again and again his face slammed into the squeezing flesh, and something hard jabbed into the back of his head. He had never felt a gun barrel pressed to his skull, but he knew it. He quit struggling. He shut his eyes.

"Is this him?" the face-squeezer said.

Another voice: "I can't tell."

"Where's Vika?"

"Vika!"

"Oh for fuck's sake," came a woman's voice from far away.

And nearby again: "Let me see him. I can't tell till I see his face." Then: "Ey"—spit sprayed with the voice—"do you know what that is pressed to your head?" Dima tried to speak, but couldn't get the air out. "Ey!" He couldn't even nod, the shoestrings were so tight. "Do you know what this is?" And, patting his calves, thighs, crotch, rear, the man repeated his demand: "Let me see him."

Easing up on the shoelaces, the fat one squeezed his arm, popped Dima's face out of his pit.

He was still bent over, his neck still twisted, one eye still mashed against the fat chest, but he could just make the other out: a bloodshot eye in a black bruise peering down from beside a scabbed-over nose, a harelip, tiny yellow teeth. The man pulled the pressure from the back of Dima's skull, showed a pistol in front of his face instead, pointed it at his forehead, as if to demonstrate *and this is how I'll use it*.

"Tell me something," he commanded.

Dima stared at the finger on the trigger.

"Tell me something!"

"I just came," Dima said, "because she told me to. She gave me a note."

The man with the gun looked at the face-squeezer. The fat one seemed to shrug.

"Fuck," the gun wielder said. Then, to Dima, "Say something else."

"I have her shoes," Dima blurted. "I—"

"From the poem," the fat man told him. "A little from the poem."

Dima swiveled his stare. He could see the bottom of the massive chin, greasy beardcurls, crimson neckfolds showing through, and he shut his eyes and tried to remember something, anything—*For you, tsaritsas of my soul . . .* —and then there was the sound of footsteps and he felt movement in front of his face and when he opened his eyes again the gun was being shoved aside and in its place was her.

Her eyes were black as Ivan's. They held on him hard as the bird's when he first took off its hood.

"Let him go," she told them. When the fat man didn't, she stuck her hand out and with it smothered as much of his huge face as she could.

Trying to shake free, the fat man spoke through her fingers: "He tried to knee me in the dick."

"He could find it?" she said, and shoved.

One final yank on the shoes around Dima's neck and—"Boing," the fat man said—his head popped up, freed too fast, all the blood that had flooded his face draining out. Dima stood, woozy, his hair wild, his frizzed beard clumped. The laces were twisted tight to his chin and he worked at them with his fingers, picked and pulled with the fury of all he didn't dare say.

She watched him like she heard it anyway and found it funny. Smiling, she glanced down. Her belt was unbuckled: the weight of the hanging end pulled apart her undone fly. "Sorry about that," she told him, buttoning it up. "I was taking a piss." Then she stepped forward and put her hands on his. His froze, fingers still in the laces. She pushed them away. Beneath his chin, she worked at the tangle. "I swear," she said, "I came as fast as I could." He could feel her fingers brushing the hairs of his throat. "I didn't even stop to wash my hands." She smiled. "Or"—she gave the shoelaces around him one more tug—"to pat my pussy dry."

She was so close that when she laughed he could smell her breath: fried mushrooms and cigarettes.

Then the weight was gone from his neck. She held the laces in a fist, shoes dangling between them like a fish she'd caught for supper.

Behind her, the pistol wielder asked, "It's him?"

Where the laces had been, a line felt sliced into Dima's neck. He reached back, pressed a palm to it.

"Thanks for the shoes." The fare collector gave them a little swing. Then reached out and with her free hand took his. She held his palm. Dropping the shoes, she reached out and held his other. "I will wear them always," she told him, and, turning to the pistol wielder, said, "Yup."

Dima felt her grip his hands harder just as he saw the flash of movement—a lunge, cloth flapping—and he tried to jerk away, jerked right into the fat man's face, teeth revealed amid the beard, before everything went dark.

There was his struggling, the rustling of whatever was on his face, the gun thrust again against his head—"I don't think he knows what this is!"—the fat man squeezing him around the chest so he couldn't breathe, someone tying his wrists.

They half-hoisted, half-helped him up small metal steps and inside what must have been a railcar and walked him down an aisle and shoved him into what might have been a booth. In front of him: the edge of a table? Beside him: the fat man? Someone else slid in against his other side. Each breath he took sucked the hood to his face. What muggy air he could get smelled like a trash can full of cigarette butts mixed with the fat man's sweat and he listened to cigarette lighters clicking and the crackle of papers and, from far off, the sounds of the workers in the rail yard, and all around the sounds of his attackers settling in.

"Why are you doing this?" he asked them.

"What?" one said, and another, "I can't hear him through the hood," and a third, "Whose idea was the fucking hood, anyway?"

Dima thought that was the woman's voice and he said again, louder, "Why are you doing this?"

The rasp of someone scratching at their beard.

"Why," the woman said, "do you stand on that statue? Why do you recite that poem?"

"What do you want?" Dima asked her.

"Why do we have to want anything?"

"This"—it sounded like the harelipped gunman—"is what your fucking friends got wrong. Purpose, purpose, purpose, purpose."

"What if what we want," the fat man, next to him, said, "is to grab you and place your head in my armpit and put a hood on you?"

"Productive, productive, productive."

"Except," the woman said, "what we want is to be able to take that hood *off*."

Dima sat there, quiet, breathing. They sat there smoking. "OK," he said. And when there was no rustling of movement towards him, no touch to the fabric over his face, he said it again: "OK."

"What we want," the woman told him, "is for *you* to take the hood off."

Slowly, he lifted his wrist-tied hands off his lap, above the table, his elbows bending awkwardly, his hands twisting to let his fingers touch the fabric at his neck. Then her hands were on his again, pulling them away.

"But first," she said, "we have to trust you." Her hands cupped his. "You have to trust us."

"You see," someone said, "unlike your fucking friends," and Dima realized it was the gun wielder again, "we don't believe in coercion, in fucking control. We believe in letting the fuck go. Doing what you fucking need to do. Me doing it. You doing it. Because—and this is the fucking point—you, us, we, humans, what we want isn't fucking conflict. I mean is it? Fuck no. It isn't competition. It's cooperation.

It's mutual fucking benefit. So why the fuck *shouldn't* we trust you? Why the fuck shouldn't you trust us?"

Because, Dima thought, *you put a gun in my face and a hood over my head.* But he only said, "What friends are you talking about?"

"Your *comrades,*" the woman told. "The ones you posed with in your poster."

"The Communists? They're not my friends. They're—"

"That's right," the fat man said. "Because *we're* your friends."

"We're your fucking *people,*" the gun wielder said.

"You just don't know it yet." The woman patted his hands with hers.

"Who knows," the fat man said, "who you might have brought with you?"

"Who might have followed you."

"Some fucking cop," the gun wielder said, "sent by the fuckers from the Oranzheria? Some guard from the fucking Dachas? National Unity thugs, National Socialist, fucking Pamyat."

"I don't understand," Dima said into his hood. "Why would anybody—"

"Because," the woman answered, "you look like one of us."

Did he? The only person he'd ever thought he looked like was his brother. But he could feel his beard bushing against the inside of the hood, smell the sourness of his sweat, and in the claustral darkness felt as far from Yarik as he could have been. His hands tried to rise, as if to grab for the fabric's edge. But hers were on them, pressing down. She kept his still. This woman who'd lured him out here, who he'd followed. "Who are you?" he asked her.

"A collector of bus fares," she said.

"A derelict," the fat man said.

The gun wielder told him, "A bum."

He asked them all, "Why would anyone come after *you?*"

"You mean to tell me," the gun wielder said, "you've never been jumped?"

Dima shook his head. The hood shook with it. "Not till tonight." The fat man laughed. "I thought you were nationalists," Dima said, and the laugh stopped.

171

"Us?" the gun wielder said.

"I thought—"

"If they were us, you wouldn't be sitting here talking about it. You wouldn't have the fucking teeth to talk through. You wouldn't . . ." And a hand was at his throat, on the edge of the hood, lifting a corner, the harelipped face close in the opening, the scabbed nose, the barrel of the gun. "Now you know," the mouth said, "what this is fucking for." Then the gun was gone, in its place a clear plastic bag filled with pieces of something that looked like scraps of shriveled skin. "*This*," the man said, "is for the cops." Then the hood was yanked down again, the blackness back.

The woman gave his hands a pat. "But those," she said, "are just our short-term problems. They aren't what worries us. What worries us long term, where the real danger lies, the threat to who we *are* . . ."

". . . is your friends," the fat man cut in, "the Communists."

"I didn't know they would take the picture," Dima said. "I didn't know about the poster. They were just . . ."

"They fooled you." The woman nodded.

"Yes," he told her.

"They tried to use you."

"Yes."

"The same old story," she said.

And the gun wielder's bark—"Spit on it!"—came at Dima with such fury he flinched. "Every fucking time, I mean since the fucking Hague, fucking Bakunin, those red motherfuckers have been fucking us over. We came for *their* revolution. We showed the fuck up. And after? They fucked us. Ours? Against the same people? Right next door? Did *they* come? Does a cat fuck a fish?" He paused, said it again: "Does a cat fuck a fish?"

Inside his hood, Dima shook his head.

"You're fucking right," the man said. "Not unless that cat *knows* it's the only way it's going to *catch* that fish, to hold that fishy still, that little fishy flopping there thinking, thinking, That cat's not so bad. It doesn't want to eat me. It only wants to *fuck* me."

"All right," the fat man said.

"*All right*? Do you *like* being treated like that? Like this guy. Like this motherfucker. Like *you*." He jabbed a finger through the hood, against Dima's forehead. "Get him on board. Fuck that fish. Fuck *us*. Until they turn around and fucking eat us. Right?" The man jabbed his finger again at Dima's forehead. "*Right?*"

"I don't know," Dima said, "who you mean by *us*." For a moment, there was just the sound of the man's worked-up breathing, Dima's own quieter breathing inside the hood. Then the man's finger was gone and the fabric was rushing up Dima's face and the hood was gone.

"*Us*," the gun wielder said, the fabric hanging from his fist. "Me, him, her."

But Dima was no longer listening. He sat, blinking, taking in the whole scene so fast he could feel it filling his eyes, as if the rush of information was what was squeezing down his pupils instead of the light— hard slants of light slicing past the crimson window drapes, painting the wall-bolted tables, the curved vinyl booths, the chrome of the bar, empty bottles glinting on dark shelves above the stools. On one table: a plastic basket that must have once held sugar or stacks of napkins but now overflowed with cigarette butts. It breathed a gray mist. The air was curdled with smoke. In the booth, to either side of him, the two men sat with cigarettes in their mouths, adding to it. Across the table the woman's mouth was empty, her empty hands still on his tied ones.

"Us," Dima heard the gun wielder say again.

She smiled a bad-toothed smile. "You," she said.

Her name was Viktoriya Kirillovna Ovinka, though she told him, "Call me Vika" as she untied his wrists. "This"—she nodded across at the gun wielder—"is Fyodor Georgievich."

"Fedya," he said, picking at the scab on his nose.

"And Vladimir Vyacheslavovich."

The fat man bowed as best he could, a small jerk of his gut against the table edge. "Volodya." He extended one huge hand to Dima. "I believe you've already met my armpit." He lifted an enormous limb, said, "Yuri Yurevich."

173

Reaching beneath the fat man's pit, Fedya flapped his hand like a mouth, let out a smoker's croak: "Yura!"

That cracked the others up.

The hood-sweat slowly drying on his face, Dima, quietly, cautiously, asked them again, "But who are you?"

"Ah," Vika said, bunching up the rope that had been around his wrists, "you mean *what* are we."

"We could be anarchists," Volodya said, "but Fedya would debate it."

"*I'm* an anarchist." Fedya rasied his hand—with the gun in it—like he was a student in some schoolroom for revolutionaries. "I'm a fucking insurrectionary anarchist. But there are definitely some mutualists in the room, collectivists, maybe—I'm not naming names—even an anarcho-capitalist."

"Who?" Vika demanded.

Fedya lifted his shoulders, held up his hands.

"I'm not an anarcho-capitalist," she said. "I'm a post-anarchist."

"Yesterday," Fedya said, "you were an anarcho-feminist."

"So today I'm a post-anarcho-feminist."

"But always"—Volodya motioned towards her with one huge hand—"and with great consistency"—held it out as if to settle everyone down—"Vika is a hedonist."

She shrugged, her small shoulders lifting her sweatshirt, the row of safety pins winking up the center of her chest. Dima looked away, tried to ignore the glint still ghosting in his eyes.

Volodya placed his wide palm across his own wide chest, as if to draw the abductee's attention back to him. "I," he said, "consider myself a gastronist. Not a gastronome. I don't love food; I *believe* in it. That society can, and should, be organized around it. But, that is, I admit, a minority view. So, if you must call us all by one moniker, then I suppose you might try Leisurists."

"It sounds so stupid," Fedya said.

"Or," Volodya continued, "my personal preference: mushroomists."

"Mushroomists?" Dima asked. Across from him Vika had balled his old wrist-rope into a tangle, its fibers a fuzzy softness between her fingers. The fat man must have gestured—Dima heard him clear his throat—because she uncupped her hands, spilled out the rope, reached beneath the table.

"Allow us," Volodya said above her rustling, "to present to you a proposition. All this blather about freedom, all this rattling on since glasnost, freedom this, a free society that . . ." Vika lifted a small plastic bag into sight. "A free society," the fat man continued as she plunked the bag down, "doesn't force its people to do what they don't want to do." She picked at a knot in its neck. "Doesn't coerce them even into doing it more frequently than they want." Her fingernails were unpainted, chewed. "Doesn't oblige some to work at jobs others wouldn't do." Dima watched her wiggle an index finger into the tied end. "Doesn't bludgeon its citizens into lives they never wanted." He could see the nicks around the quick, the red of bitten skin. "Doesn't make us work at jobs we hate." The knot came loose. Volodya reached across the table, retrieved the bag from Vika's hands. "A free society," he said, "doesn't *make* us work at all. It *lets* us. Because we *want* to. At good work. Enjoyable work. Work we like."

"In other words"—Vika spoke around a ruined thumbnail stuck between her lips—"it lets us play."

"No!" Volodya's voice was so vehement it drew Dima's look back to him. "No, my dear distracting friend," the fat man corrected her, shaking his head, his smiling cheeks joggling back and forth. "In no such words at all. Play," he addressed Dima again, "doesn't *make* anything. Nothing is *produced*. No, I'm talking about work, work that produces *and* satisfies. That *feels* like play. Shouldn't that be the point? Not just to produce as much as possible, but to do it in a way that brings pleasure in the doing? Isn't that the best work, the way we were meant to work? Play—with purpose."

Opening the bag, he stuck his face in, inhaled until the plastic crinkled around his cheeks, then peeled it away and looked at Dima again. "Behold," he said, "the heron. What gives a heron its greatest pleasure?"

Dima glanced at Vika; she was watching the fat man; the fat man was watching Dima, waiting, his chin above the bag. "Fishing?" Dima guessed.

Volodya gave Dima a look—half-amused, half-impressed—like a debater whose opponent has just proved his own point. "And a bear?" he said.

"To hunt," Vika answered.

And Fedya said, "What about a squirrel?"

"I think"—Volodya winked at Dima—"our esteemed poet has seen the point." He smiled across the table at Vika. "Cups? Thermos? Spoon?"

While she was digging in a rucksack for them, Volodya said to Dima, "Tell me, oh bard, oh scholarly scholar, why should animals have it better than us?" He waited with brows raised. Then, without looking, took the spoon from Vika.

Dima watched her put three tin cups out on the table, watched Volodya dip into the plastic bag, lift the spoon out mounded with powder, the same mealy brown as the shrivels he'd seen in Fedya's bag before. "Is that mushroom?" Dima said.

"Ah yes." Volodya, nodding vigorously, dumped the spoonful in one of the cups. "Mushroomists! You bring me back to the question at hand." He dumped a second spoonful in a different cup. "Naturally," he said, "all three of us, all *four* of us"— he gave Dima his half-surprised-half-impressed look again—"would be drawn to different kinds of work. Fedya, for example, is a magician with computers. Vika is mildly obsessed with sex." Across the table, her punch hit his shoulder hard enough he nearly spilled the thermos he had just opened up. "And violence," he added, pouring into the cups. "I—if I may for a moment unhook myself from the corset of modesty—am not merely an exuberant chef but a talented one." He finished filling all three cups. "But one thing that we all enjoy in common"—setting the thermos down, he reached beneath the table, drew out a second, larger bag—"and, it might be mentioned, also how we endeavor to support ourselves in this inexorably capitalist society"—pushed it across to Dima—"is hunting for mushrooms." He opened the bag for Dima to see. It was full of them, pounds of fungi, their brown crowns like a year's worth of moons crammed into a black dirt sky. "You might call it," Volodya added, "our co-play. Or joint work."

Fedya reached over, grabbed a cup. Volodya slid another across the table to Vika, took the third for himself. The thermos he put in front of Dima. Dima tried to peer into it. He couldn't see anything. When he looked back, the three of them had their cups in their hands, their hands raised.

Volodya nodded, made a little up-up motion with his cup.

Over the rim of hers, Vika's black eyes peered at him. "What would you do with your time," she said, "if your time was yours?"

He made himself look away. The others were all watching him, too. But, even looking back at them, he felt her stare.

"Not your *free* time," she said, "but your *work* time." And there were her eyes again. "If you could spend it at anything."

Maybe it was just the way she was with everyone, maybe it was only that these days he spent so much time alone, maybe something simple as her hair, so black, black as his mother's had been, as his brother's still was, but for whatever reason he found himself repeating her word: "Anything." He found that here, to her, he could say it: "Anything, if it was with my brother."

Vika nodded, so slightly her shock of bangs barely shook. "Then," she said, her voice low, her eyes serious, "we'll drink to your brother."

The fat man's head bobbed up and down on his fat neck. He asked Dima his brother's name, then raised the small cup in his huge hand. "To time," Volodya said, "with Yaroslav."

"To time with Yaroslav," they all said.

"And," Vika added, a small smile slipping back, "with us."

"With us," the others repeated, tipped their heads, and slugged the drink down.

It tasted so bad Dima could barely swallow. When he took the thermos from his mouth, the others were still draining their cups. As they finished they looked at him.

"You didn't drink," Volodya said.

Fedya reached out and shook the thermos, shaking Dima's hand with it. The liquid left made a small sloshing sound.

"You have to drink," Vika said, "or it won't come true."

"I'm sorry," Dima said, but Fedya was already lifting the thermos to Dima's mouth and Volodya was saying, "Not just for you, for us, too" and Vika was reaching over the table, her smile widening, her hand hunting for Dima's face while she asked, laughing, "Do you want me to hold your nose? Should I pinch your nose for you?" until he shook his head free of her fingers and the thermos free of Fedya's pushing and drank it all down himself. It wasn't until after he had swallowed, after the feeling of Vika's fingers on his nose had evaporated with the steam against his face, in the fluttery rustle of the others all clapping quietly with their fingers on their palms, that he realized what the inside of the thermos smelled like. That was when the first cramp hit.

"I think," Fedya said, "he's starting to feel sick."

"It's OK," Vika said.

"Why"—Dima's stomach clenched—"would I be feeling sick?"

"We're all feeling a little sick," she said. Dima was surprised to find her hands on top of his again, and when he looked at their faces, she was right; they did look sick: Fedya was bent over the table, breathing slowly in and out; Volodya had shut his eyes.

Gently, Vika's fingers stroked the back of his. "It's just the mushrooms," she told him. "You'll feel better in a few minutes."

But a few minutes later he was lying on his back in the aisle between the booths, staring up at the three faces peering down. In their mouths the butts of cigarettes glowed. Smoke curled around, drifted above. He watched it crawl the curve of the ceiling, felt it cling to the inside of his throat, thought he was going to throw up. As if they thought so, too, their bodies unbent, their faces retreated. Except for Vika's. She crouched down, held her cigarette out.

He shook his head. As he should have done, he knew, that first time she'd held the damp end of her stub up for him. Knew it and yet still wanted to take the paper between his lips, let the smoke soothe his churning stomach. She was right: it must just be the mushrooms. Making him

178

feel strange, his insides unfamiliar, his thoughts cast loose. All his life he'd guarded against just this thing—her, them, the allure of friends, the female touch—all he'd known would only separate him from his brother.

Around him, Dima could hear the others rustling, the clanks of the cups, squeak of the thermos top being screwed on. *Just that,* he told himself again, *just the drink.* Except—one of those loosed thoughts floating in—hadn't he felt it before he'd ever touched a drop?

Vika stood, blew out a cloud of smoke, squinted through it at the others. "I don't think he's gonna be able to walk."

From over by the booth, he heard Volodya's chuckle, Fedya's *fuck,* tried to sit up. His head went woozy.

"Nope," Vika said, "I don't think he's walking."

"Where?" he managed to ask. "Where are you going?"

And Volodya's hairy face was suddenly in his. "Why?" The blond beard bunched with the big man's smile. "You want to go?"

"No."

"You want to stay here?" Her face was blocked behind Volodya, but when Vika said, "I didn't think so," Dima could hear the smile. Then, the smile gone: "It's time."

"Time for what?" Dima asked her legs as they stepped by.

"Sorry, Mr. Boss-man," she said, "I don't wear a watch."

"Time for what?" he asked the fat man.

"Time for you to hold on, you vagabond." Volodya lifted Dima farther up, folded him over his shoulder, said, "And don't barf down my butt." And then Dima was in the air, legs dangling, head hanging behind the big man's back. He tried to struggle, shoving weakly at the shoulders, using his knees, until Volodya simply turned a little and, swinging him against a booth, whacked his head. It was a soft booth, but not as soft as his head; Dima could feel the dent it made in his skull, could feel it filling back in like foam finding its shape. That seemed strange enough he just lay still, let Volodya adjust him on his wide shoulder, watched the aisle unwind as they went out.

Out into the cool air cleared of smoke. Dima could taste its cleanness. It went through him like a gulp of ice water—he could feel it cool his stomach, his innards—and he drank it in while Volodya, holding to the railings, stepped backwards down the small metal stairs. Facing the gravel below, Dima could see each sharp shape of each rock. He could feel their gravity pulling at him, pulling as the big man dropped. He shut his eyes, clenched his teeth against the jolt to his gut. But when it came, it felt good: the huge soft shoulder shoving into him, all the bad air gushing out. It occurred to him he should have thrown up. Then it occurred to him he no longer had to.

"Where are you taking me?" he said into the broad back.

"Shh," Volodya said. And in a half-whisper, "You're like a child." He pinched his voice: "'How much longer? How much longer?'"

Dima thought he heard, over the footsteps in the gravel, the big man chuckling.

"I should spank you," Volodya said.

And Dima told himself it wasn't funny, he knew it wasn't funny, and yet he *felt* it was, and he knew that was bad, knew that *that* was what was replacing the sickness in his stomach.

"I should let Vika spank you," Volodya said. "She would like that."

Which was definitely not funny. Which was what was wrong with him in the first place. He tried to make himself feel it, bunched his brow, clenched his jaw, as if with the muscles of his face he could keep the resolve he'd found lying on the railcar's floor from seeping out, but it was gone, evanesced alongside the nausea, smoothed out with the soothing of the cramps, and trying to fake it all he felt was silly. No: what he'd felt before was the truth. *This* was false. For the fact was he was being carried on the shoulder of a man who'd just a short while ago been choking him—that was the fact.

"Vika, come!" Volodya called in a whisper cranked up for distance. "I have his ass here waiting . . ."

And as the man's words dissolved in giggles, Dima could feel them burbling off the shoulder like bubbles blown in water, could feel them against the skin of his stomach, rolling up it, tickling—and it felt good, that was a fact, too—and he lay there jouncing with each step, trying to keep his own laughter from shaking out of his nose.

"Mister Boss-man!" Volodya said, like it was a joke, and they both laughed like it was a joke, and it wasn't, Dima knew that.

"It's not funny," he told the fat man.

"I know," Volodya said. "You want to hear something funny?"

"No," Dima told him.

"Then I'll tell you something sad."

"No," Dima said again. "Tell me where we're going."

"Listen," the fat man shushed him, "there once was a time when there weren't any watches." He giggled. "Sad," he said, as if to scold himself. "Imagine: not in anybody's pocket. Not dangling from any chain. Not even clocks. Nothing. A time before the time of time. Think about that."

Dima told himself to keep his mind, instead, on where he was being carried. "Volodya—"

"Do you know when the first clock was made?"

"Vladimir Vyacheslavovich—"

"The fourteenth century. Do you know who made it?"

"Where are we—"

"Bosses," Volodya said. "In the very first factories. You know what they called their new timekeeping things?"

Dima tried to not think about it, and in his trying not to began to, and suddenly it seemed important that he answer, but all he could think was *a time before the time of time, a time before the time of time*, the phrase afloat in his brain.

"*Werkglocken*," Volodya said. "Made from—"

"A time," Dima said, "before the time of time."

The fat man puffed a wet laugh. "Nooo . . ." he said. "From bells." And with one big hand he whapped at one of Dima's dangling feet. "Bong! Time to get to work. Bong! To take a break. Bong! Better get home."

They were giggling again. "This isn't supposed to be funny," Dima said.

"Listen!" Volodya scolded him. "Before the Werkglocken, there was just the sun—goes up, goes down—sometimes later, sometimes earlier, and everybody knows when it's up and everybody knows when it's down, and nobody can say it's an inch past sunrise without it sure as hell being an inch past sunrise. Do you see?"

Dima nodded behind Volodya's back.

"They couldn't control the sun," the fat man said, "so they replaced it. Made time something that wasn't ours. Something that was spent. Not just passed, but *spent*. To spend time. That's when they started saying it."

"To spend time." In Dima's ears it sounded more sad than he could understand.

"Yes," Volodya said. "And what can be spent can be bought. Owned. They made time into something they could *own*."

A time before the end of time, Dima thought, and it sounded even sadder. Hanging there, head flopping, he watched the gravel go by a meter below his face, and it struck him for the first time in years how strange the mirror-light was—the actual light, hazy and harsh, blanched and clear—and he thought, *A dark before the end of dark.* He thought, *An us before the end of us.* He shut his eyes.

Quietly, slowly, his words shaking with Volodya's steps, he said, "Where are you taking me?"

And Volodya told him, "Home."

He thought of Yarik, then, walking away from the tram earlier that day, burdened by the plastic bags, and he could feel their weight, feel each jolt in his own sack of a body, each step thudding against the inside of his skull. His head seemed impossibly heavy.

Into it came the sound of footsteps, and then the tips of the feet flicked into his sight, one canvas shoe, the other, the first again, mesmerizing. Until he tilted his neck up, looked behind, and saw her, saw himself bent over Volodya's shoulder, butt in the air, and, shoving at the small of the man's back, he grunted, "Let me down."

It felt good to get on the ground again. His legs felt good, his stomach fine, his head wonderful.

"You feel OK to walk?" Vika asked him.

"I feel great," he said.

"Then you're about to start feeling a lot better."

He glanced at her, and it was true, and that truth was so strange it scared him back to some sense, at last. "What do you mean?" he asked.

"You'll see." She tried to take his hand.

He pulled away. "You don't like to reveal things, do you?"

"Come on," she said.

"You know why?"

"The others are way ahead."

"Because you're wrong. If everyone wants what you say they want, then why haven't we already made the world that way?" She was wearing her rucksack on her shoulders and his, too, slung over her chest, and he suddenly wanted it back. "Because," he told her, reaching for it, "it wouldn't work. It never has. It doesn't—"

She pressed her palm to his mouth. He let her, let her fingers slip over his chin, through the hair at his throat, along the flat bone down the middle of his body onto the softer place above his waist, and when they got to his waistline they curled around the top of his pants. She tugged. "Come on," she said again, "you're still unsteady on your feet."

Ahead, the tracks snaked out into the open, and beyond them there was the beginning of the access line, and, above, the sky was shaky with false stars, and in front of it all: Vika, walking backwards, pulling him.

If you could only see, she said and, *imagine if,* and her voice felt the way her hand had on his lips, and he listened to her tell him how it *would* work, how it already *had*: Ireland in the Middle Ages, ancient Icelandic thorpes, medieval cities free of rule, governed only by groups of neighbors, no laws, no central control. She told him how serfs had taken refuge there, how, centuries later, cities had cropped up again, a brief boom in anarchist communes after the Spanish Civil War. But mostly she talked of Russia. Before the Bolsheviks, the Decembrists, the tsars, the Code of Law, even the existence of the serf, here when all there was were small farming villages, the world of the mir. That was what they called the lands around each village: the *mir*, the world. The dirt streets they shared, the icehouses, ovens, woodlands and pastures and wells, all shared. One household borrowing another's horses to plow a patch of the communal fields, another bringing bread made from yet another's rye, long lines of men and women sewing flaxseeds side by side, threshing it in communal barns, butchering communal livestock, stooking communal stacks of hay: the world, the mir. And outside the mir another mir, surrounded by other fields, enclosed by other woods, another and another, unknown to any sovereign, ungoverned by any hand, a Russia made up of thousands of little worlds.

A Russia, Dima thought, *before the end of Russia.*

They had come to the rusted fence where the rail yard stopped. One after another, sets of tracks hit their concrete buffers and ended, too, sudden as time ceased. Except for one. It ran on, out, past the fence, dwindled into the distance. To either side of it a barrier of hemlocks grew, planted by the Consortium in preperatory years, a darkness-indifferent woods, branches swaying as if from a breeze blown down the access line. Dima could have stood all night watching the forest undulate if it hadn't been for the faint buzz growing in his ears. He followed the sound upward: the power line, the towers, the wires swooping and rising into the distance, cresting and falling like waves. Which would make him underwater. Which would make the tracks beneath the wires, their shadows cast upon the lakefloor. Which would mean they weren't solid at all, just strips he could stir with the brush of his hand. When he stooped down to touch them, Vika let go of his pants. The rail was solid.

He looked for Vika to let her know the news, but she was already disappearing into the shadows of the trees. Straightening up, he looked for the others. They were gone. No: he could hear them rustling in there. One by one, they came back out, the branches shifting, a shape separating from the trees, hurrying up the slope back to the tracks. Each of them carried some sort of board, wide as a spread hand, long as an arm, and, coming closer, he made out, beneath each plank, some piece of metal catching a curve of gleam. Wheels. Dima stopped, stared. Fedya was the first to set his on the rail—a heavy thunk—the others following with a clattering of metal on metal, and then a whooshing, a hiss, the sound rolling louder and louder towards Dima.

"That one," Vika called to him, "is yours."

They rode the outside rail in single file, Fedya then Vika then Dima, Volodya behind him so he wouldn't get left. Dima watched the woman in front, the way she set one foot a little back on the board, used the other to push at the ties as they flicked by—it wasn't hard; he just had to keep his balance, his distance—and when she stopped shoving and planted both feet and sank bent-kneed and low and let it glide, he did the same: the four of them flying down the rail, the trees whipping by in silent speed, a picture of the wind that rushed at Dima's face, shook his beard, went wild through his hair. Squinting into it, all he could make out was a blur: her hurtling, the rails streaking, the ties flickering by, the streams of power lines like flight paths of birds somehow made visible to him, visible as the mirrors above, and then, suddenly, he could see beyond them, through the nighttime haze, make out the Milky Way, the distant planets, the pristine blackness of space.

Somewhere his father was smoking his pipe. Somewhere he was whittling a story out of wood. Somewhere his uncle was standing barefoot in the sun in the middle of a field, his toes burrowed into the dirt, down to the coolness, down to the coolness, and what was left of his mother but love for him? What did his niece know but the softness of his beard? To whose leg did his nephew cling? Who was as forgiving as his brother's wife? What more could he want than to feel, even now, below his feet, the shaking of Yarik's shoulders before the launch into the lake, even here, the wind rushing by as they slid beside each other on their skates, to know that no matter what the world did to itself, what it might try to do to them, there were places in it, in him, in his brother, where it could never reach.

They went on. The rails went on. The trees blurred by. Nothing but the walls of the woods and the causeway between them and the woman in front of him hurtling down it and the man behind him coming on.

It was a shock to hit the Oranzheria. Its high glass plain came into view like the shore of a continent glimpsed from far out at sea. Bright as ice beneath the mirror-light, hovering above the tops of the trees, its edges stretched as far as Dima could see. Only straight ahead, where the

185

access line cut through, was there a gap. They shot into it. From beyond the buffer of hemlocks came the distant clangor of heavy machines, the roar of threshers, the din of a thousand voices, as the endless line of glass, broken only by the tops of the tallest trees, streamed by. In front, Fedya flung his arms out to either side, flipped it all the finger. Ahead, Vika did the same. Behind him, Dima knew, Volodya must be, too. He stretched his own arms out, stuck up his middle fingers, and, grinning into the wind, rocketed through.

Over an hour later, they came out the other side, blew by the outer reaches of the Oranzheria and into the sudden quiet of the still-standing woods. Not long after that, they stopped. His left heel bruised from using it as a break against the thwacking ties, Dima followed the others down the embankment into the trees. Here, the mirrors' reach was new enough that there were still birches, aspens unfurling freshly budded leaves, pines strong and healthy as if grown from Consortium seeds. Beneath the boughs they hid their rail-boards. Nobody spoke. It was darker below the canopy and he hustled to keep from losing the others behind the scrim of pines, until the scrub cleared and they were scrambling down the dirt of a dry creek bank. Walking along the sandy bottom, the sound of the woods began to change. Between the rustling of their footsteps he heard music, the distant murmur of a radio or TV.

Vika turned to him. "You want an answer?" she whispered. "Why the old way failed? Why our way never gets a chance?" Taking his hand she pulled him up, over the lip of the bank, onto the forest floor.

Through the trees, he could see colors flashing, giant TV screens. Out of the creek, he heard it: the bombardment of loudspeaker ads.

"Why do you think," Vika whispered, "the Party wouldn't let us out to see the West? Why do you think they were so scared of even letting pictures in?"

Beside them, Volodya whispered, "To make us want what we don't know we want until we want it: the genius of capitalism."

"Spit on it," Fedya said.

"Indeed." Volodya nodded in the dimness. "But admire it, too.

Because that, my expectatory friend, is the piece upon which the entire enterprise rests."

They moved off through the trees, whispering as they went.

"Always increasing," Vika said.

Volodya added, "Ever expanding."

"Fucking America," Fedya spat. "Hardest working fuckers in the world. Make three times more shit every hour than they did just fifty fucking years ago."

"So why"—Volodya lifted a bent birch trunk for them to walk beneath—"are they working *more* hours? Not a few, not even a week's worth, but *months*. Months more every year. Why?"

Behind Dima, Vika said, "Because more productivity just means more work."

"Spit on *that*."

Dropping the branch, Volodya whispered, "Doesn't make much sense, does it?"

"Unless . . ." Vika started.

And Fedya finished: ". . . for every fucking hour some wage slave works to make more shit, he's also wanting to buy more shit."

"More production," Volodya said, "means more products must be bought, means the worker must have more money to buy them, means he has to work more hours to get it, means . . ."

"He's making," Fedya said, "more fucking products."

"More profit," Volodya added.

"But," Vika chimed in, "not for him."

"Because?" Volodya asked.

"Because," Fedya said, "he's *buying* the fucking products."

They came to the edge of the woods. Scrub pines and thin saplings and the bramble-filled field that had been cleared around the outside of The Dachas. The concrete walls climbed up towards the backs of the mammoth TV screens, loomed high above the guard station set on its concrete blocks below, a green steel shell punched with a single door, the square hole of a window. It glowed, the bulb-light shifting with the shadows of men moving inside.

187

Outside, in the woods, the four of them drew close together.

"But what if," Volodya whispered, "the worker stops, stops wanting more, becomes simply satisfied?"

"Then," Fedya said, "the system is fucked."

"Or," Vika said, "it's got to make him *un*satisfied."

"What if"—Volodya dug in his rucksack—"his wants are fulfilled?"

"Then it's got to make him want *new* wants."

Out of his bag, Volodya brought a handful of what looked like swimming goggles with their sides painted black. One by one he handed them out. "The rotary phone," he said.

"The push-button phone," Vika said.

"The cordless phone."

"The mobile phone."

"The wireless earpiece," Fedya chimed in.

"Good one," Volodya told him.

"The television?" Fedya offered.

"The *color* television," Volodya said.

"The *flatscreen* television," Vika said.

"The *recordable* television," Volodya said.

"Fucking cable," Fedya said.

All three had put their goggles on. They looked at Dima, the black-painted rims and sides making their eyes, just visible behind the plastic, look lit by penlights. Fedya motioned for Dima to put his on. When he did, he found he could only see straight in front of him; all his peripheral vision was blocked out. He turned his head to face Volodya. The fat man was digging in his bag again. "What about the zerkala?" Dima said.

"Of course," Volodya answered. "Soon, we'll all want our very own orbiting imitation of the sun." He had taken out a small metal box and now he flipped the top. Inside sat a clear cake of wax. "Unless," he said, taking out a pinch, "we simply stop."

"You mean," Dima whispered, "stop wanting?"

"No." Rolling the wax into a ball, Volodya took a second pinch. "Of course you don't stop wanting," and passed the box on to Vika.

"You simply want," she said, "what you always wanted before they told you what the new thing was you were supposed to want."

"What's that?" Dima asked.

"To read a book," Volodya said.

"To lie in bed with your lover," Vika said.

"To go for a fucking walk"—Fedya gave the box back to Volodya—"in the fucking woods."

"Maybe"—Volodya passed it to Dima—"with your brother."

Dima watched the man roll his pinches of wax into two small spheres in his huge palm. Then Dima dug his fingers into the box and scooped out two of his own.

The four of them stood at the edge of the woods, listening to the small sounds of their breathing, a shirtsleeve rustling against a branch, as they pushed the plugs into their ears. Then the breaths were gone, the rustling gone, the babble of The Dachas' speakers buried beneath the beating of Dima's blood.

One by one they broke out of the forest into the open scrub, stepping single file through the grass and brambles towards the window-glowing guardhouse. When there was only Dima and Fedya left, the scab-nosed man reached out and pushed Dima into the field. Stumbling forward, he glimpsed in Fedya's other hand a pale square of caught light against the dark woods: the small translucent bag of shriveled mushrooms.

That was what got them past the guards. But why they wanted in Dima couldn't fathom. Inside, he tried to keep Volodya's broad back and boulder head in the circular sights of his goggles, but something would shove his shoulder, or make a sound loud enough to pierce the wax, and he would whip his head around, frame a black-bordered glimpse of The Dachas: a small girl turning skinned squirrels over a fire, hawking their blackened meat with a mute moving mouth; the tooth-gone grin of a drunken man, his breath hot on Dima's cheek; two more circling each other with slashing shovel-blades; a third laid out, his head stove in, a still shape that passersby stepped over, moving on.

Once, he lifted off his goggles—a blur of people shoving past, of makeshift shacks, bright billboards below the brighter flash of blasting

TVs—unplugged an ear to sound crashing over him in the same way, stuck the wax back in, pressed the goggles again onto his face.

They lived in one of the old vacation homes, the two-story building turned into a kind of crammed comune, and while Fedya took their things inside, Vika and Volodya led him up a ladder to see the view. From the roof, The Dachas looked like a dozen villages dumped on top of one another, bits of buildings half-collapsed against each other, shards of others wedged into whatever space would hold them. Up on the perimeter wall, the TV screens were at eye level. Between their pictures of leather-lined sports cars and steaming plates of meat Dima could see the dark sweep of the trees. And beyond the trees, a thin line gleaming along the entire southward horizon.

He turned to one side: Volodya laid out on his huge stomach, eyes closed, breathing slow as a hibernating bear. And to the other: Vika crouched beside him on the slope.

"What is that?" he asked her, as if with the right words he could stave off knowing what he already knew.

"What?" she mouthed, and when he pointed, she slid close and shouted so near his ear that he could feel her breath, "You have to talk like this."

He leaned in, his beard brushing her cheek. "It can't already be that close."

"And coming closer," she shouted, "every day. Won't be too long till it's here. Then they'll either knock this down and send us somewhere else, or just flatten it to one story, build right over, keep going."

"It can't," Dima shouted, "not forever."

"It has to."

"Not past the mirrors' reach."

"They'll send up more."

"It'll hit Lake Segozero."

"They'll build around it."

"It'll hit the White Sea."

"They'll go up the Karelian Isthmus."

"What about Finland?"

"They'll go north. Into the Kola Peninsula."

"And when they hit the Barents?"

"By then," she shouted, and he could feel her lips brushing his ear, "it will be outdated. They'll have invented the next model of Oranzheria." He could feel her warm gust of a laugh. "The great glass sea version two."

"And then what?" Dima shouted.

"Then version two point one." With a smile, she stood. Then stepped over Volodya and, stretching out on the roof, lay down on her back. He watched her, but she was already turned to the sky, her eyes hidden behind goggles agleam with zerkala-light, zipper teeth a twinkling track running down her chest through the darkness of her sweatshirt, the safety pins like tiny ties. Where they stopped, the fabric peeled apart: a wedge of bare belly, wavery with the flickering from the giant TV screens, and in its middle, over her navel, something round tattooed in red. He saw it now: the head of a mushroom inked into bloom over her center.

Below his hands, the tin shook. Dima turned to look: Fedya stepping onto the roof, standing up into his sphere of sight. He held something the size of a brick, passed whatever it was out of Dima's sight to someone else, while with his free hand he reached into his pants' waist, drew the pistol out. Then he was there, filling the frames of Dima's goggles, patting the air with his palm—*get down?*—until, with a shove of the man's hand on his shoulder, Dima lay back. Stradling him, Fedya raised the gun, pointed to it, to Dima. Dima lay still. The man above him tapped his own goggles a couple times, then swung his leg over Dima and lay down beside him on the roof. Cheek laid flat against the metal, Dima could see Fedya's face less than a meter away. Fedya didn't look back at him. Instead, the man slowly raised his hand until his arm was a straight line from his shoulder to the sky.

Dima felt the shot—the jerk of Fedya's shoulder shuddering the tin—as much as heard the sound: someone hammering a nail in one hard bang. Without dropping his arm, Fedya turned to Dima, grinned. "Fucking zerkala!" he shouted.

191

Dima nodded. "Fucking zerkala!"

The second shot didn't come as a surprise. But Volodya's voice booming in his ear did. He jerked his head around, knocked his nose into the fat man's cheek. Volodya laughed—Dima could feel the beard shaking against his face—but when the man leaned to his ear to shout again, his voice was serious.

"You ever hear," he shouted, "of 'propaganda by the deed'?"

Dima shook his head.

"One day," Volodya shouted, "we're going to *do* something. Something more powerful than any ad on any TV. We're going to show the people that it doesn't have to be this way. That we can change it. You want to know how?" Volodya pointed up, his huge arm like a missile launcher, his fist the missile, his pointer finger its tip. He aimed from mirror to mirror to mirror. Into Dima's ear, he shouted, "We're going to turn them off. All of them. All at once."

On Dima's other side, a third bang cracked the quiet of the wax plug. Dima turned away from it, towards Volodya to shout his question, but Volodya was already at his ear, answering it.

"Break into the control room," the fat man shouted. "Redirect the bastards so they can't shine their light down."

Another shot shook Fedya's shoulder, shook Dima's head.

"But," Dima shouted in Volodya's ear, "won't they just direct them back?"

"That's the point. One night, maybe just one hour, even just one minute. Like one giant wink. Aimed at the whole city, at the whole country, telling them, *us*, we can change this. We can do what we want to do. What we *need* to do." Another pistol crack. "We just have to do it." Dima could feel the man's grin coming through the beard hairs against his cheek. "And that, *that* is going to be some serious propaganda by the deed."

But when Dima turned to look at him, the man lowered his arm and pointed for Dima to look the other way. There, Fedya was knocking the spent shells out of the revolver's chamber. They hit the roof, bounced: six shiny gleams silently rolling towards the edge of the tin.

When Dima looked back at Fedya, the man was loading fresh bullets into the chamber. He held the gun out to Dima. He put it in Dima's hand. He rolled close enough to shout.

"Try it. It feels fucking good." And when Dima closed his fingers around the grip, Fedya told him, "Aim for a different one each time. You can almost convince yourself you're hitting them."

It was true. He held the gun in both hands and extended his arms straight above him and the tip of the barrel seemed to aim at a mirror all by itself. He pulled the trigger. The gun nearly shot out of his hands, jerked back, yanked his arms up, slammed against the roof above his head. He looked at Fedya. Fedya was grinning like he'd just watched one of the zerkala come crashing down. The others were looking at him the same way. And when he turned back to the sky and looked up at the mirrors, it did seem like one of them might be missing, like there was a little more black. He aimed the gun again. The false stars shimmered, their reflected light shaking, as if they knew what was coming. He covered one with the revolver's barrel and let loose.

A Deeper Breath

The sun had been up for hours by the time he got home. Riding the tram back to Avtovskaya Street, he could hardly keep his eyes open, nearly missed his stop. Halfway up the stairs, he had to sit, head pounding, all his muscles aching by the time, at last, he opened the apartment door. The rugs were rolled, clamped, the morning brightness streaming in as the mirror-light must have done all night. His mother was slumped over her sewing machine, the thread pulled out and strung from the needle to her lap like a strand of spiderweb catching the sun. He watched it. It did not move. *Mama*, he tried to say, but his throat wouldn't, and he was crossing the room, and the string still didn't move, and he was about to reach out, shake her, when her head lolled a little farther onto her outstretched arm. She sighed, went back to her slow sleep breath. At first, he couldn't tell what she'd been sewing—a bunched-up ball with a cuff sticking out—and then he saw the pile of unsewn gloves, all the mismatched pairs she'd stored since he and Yarik had been young, saw beside them the pile of ones she'd stitched shut finger by finger into fists.

In the flesh of his palm, he could still feel a faint bruise: the pistol's kick. Standing in his mother's apartment it seemed too strange a night to have passed through his life only hours ago. But there were his wrists, raw from the rope. And there was Ivan, his tawny feathers mashed against the balcony doors, his body bunched as the gloves and just as still.

Dima was halfway to the bird before it burst into motion, jerked one way, the other, exploded in a fury of feathers and feet—and was still again. None of which distanced it from the glass. When he was closer yet, it did it all again—the wild flapping, the yanking side to side, the collapse into quiet—and got no further. It wasn't until he was at the doors, about to throw them open, and it had recommenced convulsions, that he saw it had somehow jammed its beak between the panels, gotten stuck. He watched it thrash, body leaping, wings awhir, head like a peg pinning it to the door. How long had it been like that? He knelt down, stared into its crazed eye.

Like hers in more ways than just how black. She'd taken him back by herself—the only Leisurist who worked and lived outside The Dachas—bribing the guard with psilocybe, leading Dima to the tracks. They'd skated slower, lifting their boards off at the sounds of coming trains, hiding in the scrub, riding again into the Oranzheria just as the glass was beginning to blush, leaving it in full golden glare, getting to the rail yard so late the tracks were already hot to the touch. She had showed him. Crouched before they made their run across the yard, she'd pressed the tips of her fingers to the rails, lifted them to his forehead, dipped them to the metal again, and one eyelid, the other, dipped them, his lips. He had kept his face utterly still.

Now, it felt already half-asleep. But, staring at the hood that hung from a door handle, that he should have put on the bird last night, he refused to let his eyelids shut. Standing, he tugged open the door, cornered the Golden Phoenix, and scooped it up. He held it tight to his chest, ran his fingers over its beak, stroked the quivering neck until its heart, beating against his forearm, began to slow. On all the other balconies, the flower pots had sprouted—new green leaves growing fast—but if there were any buds they were too far away for him to tell what kind of blooms they might become. When the bird was calm, he slipped on its hood. Inside again, he unclamped the rugs, rolled them down. He carried his mother to her bedroom. She woke in his arms.

"Good morning, lyubimy," she said.

"It's nighttime, Mama," he lied.

When he woke, the rug over his bedroom window was speckled with the same bright spots of the same tiny holes, but the thin strings of sunlight were slanted the wrong way. He watched them stir on the blanket over his feet. Then he kicked them off and rose and rolled the rugs up and filled Ivan's bowl and took it out to the balcony and untied the hood and, listening to the rooster crow at the sinking sun, he felt sick. When the bird at last quit he gave it the bowl and watched it eat. He knew he should do the same; he didn't think he could. Instead, he put the rooster's hood back on, went back inside, rolled back down the rugs, left his mother sleeping, went out to catch the bus.

Under the glass, at the far end of the Oranzheria, at his brother's stop, at the time his brother always got on, Dima waited as the bus emptied of workers heading to their shifts, refilled with ones returning home, his hand spread on the seat beside him, holding a place for Yarik. He told himself the tremor was just the bus, but when it shook away from the stop without his brother—he must have been kept late—Dima felt a stab of relief. And that felt more wrong than everything else. Until, as they circled around, he caught sight of Yarik: his back to the bus, his hard hat on, standing as still as the shut-down backhoe beside him, its shovel arm drawn into itself.

The next morning he wasn't at the Oktrovskogo Avenue stop, either. Dima waited in the sun while three buses came and went, the heat dampening his shirt between his shoulder blades, and then he turned and walked down the concrete pathway to the concrete building and up the five flights of stairs to the apartment door.

"He's at work," Zinaida told him.

"No," Dima said, "he didn't get on the bus."

"He takes a different one now."

"Which?"

His brother's home was quiet, the children gone to school.

"I'm sorry," she told him, "I have to get ready."

"What number bus?"

"I'm already late."

"Zina," he said, and would have asked her, *Why? Why was Yarik taking a different bus?* but the sadness on her face stopped him.

"I'm sorry," she said.

That day Dima stayed away from the statue, from the railroad station, from tram number 119, off all the buses except the one he took that evening out to the Oranzheria only to find this time his brother wasn't at the stop at all. He took the bus back alone again, went again up the stairs to Yarik's apartment and knocked and no one came to the door. He could hear the baby crying inside. He knocked another time, waited, put his forehead to the door, said to the wood, "It's Dima."

He was on the first step down when he heard the bolt. Through the open crack the baby's wails came so loud he imagined, for a second, that the noise had blown the door open on its own. Then, he heard "Dyadya?" and saw Timofei, his blond hair feathered up off the back of his head, stirring, as if it, too, could feel the baby's wails.

Dima crouched to his nephew's height. "Is your papa home?" The boy shook his head. "Is your mama?" The boy nodded. Shutting the door behind him, Dima stood in the foyer, in the full blast of the caterwaul, waiting for Zinaida to come out. Next to the coatrack, right at the height of Dima's eyes, he could see a new hole in the plaster wall, as if someone had punched it with a fist. Something tugged at his hip: Timofei, standing on his slipper toes to get his voice closer.

Through the howls, the boy told Dima, "Papa had to take the long way home."

Dima crouched, his nephew's hands moving to his neck, his own folding around the boy's back. "Why?"

197

"Mama said so." The boy scrunched his small fingers into Dima's beard, tugged his face down even closer, said, as if it was a secret, "Last night he was sick."

"Your papa?"

Then his nephew's breath was on his ear, whispering. "He was drunk." Timofei gave a giddy smile, as if to cover the worry in his eyes. "It was the computer."

"The computer?"

As Dima made his way towards it, the dark screen blinked on, Timofei already standing on the chair, clicking at something. On the screen a video began to play.

Leaning over the boy's shoulder, Dima saw an image of the night sky, the zerkala drifting through the bleached-out dark. Over it, a voice, shouting: *Fucking zerkala!* He knew that voice. Then another, a little quieter, harder to hear—*Fucking zerkala!*—that he knew even better. Still, when his own image flashed onto the screen, he jerked. It was him on the plinth, shouting along with the shouting crowd, *My head still rests upon my shoulders! I still wield my sword with skill!* Dima could feel the blood draining out of his muscles and then the frame froze and a voice said over it, *One day we're going to do something* and a prickling started in his blood's place. *We're going to show the people what can be done. That it doesn't have to be this way. That we can change it.* There was Volodya's goggled face. *You want to know how?*

Even before the camera panned, before he saw them on the roof, before he heard the shots, Dima's stomach started to hollow out. The video cut close on him, the pistol jerking in his hands, its muzzle flashing above his face. Over it white words scrolled: THE POET OF PETER THE GREAT SQUARE. And there was Volodya again—something about a revolution—and the mirrors again, and then Fedya's wild face screaming *Fucking zerkala!* and the camera pulling back to show Dima next to him saying it, too. One last revolver boom. The screen faded halfway to black, and froze.

He could feel Timofei gripping his beard, the pull of the hairs, the sting. Slowly, he reached up, found his nephew's fingers, squeezed them tight in his own fist.

He didn't wait for Zinaida to come out. He didn't wait for his brother to come back. He unhooked his nephew's fingers from his beard, and kissed the boy's head, and got his shoes on, and into the stairwell, and down, and out to the courtyard, and then he had to sit. Holding a rusted bar, he lowered himself to the edge of the old carousel. It groaned, tilted into an even steeper slant. His fingers pressed into his forehead. His head gave up its weight. Beneath him, the iron disk slid a little, as if about to spin; it might have already been: whirring, listing, the ground trying to pull him off. He could feel the abyss. They were standing at its edge and he could feel the world pushing him, feel it pulling his brother back, and he took his hands from his face and held hard to the carousel, as if to stop it spinning. It creaked, slid a little again. The metal was still warm from the sun. He pressed his palms against it.

And felt her fingers on his shut lids. She had been the only one who wasn't ever shown, who'd stayed behind the lense, out of the frame. In the air the wires over the tramline began to shake. The clatter of contactors on the wires, the shriek of brakes. He opened his eyes, watched the tram pull up, let passengers out, pull away again. The next one, he knew, or the one after that, would bring his brother.

Dima stood up. Before those doors opened to Yarik stepping out, before another thing could jolt them, he would leave. And tomorrow morning he wouldn't try to meet his brother at the bus stop. He wouldn't try to meet him after his work. He would give him some time. He would take the time to get himself back level. He would wait.

That night, lying in bed beneath faint motes of mirror-light, he tried to clear his mind of the thing that had knocked him off balance. Because, taking the tram home from his brother's, he'd been unable to keep from staring at some other ticket collector's yellow vest. For the rest of the ride he had shut his eyes. And seen beneath it, beneath her sweatshirt, below the safety pins where the halves of the zipper fell apart, to the thing he'd glimpsed two nights before: that small red navel tattoo, that mushroom blooming from her belly. Out on the balcony, he had seen her close-buzzed hair in the tiny ruffled feathers of Ivan's neck and paused—what would it feel like to brush his fingers along the curve of her head?—before he tugged the hood down. Now he turned to the wall. The cot creaked under him.

Some two dozen years ago, in those nights after he and his brother had returned to their childhood home, when they were eleven, twelve, barely beginning to molt their boyhood, Yarik would turn away from the room, and, lying on his cot, whisper stories to them both. Stories about the tsarevnas, maidens, Alyonishka with her golden hair, Lyudmila in her nightgown and her braids, her alabaster bosom, Ruslan tearing open the nets that bound her, peering at her sleeping shape— *but did he really just keep watch,* Pushkin had wondered, *in thoughts of love, without the deed?*—and how, in Yarik's tightening voice, the wondering would end, the knight would take her, what he would do to her, what she would do for him, the way she'd feel. Listening to the creaking across the room, Dima would attempt to imagine it, too. Would shut his eyes and try to learn from his brother's sounds, time his hand to that. Until they grew older and Yarik stopped telling the tales, quit talking at all once the lights were off, would just turn away from Dima in his cot and silently face the wall.

In the years since then, Dima could count on one hand the number of times he'd let the idea of someone else get deep enough in him he had to work to pull it out. How had she done it so deeply now? Because she watched the world same as him, rode all day on the trams seeing it slide past the windows? Or with that raven wing of unbuzzed bangs, had she, like the Kievan prince who, shaped as a crow, would alight before an unsuspecting maid, swooped down on him?

Eyes shut, facing the wall, he tried to shake her off the only way that he knew how. To yank her away, make her release her grip, force her from his mind, cleanse himself, spill her out.

When he was finished, he lay with the sheet tented off him by his bent knees. Over by the window, beneath the artificial night of the rug Dima had hung, Yarik's cot was still there, the holes in the old kovyor above it letting through just enough light to show the mattress bare as it had been for years. Had Yarik ever lain there, his sheet around his knees? Had he been able to empty himself of thoughts? Had he even tried?

Outside the window some cloud smothered the sky. The holes in the rug dimmed; the mattress disappeared into the dark.

The night that Yarik met Zinaida they had been at the dom kultura. One moment his brother was out by the bonfire, then gone. It was the eve of Ivan Kupala. Soon women would wander to the woods, pretending to search for the Chernova Ruta. He knew none of them believed in it—the fabled fern blossom, its once-yearly bloom, its augury of love's success—knew they wanted to be hunted instead: the candles in their hands beacons flashing (*find me*), the garlands in the hair of unwed girls whispering (*take me*) to young men who would watch, who would wade out towards the trees, who, for now, still stood around the bonfire, waiting, whooping while they jumped the flames, the night streaked with the red blurs of their boots.

But Dima came into the light looking only at the faces. He could feel the heat growing on his own. Smoke filled his throat. He turned to look towards the woods again. From far off, over by the Kosha's bank, there came a cry—*Hai!*—and singing: *On the Day of Ivan-Kupala. . .*—he could just make out the women's voices—*. . . her fortune sought . . .* the cluster of them by the water . . . *plucked the flowers to make her garlands . . .* the moonwhite blooms they pulled out of their hair. Between them and him the field was lashed with shafts thrown by the dom kultura's windows and in them he could see the spark of a button, a pale knee jutting, eddies in the grass. *She strewed them on the river's breast.* Something jabbed at Dima's ribs. A bottle, a hand passing it to him. He took it, turned back to the fire, drank.

By the time the call for the Cossack dancing came through the crowd, his belly was warm, his chest hot beneath his fire-baked shirt. He could feel the smoke in his skull, stuffed like padding between bone and brain. Someone asked him if he was going to dance. Someone asked him where his brother was. He had long since ceased to feel the burn of the vodka on his throat.

Inside, the crowd was already packed against the wall. He pushed his way through, found a space just large enough for him. The band began to tune. To Dima's right, a farm couple clasped hands, crouched down. To his left, three men in machinist coveralls held each other's forearms, right legs jutting from their circle like spokes. He stood above the floorful of squatted dancers, staring into the wall of those who'd come to watch. The singer coughed. Someone shouted something about him, his brother; it sent a murmuring through the crowd. He lowered himself. And when the first note wailed, he threw his boot out with the rest, drew it in with them on the next beat. He didn't know what to do with his hands, held them out a little from his body, awkward and jerking as if, without anything to grip, they'd ceased to be a part of him at all. His legs, too, moved on their own, jolted him so hard he could feel his brain thud, and he tried to focus on nothing but not falling, to think of nothing but the kick, the kick, the kick. Next to him, the group of machinists tangled up, crashed guffawing to the floor. Half the dancers were already down, others walking wobbly legged off into the crowd. His own legs had begun to shake. He watched them like they were strange animals latched onto him to keep themselves from falling, felt resentment that they might pull him down as well. When he next looked up, the floor was emptier again, a few red faces left, clenched teeth and strained necks and some shouting in pain along with each kick. He reached down and put his hands on his thighs, felt them working, was flooded with regret for his resentment the moment before. He was glad to help, glad to have them, would make his purpose to pull them through.

He would not have looked up again if the clapping of the crowd hadn't broken suddenly apart. It quieted like a rainstorm petering out, then roared back with the wildness of hail, loosed from the rhythm of the band, mixed with shouts that rose up through it. Over by the entrance, people were parting, pushing others behind them, making way. Through the cheering crowd there came a woman, her head thrown back in laughter, flowers scattered in her swinging hair, her arms held out as if for balance, she shook her way strangely forward, jerking and leaning and righting herself and jerking forward again, until the last line of revelers between her and Dima broke away and he saw the cheers of the crowd hadn't been for her alone.

Beneath her crouched his brother. Yarik came into the clearing with her on his shoulders, his arms squeezed tight around her legs, his own legs kicking, out and back and out again, heels hammering the floorboards in synch with Dima's own. Dima could feel their blows in his knees. He could feel the shaking with each kick that brought his brother closer. The tendons stood out on Yarik's neck, and Dima could feel that, too. On his own shoulders: her weight. A spike of pain shot through his legs. But his brother was beaming, his eyes all laughter. Beneath her laughter, her head thrown back. Her hair was tangled with leaves, Yarik's boot soles clogged with mud. And with each shake their bodies made, Dima watched another piece of the forest fall to the floor.

Now, each day, he stayed away from the statue, kept clear of the lake, off the city's streets, abandoned the trams, the markets, anywhere he might be found by anyone who might try again to grab a hold of him. Each morning, instead, he took the bus to the only place he knew for sure she wouldn't go. The whole ride out, he sat hunched in the back, a hood pulled up, pretending to sleep. But once the bus entered the Oranzheria, he felt safe. Maybe a worker would glance his way, befuddled by the lack of hard hat. Maybe a foreman would jab him with a glare. A few stared, as if to locate the familiarity of his face. He learned to steer clear of where they were. And once he found his routes, his paths, it was so pleasant beneath the glass. On sunny days, it was strip-off-the-overshirt hot. He strolled the road in sleeveless tee, his shadow ambling beside him in the dirt. Men working in dusty fields, grayed skin striated with sweat, paused, watched him, worked a little more slowly when he was past. Sometimes he whistled a tune.

On rainy days the great glass sea became an endless awning, a translucent roof drummed hard by downpours, soft by drizzles, all the Oranzheria his porch. He would find a patch of grass beside a collection pipe, lie down, and listen to the rain spill down from duct to cistern: some days the babbling of a brook, others the muffled roar of a waterfall in a glade. And high above him, on the glass, there might stand a laborer in wet-weather gear, his poncho shedding rain like the canopy of a tree, his boot soles still as roots, his shadowed face staring. Until another splashed over to send him back to work. While, below, propped on his rucksack, leg crossed over knee, rereading books from his and Yarik's school days, Dima might look up to see the foreman shouting down. But through the glass, the beating rain, he would not hear.

There were times someone from security would approach, tell him he had to leave. He would put away his book, put on his shoes, catch the next bus, take it to another sector. Sometimes, when he stepped off he would think that he could feel his brother. He would stand very still, surrounded by the scents of new corn silk or water-soaked soil or wheatheads baked dry in the sun, and let his beard grow heavy with the humidity, his arm hairs brown with dust. Sometimes he thought he heard Yarik's voice. Once, he was sure he heard his laugh. He sat where he was and listened and when he heard it again, he didn't call out, didn't get up, simply laughed silently to himself. And pictured Yarik hearing that. Sometimes he liked to imagine Yarik feeling that he was near, liked to picture his brother taking a deeper breath. And Dima would take a deep breath. And that was all. He never went to look for Yarik. He would wait till his brother was ready. Till the trouble he had caused had died down. Till one day soon, when his bratan would come and find him.

The day he did it was hot, the beginning of July. Dima had hitched on the back of a supply truck and, climbing out of the hot wet air beneath the tarp into the hot drier air beneath the glass, he headed straight for the Kosha. Between him and the river was a vast field of corn, and while he waded through the waist-high stalks he unbuttoned his shirt, stripped off his sleeveless, and by the time he got to the bank his back was bare and he was tugging at his shoes. Not thirty seconds later, he was in his underwear. Then he was swimming.

He splashed out to the deep, tussled with the current, flipped on his back, floated downstream in tandem with a duck, flipped again and dove under, and when he came up, something smacked into him. Neck stinging, he swept his water-bleared eyes over the surface: a dark, wet shape, pointed as a snake's head. He jerked away. And amid the sound of his splashing heard laughter. At the same moment, he knew what had hit him was his shoe. He whipped a look around for it—saw the men on the bank, the one holding his clothes—and slashed downstream after what he hoped was a glimpse of its sinking shape. Diving, he felt the laces, the leather, came up coughing with it.

On the bank, the men cheered. And the one with his clothes threw his other shoe. He threw it as far from Dima as he could and still be sure it landed in deep water. Turning, Dima scrambled through the current. Halfway across, breath gusting out and coming in half water, he lost sight of it and stopped. The men on the bank booed.

A dozen hard hats standing there, and more coming down the field rows at a jog. They were calling to each other. The calls sounded happy. At the edge of the bank, a foreman stood holding his clothes.

"You don't want your shoe?" the man shouted. "How about your shirt?" It hung from his hand, flapping a little, like something he had by the throat.

"Those were my only shoes!" Dima shouted.

The man's face leapt with mock surprise. His whole body bobbed a little with it. "Why would you need shoes?" he called back. "Aren't bums supposed to be barefoot?"

When he threw the shirt, it spread out, caught the air, dropped close to shore. Dima watched the current sweep it into the reeds. One of the laborers waded out and grabbed it and flung it farther. Watching the river whisk it away, Dima could feel all his muscles tiring. When he shouted back at the man on the bank—"Please, nothing else!"—his lungs were working too hard to add much sound to his breath.

"What?" the man shouted as he threw Dima's pants. This time he'd balled them up. They soared within reach before opening, stopping, falling. Dima didn't even watch them slip away. He just started swimming for the shore.

In the time it took him to get there, the man threw his undershirt and socks and his *Dead Souls*. The book hit him in the ribs as he was splashing up out of the water. When the foreman reached down and snatched his rucksack, Dima rushed him, got a hand on the bag, turned to fish it from the reeds.

But the foreman grabbed his shoulder, turned him back. "Why don't you just get the fuck out of here."

"OK." Dima turned again.

Again, the foreman stopped him.

"Why the fuck did you come here, anyway?" the man said. "What the fuck are you doing here?"

"Nothing," Dima said.

"Bullshit," the foreman told him. "Nobody does nothing."

From the crowd came someone's shout: "Maybe he's waiting for his buddies."

And another: "So they can put on their goggles together."

"And their capes," someone else called out.

"And change the world," the first one said.

Then they were laughing.

The foreman wasn't. He said, "You waiting for your buddies?"

"My brother," Dima said. It just came out.

"Who's your brother?"

Dima could hear some of the workers shout out Yarik's name and some shout the last name he and his brother shared and he said, "All right, I'm going."

But the man's grip on his arm didn't loosen. "Why don't you just stand here a second."

"I'll go."

"Why don't you let these guys get a good look at you." The man turned to the others. "What do you think, guys? Does it look so good

206

now, being a bum? You think I don't hear you bitching? Oh, that's a good life. That's a easy life. Oh I wish—"

Dima tried to jerk his arm free and the foreman shoved him backwards into the mud and before he could scramble up again the man was over him.

"Stay the fuck down there," the foreman said. And to the men, "You wish you could be useless as *that*?" He swept a hand towards Dima. "What if this country was full of men like you? We should stomp you out." And he raised a boot. Mud from its sole spattered against Dima's chest. He started to jerk away, but the boot came down, slammed into the mud centimeters from where his hand was splayed.

"We're going to get back to work," the man said. "And you're going to get the fuck out of here. And you're not going to come back."

Then he turned and started through the men back up towards the cornfield. The men went with him. In the cornfield, the ones who had not made it to the bank stopped and watched the others come. A few asked what had happened, but most had made it close enough to see over the bank where Dima sat in his underwear, elbows hooked around his knees, chest sunken, his face looking up at them, up at the face of his brother, before Yarik, too, turned and started away.

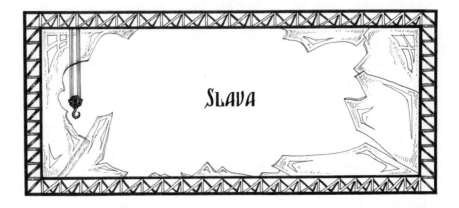

Slava

He could not seem to leave that riverbank. Sending his crew off to punch out that evening, the shoulders Yarik had slapped had been the ones wedged against his in the crowd above the river; the necks his hand cupped, the same that had stretched to see the spectacle. Sitting on the stool by the front door, putting on his slippers, he had watched that shoe sink out of sight. All supper he couldn't stop thinking how thin Dima had looked. When it was time to put Timosha to bed, his son, undressed to his underwear, had run from him, playing their nightly game—the frightened muzhik fleeing his undead dog—shouting for his papa to give chase. He had stood stiff-kneed by the hole punched in the wall, trying not to match it with another. Even now, watching his wife stark naked beneath him, Yarik could not stop seeing his brother.

Yes, he told himself, you can.

The sight of her had always seemed to strip his thoughts of everything else. The first time he found that out he'd been standing just as still, but alone, listening over the pulse in his ears, his too-loud breath, to the others moving through the woods at night. They carried candles,

208

lanterns, a few flashlights. His own was dark. In the blackness beneath the trees, he'd felt the beam drawing eyes to him, told himself it was just superstition—*foolish!*—and felt the eyes—*a festival to draw the spirits of the drowned!*—and stopped—*rusalki rising from the rivers*—shut his flashlight off. Only in fables did wraiths claim companions for their suffocated souls: he knew that. What he hadn't known, hiding there in the dark, listening to the others whispering through the underbrush, was how she'd found him.

They'd flirted across the bonfire earlier that evening and, as she took shape behind a candle, it occurred to him he had only ever seen her face in firelight. Holding her candle closer to his, she'd asked him what was wrong. It must have been his shame at the fear he knew she saw that made him tell her about his father. It must have been the heart in her that he would grow to love that made her take his hand.

But emerging from the woods, he had heard, beneath the sounds of women singing, the gurgle of the Kosha's current flowing by beneath. He'd pulled his hand from hers, stepped back, asked, *Where are you taking me?*

And taking his hand again, she'd told him, *To the river. So you can look in and see nothing there but us.*

Now, he stood at the edge of the mattress, looking down at only her, his dark belly hair still wet from the bath, the sting of the after-shave all but gone from his face, his hands holding her feet, his fingers curled over her toes, concentrating on the feel of her with everything he had. It was their Sunday night ritual: once a week, after the seventh workday had come and gone, and the next seven were about to start, after supper and putting the children to bed, after the housework and the paperwork, even if Yarik's neck ached just holding his head, even if Zina's eyes itched with needing sleep, they made the time to make love to each other.

He would press each of her fingers to his lips, pinky to thumb, one by one, slipping them into his mouth, telling her with his tongue *I know this crevice, I remember this crease.* Each place on each foot he would match with some part of him: the heels of his palms fitting

209

her arches, his tongue between her toes. Slowly, he would work his way along her arms, the soft insides of her elbows, her collarbone rising and falling with his own breath, so that by the time he kissed her pulse through the heat of her thigh, he could feel his own blood pumping at his neck. And she would push him onto his back and put him in and go at him with a fury like all his touches packed together, balled up, and burst.

But that night, beneath her, his brother at last shoved from his mind, he could not keep from confronting himself: his mouth mashed against his wife's sweet-scented neck, he saw his own, raw and red, the after-shave slapped on to hide his smell; his face hidden between her breasts, he pictured his own chest, a mangy pelt, nipples pink as sores; trying to stay inside her warmth, he imagined his own blood-filled sex, his hang-ing sack, thought *how grotesque*. As she surely would have thought if she had seen her husband that day on the bank. As, surely, his brother would see him now. That made him pull out. She reached down, bent for him, but he lifted her face in his hands and shook his head.

Hours after she had gone to sleep, he was still in the kitchen, still sitting in his robe and slippers on the chair he had dragged to the win-dow, his arms still crossed on the sill, another cigarette smoking in his hand. The teacup on top of the stove was stuffed with butts. Beside it, the percolator he'd brewed the coffee in was empty. The sweet-cheese pie he'd taken from the fridge was gone but for a few lumps stuck to the cardboard disk. On the windowsill, beneath his crossed arms, lay his uncle's old snub-nosed revolver. His home was quiet. His daughter asleep in her crib, his son in his bed.

He was imagining a dog like Dyadya Avya's stretched out beside his sleeping boy, Timosha's face buried in the wolfhound's side, thick fur fluttering with his breath. He imagined the dog following Polina as she toddled around the house, nudging her with its nose. He could almost hear the clacking of its nails, the thump of it lying down by the stove, the quiet keening it would make in its dreams.

Maybe that was why he had taken out the gun: to help him re-member what it was like inside their uncle's izba. Or maybe to bring

210

him back to the first time he had held it, that night when he and Dima had snuck it down to the lake, back when they were boys, when it seemed possible to take care of anything—even the Chudo-Yudo, even their father's soul—together. Whatever it was, once he had brought it out, he hadn't wanted to hold it. He had set it on the sill, covered it with his arms. He had not looked at it since. But he could feel it there, pressing its cold shape into his skin.

Outside, the traffic rumbled. Voices from the bus stop floated up. A vacuum in the apartment upstairs droned. There came the clatter of a trolleybus. He wondered if his wife and kids could ever get used to wind in the trees. If they could sleep through the sounds of the peepers, crickets, rain on the roof. Dogs, and their distant yipping, mice in the walls, night birds, the clamor of morning. Why not? Zina hadn't lived in the city until she met him. She knew the joys that could come from a childhood spent in the fields.

Lighting another cigarette, he went through all the new things in his home—the washing machine, the computer, the color TV, their electric toothbrushes, Timosha's little rucksack with wheels, plastic flowers for the vase in the vestibule, the vase, matching slippers for Zina and him—and as he thought of them, he made them disappear. Pictured them simply gone from the rooms. It seemed easy. Until he pictured Zina finding out. Because, of course, she also knew the misery that could come from a childhood in the fields. It wasn't just him that had brought her to the city. And who was he kidding: he'd wanted all those things, too.

"Well," he said, aloud, "sometimes you don't get what you want." He watched the tip of the cigarette burn. Sometimes, you have to choose between what you want and what you need. He ashed over the window ledge, took a draw, held it in his lungs. The problem was sometimes it wasn't so easy to tell which was which.

From far out over the city, the bells of the Alexandro-Nevsky Church rang. Faint, low gongs. He wished he could walk through the heavy doors into the cool dark nave, crowd with the worshippers against the walls, and in the undulating drones of the priests feel just a little of Zina's belief. He wished he could light a candle and whisper a prayer and know that it was heard, out of his hands. Every Sunday evening, when he got off work, he went to Alexandro-Nevsky with his wife and, standing there, bowing, murmuring in time with all the others, prayed to feel God's hands on his shoulders, for them to gentle him along a path he didn't have to create for himself, to lift his family in their palms, to fold protecting fingers around his brother. But, outside again, he only felt the surety in his wife's hand holding his, the strength of her grip.

And if he were to go in there this morning, he knew he would only stand beneath the icons' stares and feel the hard floor, the empty cavern, that in the bearded visage of each priest, he would see his brother's face. He would feel the chill dawn air on his own smooth cheeks, the shaking of the road beneath him, the soil under his hands, the body between them, and the word *bratishka* on his lips, *I'll take care of you* in his mind. *It will be OK.* It wasn't. He hadn't.

It was then he realized that he was staring at the gun. The old Nagant revolver lying there. A small pistol, its barrel sawed off short, the dull metal scratched, its wood handle worn. It looked almost as old as the cowboy guns on the billionaire's desk, like something from before the Great War, maybe even before The Revolution, and, wondering where their uncle had gotten it, he reached down and unlocked the gate and let it fall open. He rolled the cylinder one click. It was loaded. Click. And loaded. Click. All seven chambers full. It had been empty that day that they had fished it out of the water; Dyadya Avya had emptied it. But who had loaded it again? He couldn't remember if he and Dima had done it afterwards. Why would they have? Or had their mother? Sometime in the years after her husband died, after Avya died, after the farm was gone, her pension gone, the system she had lived her life by, the world she knew how to live in, gone, had she done it then, some night, loading it alone? Left alone by her son who had gone, too. Who no longer visited, never called. Sometimes he thought he'd take the tram over, visit for an hour. Sometimes he sat by the phone, imagining his brother's hello. *Put Mama on,* he'd say.

212

Then set down the receiver, get up, walk away. Ever since he'd been a boy she had seen through him, known she had to push and push or he would fail. *It's Yarik!* Dima would say, his voice shot through with joy just at the fact his brother hadn't failed him, too. But she would see, would know.

He thought then that he understood his father better than he ever had before. The hours he had spent hidden in his ice fishing hut; the way he would head for the balcony to smoke his pipe, shut the door behind him, close his eyes; how much he must have needed the release of the dancing, relief of the drinking, those nights out at the dom kultura. There were times Yarik had hated him for being gone. Hated him even then, as a child, before he had been gone for good. And afterwards. And now. There were times when he hated his mother, too, for giving in to her grief, his uncle for giving up, his brother simply for being there on that pile of dirt in the back of that truck needing him to say *bratishka*. Needing him to be a bratan. *I'll take care of you.* He had been ten.

Looking down at the bus stop, the crowd pushing onto the tram, watching how fast the ones who disembarked walked away, crossed the street, the cars refusing to so much as slow, it seemed to Yarik his forebears had passed on to him a flaw in their hearts that with each beat of his own he had to struggle to suppress: what had permitted his father to fail at even finding a way out of the ice; what had let his mother succumb to her collapse, leave her sons to take that on their shoulders, as well; whatever weakness in Dyadya Avya had allowed him to abandon his almost-sons, led him to the riverbank, given its assent to the gun, the trigger, his finger.

A bang. Yarik jerked, eyes snapping shut. It was only hearing the skitter across the floor, opening his eyes to see the pistol slide beneath the couch, that he realized it had not gone off, had just been shoved off of the sill, that his arm had done the shoving. From beneath the couch, against the wall: a muffled thud. He felt it as if the gun smacked to a stop against the inside of his skull. Turning back to the window, he lowered his head to the sill, smothered it under his crossed arms. The last thought he had before falling asleep was that maybe he should not have taken the gun from the chest in his mother's home; maybe it was no safer here with him than with his brother.

But when he woke it was into a feeling of peace. Some noise from outside must have brought him back. He couldn't have slept long; the mirrors were still sinking below the earth's edge. Inside the apartment it was as quiet as before. He listened to the silence of his family sleeping. He felt hungry, and emptied out, and light, and at ease. He tried to remember what he had dreamed, but all he could bring back was that it had been about his brother and him. Maybe they had been crouched together, in the dirt, in a row, in a field; yes: using their fingers to push holes in the soil. And he had woken up with this unexpected calm. He rose and opened the refrigerator and stood in its chill, its yellow light, and all he could see clearly was that he had no choice at all.

Later that morning, when he told his manager that he was quitting, the man looked at him with relief. Still, he gave Yarik the obligatory *sorry to see you go*, didn't bring up the way he must have seen Yarik's crew ignoring their foreman's orders, heard the jokes they cracked at Yarik's expense, didn't tell him that ever since his brother had become a problem he'd been wanting to fire Yarik anyway. He just pushed back from his desk and opened the door to the anteroom, asked Yarik to step out there, said he had to check on something. "It'll take me less than five." But half an hour later, when the manager finally emerged from his office, the look of relief was gone. "Wait here," he said and, "Welcome back," and shut the door again.

"Here" was inside a mobile trailer rolled to the edge of the Oran-zheria: toilets and a cafeteria and the sector manager's office and the tiny anteroom Yarik had been put in, all of which in a few weeks would be rolled forward again as the glass spread north. The anteroom was carpeted, air-conditioned, smelled faintly like boiled potatoes. Yarik sat on the faux leather love seat below a framed photograph of the Chinese Great Wall. Across the narrow room the Pyramids hung. Behind his head, he could hear the sounds of a crew—his?—getting tea in the next compartment over. Outside the trailer there were the rumbles of a backhoe, a compactor, all the work going on without him. Inside the office, the manager was on the phone, his voice coming through the door loud enough for Yarik to make out that he wasn't happy, but not why.

Across from him, beneath the Pyramids at sunset, a flowing script read *Nothing bold was ever built without someone deciding where to lay the first stone.*

His brother, him, a field, a row. What were they poking into the earth? Seeds? Fertilizer? Just making holes?

Half an hour ago he had been so sure of what he had to do. Now, he could feel doubt creeping in again. What would his wife think? How would he explain it to his son?

He was still staring at the photograph on the wall when a roar turned his head. It sounded way too close, as if someone was trying to park an earthmover outside the trailer's door. Then it didn't sound like they were trying to park. Outside: shouts. Yarik was up just in time to be knocked back onto the juddering couch, the whole trailer lurching with the manager's shout, the Pyramid picture crashing to the floor. Right on the other side of the thin wall the engine rumbled. Around the entrance, part of the trailer's metal had caved in, the door cracked along a bottom corner, half off a hinge. Yarik got up, yanked it open.

There was the dozer's shovel, its maw so close he could have grabbed the top of the blade in his hands, its cutting edge buried beneath the trailer, its lower jaw crushed through the stairs, and the stack blowing smoke and the heat gusting off the grill and the bars of the open cab shaking at the idle, and behind them, in the operator's seat, looking back at him, Boris Bazarov. His sunglasses were crooked on his nose. A few long shocks of hair had fallen in front of his face. He swept them behind his ears, straightened his shades. "My God!" the billionaire shouted over the diesel noise. "Who the hell let me drive one of these things?"

Then he was climbing out of it, the engine still rumbling, hopping down onto the treads and into the throng. He took the hands held out to help him as if they were offered for a shake, clapped necks, punched shoulders, said something that drew from the men a few wary smiles and from the billionaire his own laugh. Bazarov slapped the side of the machine—"Any of you guys know how to back this thing up?"—then turned to Yarik. "I bet you do," he said, "but you stay put. You I want to talk to."

While one of the workers climbed into the dozer's cab, Bazarov stepped up on its push-frame, grabbed a cylinder, lifted a brown boot over the shovel blade, and clambered through the doorway, matching string tie swinging. His shiny suit was dust dulled, smudged with grease. He stilled his tie, held out his hand. Yarik took it.

"Hold on," the billionaire said.

Behind them, the dozer revved, backed up. The tilted trailer slammed flat again.

Letting loose his grip, Bazarov cranked his neck to watch the bulldozer backing away. "I was at the head office," he said. "Came quick as I could." Then, turning back to Yarik, "Are you trying to go DOMO on me?"

Yarik shook his head.

"Do you know what DOMO means?"

"No," Yarik said.

"Downwardly mobile," Bazarov told him. He said it in English, and he reached by Yarik for the door handle and said it in Russian— "*Nizhnyie dvizheniya*"—and shut the door behind him.

The room was so small that the two of them filled it. In the office door, the manager stood, making it smaller.

Bazarov took off his sunglasses, his stare on Yarik. "I give you a good job," he said. "I give you a good salary."

"It's not the money," Yarik told him.

"I give you my friendship. I have you over to my home, take you out on the lake, show you my secrets, I set you up."

"It's not something I want to do."

"Bullshit," Bazarov said. "You're making the decision."

"I—"

"You're deciding to do it." He looked past Yarik's shoulder, and the manager said "Excuse me, please," and Bazarov stepped to the wall, looked at the broken glass fallen out of the Pyramids' picture frame, told Yarik, "Or not to do it. Because nobody chooses to do anything they don't want to do. At least not here, not now." He picked the frame up. "Not men like us." He set the picture back on its hook. "Men like us sometimes *have* to do something we don't want in order to get something we *do* want. But that means we want to do it. Because it gets us to what we want. But"—he turned, looked at Yarik again— "we already know what you want. Remember?" Behind his back, another piece of glass fell to the carpet. "And this, Yaroslav Lvovich, is not the way to get it."

"I'm not doing it for myself," Yarik said.

"Bullshit again."

"If I may, Mr. Bazarov." It was the manager. "This doesn't concern only him. You may have heard about the trouble his brother is causing, a video . . . this kind of . . . well, there was an incident here yesterday. A disruption. Caused by his brother. It's become, I'm afraid, untenable, actually. It's actually only the responsible—"

"This"—Bazarov cut the man off, not looking at him, not talking to him—"must be the manager . . ."

"Nikitin," the manager said.

". . . who called the branch director . . ."

"Eduard Nikitin."

". . . who called the personnel director, who called my secretary, who was supposed to tell me—who *told* me—that you," he said to Yarik, "were going DOMO. That you were a flight risk."

"Yes, sir," the manager said.

"He did the right thing," Bazarov told Yarik.

"Thank you, sir," the manager said.

"But," Bazarov said, "he's still going to lose his job."

From behind the manager, somewhere in his office, came the drone of the air conditioner, the rattle of it shutting off.

"Why?" Yarik said.

"Because," Bazarov told him, "you're going to take it."

While the manager stood in the doorway and tried to argue why it wasn't right and then to explain the complexities of the position and finally to plead, Bazarov laid it out—how soon Yarik would start, what his duties would be, how many foremen he would have under him, how many laborers in his section, how much more money he would make—until the manager came out of the doorway into the anteroom and tried to shove himself between his former boss and his former employee, to make Bazarov look at him, hear him, and Yarik said, "I can't. I'm sorry, I can't."

Bazarov turned, walked away from the frantic manager. He opened the exit door and stood in it, squinting into the brightness outside. The manager followed him. Yarik stayed where he was. From behind the two men, he could see the billionaire pointing to something. The manager went quiet.

"Well?" Bazarov asked the man. "Can you bring it down?"

Yarik tried to make out, through their figures, what they were looking at.

"I didn't ask *will* you," Bazarov said, and the manager said something that Yarik couldn't hear, and Bazarov didn't answer, just stepped back into the room and put his hand on the door edge, as if to swing it shut and waited, and the man slowly made his way out and down the wrecked steps to the ground.

Watching him, watching the laborers beyond, the landscape of his worklife framed by the open door, Yarik could not understand how he'd so quickly become separated from it all. Something about it all felt wrong. Not just what he had witnessed with the fired man, not just the unfairness of how it had been done, but the fact that Bazarov had come here to do it. That his boss seemed to have put in place some standing order to report on all that Yarik did, to relay news of his actions up a chain of command. Maybe it was his dream, maybe his decision, maybe simply that Yarik was looking out at fields soon to be plowed and planted, but as he wondered what was in him, what he might have, that could have brought all this about, the only thing that came to him was the farm. Which wasn't even his. Which was nothing more than a possibility planted far in his past, a half-hopeless dream of what might be. Surely, with all his information, all the effort he'd already spent selecting Yarik for *something*, surely the billionaire knew that.

"What's a setback," Bazarov said now, "but a new beginning?" He still stood in the door, his back to Yarik, and Yarik wasn't sure if his boss was talking to him or to the man he'd fired. "A chance to go even further in a new direction. Any successful man knows that. Any failed man knows it, too, just learns it too late. If he's smart, he'll turn this into an opportunity. No"—he patted the door—"he'll *recognize* the opportunity I've given him. If he doesn't, then I didn't want him working for me, anyway."

Yarik could see, past Bazarov in the still-open door, the manager making his way across the lot, his suit pressed against him by the wind, his tie fluttering from his neck.

"He's lost his job"—Bazarov turned back to Yarik—"whether or not you choose to take it." He let go the door, left it open. "So why are you still looking at him?"

But when Yarik refocused, Bazarov was gone from the doorway. He had stooped to the carpet, and he came up holding a clear glass shard in his hand. A jagged shape half the size of his face.

Through it, he looked at Yarik. "It's about seeing the opportunity," he said. "It's always about seeing the opportunity." He lowered the shard till his eye looked over it. "Khodorkovsky." His breath blew against it when he spoke. "You've heard of Khodorkovsky. What would Mikhail Khodorkovsky have become if he hadn't been denied a defense job because he was a Jew? Would he have become one of the richest men in Russia if he hadn't looked around him and seen what he could do *instead*? Would he ever have started his Center for the Scientific-Technical Creativity of Young People?" Bazarov laughed, shook his head. "What we did back then to avoid saying the word 'business,' right? And Friedman? The head of Alfa Group? You know how he started? Hawking theater tickets. Organizing the hawkers.

A theater mafia. By the time he graduated university he was director of a hundred and fifty students all over Moscow, buying up tickets, bartering them on the black market. What is that?" Holding the glass between his thumb and forefinger, he touched one sharp corner to the flesh below his eye. He asked again, "What is that?"

And Yarik answered, "Seeing the opportunity."

"*Taking* the opportunity. More than just the vision to see it." Bazarov jutted the shard towards Yarik. "The balls to *take* it." Bringing it back until it was an inch from his mouth, he breathed on the glass, fogged it, and when it had cleared again, said, "You know how long it took me to make my first two million?" He tapped a jagged corner against his front tooth. It made Yarik wince. "Seventy-two hours. Two million American dollars. I was given a chance to arrange a transfer. Roubles to dollars, Russia to the West. Just making a trade. But this was the first month of the new economy, and between the official exchange rate and what the market would pay there was a little difference. Ten percent. Which I pocketed. Sure, I'd done it before—a thousand here, a few thousand there—but never on a twenty-million-dollar exchange. You know how much I would have made if I had hesitated? Nothing. Everyone who means anything has a story like that. That was how it was. Now, it's not so easy to get that kind of shot. But there still are opportunities. There are chances. This here, now, is one for you."

"I know," Yarik said. "What I don't understand . . . I don't understand why now, why—"

"Yaroslav Lvovich," Bazarov said, "you don't decide when the opportunity comes. You decide only if you will take it. *I* decide when it comes. Because I'm the one offering it. All I can do is give you what you need to take the next step. You have to take it. I can give you the cornerstone, my friend, but you have to decide where to lay it. What kind of life you're going to make with it. Maybe your life is destined to be little. Maybe great. But you can't know until you start building. And you can't start building until you lay the first stone."

Yarik could feel his smile betraying him, and he tried to tamp it down, flatten his face back out.

"What?" Bazarov said.

"Nothing," Yarik told him, and saw the man's eyebrows rise and knew that was the wrong thing to say and followed it fast with, "It's just the thing about the stone. You got that from the poster."

For a moment, there was only the sound of the work going on outside, the air conditioner whirring. Then Bazarov's lips split, and his teeth showed and he tapped at them again with the corner of the glass. His smile spread. "That is the kind of thing," he said, "I would have said back in the nineties." He barked a laugh. "Look at you! Going from laborer to foreman to manager to *this* in just a few months. You're having your own 1992 right here in my Oranzheria."

"That's what I don't understand," Yarik said.

"What's there to understand?"

"Why me. Why you seem to like me—"

"Seem? I'm offering you your opportunity. Take it. Unless you think it's going to bite you when you grab on." He grinned again. "You think I'm going to bite you?"

"No," Yarik said.

"You sure?" And in one quick move he lifted the piece of glass to his mouth and, peeling back his lips like a dog, chomped his teeth down on a corner. For a second, there was just the man clenching his jaw, and Yarik staring at him, and then Bazarov's laughter burbled out around the glass and his lips shook and he dropped the glass and his laugh exploded in the room as if the shard he'd yanked from his teeth had been a grenade pin. "What makes you think that I like you? Because I ask you on a hunting trip? Because I tell you I want to see you stand in front of a two-hundred-kilogram boar with nothing but an old revolver? That *I've* loaded?"

"I only meant—"

"With how many bullets? Maybe"—he shrugged—"just one?" He held up a single finger. Then tapped it lightly against Yarik's chest. "I like your *history*, cowboy. I like the story behind you, *of* you." He smiled. "Oh, don't look so glum. I like you all right, too." And his smile spread to his eyes. "Come on, lyubimy," he said, "let's take a little lovers' walk."

They went straight through the work zone, Bazarov cutting across it casually as if it were a meadow in the woods. Not long ago it might have been. It had definitely been forest. Up ahead, out from under the glass and girders, in the open air at the edge of the Oranzheria, the loggers were taking the next trees down. A long line of quivering firs and spruce, each shaking as a saw bit through. All along the forest edge they dropped in booms, the wall of green calving like the cliff-front of a glacier. Between the loggers and the two of them roamed the machines, scaly-plated and shovel-toothed, backhoes clawing logs into piles, cranes dipping hydraulic heads into the stacks, lifting felled trunks one by one. In their wake the chippers came on wheels tall as the men beside them, and before them the ground was cleared of all but churned earth the stump-pullers tore apart into massive holes.

Bazarov made his way through, leaving room for Yarik to walk beside if he could keep up. When he came even, Bazarov said, without slowing his stride or turning to look, "I'm the one who should be glum. All these stories about everyone else and you never even ask me how I got rich."

"I thought," Yarik said, "you made your first two million—"

"That's an anecdote," Bazarov told him. "That's not my history, my story. How I got from then to now, there to here. Who I am."

But before Yarik could ask, the billionaire had spotted a hard hat coming their way, veered into his path, stepped in front of him so fast the kid—barely older than a boy, carrying a tray crammed with enough tea glasses for his entire crew: a new hire's chore—nearly smacked straight into his boss's chest. For a second, the two of them stood there, each gripping a side of the tray, the tea spilled into a pool around the cups, the cups rattling, the kid's face shifting from about-to-slug-the-sonofabitch to shock to worry to a half-swallowed, "I'm sorry."

Bazarov's shrug made the tray jerk. "Friend," he said, "what's your name?"

"Sergei."

"Seryozha, my friend, it looks like we better turn around and fill these back up. Here"—he tugged the tray free—"let me help you," and they were all three walking back the way the kid had come, Bazarov carrying the clattering glasses, the kid glancing at the spilling tea, Yarik watching them both, trying to keep up.

"How old are you?" Bazarov asked.

"Eighteen," the kid said.

"Eighteen." Bazarov said the age as if it made him happy. "When I was eighteen, I was . . ." He nudged the kid with an elbow. "I was carrying coffee back and forth just like you. But"—he shot the boy a reproving look—"I wasn't doing it for free. This was in Leningrad at the Institute of Engineering and Economics. I wasn't a student. I couldn't get in." He winked at the kid, flashed a mock-shocked face at Yarik. "But I knew students. And these students were always complaining about tea: having to leave their studies to buy it from the corner teahouse, out and in, in and out, every hour. So for a few roubles, for a while, I was a one-man mob in the tea-delivery black market. Until word spread to other study groups. Soon, I had to hire my roommate to make the tea. Other friends to deliver it. To *other* universities. The Polytechnical. The Institute of Technology. A little illegal *spekulyatsia* of my own." There was the noise of the work all around them, the clanking of the glasses on the tray. He shook his head. "I know," he said, "you're thinking, *This guy is full of it.*"

"No, sir," the kid said, "I don't think you're—"

"But he does." Baz slid his look to Yarik. "He's thinking, *He carried coffee, not tea.*" They had reached the cafeteria trailer, and Bazarov stopped. "But, Seryozha, these students, they were, in secret, fans of the West. In secret they liked to smoke Marlboros. They liked to read Ricardo, Mill, Adam Smith. They liked to drink coffee."

The kid glanced at the cafeteria trailer.

Bazarov rattled the glasses. "OK," he said, "I'll give you the quick and dirty, as the Americans say. By the time those students were scrambling to put what they'd been reading to practice, I was importing green coffee beans by the sackful. Also, inside the sacks, I hid diamonds." He raised his eyebrows at Yarik, at the kid. "Not for myself," he assured them, "but for the men who paid off the customs agents for the

lying documents that let me bring in my shiploads of beans, untaxed."
Bazarov handed the tray back to the kid, plucked off a half-full glass,
handed another to Yarik. "You know the place called Kofe Khauz on
Lyzhnaya Street in town? Or the one on Chernishevskogo Avenue? Or
maybe the Kirov Square branch?" He winked, held up his cup, and, in
one shot, drank the cooled tea down. Replacing his cup, he asked the
kid, "Want to know why I told you this?" He took Yarik's glass and
put it on the tray, too. "So that, when you bring the full cups back to
your buddies, you'll tell them you want ten roubles each for doing it.
And tomorrow you'll tell them twenty."

When they had left the kid and the trailer and were walking fast
again towards wherever Bazarov was taking them, Yarik told the billionaire he hadn't realized the chain of American-style cafés that had
cropped up in Moscow, St. Petersburg, even, in the last few years,
Petroplavilsk, was owned by him.

"It isn't," Bazarov said.

"Or that you started it."

"I didn't."

They walked in silence, passing workers passing them the other
way, until another—a sack of concrete on one shoulder, a shovel on
the other—seemed to grab Bazarov's eye. The man's face was slit from
ear to lip by a raw scar, forearms blue with amateur tattoos.

"Now to him," the billionaire turned to Yarik, "I wouldn't have
told that lie." He flipped Yarik a smile. "To him I would have told a
different one. Maybe I would have asked where he got his scar. Then
I would have told him a secret of my own. A secret that showed the
real me, something that he would take home with him and hold up
against himself and recognize." He peered ahead into the distance. At
what, Yarik couldn't see. "I would have told him I was there: Moscow,
the putsch of '93. That I was in the squadron they sent across the
Moskva to seize the mayor's office. I would have been twenty-seven
then. Penniless. In the parliamentary police. We hadn't seen wages for
months. I would have told him about storming the old Comecon building, being sent into the basement to see if anyone was hiding, about

what I found, instead. You know what was down there? Vouchers. Privatization vouchers. Eleven million of them. Worth fifty-five million American dollars. Tied in bundles wrapped with condoms. Honest to God: condoms. And all of it behind a flimsy wooden door, a cheap little padlock. The fact that none of my fellow countrymen storming into that basement thought to bust down that door still makes me ashamed to be a Russian. *That* was a lack of seeing the opportunity. *That* was a failure to seize it. If I had been there"—he turned his hands palm up—"that would have been the way I got my start." He shrugged. "Or at least that's what I would have told a man like that."

Still staring ahead, Bazarov raised a hand, as if signaling to someone. Someone standing beside a distant crawler-crane, the iron boom rising high over the scaffolding of the Oranzheria's unfinished edge, the outrigger big as a dump truck on treads, its cabin window open beside the small dark dot of a man. A man wearing a suit. A suit the blue of the one Yarik's manager had worn. Bazarov dropped his hand. In the distance, the man turned from the crane, started walking away. Even from afar, Yarik could hear the whir of the winding drum starting to lower the line.

Listening to it, walking towards it, Yarik asked the man beside him, "What would you have told me? That you made your first two million dollars in seventy-two hours? That your mother was a seamstress and your sisters died in a fire? That you would show me things you'd never even shown your son?" He kept his eyes on the crane, the figure in the suit leaving. "That there was some way I could keep this job, and keep my brother, and I should trust you?"

"You see," Bazarov said, "I told you I knew I liked you. I wasn't lying to you then, not about the millions, or my mother, or my sisters, or Pavel, and I'm not lying to you now. Half of success is knowing how to lie, Yarik. The other half is knowing when not to. And the key to that is *who*. Ask yourself: Why, if I wanted to deceive you, would I have just given you a demonstration of my methods of deceit?"

They were nearing the crane now. Yarik glanced up at the end of the girders, the beginning of open sky, the boom way up there, and, coming down on the line, swaying a little in the grip of its lower sheave, a square-sided metal bucket, huge and dark against the brightness of noon.

"I don't know why," Yarik told him.

"Because," Bazarov said, "it was never in doubt that I liked you, that I trusted you. What you were asking is why I *need* you."

They were a dozen meters from the crane, and the bucket was less than that above and dropping fast, and Bazarov walked to its shadow, stopped, turned to see if Yarik was coming. Yarik stood a few meters back, listening to the whine of the line lowering the bucket, watching the shadow shrink fast around the man.

"Why I need you," Bazarov said, "is *your* history. *Your* story."

The bucket dropped so close to the billionaire that Yarik could see his body shake with the quiver of the ground. Bazarov didn't even shift his feet. He didn't shift his gaze from Yarik, either. Then he turned, placed his hands on the bucket's rim, pushed himself up, and, easy as stepping over a low fence, swung his legs in. From inside the bucket, he looked back at Yarik. "Come on," he said. "Get in. I'm going to tell you the story of you."

There was the unmistakable weight of the bucket beneath him, the solidity of the rim in his hands, and yet the tug of the line, when it lifted them off the earth, made even the heavy steel under his boots feel fragile. The winding drum moaned; the hoist rope sang; the bucket swayed a little. He watched its shadow slide on the ground, open up beneath them, spread wider as they rose.

"Yaroslav Lvovich Zhuvov." Over the noise of the crane's hydraulics, Bazarov had to half-shout. "Big blue eyes, black black hair. From good Karelian stock. Son of a good Russian fisherman, a lover of our great poet, our great drink. Son of a good Russian woman who worked hard all her life in our textile plants, on our local army base. Son of Petroplavilsk, of our city."

Down below: their own shadows, side by side, jutting out of the patch of shade cast by the rising bucket. Their shapes rose with it. A strange sensation: even as Yarik's shadow shrank from him, there it was among the men below, growing larger.

226

"But," Bazarov continued, "a son of the countryside, too." Bazarov waved his hands at the sinking trees, the fields they couldn't yet see. "Out there"—he brought his hand back, made a fist of it—"in here"—gave his chest a gentle knock. "A boy of the woods and pastures. A farm boy. Pulling potatoes. Whistling as he works. Until . . ." Bazarov smacked his hands together. "Tragedy. Papa: dead. Mama: gone mad with grief. And yet, raised by his loving uncle—that stout kolkhoznik, red-chested man of the soil—he struggles on."

Yarik watched the ground slip away, watched the shape of the bucket stretch with the changing slant of the sun.

"But what," Bazarov said, "what, in the hard times that we all knew, the great collapse we still feel *here*"—again, he thumped his fist against his chest—"what, in those times, was a penniless boy, practically an orphan, an orphan raised by an uncle who was—let's face it—afflicted by that devil all our Russian families know, an orphaned peasant boy alone in a drafty izba with his drunken uncle unable to make ends meet, what was he to do?"

And there was Yarik's own shape stretching, too, already almost unrecognizable as something made by him.

"Persevere!" Bazarov raised his fist between them, shook it. "Survive! Make it through one day after the next until, finally, there comes a day that is different. Over the city"—Bazarov swept his hand like the whole world was drawn on a page and he was flipping it—"there appears a new star. His wife? And another. His child? And soon a whole sky full of them. The zerkala. The Oranzheria. Where our Yaroslav . . ." Bazarov paused. "Shall we call him Slava or Yarik?"

But Yarik was silent, looking down at the tops of the trees where his shadow had been broken up and swallowed by the woods.

"Where Slava," Bazarov went on, "signs up to work. He works hard, our Slava, a new husband, a new father. He works well. Is he rewarded? Not right away. But"—Bazarov held up a finger, let his smile break out behind it—"eventually, after a few years—but not so many years; really, not very many at all—his hard work is, yes, at last, recognized. He is promoted to foreman. Then to manager. And next . . ."

Yarik could feel Bazarov looking at him as steadily as he was look-ing down, and when he lifted his eyes Bazarov let go of the bucket's edge, raised his hands, palms up.

"Next?" Yarik said.

"I don't know," Bazarov said. "Is there a next? Or does he throw it all away?" Palms still raised, he leaned back against his side of the bucket.

Through the metal, Yarik could feel the slight shake, an almost imperceptible shift, and he leaned a little against his own side, as if, though his mind knew it wouldn't tip, his body was telling him it might.

"I hope not," Bazarov said. "Because that story? That history? That's a history almost everyone here can relate to. That's a story people will take home with them. *These* people." He leaned over the edge, looked down, and Yarik, feeling the bucket shift again, looked down over his edge, too. "These people will hold that story up before them. And in it, they'll see themselves."

Down there, the yellow hard hats of the logging crews floated amid the forest, the green pines and bright birch leaves, like bees in a field, the roar of their chain saws reduced by the height to a buzz broken only by the rumbling of the machines, the crack and crash of trees coming down. All along the edge of the woods they fell, and looking at the trunks laid out on the ground it was almost as if the ground itself had flipped ninety degrees and the line of fallen trees down there was the new forest's edge, and for a moment Yarik felt he couldn't tell if he was leaning over at all, or standing straight. . . . But there was the ground, the churned soil, the skidder machines dragging the logs across it, and the tub grinders chewing them to pulp and the graders rolling over the dirt to push it flat, and then the girders going up, the bright metal scaffolding reaching out from the south, and he had the feeling again of the earth being tilted, as if the scaffolding was rebar at the top of a skyscraper, erected upwards into a muddy sky and, far below, the finished exteriors gleaming with glass, towering too high, too far from the ground, to even see where it was rooted to the earth.

"You were right," Bazarov said, "it is beautiful."

Yarik looked up from the sight.

"The first time we met," Bazarov reminded him. "You said it should be turned into an attraction. Not just someplace people worked, but a place people wanted to come to. You were right about that. Just not about *which* people." He smiled at Yarik. "It's OK. You haven't seen the surveys. You don't have a team devoted to figuring this stuff out. You haven't studied the past fifty years in the part of the world we're trying to outdo. Productivity, retention rates. Do you know the secret to their success?"

"Whose?"

"Tomorrow. The belief in tomorrow. That it will be a better day. Work hard, play fair, make something of yourself. The chance to get ahead, to climb a little higher. Or at least the fact that they believe the chance exists." He turned and spread his arms and leaned farther out over the edge and flapped them—once, twice, big slow flaps—and when he turned back he was beaming. "Fly high!" he said. "You're going straight to the top!" He squinted at Yarik. "Don't look at me like you don't know what I'm talking about. You've been there. You *are* there."

"I don't know what you're talking about," Yarik said.

And standing in that steel bucket in the sky, their clothes bright in the blasting noon, one's head dark as a distant bird, the other's a speck of sun against the blue, Bazarov laid it all out: how his managers had come to him, the warnings they had brought of the rumblings they had heard, the laborers growing dissatisfied, the workforce that had been so grateful in the first years now starting to raise complaints—hours, pay, safety, breaks—how beneath it all there was the same murmuring stream: What now? Where next? Is this it? *No*, he told Yarik. Not for them, not for the Oranzheria. They just had to make the workers see it. They had to make them believe it. They had to show them him, Yarik. Posters, flyers, billboards, TV. A publicity campaign built around his story.

"You mean Slava's story," Yarik said.

"OK." Bazarov shrugged. "But *your* face." Beneath them: the sound of all the work. Above: a breeze whistling through the cable. Then

Bazarov reached out, slapped Yarik on the shoulder. "Holy shit," he said. "I've got it. Yaroslav Lvovich, I have got it. And you gave it to me."

"What?" Yarik said.

"Next," Bazarov told him. Between their faces he swiped at the air with his hand and, as if the word had appeared in its wake, said it again: "Next." Pushing his sunglasses down his nose, he stared at Yarik. "The slogan!"

"Next?"

"You were the one who said it," Bazarov nearly shouted. "What's next? Who's next? How much next? What more next? All the questions are in that one word. And all the answers are in you. In the story of Slava. Because by the time we're done with it, they"—he stabbed a finger over the edge at the workers below—"they will see you, but they will think to themselves, *Me.*"

"OK," Yarik said.

"Good!"

"No," Yarik told him, "what I mean is, OK, then let me ask you something: What's in it for me?"

Slowly, the hairs of Bazarov's goatee shifted around his mouth; they spread and rose and then his teeth were a thin strip of glint flashing in the sun. "Cossack," he said.

"I mean," Yarik told him, "that I don't see how any of this . . ."

"Cowboy."

". . . changes any of the reasons that today I came in to quit my—"

And Bazarov punched him. He punched him in the upper arm, hard. "Fucking cowboy," Bazarov said. His laugh burst out so loud, a roar so forceful Yarik could swear he felt the bucket shake. Then he was sure of it. Clamping a hand to the metal rim, he stared at Bazarov. The man gripped the sides, swinging his weight back and forth, back and forth, laughing, shaking his head, saying, "You fucking cowboy, you fucking cowboy," until they were swinging, the wire jerking above them, Yarik's stomach beginning to lurch.

Then just as suddenly, Bazarov stopped. His laugh petered out to a breathing through his bared teeth. "What's in it for you, you fucking cowboy, is that you get to be the answer. And since we always have to have an answer, you always get to be next. Do you understand?" The bucket swayed back and forth, back and forth. "What I'm saying is you don't just get promoted to manager today, but you get promoted tomorrow, and after that, and after that. You *have* to. We *must*. As long as we're running the ads, as long as, in their minds, your face is what they see when they see the possibility of *next*, and in your face they see their own, you don't have to worry about how you're going to do your job, about what your crew will think of you, about what they think of your brother. They'll want to *be* you."

"But don't you see . . ."

"Because you'll have a lock on what they really want. Upward mobility. Going straight to the top. A lifetime guarantee on the American dream."

The bucket swayed. Yarik stared at its iron floor between their boots. "Don't you see," he said again, "that's what's wrong with the history you told."

"What?"

"My brother."

This time it was Bazarov who, for a moment, was quiet. Finally, he said, "What about him?"

"You left him out of my history."

"I left him out of Slava's history."

"But people know who he is. Dima is . . . Dima's the reason I came here today to quit. People know he's my—"

"I know all about your brother," Bazarov said. "I knew all I needed to know the first day I met him—met you both. I've seen the video." He grinned, stuck his hand up, made a pistol shape with finger and thumb, said, "*Puf! puf! puf!*" Dropping his hand again, he gave a shrug, let his eyes roll. "Ridiculous," he said. But when he looked back at Yarik, he wasn't grinning. "And maybe a little dangerous, too."

"But he's my brother," Yarik told him. "I can't—"

"He's not the part of the story we would leave out," Bazarov said. "He's the part that makes it beautiful. Because, without him, Slava, your story is just one of hard work and luck. But that's not how the world works. And no matter how good you make a lie, if it's not how the world works people won't believe it. Luckily for us, the way the world works *is* the way your story works. A lot of hard work and a little luck but, mostly, a moment of opportunity and the decision to take it."

Yarik looked down at the iron floor again. "I'm sorry," he said.

"Choice, Slava."

"I think the swaying is getting to me."

"It all comes down to choice. Who chooses to be next, and who chooses to be passed by."

"I think we should go back down," Yarik said.

"Sometimes," Bazarov told him, "I think this whole country wants to go back down. Our nostalgic Russian soul. Sometimes I think it's going to sink us all. I understand: it's a hard thing, this choosing. We didn't used to have to do it. In The Past Life our choices were made for us. But now we live in a different world. And in this world everything depends on the decisions we make. And what better story of *that*," Bazarov told him, "than two brothers, twins, who choose so differently."

He could see the tips of his boots and the tips of Bazarov's pointing towards his, and he kept his eyes on the stretch of empty steel between them.

"What better way," Bazarov said, "to show the consequences. One brother who chooses hard work and ambition. The other who chooses to slough off both. What better way to quash whatever effect your brother might have, those like him might have, those using him wish to have, on all the workers like you both. What better way than simply to show them *you*. You in the suit and tie of a section manager. In your manager's car."

"I'm not a prop," Yarik said.

"Of course not," Bazarov told him. "A prop doesn't get to choose the direction his life will take."

On the steel, a scattering of dirt and stones shifted back and forth, pebbles rolling, stopping, rolling back.

232

"Yarik."

At the sound of his name, Yarik lifted his gaze. Bazarov's was already on him.

"You think," Bazarov said, "that I don't know how hard this is? You forget: I also had a sibling. Two." In his eyes there was an openness so unexpected it made Yarik want to look away again, but the man said, "I told you that they died," and he couldn't. "A fire. I didn't tell you it was my fault. Well"—Bazarov sighed—"at least I *felt* it was. I loved them." He raised his eyebrows, as if there was no way to hide a thing like that. "When it happened," he went on, "I was away. Like our father, who was never home, who was never *anything*. Except drunk. I was in Moscow, trying to make my business . . ." He winced. "If I had been there, I know I could have saved them. I *know* it. The way I know I failed them because I wasn't. For a long time after, I thought *I* was a failure, felt it no matter how well my business did, maybe even *because* my business . . ." He shook his head. "But now I don't. Now I think of my son, his secure future. His mother, who I support. *My* mother, who didn't have to wreck her health with work, who doesn't have to worry in her old age. I think of the mothers and children and loved ones of all the people who work here." He opened his arms. "So many who I've done good by. *Because* of my business. Was it worth it? I can't think of it like that. I can only know this: I chose to live up to *them*. To all those other lives. Sometimes, you have to choose to fail. To let one person down. Or even two. So you can live up to *everyone* else. Especially yourself."

When Yarik dropped his gaze back to the bucket's floor, the dirt was still, the pebbles stopped.

"I can't tell you what to choose," Bazarov said, "but I can tell you this: whoever you do let down, don't make it someone who you know won't let you down. Those people are rare. I know: I've spent my life looking for them. Yarik," he said, and Yarik shut his eyes, "find the person who is already holding you back, who is already failing you. Because I know this, too: I wasn't the only one who failed my sisters. There were so many others who might have saved them. Including, hard as it is, themselves."

With his eyes shut, Yarik could still feel the bucket's swaying inside him. And when he shook his head, it was worse. The scrape of Bazarov's bootstep, the sense of a weight come closer. From far below, there rose the sound of the logging crews, the earth-shaking thunder of all the trees falling along the forest's edge.

"I know it's hard."

Yarik felt the man's hand on his shoulder. It was bruised from the punch and it hurt and Yarik didn't pull away.

"And," he heard Bazarov say, "it's going to get harder."

That evening, when Yarik pushed open the door to the stairwell of his home, he heard footsteps climbing somewhere on the flights above. It could have been any woman's heels clacking, but it wasn't; it was his wife's; he knew it in his body. His boot-thuds banged up the stairs, reverberating like a whole flightful of men, so loud he couldn't hear if she had stopped, or kept on towards the neighbor's door, where, just home from work, she would retrieve their children from the old woman, which she could not do, which he could not let her do. By the time he reached her there on the landing, grabbed her around the waist just as she was about to knock, he was gusting so hard from running up that he could not get out any words.

"What is it?" she whispered.

He took the hand that she'd touched to his face and put his mouth to her fingers and breathed.

"What's going on?" she said, and he told her, "Don't get them" and "Leave them for a while" and "Downstairs."

In their apartment, he pressed her against the wall, shoved up her work skirt, got her hose down. "What is it?" she asked him, again, breathy and quick. "What is it?"

"I got a new job."

"A raise?"

"A new job," he repeated, and then, "a better job. Bigger, more money, more . . ." And then he was in her and she was saying, "How? How?" the way she had said "What is it?" before, but he was staring above her head at the hole in the wall and he couldn't speak. "How?" she said, "How?" and each time she said it he grew softer and softer until he had to push his pelvis all the way against her just to keep from slipping out and still he ground away, refusing to stop, trying long past when he knew he could not ever come, could only keep pushing, keep staring at the pieces of plaster broken inward, the chunks of it missing, the black place in the middle the size of his fist.

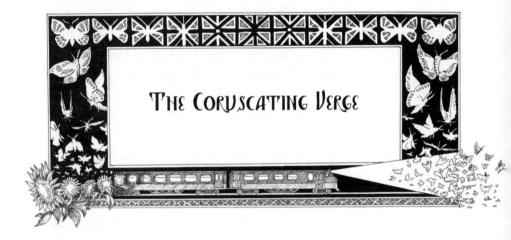

The Coruscating Verge

The day before, it had been Dima staring down at the holes his hands had made, the strange shape his splayed body had imprinted in the bank. Mud had clung to his neck hair, slicked down his back. In his underwear, he'd hunted the shallows for the rest of his clothes. By the time he'd given up, the mud had dried to a crust on his back, silt sifting down into the water with each step. Sliding his bare arms through his rucksack's straps, he knew it would be a long time before he saw his brother again. Knew, splashing south in nothing but wet underwear, it would be a while before he'd want to.

He stayed close to the bank, screened by the reeds, until the river turned and, climbing out, he made his way along the drainage ditches, through the woods, up the embankment of the access line. At the tracks, he stepped onto a rail, hoping to relieve his root-and-rock-torn feet. Instead, the steel seared them. Scrambling off, he stood looking at the burning metal, the smear of blood from his gouged soles bright in the sun. But it was on his face that he felt the heat. His forehead. His eyelids. He shut them. Her fingertips.

He had intended to take the tracks back to Petroplavilsk, to hide

236

between the walls of buffer woods until, beneath the less revealing mirror-light, along the city's side streets, he could, unclothed, sneak home. Where these days his mother hardly seemed to know him, where his brother no longer came, where the only soul he ever spoke with was the bird. *Home.* He could hear Volodya's voice, could feel again the sadness with which the word had filled him then. *Because,* the fat man had said, *we're your friends.* And Fedya: *We're your people.* And Vika, too: *You just don't know it yet.* But how could they be after the way they'd used him? The memory made him want to sit down, stay there, stop thinking. Because how was what his brother had done, or stood by and let be done to him, any better? Dima took a step, as if to shake the thought, leave it behind. Because if that was true so was this: all his life he'd never felt the need for friends, could never comprehend how others created out of nothing anything close to what he and Yarik had always simply had. *Have,* he told himself. But when he took another step it was in the oppsite direction. Away from the city. Down the tracks towards a distant place where they seemed to disappear.

And here he is, this tall skinny man, all shaggy hair and black beard and bony body and underwear, trying to step from railroad tie to railroad tie. Strange storklike stride, awkward and long. And sometimes, when the trees darken him with shade, when their shadows erase a section of sun-gleamed line, he steps up, balances on a rail, sets one foot before the other, lifts his arms.

Hours to reach the end of the Oranzheria, and an hour's walking after that, and all the while he watched the woods for the spot where they'd turned off. Any other time of year the tracks and forest would have been already illumined by only mirror-light, but here the midsummer sun still hung in the tops of the trees, its redness slivering through their boughs, shadows masking the wood's edge from Dima's memory. Still, he recognized the sound. That far faint whine of wheels-on-rail. Even as he turned, he knew, somehow, it would be her. A small dark spot coming on. Beneath the already risen mirrors, below power lines strung like strips of sunset, amid the growing sonance of her speeding rail-board, she took shape: jeans flapping loosely at her legs, metal glints all up her sternum, her hood blown off, her bangs flying, her face suddenly there.

In the silence left by her heel-thudding stop he felt her eyes all over him. His underwear, his nothing else.

"The poet"—her hands sprung open, as if presenting him—"reappears!"

He resisted the urge to swing his rucksack off his shoulders, bring it around to cover his chest. "I was just out here . . ."

"Just out here?"

". . . looking for the place where we got off last time."

"And to think," she said, "all this time we've been looking for you." She flicked a finger against his bare chest. "What happened?"

He folded his arms over the place where her flick had hit. "Why don't you tell me?" he said. "Why didn't you tell me what you were doing?"

"Me?" She pushed her shock of bangs out of her eyes. "I was down at the park waiting for you to pick up the story."

"I mean the video."

"Oh."

"Why—"

"Then you mean us. The way we opened our group to you, risked smuggling you into our house, showed you everything that we're about. Gave you our trust. Not to mention the gun. Which you shot."

Beneath his folded arms he could still feel the faint knock of her finger. "You used me," he told her.

"True," she said. "Though I don't remember using you quite as hard as this." This time her finger found his belly. "What I want to know," she said, "is what happened to Dima." Dropping her hand, she plucked his underwear waist, let it snap back. "To his clothes."

Watching her smile he knew he wouldn't tell her. But when she reached to him again her smile slipped away. Beside the hurt where he knew his jaw must have begun to show the bruise, he could feel her fingers hovering.

238

"To you," she said, the last of the mirth leaving the black of her dark eyes, something seeping in its place that he hadn't seen before, but that, seeing it now, made him want to see it again. Maybe it was simply that—the wish to hold her almost-softness there, the fact that as he spoke it stayed, softened even more—that made him tell her all that had happened, from the foreman's first words to the spectacle of him sprawled out in the mud. While he talked she seemed to take him in anew, too. Maybe it was only his cuts and bruises—she touched the skin over his jaw, stared at his torn-up feet—because when he was done she sat down on the rail beside him, started unlacing her shoes. Then, tossing them onto the gravel, she stripped off one of her socks.

They were striped, purple and gray, far too small, and when, sitting on the rail, he'd worked them over the wreckage of his feet the heels hung from his soles in two loose flaps. Retying her shoes beside him, Vika reached over and swatted one of the wattles. Then grabbed his foot and, shaking it, let loose a burst of rooster's crows. Laughing, she stood. "You know what they say about big feet." She kicked his other one. Waited. Rolled her eyes. "Of course you don't," she said, and, dropping her chin, peering down at her chest, started popping open her row of safety pins.

Standing, he told her, "It's OK," set an outspread hand over hers, as if under his fingers her own would have to stop. But they kept moving beneath his skin so that he couldn't help but be more aware of hers. "I'm not cold," he told her.

"You will be," she said.

He could feel each pin unlatch, as if what she touched transferred straight through to his fingers. Then her fingers were out from under his, working lower, and there was just her chest beneath his palm. He drew his hand back. Bending a little forward, she shucked the sweat-shirt off. Struggling with the sleeves, her arms hooked behind her, and he could not help but see the way her breasts pressed against the undershirt she wore, the way age had torn it at the neck, the under-arms, thinned the fabric nearly to gauze: twin circles dark as new

239

moons showing through, and, below, where her navel would have been, another—faint shadow—red as Mars.

When he looked up from it her eyes were looking down. They seemed to take him in a little lower than where he'd stared at her. He tried to shift away from her grin. "I guess it's true," she said and tossed the sweatshirt to him.

Tying it quickly around his waist, he turned it so the back hung down in front, an oversized loincloth equiped with a hood. That just made her laugh again. And setting one foot on her rail-board she gave her haunch a slap. "Come on," she told him. "There's room on here for three."

They rode together, him behind her, both with a foot on the board, her pushing at the ties with her other, his sock-foot hovering help-lessly. The ridge of her hips rocked beneath his hands, the neck of her shirt blowing open at her nape. Every now and then her leg, reaching back, would brush into him, rush his blood, until, to slow it, to steer his thoughts back to something that would set him straight, he told her the thing he had left out before: that his brother had been there. "On the bank," he shouted into the wind, "watching." Saying it hurt so much it worked: he could feel his blood drain out, and, suddenly, he wanted to lean forward, rest against her back, let her support him for a second. Instead, he just shifted a little closer, shouted over her shoulder a little more: how worried Yarik was, how he hated knowing that, the way his brother couldn't comprehend the choice Dima had made. "Sometimes," he said, "I see the way they look at me. Such hate. And I think I understand." Speaking so close that her bangs fluttered back almost into his eyes, he told her how, walking the rails that afternoon, he'd wondered if the foreman who'd berated him had been right, if there was something wrong with him, some-thing skewed, a flaw in who he was, a moral failing in how he was choosing to live his life.

"That," she shouted back, "is so fucked-up!"

For a second he thought she meant the way he'd turned to his brother in order to distract his mind from her, but she went on—"The morality of work!"—and, though he could feel their speed in his beard, in the breeze they made together, it seemed, as he tried to catch snippets of the words blown back at him—". . . once they make you think like that . . . policing yourself . . . mind-set of slaves . . ."—as if it were her voice itself that shook his beard, brushed against his shoulders, his bare chest. "Capitalists," she said, "Communists," and something sank in him—that he had told her what he had and she'd replied with this. Staring down at the rail slipping by beneath them, the ground a blur, he heard her saying, ". . . all they have in common . . ." and, in the smoothness of their glide, felt a tremor, faint and passing fast, but undeniable. "Coercion," she said. Up ahead, where the woods followed the tracks around a curve, the last red of sunset reflected on the trees washed out with a brighter light. The branches lost their shadows. Around the bend a star flared on. "Economic." He glanced from the light to her. "Political." He looked ahead again. "It's all the fucking same." Behind the headlight: two sky-lit windshields, a massive bank of shadowed steel, the train all heavy hurtling velocity. She was saying something about consumption, production—". . . same as what is worshipped now . . ."—and Dima's foot was hovering in its sock, about to bang down, slow them—". . . the same slave idea . . ."—shove himself free, when the horn blast blew and the board juddered and the speed rattled out from under it, bursting towards them instead in the shape of the train, and she was off, him stumbling after, the two half-scrambling, half-tumbling down the embankment, his rucksack slapping at his back, her rail-board slamming into the gravel as they slid to a stop, flipped onto their fronts, watched the train crash by above.

Beneath its thunder, Vika slid close, her face closer. "Look at them," she shouted. And if he swiveled his head to watch a window, he could see the dim shapes of passengers. "They're the ones whose lives are skewed."

The wind blown off the train was cold, rushed over his skin, prickled his flesh everwhere except his ear; there, her breath was warm.

"Fucked-up," she said, "as my family." He would have looked at her then, but his ear didn't want to leave her breath. "My grandmother was a Hero of Socialist Labor. My father was awarded The Order of

Labor Glory. Had the medal. For making shit that no one needed. But making a lot of it, working hard at it. Virtuous as your brother." He looked at her. With his ear towards the tracks, the thunder was louder. "You know where my father was today?" she shouted over it. "Mongolia. The Gobi Desert. Mining. His big chance in the new life. He left three years ago. My mom went with him. And fuck me."

And fast as thunder rolling away into the sky, the train was past.

"I was sixteen," she told him over its receeding wind.

In the quiet, he asked if she ever saw them.

Her smile was a short, aborted thing. "It's six thousand kilometers from here."

"Don't you miss them?"

Turning to the tracks, she pointed at the quickly disappearing train, showed him the shape of someone clung to the last car's ladder: faint face of a figure twisted around, as if to watch them back. "You and me?" she said, her breath on his ear again. "We're the ones trying to live right. To live straight. The way others look at us? The way they treated you today? It's because they know it. And they want it, too."

Then the train was gone and her breath was gone and on his beard he felt her hands turning him to look at her and her face was so close. "Dima," she said, "there's nothing wrong with you." So close he could barely focus on her black eyes, her bad-toothed smile. "Except"—her fingers touched his shoulder, brushed down his arm—"that you're all bumps." Her touch vanished only to reappear on the bare back of his thigh. "A plucked bird." She pinched his hairs. And, pulling back into sharpness, said, "Don't you have *anything* in here?" This time the tug came from his rucksack strap. He shook his head. But she was already asking, "What *do* you have in here?" Up off her elbow, she rose, swung a leg, was suddenly over him, sitting on his back. While she unbuckled the straps he tried to breathe. Her crotch pressed down on his rear, his underwear so thin he could feel the roughness of her jeans, her thigh muscles tightening with each yank of a strap, the way her whole body shifted over him when she loosed the top and leaned forward to peer in. An armful of soybean pods he'd stolen from the

Oranzheria, a sack of strawberries, a few cucumbers lost among the pilfered ears of corn, smothered by the heavy head of a sunflower he'd snapped off to harvest its seeds back home. Nothing that would explain why, without another word, she sat back, stood up, stepped off. He watched her shoes pass by him: small cascade of stones. By the time he'd gotten to his feet she was halfway to the tracks.

"Where are you going?" he asked.

She turned back. Behind her belt, against her belly, she'd shoved the sunflower bloom, the big head mashed halfway inside her jeans, the other half a golden mass of petals spread in a semicircle over her middle. "To our picnic spot," she said and, turning, climbed the rest of the way up to the rails.

From afar it glittered, the border between the mirror-lit world and the darkness of the one beyond, shimmered as if all the stars lost from view inside the city had been swept out to the edge in swaths of dust. But it was insect wings. Billions of them. Drawn each night towards the perimeter of that perpetual light. A mass migration met by the birds and bats who fed on it. In flocks thick as fog they circled the inside edge of that outer ring. While the moths and beetles and winged bugs flew in, a lepidopteric storm, ceaselessly swept into the coruscating verge.

When Dima and Vika first arrived, the line between the mirrors' sphere and the rest of night was still blurred by the last lingering of near-solstice light, but as they sat at the edge of the bog where she had brought them they watched the border of insects and birds begin to build itself in the air around. Slowly, the zerkala's glow seemed to grow more bright, the darkness sifted down beyond, while over the wide open soggy field, the stunted plants and small reflecting ponds, the glimmering gathered: a thin gauze laid over the darkening distance, slowly thickening into a cloud until at last it was a shaking wall of wings. From far out in the field the sound blew back to them: an ocean washing up against the rock on which they sat. In silence. For hours.

It must have been past midnight before she spoke. "If you were working," she said, "you wouldn't be here."

243

He had untied her sweatshirt from his waist and put it on, the sleeves too short, the shoulders too high on his, the front stretched across his chest, clasped there by the couple safety pins that reached. Against the chill in the air and the warmth of her so near he had lain the rucksack across his lap. In hers, she held the sunflower head.

"If I gave a shit about my work," she said, "I'd be sleeping." Her fingers dipped, picked out a seed. "Instead of here with you." She split the shell. "I never would have stood around in the park." Flicked the husk. "You never would have stood there on that statue." Slipped the seed between her lips. "We never would have even met."

He watched her chew.

"You know what sucked?" she said.

And he looked at her eyes again.

"Waiting there for you." She dug at the sunflower head. "For days. Along with everyone else. Though they gave up, quit coming. I was there today. Just like yesterday. Just like the day before that."

"Why?"

This time she handed him the seed. "The same reason they all were. Only I cared about it more."

His fingers turned the hard shell. "It's just a poem," he told her. "Just a foolish—" She reached over, snatched the seed back from his hand. He said, "It doesn't even mean anything."

"It does to them. To us. To listen to it. It's not what it's about," she told him. "It's what it *is*. It reminds us, standing there, drifting off from everything else. Maybe of how it was before. Maybe how it could still be. Not the fable. Not the fucking poem. But the time to listen to it. The kind of life that would let us." She turned to him, leaned in, and he could feel the weight of the seed head slide against his leg, the petals slick and soft on his skin. "All those people?" she said. "They didn't come for a poem, Dima." She was so close, now, that she had to reach out with her empty hand and spread it against his chest to hold her weight. "They came for *that*. They wanted *that*." In her other hand she held another seed. "They just didn't know until you showed them." This one was already shelled. "You made them feel it," she said. "And then?" She held the seed an inch from his mouth. "You disappeared."

He could feel the air compressed between her fingers and his lips. He could feel the slight shaking of her spread palm with each thump in his chest. He could feel the weight of her entire body hovering over him, her shock of bangs hanging down into the place between their eyes, her breasts filling in the space his bowed body left. He could feel that, too, how his own chest had gone concave, his whole self bent, as if afraid to let hers touch him. But mostly what he felt was how her whole self bent to make sure she did, how she twinned her shape with his.

"But"—he watched the word blow her bangs—"isn't that the same thing that they do, that you're against? The way we're made to want something we didn't know we wanted until they—"

She pressed the seed against his lips. "No." She shook her head; her bangs brushed his skin; he let the seed slip in. "That's making a new want where there wasn't one before. This is just uncovering a want that was always there. Maybe forgotten, or burried, or blocked out, but *there*." Her hand gave his breastbone a little push.

Looking away, he watched the far-off ring shimmering around them, the swarm of insects beneath the swirling birds, stared across the bog to where the wall of their glistering bodies shook. Beyond it: blackness. At first, when they'd come here and sat on the rock and seen the border between the long dusk and real night solidify before them, he'd wanted to wander out there, past it, beyond the verge. But now something about the idea scared him, seemed suddenly too huge. And he was afraid to look at her, to see the disappointment he knew would be in her black eyes. Instead, he thought, he'd give her what he could. He tried to remember the poem where he'd left off, the start to the second canto, the lines that spoke to the ways of warriors compared to poets compared to lovers, and, swallowing the seed, shaped his lips into the name *Rogdai,* tried to start the story of the rival suitor. . . . But couldn't. It had been so many years since he and his brother had lain beneath that blanket of mushrooms, so long since they had filled the warren's air with their renditions of the fable, and, still, it felt so real, so true, strong enough to make this now feel wrong.

"It's OK," she said. "You don't have to. We don't need to. Not anything." And, taking her weight off his chest, telling him, "Not even touch," she filled him with a worry that felt even worse: somehow she'd read him, known him, the way that, once, only Yarik could.

"In Mongolia," she whispered, her face still close, "among the herders, they learn to recognize each other's smell. That's how they know their friends, their feelings. They say hello like this." Smiling, she dipped her face beside his, sniffed a cheek, the other.

He felt his own smile break.

"Here," she said, leaning down with her face turned so that her neck nearly grazed his nose. "What do I smell like?"

He breathed in. If there was a faint redolence of mushroom and cigarettes and something fresh and sharp as a radish newly bit, on her it still seemed unlike anything he'd ever known.

When he stayed silent, she returned her face to him. And leaning in to place her nose close to his neck, whispered, "You know what you smell like?" When he shook his head, he could feel the blood throb through the bruise in his jaw. He could feel her breath brush the tender spot of skin when she told him, "Me."

The Way the World Works

Now, Dima was out under the zerkala again. It seemed to him the Consortium must have sent more up: they filled the sky, a city of lights above the city of none, as if the souls of all the disused streetlamps of Petroplavilsk had taken residence in the heavens. Beneath them, Dima walked the long walk to his brother's home.

Again, he had returned to his own just before morning. Again, he'd slept through the day. And waking in the late afternoon across the room from Yarik's old cot, in the same strings of sunlight coming through the window-hung kovyor, he'd felt the weave of them, him and his brother, the threads that all their lives had held them together, fraying—the day they'd sold their father's boat, the evening Yarik first saw Zinaida, the hours Dima had spent with Vika last night: these were the moments that pulled the loose ends of life—and, rising, he had known they had to see each other, to talk, whether Yarik wanted to or not.

By the time he got to the building it was late enough Zina and the children would have already eaten supper, late enough Dima could be sure his brother would be there. He'd found a pair of peeling boots to replace his lost shoes, and the tape that he'd used to hold together the sole of one had come undone. The rubber slapped with every step on every stair. On the landing, he paused. Through the apartment door he could hear the baby crying, dishes banging in the sink, Yarik shouting at his wife that she was going to break something, her shouting back that he was one to talk.

When Dima knocked, all the noise but the baby stopped.

"Bratets," he said, "it's me."

There was whispering before his brother came to the door. Yarik had on a bathrobe and slippers and his hair was wet. The hallway light showed the trails trickled down his temples, his neck.

"Hello, bratishka," Yarik said.

"Hello, bratan."

It seemed like such a long time since he had seen his brother. Now, standing so close, last night seemed even farther away than that. Or maybe just seemed smaller. Maybe, back beside his brother, he already felt a little less scared of it, a little more safe. Some neighbor below opened a door, shut it, started down the stairs. Dima reached out and took Yarik's hand and lifted his arm and put his brother's palm over the back of his neck. Footsteps down a second flight, a third.

Yarik squeezed a little. "Come in," he said.

A color television flashed from the living room, flickering over Polya's scattered toys, and there was Timofei, sitting crosslegged on the floor before a video game, nearly unrecognizable in the crazed light of the screen. The coatrack had been moved. Dima didn't see why until he reached to it, ran his hand down the post their father carved, his palm slipping over the spirals, slowing, going still. There, at eye level: a second hole in the wall.

"It was like only having one shoe." Yarik forced a smile. "I needed a pair." And then he realized what he'd said and his smile twisted, as if trying, too late, to change the words. He looked away, opened the sideboard, turned back with a bottle in his fist.

The sound of his brother pouring the vodka into the glasses was the same, the show on the TV the same, the old oil scent from the kitchen, the way Zinaida sighed heavily over the dishes the same sound of forbearance that Dima had grown to know was her weighing the good and bad of the life she'd made with Yarik and deciding it was, in the end, OK.

His brother finished screwing the cap back on the bottle and matched her sigh. As if he had been listening to his wife and knew that it would go on as it did—his marriage, his kids, his day after day—and that that was, in the end, OK, too.

For the first time, Dima thought he understood why someone might want it, the ways it could seem nearly enough, how tempting it must have been for Yarik. Might even be someday for him.

"What are you smiling about?" Yarik said, the two glasses in his hands, his wet hair dripping.

"It's just," Dima said, "you look contented."

Yarik's eyebrows rose. "You look like you got attacked by a rooster."

Dima felt his brow mimic his brother's, saw Yarik see it, his brother unable to stop a real smile at the sight. And, watching that, Dima felt the same pull at his face. He winced: the pain in his jaw where the shoe had hit.

As if he hadn't noticed, Yarik handed Dima the glass, made as if to put his arm around his brother's back, but checked himself, unsure of what else might be hurt. "Come here," Yarik said, instead. "Look."

They stood in front of the hallway mirror, Yarik a little behind Dima, the glasses in their hands.

"Not at me," Yarik told him.

Dima glanced at himself, then back to his brother.

"You don't even see, do you?" Yarik said. "When was the last time you got a haircut? It looks like Mama did it."

Dima shrugged.

"Oh my God. I was joking." Yarik tugged first one of Dima's ears, then the next. "And you managed to keep *both*?" His hand slid around to Dima's face and brushed his beard against his cheeks, all telltale gingerly when it should have been a squeeze. "Are you waiting for her to give you a shave, too? Or are you training to become a priest?"

How hard Vika's hand had pressed his chest, how quickly she'd reached for his jaw, how strange the way whatever was in him pushed the comparison on his mind. "It's OK," Dima said, as if his voice might clear it away. "It's just a little sore."

But it was Yarik's fingers that drew back. His brother wiped them on his robe. His eyes had left Dima's face in the mirror, and he held Dima forward by the shoulder, as if to look at the whole of him, as if to hide behind his thin shape. "What are you eating?" he asked. "What is Mama making you for supper? What in God's name are you bringing her to make?"

"We have enough," Dima said.

"Enough? How long can rooster soup last?"

"I wouldn't eat Ivan."

"I bet your neighbors would. Is it still crowing?"

"Yarik," Dima said, "when are you going to stop taking a different bus?"

Yarik took a sip from his glass. He looked like his whole face felt bruised as Dima's jaw. "I can't talk here," he said. "I can't *think* in here. Listen to that!" He motioned to the living room with the noise of the kids and swept his hand onward to the kitchen with the racket of the dishes, and the movement allowed him to turn away from Dima. He took another drink. "You named it Ivan?" he said. "Like the dog?"

"Yarik—"

"Let's go up to the roof." And, passing by the sideboard, he took the bottle. On the roof, he dragged the two deck chairs over, dropped himself into one, lay back against its low recline, the plastic footrest sagging with the weight of his heels, and, letting the bottle clank next to him, told Dima, "Sit." They sat beneath the mirrors sliding across the dome of the sky, amid their reflections in the surrounding rooftop solar panes. From up there all of Petroplavilsk seemed to be drifting.

Sitting there, beside his brother again, Dima could feel it. Not only the way that life had tried to carry them apart, but how far he had begun to drift himself. For a moment he was afraid to look at Yarik. He had missed his brother so much.

"I know," Yarik said.

And Dima turned to see: in his brother's face there was the same thing his brother had seen in his.

But, clearing his throat, Yarik tried to turn it into something else. "I know," he said again, "that it must be hard. You must need money."

"No," Dima told him.

"For my brother, my mother, I can find—"

"All your brother wants," Dima said, "is that you save." And, saying it, he knew it was true. All he wanted was to live life beside his brother. And all they needed to do it was the farm. "Save, bratan, so we can—"

"That's what I don't understand," Yarik said. "By now, *you* must have gone through so much of what *you'd* saved. If you'd only kept working, if you still had your half . . ."

"I have it." Dima set his glass down. He lifted his bony hips, reached into his back pocket, drew out a folded bit of cloth. "I haven't touched it." Inside there was a handful of half-smoked cigarettes sallow in the mirror-light. He picked through the pile for the longest stub, found it, put it to his lips, and, cupping the remaining butts in his palm, offered the clothful to Yarik.

His brother looked at it. Dima followed the glance. The stubs were shaking. Then Yarik's hand cupped Dima's fingers, folded them closed around the cloth.

Setting his glass on his belly, Yarik reached into the pocket of his robe. He brought out his own pack of cigarettes, drew out two, gave one to Dima. Lighting a match, steadying his glass, he reached over. In Yarik's fingers the flame shivered. Watching it, Dima inhaled, let go of the first smoke.

"Bratets," Yarik said, "what *do* you eat?"

"Food."

"How do you get it?"

"Mama's apartment is full of things we don't need."

"And when you're down to the things you do need?"

"Each thing that I get in trade," Dima said, "I ask the farmers about. How to plant it. How to grow it." His brother swapped the cigarette for his glass, looked at him over the rim. "We already know most of it from when we were boys."

"Dima," Yarik said, "how long do you plan to survive on a dream?"

They sat with their cigarettes burning down in their fingers.

"I have a boy now," Yarik told him. "A daughter. A wife. You think I can support them by trading things?"

"You don't even have to trade for most of it," Dima told him. "Most I just find."

"Oh," Yarik said, like the word had gone through him and cramped somewhere inside. He drew on the cigarette and sighed the smoke out and then reached down and ground the stub against the roof. "You're feeding our mother off trash." He handed the stub to Dima. "You want me to feed my family on trash?"

Dima took the stub and ground his own out and drew the cloth out of his pocket and wrapped the two in it and put the cloth back, and while he did his brother watched him, and while watching him Yarik drained his glass.

"Before the Oranzheria—" Dima started.

"We were kids," Yarik cut him off. "Now we're not." He waited while Dima took a drink from his half-full glass. Then he reached to the bottle and unscrewed the top and poured it for himself. "It's part of growing up, bratets." He poured Dima's glass full, too. "It's the way the world—"

"It doesn't have to be," Dima said. "It didn't used to be. It wasn't the way the old mir worked."

"The mir?"

"It wasn't how Dyadya Avya worked."

"The mir of the peasants from centuries ago?"

"On Dyadya Avya's—"

"On Dyadya Avya's we lived like animals. On the mir, they—"

"And why not?" Dima's hand jerked with the words, the vodka spilling onto his fingers. "Animals *like* their work. A heron likes to fish."

"What is this," Yarik said, "something you picked up from the people you've been hanging around with?"

"A bear . . ."

"Dima . . ."

". . . to hunt."

"What the hell are you talking about?"

"Squirrels—"

"Right," Yarik said, "I'm sure squirrels fucking love to collect nuts. But we're not squirrels, bratets." He took a slug from his glass. "I mean, Dima, look at us. Look at fucking *them*." He waved a hand at the zerkala above. "We're not wild animals. We're fucking house cats. And you know what a house cat wants? To sit on its ass and lap from a bowl of milk. A bowl someone else has brought for it. But if there's nobody to bring the bowl? Until we make enough money to pay someone to bring it, bratets, we can't just do what we want." He set his glass down on his armrest with a dull clank.

Slowly Dima drank his empty, too. Then he reached down and unscrewed the cap on the bottle and refilled his brother's glass, refilled his. "If we could just buy the farm," he told Yarik, "we *could* work at what we want, we'd—"

"We'd what?" Yarik said. "Plow up the old fields? Grow some flax? Some turnips? Spend all day hunched over with a hoe like Dyadya Avya? Do you think he *liked* pulling turnips? Do you think those farmers you talk to, are they, with their backs bent from a life of it, do you think they're happy?"

"I think they're happier than us."

"Not for long."

Dima looked at his brother, the vodka stinging on his lip.

"These farmers," Yarik went on. "They're in the old market?"

"Yeah."

"And what do they sell? What do they have left that can grow? Who can grow it? A few so far out they're not yet affected by the zerkala? A few who scratch together enough to buy their seeds from the Consortium? And the rest? A few cucumbers that don't need the dark? A few onions? It's not like Dyadya Avya's anymore, Dima."

"If they can—"

"How many? How many are there?"

"I don't know."

"Not as many as there used to be."

"No."

"Not nearly. Next year there will be none. Every month it pushes out another kilometer. *I* push it out another kilometer. Another hundred hectares of fields. How can they compete? Bratishka, how could you?"

"We—"

"No," Yarik said. "No." He drank, swallowed. "It has to stop."

The glass on Dima's thigh felt too heavy for him to lift it off. "What?" he said.

"What other people must think," Yarik told him. "When they see you digging through the trash. When they see you riding the bus like a bum all day long."

"I'm not a bum."

"Like a beggar."

"I don't beg," Dima told him.

"And you think that would keep you out of The Dachas?" Yarik slugged back the rest of his drink. "Do you ever wonder why you haven't been put there yet?"

"Why would they put me there?"

"Why *wouldn't* they?"

"I don't think—"

"*I* do," Yarik said. "Zina does. Because we know what would happen without the six thousand roubles I pay the police to keep you out."

Dima sat silent.

"Each month," Yarik said. He slid his gaze to Dima, his glass squeezed in his fist. "I know what you're thinking now."

"Six thousand roubles a month."

"And it's not 'thank you.'"

"Yarik," Dima nearly whispered, "have you managed to save anything at all?"

The glass banged down on the rooftop. "*That*"—Yarik let go, as if it had broken—"is what has to stop."

Again, Dima drained his glass. He watched Yarik over the rim, and then through the empty bottom, and then he set the glass on the concrete beside his brother's. Looking at the two glasses standing still and empty there, he said, as slowly as he'd drunk, "What are you saying?"

"I'm saying . . ." Yarik clenched his empty hand, let it fall open. "When you say the difference between us and animals, Dima, is that they get their joy from their work, that we get none, I'm saying maybe they get their *purpose* from it, bratets. Maybe their purpose gives them joy. Maybe, bratets, maybe it just turns out you and I . . ."

"You're saying you're not a bum."

"Maybe we're just different kinds of animals." Yarik's eyes stayed closed. He waited, as if for Dima to speak, and when he did—"You think your brother's a bum"—Yarik reached for the vodka. Beneath his fingers, the glass rattled.

"But I'm not." Dima sat there, staring at his brother. Then, slowly, body stiff with the effort, raised one leg, held his foot up off the footrest of the chair. "See?" he said, and his voice, shaking like Yarik's cup, made of the word a command. "I even found some old shoes to fix up." The boot stuck there, tape around its sole, motionless in the air between them. "And you know," Dima said, "beggars don't need shoes."

Yarik stared at his brother's foot the way Dima was staring at him. Then, emitting a small squeezed groan, he leaned forward off his chair. He put his hand on Dima's foot and, for a moment, rested it there. He looked like he was going to say something to the boot. But he just pushed it, gently, back onto the footrest. And filled their glasses again. And when he was again sitting back beside Dima, he said, "Do you know what would have happened if I had helped you?"

"It's OK," Dima said.

"No," Yarik said. "No, it's not. Even while I was standing there, not helping you, even then I knew it wasn't OK, and I hated myself, I fucking hate myself for standing there, and still, I know, I know that if I had, if you understood that—"

"I understand."

"No, you don't."

255

"I don't care about—"

"*I* care," Yarik said. "Dima, today I took the number six. I had to get it half an hour earlier because I had to transfer to the number three." He looked like he would take a drink, but his hand simply rose and fell and never reached his mouth. He said, "I have to transfer to the three because you're not on it."

Dima reached over and touched his brother for the first time since they had come up on the roof. He put his hand on Yarik's forearm. His thumb rubbed lightly at the softness of his brother's arm hair. "I know," he said, "like every day the past two weeks." He smiled a small smile. "But it will be OK now. I've stopped going to the square. I've stopped reciting the poem. I won't see any of those people anymore. Nobody. Just my bratets." He let his fingers squeeze his brother's wrist a little tighter. And when Yarik's other hand pressed down on his, Dima shut his eyes. So it was a motion he felt more than saw—the weight of both their hands, Yarik's fingers stilling Dima's thumb, then the breath of air beneath his own palm—when his brother lifted Dima's hand off. But he opened his eyes in time to see the small shaking of Yarik's head.

Somewhere, a flock of geese was flying. Yarik turned away, as if to look for them.

"You're right," Dima said, "I don't understand."

"I know." Still looking up at the sky, Yarik ran a hand through his short, wet hair. "That's the problem." He ran it back again towards his forehead, and in the light of the mirrors his hair sprayed a fine mist over his fingers and dampened his forehead and there were tiny drops glinting on the hairs of his eyebrows, on his lashes, when he closed his eyes. "You know who lived like an animal?" he said. "Papa."

"He was happy," Dima said.

Yarik breathed hard through his nose. "Mama was so miserable. We were so hungry. Selfish!" His whole brow jerked: a mist of fine drops shed. "How could he have been so selfish, Dima?" Then he opened his eyes and took a drink and swallowed, and when he was done, he said, "Today, I went to the Oranzheria to quit."

Dima's throat closed down to a whisper: "Because of me?"

Yarik finished his drink, set the glass down so carefully it made no noise at all on the roof. "I didn't," he said, and poured himself another glass. "Quit." He said the word as if it was a joke of a word, and drank, and said, "Hired as foreman the day before *you* quit. And as manager the day *I* try to."

"They're going to make you a manager?"

"Maybe," Yarik said. Then he said, "Yes." He stared up at the sky, as if still searching for the geese among the mirror gleam. "Unless I say no."

"Why would you say no?"

The breath he let out seemed to take half the weight of his body with it. And the way his body sank into the chair it seemed what was left was still too much. "Listen to them," he said. "Do you think they navigate by the stars? What if they navigate by the stars?" Then he dropped his chin and cleared his throat and took a drink again and looked at his brother and said, "It's just temporary."

"What is?"

"Just a precaution. A condition. That's what he told me: it's a condition."

"Who told you?"

Yarik shut his eyes and put his hand over them and held it there.

"Who told you?" Dima asked again.

Beneath his hand, Yarik shook his head. He took his hand away. His eyes were open. "He told me it was the only way. He said, 'What if the men in your section see him lounging about? What if they see you together? What would that do to our story?'" He breathed out a small breath through his nose. Dima could hear it hit the drink close to his brother's mouth. "They won't, I told him. 'What if he comes to visit you?' he said. He won't, I told him. He said, 'What if you're seen with him riding the buses?'"

The geese were right above them now, their sounds so loud that when Dima said, "For how long?" he could not tell if his brother had heard him or not.

"What the hell do you think they steer by?" Yarik said. He was still

257

looking up at the birds. "It can't be by land. Because every year the land is different. What the hell must they think of the Oranzheria? A huge lake with no water? Ice in the summer? They must hate it. One year it was just there. And they looked for the fields, and they were farther than they should have been. And when they came back, on the way south, the lake was even farther. And the next year, the distance from the lake to the fields was farther again, and it must have kept on like that, for years, the glass growing, them coming back. Until one year it will be too big and they'll have no place to land at all."

Dima reached over and touched his brother on the shoulder. "For how long?"

"Or anywhere," Yarik said. "That's what he told me today. That was his condition: or anywhere."

"How long is temporary, Yarik?"

"Not just the buses. Not just in the Oranzheria, he said. He said, 'What if you're seen with him anywhere?'" Yarik looked at Dima. "'I won't be,' I told him."

There was the sound of the geese, and of the traffic below, and of someone shouting in an apartment, muffled, as if through a closed window, and loud, as if the shouting was out of a fury or a sorrow that could not be contained by windows or walls or that could ever go quiet. And then it stopped, and there was just the sound of the traffic and over it the geese. Yarik reached for the bottle, poured another glass, and, shaking his head, sucked the edge of his hand where the vodka had spilled. Through his fingers he said, "Why did you have to make that video? That poster?"

"I didn't know—"

"How could you be so stupid?" he shouted, and the echo came back like the shouting from the apartment a moment ago, and after it the geese seemed to have gone quiet, or simply gone, and Yarik bunched the sleeve of his robe in his free fist and squeezed, hard. "I'm sorry," he said. The spilled liquor dripped. "I don't know how long."

"When will you know?"

"When I tell him to go fuck himself. When I've made enough, when my job is safe enough, I'll tell them all to go fuck themselves." He drank the rest of his glass and smacked it down on the roof beside him and lifted the lever on the deck chair so that the back slapped flat beneath his weight and he lay there looking up at the sky. "Then fuck the bus," he said. "They'll pay me enough I can get a car. I'll *have* to get a car. They'll expect a manager to have a car. They already expect a fucking foreman to *look* like he *could* have a car." He rubbed at the skin below his jaw. "I shave both ways, now," he said, his voice tight with the stretch of his neck. "First up, then down. I never fucking did that in my life. Zina likes it. She likes the way clothes smell coming back from the dry cleaner. When she goes to the station she likes having to look like she could be a foreman's wife. She holds Polya between us in bed and brushes the baby's cheek against my cheek and whispers things to her about the kind of life she's going to lead. She lets Timofei use my aftershave. Aftershave! Since when did I ever use fucking aftershave? She dabs it on his chin. She tells him once we send him away to school, to a private school, he'll have to do his part, too. Why? he says. Because it's for you, she tells him. And she puts the aftershave on his chin." Yarik slowly lowered his glass to the concrete next to him. "Don't ever have children," he told Dima. "Don't ever have a wife. You love them too fucking much."

Dima set his glass down, too. "I already have a brother," he said. And, when Yarik looked at him: "It's OK. You can go back to taking the number four."

Maybe high up at the edge of space one of the mirror wings was shaking. Or maybe down on the roof, in the pallid light, it was his brother's face instead. "I won't see you in public," Dima told him. "Until your job is safe. Until you say. I'll only come by here." It was his brother's face. "It's OK, Yarik. I'll come by at night and help with the children. I can cook. I know how to make a hell of a cabbage soup."

When his brother spoke, the sound made the shaking of his face seem worse. "I don't think . . ."

It was as if the thing that was working in his brother's face had slipped into Dima's, too. "What?"

"Zina came back from church," Yarik said. "The priest. She said he talked to her about you. About the children. What people will say. The lessons they'll learn."

"What lessons?"

"She said . . ."

For a moment Yarik's face seemed about to break, and Dima could see his mouth working to keep it from shaking completely apart and when Dima spoke his voice came out louder than he expected: "You'll come to Mama's then."

Yarik shook his head.

"You'll come."

"No," Yarik whispered.

"Yarik—"

"I think for a while . . ."

"Don't say it."

"For a while we should not see each other, bratishka."

And Dima had to look up at the sky. He tipped his head back as he would to keep the blood from dripping out of a broken nose, and stared through the ache in his eyes. He could hear the geese again, faintly, and there they were, already so far he could barely make them out, moving eastward, into the distance, and against the movement of the zerkala drifting to the west they seemed to be going so fast.

"Then," his brother's voice said from beside him, "we'll see each other all the fucking time. I swear. Dima, I'll be making enough that I can save, really save. I made him a condition, too. He pays to keep you out of The Dachas. Six thousand roubles a month. And that's nothing! Nothing compared to what I'll be able to put aside! I'll be saving sixty thousand a month, maybe more. In a year—just a year—I can have enough to buy Dyadya Avya's. Dima, it's the only way. Can't you see that? Without it we'll never do it. Zina's never going to be a farmwife. She's never going to let her children grow up hoeing weeds. *I* won't let them. *I* don't want it. But I want to be with you. Dimochka. Bratishka,

I'll make enough to build a second house out there. A real dacha, like the rich men have. A country home. Next to you and Mama in Dyadya Avya's old place. In a year, Dima, I'll be able to buy it for you *myself.*"

Dima rose then, and steadied himself on his feet. He didn't even realize he had made fists with his hands until Yarik rose, too, and put his own big palms over each of Dima's knotted ones. For a moment, Dima just let them stay there, feeling them on the back of his, and then they lifted, barely the beginning of a lift, the faintest cool air coming between their skin, and Dima's hands unclenched and grabbed his bother's and clenched again.

They stood like that for a long time, long enough that the last sounds of the geese were covered back up by the sounds of the traffic. When they could no longer hear them at all, Yarik said, "Is it a long crower, Dima? Like Dyadya Avya's? Do you remember how long his rooster would call? Does Ivan call as long as that? As long as the one out in the lake? On Nizhi? Dima? Bratets? Bratishka?"

In the apartment nearby where the shouting had been, or another one below, or one across the alley in another building, someone had turned the television on. It sounded like the news, or an interview, or, anyway, some man talking numbers. Slowly, Yarik forced his own hands open, loosening his brother's grip around his fists, straining against Dima straining to hold them still, both, for too short a moment, failing.

Towards Winter

That night, crossing Ostrovskogo Avenue, Dima stood on the concrete island between the trolley tracks, waiting for the eastbound four to pass. It came on through the mirror dusk, wheels clacking, contactors zipping on the wires with a sound like the air being slit. And when the westbound four slid around the corner, too, he could feel the sound blasting at him, pressing at his front and back, solid as a pair of palms trying to hold him still. He watched the riders in the windows: weary faces, shadowed eyes, sleepers and gazers and all of them passing on without any sign they had seen him. Then the roar was gone and the dragged walls of wind fought his coat, whipped his hair, blew the track trash so it leapt and shook as if strung along behind. Slowly, so slowly it took him hours, letting each foot shuffle forward at the pace it wished to go, he walked home.

And from that day, he ceased to hide from the city's sight. No longer did he keep to quiet laneways, dark alleys, the hidden corners at the back of buses. Of what consequence, his concealment? In fear of what result? So long as he stayed away from his brother. There was who he and Yarik had been before, and who they one day would be again, restored to themselves on their old land, and in between, he knew, his own self had become their greatest danger, his presence in his brother's world the only thing to dread.

Now he haunted all of Petroplavilsk on foot. How many saw him from the windows as they passed? His beard blowing, his hair a tattered flag, his cheekbones hard and thin as the edges of a soup bowl, his eyes in the sun so blue. How many watched him where he stooped in Pervomayisky Park, beneath the heavy greenness of the late summer leaves, the grass around him scattered with sticks small and white as broken birch twigs, a hundred half-smoked cigarettes thrown out. He plucks them, gathers them in his palm like berries, fills his coat pocket, slips one between his lips and lights it and draws. The smoke drifts through his beard like forest fog. How many saw him slip into the rain-dark alleys between apartment blocks, his soaked coat and hair disappear into a dumpster's mouth, emerge again to sling his rucksack on, swing a leg over a metal side, slosh back onto the street. What passerby noticed the flick of the rod, the singing line, the shape squatting on rocks beyond the guard wall of the pier, the silver flash of a fish slapped down and brained? Who heard the singsong chortling voice blown in off the lake on the breeze?

It seems to him most days that the answer is no one at all.

Certainly there is no one in the echoing National Theater, where he sits in the velvet-shedding seats, beneath dead chandeliers, prying the shells off foraged walnuts. The thin autumn sunlight streaks in through the gap left by the pried-open exit door, touches the bare stage, makes its way slowly across the rippling folds of the endlessly still curtain. The sound of the husks dropping to the floor is thunderous.

Certainly no one else stands on the cold tiles of the cavernous gymnasium, the wall cracks lumped with lichens, its vast pool murky as a lagoon. No one else strips down beside him, drops their clothes, leaps boylike into a splash so huge it spatters the wall. No one hears his whoop, his shriek, the chattering of his teeth after.

Now the only places from which he stays away are the ones where he used to go before, where the only people from whom he hides would expect to find him. For a while they wait down by the lake. Business-men watching from their windows. Trash collectors sweeping past the square. A few thugs still brave the threat of cops, give out feeble shouts, old slogans, light sad, smoky fires in the garbage cans. For a while, the Communists drape the statue with their banners, paste it with fly-ers of him, play bright tunes on old brass horns, their even older lips unable to keep the notes from sliding into sorrow. Some hangers-on post torn-out pages on the plinth. Some climb up, read Pushkin from their books. Some try reciting words of their own. None last. Nobody listens. A few people boo. A few days later there are only a couple stragglers camped out. A few after that the cops take them away. To The Dachas? Is that why the three figures who all this time have sat beneath the trees, waiting, watching, finally leave?

And then the great tsar has the plinth to himself. Nobody clings to his bronze body but the jaegers and crows, alighting spread-winged, ruffling, looking over the ever emptier square. The old men and women in their Soviet scarves and pins have retreated again into the aspens' shade, the sometime cannonade of empty bottles dumped into their plastic drums. In the old library there is not even that much sound. It has sunk back into silence, darkness, the weary patience of books deprived of hands to pull them, pages waiting to be turned. Behind the rail station, the access line is two long threads of mirror-light strung out, unbroken by even a sliver of his shadow. If the railcars wake from their rusty slumber, it is not from his footsteps on the gravel. Even the trams, the buses, the trolleys are empty of him now; he shuns them the way on sidewalks others shy from him. And if he sees a ticket-taking woman peering out an opening door, he turns his face away, turns down the next side street, disappears.

Sometimes, on the days he walks out to the Oranzheria, he feels like he is being followed. Sometimes he hears footsteps in the dirt, a voice—*Mister Boss-man!*—barking from the breezeway between buildings. *Gave you our trust!* from the darkness beneath the access line trees. But when he shouts in return for it to leave him be, there is just the quiet of the hemlocks, a cat mewling, a child mocking him back. When he looks behind him, there is never anyone else walking on the road. Just the roar of a bus, the rumble of a truck blowing by, dust clouds in their wake, him making his way through.

There's nothing wrong with you, she'd told him, and keeping to himself, steering clear of everyone else, he can feel it's true. Except for when he lets his thoughts stray into memories of her. Then he feels the threads inside him start to unspool, holds tight to the ends—*You made them feel it*—gathers them to his chest—*then disappeared*—tries to keep them from spilling any more. Sometimes, walking in the buffer trees between the city and the sea of glass, he thinks he hears a railboard's whoosing along the hidden tracks. He pauses, closes his eyes, listens to the rustling of the fallen leaves, the calls of crows drawing autumn towards the coming winter.

And then he passes through one of the worker's doors, and the sky is sheathed. The crows are blown away, as if on some mad gust, gone. There is the rolling song of a bunting. The *chif! chif!* of a warbler. Above the vast yellow plain of rapeseed flowers blue-winged thrushes dart. He strips off his coat, hangs it on his shoulder. By the time he has reached the cornfields, the vast stretches of soybeans, he is sweating. He dissolves into the high green stalks, nothing left but a faint rattling. He flattens onto his belly, becomes a wispy trail of dust moving down brown soybean rows. Emerging with his rucksack full of stubbled pods, heavy with a dozen ears, he waits in the crop cover for a truck he can jump, lies pressed against the pile of topsoil beneath a tarp or hunches inside some section of a giant water main, and when he reaches his brother's sector, jumps off. He hides where he can see the buses stop, watches the workers gather, so many their hard hats bulge like fish eggs floating in a sea of their blue coveralls. Sometimes he thinks he can feel his brother. Sometimes he sees him a moment later: his own face fuller, his own black hair shorn short. It is all he can do not to call out.

Sometimes he thinks he hears Yarik calling to him, distorted by all the distance, muffled by so many days since they last spoke, time like water in his ears. A shout small and wavery as it was from inside their

265

father's fishing shack, from on top of the ice around the hole, as he had heard it that night, long ago, sinking into the cold water below. Down beneath his feet it was churning, and beneath the churning it was black, and his eyes refused to look anywhere but there, down where the thing must be that had grabbed him, that would come up out of the blackness and grab him again. If he had air in his throat, it would not out. If he had strength in his lips, it would not move them. How far down did that darkness go? How deep would he sink before he could not even tell what was down at all?

Sometimes he wishes his mother would die. Sometimes he feels she is the only thing still holding him to this world. Once, he walked all the way to the Oranzheria's edge and beyond the glass and into the woods and stood there, listening to the fury of the chain saws behind him, feeling the air shake with the crash of the trees, looking out into the dark still green, and almost stepped forward, and forward, and another step, another. He has swum out into the lake, swum until his arms couldn't move him anymore, and lain on his back, and looked up at the clouds, and let the waves return him to shore. There are nights he cannot sleep, when his mind is tumid with ghosts of the living, when nothing he does will ease the ache, when he goes out onto the balcony and crams the hooded bird against his chest, his cheek to the twitching felt, and whispers to it, *One day*, whispers stories that cut them loose from everything, in which everything has cut loose from them—*One day*—stories that hold within them no humans but him. Sometimes, then, he thinks how easy it would be to just keep sinking.

But nothing had grabbed him from below to drag him under. His limbs had moved, and the air had bubbled from his mouth, and his eyes had followed the bubbles as they floated up, and one day his mother would die, without his wishing, despite his desperation that she not, and the thought shook through him and cramped his lungs and seized his muscles and sent him kicking. Back up, up there where he could see a small spot shaking, blinking out, back on, yellow, burning. One day, he would sit again on the couch between his niece and nephew, tell his stories into their soft hair instead of the bird's feather-pricked hood. Like a small spot of oil lit atop the water, flickering, burning bright, and all around it the vast field of faint blue ice that was the moonlight coming through. One day, he would take off his shoes and walk barefoot in the hot dirt of the fields his uncle had walked before. He could feel his boots come loose, slip off, sink away beneath him, and he kicked at them, kicked, and one day, his brother would come back to him, his brother whose hand had been the thing to finally grab him, from above, by the hair, then by his hood, at last hauling him up.

Once each month, every month since he had last seen Yarik, an envelope appeared in the mailbox downstairs. On it: *Galina Yegorovna Zhuvova* and the apartment's address put down in ink. It looked like the stamp that years ago Zinaida had bought for the tags on his mother's clothes, back when they had all begun to worry she might wander off. Inside the envelope there was never anything but the cash. Six thousand roubles in thousand-rouble notes. They were stacked the same side forward, the same edge up, the way Yarik always stacked bills in his wallet, and Dima would turn the envelope over, looking for another sign—even just the smudge marks of dirt-ingrained fingers, even a scent. But there was nothing.

The only other mail that ever came was his mother's meager pension check, or bills, the one not nearly enough to cover the others. The bills he saved for kindling. The envelopes he carried to the bank. He dreaded going there, where customers gave him glares, glanced at each other, sometimes derided him aloud: *Your comrade calls you!* one might say, or turn in line and whisper from the video—*It doesn't have to be this way*—or even recite a line of poetry—*Lyudmila? Where is Lyudmila?*—and ask him, mocking, why he'd stopped. At first, the tellers tried not to serve him, timed their breaks with his turn at the window or called the person behind him to step up. Once a guard wouldn't let him in—*I thought you didn't believe in money*—and Dima had to bribe him with a thousand-rouble note. The man must have shared it with the tellers: after, they served him without complaint. His mother's pension he placed in her account. His brother's remaining five thousand roubles he deposited into his own. Once there, it was untouchable; he never took a rouble out.

It was a rule he'd formed the first time he brought the envelope to the bank, sworn it shuffling along the street beneath his brother's disapproving stare, his eyes turned from the gritty wind of passing buses plastered with his brother's face; he had crossed Ilyinsky Square that day with his gaze a broom brushing the pavement before his feet, never lifting, not even at the coaxing of Yarik's voice: *Look up! Look ahead!*

His brother was everywhere: on the loudspeakers topping defunct streetlamp poles, smiling down from billboards above the shuttered theater, blocked the train station's red-starred spire, wondered aloud *Who's next?* in bright blue letters beneath the tip of his bright blue tie. His teeth were straight and white, set in a smile, asking, *Why not you?*

Each afternoon Dima went to the Universitetski Rynok, to the metastasizing kiosks that swamped the fountain, into the swarm of mongers and shoppers gathered around the tsar's bronze ship. Through the throngs, Dima could just make out the ground-level billboard that stretched the length of an entire wall. Five lifesize likenesses of his brother, progressing left to right: Yarik on his knees, draped in peasant's rags, bent double to pull a weed; Yarik crouched in coveralls and hard hat, reaching with a wrench, as if another's hand might pull him up; then he was standing, hunched over a clipboard, his foreman's windbreaker embroidered with SLAVA above his chest; and at last he stood unbent, straight shouldered in suit and tie, briefcase in hand, shiny black shoe lifted, as if to stride right past the building's edge. But he was blocked by one more image: his own silhouette, or any silhouette of any man, outlined in gold and filled with a mirror that reflected back whoever passed. Most who did stopped. They turned, walked close, fit themselves into the shape, who they were staring back from within the golden shimmer of who they might become.

Once, Dima had stood like that, his body encased in the outline of his brother's—his taped-together boots filling the space for Yarik's shoes, his ragged pants fluttering in a wind, his shirt so thin dark patches of hair showed through like bruises beneath etiolated skin, his shoulders shrunken too small for the silhouette, his tangle of beard too big, his face, in the hard late sun, a landscape so shadowed with hollows it seemed to him hardly a face at all, no more his than the faces of his brother peering out from the wall to watch him, this Slava's gleaming smile, his carefully coiffed hair. Only the eyes in their depths were Yarik's—and feeling them on him Dima had tugged his body loose of the silhouette, turned from his reflection, hurried away.

The first to go was the cooking gas. One evening he came home and found his mother at the stove holding a match to the burner. He watched the flame reach her fingers. She shook it out, dropped it on a cutting board, lit another. On the board there was a pile burned to blackened ropes.

By then, she shouldn't have been cooking, anyway. Her hands shook too much to chop; one day he would open the door to her wailing, the counter slick with blood. Twice this month she had forgotten to add liquid to the soup; he'd found the pot billowing smoke, cabbage sludgy in the bottom, a fire about to start.

After the gas was turned off, he made them supper. Usually it was cold—the edible leaves from a half-rotted cabbage, cheese with the mold sliced off, stale bread turned to crackers in the toaster—but sometimes he carried kindling out to the balcony. Ivan would flutter with fury at his invasion of the space. He'd wrestle the hood on the bird, tie it to the railing. He had traded away the couch, but he would set a pillow on the ground, lead his mother out by the hand. Her eyes would widen at the fire. "Oh!" she'd say, as if he'd given her a diamond. Sitting crosslegged on the concrete, they would watch it burn, its flame dim in the zerkala's glow.

"Is it the white nights?" his mother would ask.

"Yes," he'd tell her, though they had come and gone months ago.

He had been glad to see them wane. Back in summer, out on the balcony, waiting for the sun to set so he could slip the hood over the rooster's head, he'd watched the last of the natural light, the sanguine sheen lingering on the leaves of all the potted plants on all the

269

balconies, that faint color the closest they had come to flowering. No buds had ever formed, never a single bloom. All the long hour it had taken the redness to drain out of the clouds, he'd tried to imagine what had gone wrong inside them, tried to keep his thoughts away from that night on the other side of the solstice, to steel his mind against it, keep the pins from popping open beneath his fingers, from feeling the flick of her finger against his chest, her hand there, pressing. But as the nights grew longer, day's end realigning more and more with the mirrors' rise, the color leaching more quickly from the sky, the plants withering away in their pots, the weight on his chest had become less a feeling than the memory of one, then at last simply something that might have happened to another him, in another life. This one was so much simpler. Out on the balcony, in front of the fire, sitting beside his blanket-wrapped mother, beneath the perched and hooded bird, he was grateful. What could be better, after a week of cold salads and coagulated cheese, than the crackling of fish skin when he put it on the coals, the smell of its flesh cooking? What could sound more gratifying than the hums of pleasure his mother made as she picked clean the bones? "Good," she would say, looking up, her eyes crinkling. He would lean over and kiss her cheek, beneath his greasy lips the softness crinkling, too.

And if it rained, or sleeted, or simply was too cold, they would sit inside and listen to the radio. In the bare apartment it had taken on the feeling of furniture, and he would carry it, cord dragging behind, to whereever his mother was—the sewing machine, the bath—and tune it to the Rachmaninoff or Mussorgsky that she liked. Between every piece, advertisements blared. The last notes of *Lilacs* were trickling away, and Dima had reached out to turn the volume down, the first time Yarik's voice came on. His fingers stilled.

You know me, his brother said.

A salvaged pirozhki slipped off his mother's fork.

I'm your neighbor, your friend, your husband, your son.

His mother stared at the radio: "Yarishka!"

I used to be you.

270

"Your brother," she said.

Dima nodded, not wanting to cover any of the radio's sound.

Before I joined the team at the Oranzheria . . .

He shut his eyes, tried to strip the words away, to pare the voice down to just vibrations, to feel them on his face.

Next! The word seemed to break against him. The Consortium's theme song swelled.

Electricity was the next to go. The company warned him, but the letter seemed from such a distant entity, so far removed from what life had become, that Dima couldn't work up much worry. So long as they still had heat—the steam that had all his life run through the pipes of the entire building—they would be fine. Without lights they would simply go to bed when the sun set. They would rise with it. Without power the radio could no longer haunt them. He sold it. The toaster, too. Traded the plug-in clock. In Dyadya Avya's box he found a wind-up watch. That night, he turned the tiny knob with his thick fingers, listening to the sound of its spring tightening.

And in the morning, he carried the new electric samovar out to the bus. Back when his brother had brought it over, he'd taken his mother's old coal-burning one and traded it away at the Universitetski Rynok. Now, he waded through the crowds, searched for the same kiosk, the samovar propped against his chest, his thinned arms straining with the weight, until at last he saw the stall, hurried to set the samovar down.

"Hey!" The stallkeeper's voice was harsh as a gull's. "Take that off my table."

Hefting it again, he told her he wanted to trade it.

"A samovar?" She laughed, said she should have never taken his old one. "Just to get rid of it," she told him, "I had to throw it in for free with one of these."

On the long table of goods for sale sat some sort of white machines, larger than toasters, smaller than microwaves, cords hanging like limp tails.

"What are they?" he asked. And when she told him "bread machines" he stared. "For baking bread?" he said.

271

Modes for low heat and high, the stallkeeper told him, settings for half kilo loaves and full kilo ones. "This can even do two-thirds of a kilo." Round shapes, rectangular, baguettes, sweet cakes, keep-warm features, variable crust colors . . .

"You mean," Dima broke into the stream of her salespitch, "like an oven?"

She glared at him. "These do the baking *for* you. While you're at work. Which you'd understand if you weren't a bum."

He could feel the samovar reflecting the low sunlight onto his neck, his face. The edge of its base dug into his fingers.

"Get out of here," she spat, "before I throw a rock at you."

Carrying the samovar away, he heard her say beneath her breath, *Feed them once, they come back forever,* but he was thinking of long ago, when he was a child, of the early morning every week he had accompanied his mother and her baking kooperativ. Of how, before light, thirty or forty neighbors—parents, kids, the whole apartment block—would walk together down the still-dark street, passing among them thermoses of tea, steam rising as they drank. He was remembering the bread factory, its huge ovens, everyone stripping off their coats and rolling their sleeves, and the smell of the baking, and how, when it was done, they would cut the steaming loaves, everyone—his mother, her friends, the neighbors he called aunt and grandmother and grandfather—eating a slice right there, their eyes shutting for a second, faces flushed with the heat.

At home, each evening, he would take the toothbrush from his mother's shaking hand and squeeze the paste on for her, stand beside her at the bathroom sink brushing his own. A little longer, he would tell her, and, after, with a washcloth, wipe spittle from her chin. In her bedroom, she would give the mattress a pat. He would climb onto the comforter, lay back beside her, listen as she told him stories of his childhood. Sometimes, she confused Yarik and him. He let her. Sometimes she seemed to think they were still little. "Which one," she would say, "would you like tonight?" And he would shut his eyes, hear in her age-deepened voice, her "Zhili-Byli . . ." at the beginning of a tale, the sound of his papa from so long ago. In his own, his brother's boyish whisper, "One more."

Afterwards, every night, Dima would sit in the living room on the floor beside the phone and call.

The first time Zinaida had picked up.

"It's Dima," he said.

"Hi," she said.

"How are you?"

"He's not home," she told him.

The next time she heard his voice and hung up.

When they stopped answering at the time that he would call, he started calling an hour later, or in the morning, or as soon as he knew Yarik would return from work.

Sometimes he got Timofei. "It's your Dyadya Dima," he would say.

"It's Dyadya Dima!" the boy would shout. And the phone would go dead.

After a few times, he called and simply said, "Hello."

"Hello, Dyadya," the boy had said.

Dima had paused. "Who?"

He could hear the boy's breath come close to the phone. "I know it's you, Dyadya," Timofei whispered.

"Is your father at home?" Dima asked.

"Yes," the boy whispered.

"Put him on the phone."

"OK," the boy whispered.

He sat there, feeling his rib cage jerk with the convulsions of his heart. Until the line went dead.

Still, the night he picked up the receiver and heard no tone he panicked. He tore out to the hallway, knocked at his neighbors' doors. At each, he heard footsteps, saw dark spots where their shoes blocked the light, felt them peer at him through the small glassed hole, watched the light fill the crack of the door again, listened to their footsteps retreating. It was no different downstairs on the third floor at the Shopsins'.

Except that this time, when he saw the darkened patches beneath the door, he said, "Gennady!" The footsteps started away. "Do you still want the apartment?" They stopped. He heard them come back.

"Dmitry?" Gennady said, as if he hadn't already known. "Are you . . . ? Is she . . . ?"

"Can I use your phone?" Dima said.

"Is your mother . . . ?"

"I need to use your phone."

"To call the ambulance?" His voice sounded tight as Dima's.

"Yes," Dima said.

The clack of the bolt, the rattle of the chain.

Inside, the apartment seemed so full, the walls so covered, the rooms so cozy with furniture, the light of the lamps so warm, the whole place so much a home, that, following Gennady into the living room, Dima almost wished it was true, about his mother, if only so he could sit in the room and Gennady would bring him a glass of vodka and put on the tea, and he could lie down on the couch and lay his head on the cushion where Gennady's wife was sitting and nobody would tell him he couldn't. But she was already standing, smoothing her skirt, saying to Gennady, "Oh, now you're letting in the building's bum?"

"Masha!" Gennady tried to hush her.

"Why don't you ask him to bring his fucking rooster?"

"It's his mother." Gennady handed Dima the phone as he whispered to his wife. "She's dying."

They watched him dial. Four long rings. Someone picked up and he started to speak and whoever it was put their receiver down.

"They aren't there?" Dima heard Gennady say in one ear. In his other: the dial tone.

"What kind of a city do we live in?" Gennady was nearly shouting. "The ambulance—"

"Yes," Dima said to the dial tone. "I need an ambulance. My mother." He felt his eyes swell and knew he would cry if he didn't stop.

Gennady stared at him.

Into the phone, Dima whispered, "What if she *was*, Yarik?"

"What?" Gennady said. And then, coming close to Dima: "Three-eight-one-seven Avtovskaya Street, apartment number—" Dima hung up the phone. "You didn't tell them . . ."

"What are you worried about?" Dima said. "You don't *want* them to save her."

He was halfway to the door when he heard Gennady's wife shout, "Who did you call?"

Then there were footsteps thudding and Dima's arm was yanked backward and there was Gennady's face, furious. "She's not dying at all," Gennady said.

"No," Dima told him.

"Who did you call?" the man's wife shouted.

"Listen, you bum," Gennady said. "You fucking tramp. I should have climbed up to that fucking balcony months ago . . ."

"Who did you call?" his wife shouted.

". . . and tore the head off that fucking rooster. If we didn't have a deal . . ."

"Who—" his wife began again.

But Dima shouted back at her over the man's head, "The same person I'm going to call from here when I come back tomorrow."

"Oh," Gennady said. He breathed the word like he was clearing his lungs for all the worse words coming. "Oh," he breathed. "I'm going to fucking teach you a—"

"Or"—Dima jerked out of the man's grip—"when my mother does die, you sonofabitch, I won't sell you a single knob off a single door."

Back upstairs, he shut that door behind him and stood with his fingers still on that knob, looking at what he had done to his mother's place. The coatrack was gone, the bench beneath it gone. There were only the nails he'd banged into the hallway wall, the two coats hanging. In the kitchen: a greasy square on the wall where the stove had been before he'd sold it. The living room was carpetless but for the rugs hung over the windows. They were still rolled, mirror-light spreading over the emptiness: the bare sockets, their covers unscrewed and bartered; the broom leaning alone in the corner; the clothes his mother had stitched up piled on the floor. She was still working at the old foot-powered machine.

"Mama," he said.

She glanced at him, then back at her work, as if she didn't know he had been gone.

He watched her pick a skirt from the pile of ones he had reopened. Carefully, she squeezed its waist together, slid the two parts beneath the metal foot, lowered the needle, began to sew it closed again.

He rushed to her, then, yanked the skirt out of the machine, the thread stringing out with it and, grabbing his mother by her arms, dragged her up out of the chair and shouted into her close face, "Why are you doing this? Why are you doing this?"

Her eyes widened. She opened her mouth. "Who are you?" she screamed.

"Mama—"

"Who are you?"

His fingers slid off her arms and she jerked as if she meant to flee him, but he wrapped himself around her, pulled her to his chest, said into her hair, "It's Dima, Mama. It's Dima, it's OK."

He could feel the wetness of her mouth coming through his shirt. He held her tighter. Against his chest, she said something and he pulled away, looked down at her.

"Yarik?" she asked him.

"No," he told her. "I'm Dima."

"Where's Yarik?"

"He's at work."

"He should be home by now."

"Yes," he said.

"He comes home and I make him cabbage soup and we listen to 'Ochi chyornye.'"

"I know," he said. "But I'm home now, Mama. OK?" He held her face in his palm and kissed her forehead and said, "I'm home, Mama."

Around her eyes the skin was still red from her fright, but her eyes were calm. He watched them fill with something like happiness.

"Good evening, lyubimy," she said to him.

"Good evening, Mama," he said.

She sat back down at her machine, shook her head at the mess of the thread. She found her scissors and cut it and threaded the needle again and put the skirt back under the foot and began to sew. All the time he watched her. When the chattering of the needle had settled into its rhythm, he sank beside her, sat on the floor next to her chair, put his head in her lap, and could almost hear her ask, the way she used to when he was a boy, *What happened?* Beneath his head, her thigh rose and fell. Then stopped. He looked up at her. She was looking down at him. Her fingers stroked his hair.

"How was work?" she said.

She never left the flat. Had not for nearly six months now.

"Mama," he would ask her, "why don't you come with me to work today?"

They would be out on the balcony, Dima brushing away last night's ashes with his boot, his mother cocooned in the blanket he'd wrapped around her against the cold. "I have too much to do," she would tell him, or, "I'd just be in your way," or her hand would simply shove free of the blanket and grip the railing as if she thought he'd try to take her outside by force.

Once, he had. Carrying her down the stairs—back cramping, thighs shaking—and out onto the sidewalk. His arm around her shoulders, her arms hitched stiffly at her sides, they had watched the people pass.

"Why is everyone in such a rush?" she'd said.

He'd shrugged, asked her if she wanted to ride the trolley with them. She looked at him like he'd gone mad.

Sometimes he worried that she was. That the affliction from their father's death so many years ago, the derangement that had taken her from them for that long year when he and Yarik turned ten, was coming back.

The day her husband died, she had been at work. A secretary at the army base on the outskirts of the city—typing letters, scheduling meetings, making the country stronger in a thousand tiny ways: each envelope she sealed, each call she made, each movement part of the Party machine. How she had loved it. And how hard it must have been to know her husband couldn't, to understand the man she'd married had become a fisherman who brought home no fish, who spent his days alone on the ice, doing nothing, that the fact that she still loved him could bring her such shame. Such resentment. She had stopped asking her husband to come with her to community cinema nights at the base, went to dinners with officers alone, worked late solely so he would get home from his day doing nothing and find her still gone. The way she did the night she returned to his drowned body instead.

Climbing the last stairs, hearing the voices behind her apartment door, opening it onto a crowd of turning faces, she must have known some tragedy lay in wait, must have wondered, for a moment, worse than any other, *Who?*

They had lain the body out, wrapped it in towels soaked through and clinging to the shape of her husband's corpse. Beneath, the kitchen table buckled with lakewater weight. The floor gleamed from a mopping. She would have seen her husband's brother standing with the mop head in his hands. He was wringing it. In the light from the overhead bulb, the water was a sheen on his forearms. She would have seen her small sons, sitting on chairs, their eyes at the height of the crowd's hanging hands, their bandaged feet before them. She would have seen the place where the towel had slipped and fallen away: a small spot, no bigger than the palm of her hand, a hole so black it would have seemed as if the towels encased nothing more than an emptiness inside, until, slowly, she made out the pitch-black strands of his wet hair.

Dima could still remember the look on her face. Because, for the next weeks, it had refused to leave—lived on in her eyes, endured in the set of her mouth, abided even in the way she breathed—while all around it the rest of her face changed.

She went to bed that night and did not get out of it on her own again. Not to go to the funeral. Not to march from the old country church to the hole in the earth of the kolkhoz. She did not hear the goat-skin *volynka* play the funeral march, see the coffin carried past the neighboring farms. She did not hold her children while the casket was closed. She did not go to them that night when their uncle brought them home. In the morning, she did not go to work. She did not cook them breakfast, or pack them lunch, or make them supper after school. She did not ask them how their day had been. She did not speak. By the time the sanitarium sent its grim-eyed men, her hair had gone white, her skin shrunken on the bones of her face, her lips shriveled as if she'd aged a decade.

And Dima, not yet ten years old, nearly two dozen years ago, long before he ever imagined losing his brother, hadn't been able to understand. Now, watching a different kind of hole opening in her, Dima knew something he couldn't understand was happening again. More and more she was becoming like she'd been then: her refusal to ever leave the house, the times she seemed unable to even acknowledge him, even the manic sewing. One day, he took her machine away. The ceaseless chatter of the needle, the steady pumping of her foot; the way she went to it first thing in the morning, tying her robe around her; the way she was still there when he got back at night: it was all too close to how he remembered her, to the sanitarium from so many years ago, to the faint shaking he could still feel in the air amid the ceaseless stabbings of the workroom machines when he and Yarik would walk hand in hand down the hall to visit her in that small gray room with its drab padded walls, the black-barred windows, their mother motionless on the hard bed.

The first time he came home and found her with the box, he thought she was going to be all right. Thought it might even be useful, almost as if she were making a gift for him. Of course, it was really for the rooster. He leaned against the doorjamb and watched the two of them.

It was autumn, the coldest day yet, and his mother had brought Ivan in from the balcony, tied him to the hissing heater. On the floor, beside where she knelt, she had placed a box of soggy crackers, and while she worked she would pinch some of the meal, roll it into a ball, toss it to the Golden Phoenix. It would peck it off the rug, cluck at her.

She would cluck back. She did remarkable imitations of its sounds. She did it, he could tell, almost without knowing. All her attention was on the box.

A big cardboard box, overturned and empty of all but what she had put in it: a thin brown blanket folded to make a floor, a pillow from the long-gone couch become a bed. With her heron scissors she had cut a doorway in one side and a window in the other. Beside the entrance, she had written the word ZHUVOV, as if the rooster deserved their surname now that it would sleep inside their home. Which, that night, it did.

But when Dima came home the next day, she was working on the box again, lining its inside walls with gray-green wool cut from her old army secretary's coat. He had tried to pretend it could have been any color, tried to pretend the skin beneath his beard, around his jaw, over his throat, wasn't tightening.

That night Ivan ripped the lining apart and all the next day she had to reinstall it, and he had been able to go on pretending. But the next morning he saw what she'd drawn with marker on the pillow: black outlines of a turned-down sheet, of two small pillows at the head. And that night he came home to her constructing bars. They were black bobby pins that she had shoved into the cardboard windowsill. He watched her put the last ones in place. Then he knelt down and slowly, silently, pulled each back out.

WHAT HURTS

It was the end of October when their mother began refusing to get out of bed. The first morning Dima let her be, brought her eggs boiled over the balcony fire, sat at the foot of the mattress, eating from his own plate while she picked at hers. But when he came back at the end of the day, she was still there, sitting on the pillows the way he'd propped her up ten hours before, everything about her seeming asleep except her open eyes. All the next day he stayed home, trying to coax her onto her feet. He moved the kitchen table to the living room, in view of her doorway, poured glasses of steaming tea, set out plates of blini straight from the pan, each pancake filled with the last of the cheese. He sat there oohing and ahing over the smell, urging her to come try the way the wood smoke made the dumplings taste even better than the ones she used to make. "You don't believe me?" he said. She leaned over the bedside and spat.

He brought the rooster to the edge of her room, stood there stroking the soft feathers of its chest.

"Bring him to me," his mother said, scooping the air with her arm.

Instead, Dima turned and took the Golden Phoenix out of sight, stood just to the side of her door talking loud enough she couldn't help but hear. "I don't know why, Ivan," he said. "Maybe she just doesn't like you anymore."

By that night he had begun to worry something was wrong with her legs. When he pulled the covers off, her whole body—so small! so shrunken!—tightened at the cold, her hands flapping for her nightgown's hem. He wrapped his fingers around her feet, began to feel her bones.

"What are you doing?" she asked.

"Does this hurt?" He moved up to her ankles.

But she only repeated it—"What are you doing?"—more and more anxiously as, searching for something knotted or bruised, he probed the sagging muscles of her calves.

"Do you want to go to the hospital?" He said it as a threat. "Do you want to be locked in a room?" His hands working up the brittle bar of her shin. "Do you remember what that's like? Hm? Mama?"

All the while, her saying, over and over, "*Chto ti delaesh?*" until his fingers found the hollows around her knees and her hands flew from her nightgown, grabbed at his, and she cried out, "What are you doing, Dima?"

"Trying to see if you can stand!" he cried back.

And, just like that, the panic left her eyes. Her body relaxed. Her hands left his. He let go of her knees and watched as she slid out of bed and put her bare feet on the floor and stood. She smiled, as if she expected him to be pleased. Then she climbed back in the bed and reached down, drew up the cover, lay there again.

And again, the next morning, she refused to get out of bed.

"All right," he told her. "OK."

When he came back into her room he had thrown his winter coat over blue coveralls. He wore the yellow hard hat for the first time in half a year.

By the time the autobus came she had quit struggling, gone limp in his arms where he sat at the stop with her held on his lap, and by the time he was carrying her up the steps towards the driver, she had quit shouting at him, too. The sky was a heavy stillness of clouds dark and full as insects too gorged to move, and they rode beneath it, through the cacophony of shouts and horns, along streets kaleidoscoped with the colors of all the new cars roiling among the furious currents of the crowds, his mother's eyes growing wider and wider, her face more and more slack. Until, nearing the outskirts of Petroplavilsk, her face started to contract. He watched her brow bunch, followed her stare. And realized this was the first time that she'd seen it.

Out over the Oranzheria it had started to hail. As far as he could see, the pebbles of ice hit the glass, bounced, leapt. From that distance it looked like there was a line in the air a couple stories up from the ground where the hail decided to stop and dance.

He leaned towards his mother. "It's a greenhouse," he told her, close to her ear. "The largest in the world."

Then the hail swept towards the bus and the bus met it and there was a thundering on the metal roof so loud that, even bent so his cheek was next to hers, he couldn't hear what his mother said.

"What?" he shouted.

"Are we going there?" she asked.

"Yes."

"Is that where you work?"

"It's where Yarik works."

"Are we going to see Yarik?"

In the first quiet after they had gotten on the bus, after she had stopped struggling and he could sink back against the seat, he had let himself imagine maybe they would: Yarik would hear of them, or see them in the bus's window, or would just know. But it wouldn't matter; he wouldn't come. "No," Dima told his mother. She looked at him as if he had not answered anything, and he shouted, "Not Yarik."

The last word cracked loud over the suddenly quiet inside of the bus, the banging of the hail gone abruptly as it had started. In its place there was the distant muffled remnants of its thunder. Through the bus window, he could see the hail bouncing off the panes of glass above.

When he pulled the bell cord the driver glanced in his rearview, then kept driving, as if he had misheard. Dima tugged the cord again. As the bus slowed, he could feel all the laborers on it looking at him. The whole ride he'd been worried one of them would say something, come over, make a scene that would get his mother shouting again. Maybe it was because of her that they hadn't. Maybe it was the way his face in the last months had almost disappeared beneath his beard. But now one of the men in the seat behind them leaned forward.

"Where you trying to go, man?" he said, as if the one destination it couldn't be was the place where Dima had asked to stop.

When the bus pulled away, they stood looking through its dust across the road to what remained of the sanitarium. He hadn't expected much to be left—maybe the outlines of its foundation, maybe the two old lampposts that had stood sentry at the road, maybe nothing more than the feeling of the place hovering over a new-turned field. But there it was. Or at least the lower half of it. The entire cloister had been truncated five meters up. The top of the bell tower had been shaved off, the belly of the glass sky nearly brushing the old slate. At the corners of the garden wall, the turrets rose towards the sealed-off sky, their gray stone ending abruptly as the barrel of a gun. The building itself had been relieved of its entire roof, the whole second story gone. The old oaks that lined the drive had been de-canopied, flat-topped as a hedge.

And yet, they were still there. Ivy still crawled the walls. The tall windows had been freed of bars, but they still gazed out on the grounds as solemnly. There was a new coat of paint on the big double doors, but they were still black, still sat atop the wide stone steps, and Dima wondered how it would all affect his mother. After all, that was why he'd brought her. She who had not been back since her release two decades ago, who would not even pass by it to visit their father's grave, not even to see Dyadya Avya before he died. If anything could pull her mind away from where it seemed determined to go, it must be this.

She stood in the glass-muffled drumming of the hail, staring at it. On her face there was a faint film of dust from the autobus. She touched her fingers to the hollow of her old neck, left a small muddy smear. He was about to reach out, to steady her, when she took a step forward and started across the road. There, where the wall broke to let the driveway through, he could see the new sign: SPACE REGATTA CONSORTIUM, PETROPLAVILSK HEADQUARTERS, MANAGERIAL OFFICES OF THE ORANZHERIA DIVISION.

"Ma'am?" the guard said, stepping out to meet her.

"I'm going, I'm going." She brushed his hand off her shoulder, said, "I can find it myself," and kept on.

"It's OK?" Dima said, drawing up to the guard. He meant it as a statement but it came out a question.

"She can't go in there," the guard said.

"Look at her," Dima told him. She was walking faster than he'd seen her move all year.

"What sector do you work in?" the guard asked him.

"She's my mother."

"Why is she here?"

"She has to use the restroom."

"No, why did you get off here?"

"She's going to have an accident." Dima started after her. "We'll be right out."

He had to jog to reach her before she got to the steps. Helping her up them, he asked, "Are you going to be OK, Mama?"

"I know my way," she told him. "I wouldn't forget it in a million years."

"Are you all right?"

"Fine, fine," she said with the same irritation that the guard had stirred in her.

But, inside, Dima wasn't. At first he thought it was the stares: the foyer boomed with the footsteps of all the men and women crossing, heels clacking, doors whacking open, smacking shut. They threw glances at the big-bearded laborer, the old lady sweating beside him in her coat, at others rushing by as if to see if they would say something. Nobody did. Where there had been the nurses' desk vending machines now stood, the old green walls repainted yellow, hung with huge pictures—blowups of the zerkala line, Banner 1 to 1.5 all the way up to the 8 series satellites they were launching now—but it was the light in the place that felt most strange. Dima's neck craned back. Panes of pellucid glass. The frenzied battering of hail. There was no ceiling but the same that roofed the open fields outside.

When he looked down again, his mother was shuffling away through the rush around her. The hallway she entered was less crowded; he could feel the space opening around him as he followed her, as if he were growing smaller with each step. The wood floor was the same worn wood. The shoe racks outside the rooms the same brass racks. In the vast workspace the long tables of sewing machines were gone as the inmates who had worked at them all day, a maze of cubicles in their place, and as he went on behind her down the hall, he could hear the ceaseless chattering of keyboards, the paper whispering like cloth.

She stopped, turned, tried the handle of a door. Through the gap it opened, she disappeared. In the moment before he followed her inside, he reached for his brother's hand. His fingers floated in the empty air. Then he closed them and buried them inside his coat pocket and, with his other hand, shut the door behind him.

At the sound, she looked at him. "Where is everything?" she said. "Where has it all gone?"

In his pocket, his hand squeezed on itself.

It was an office, now. Cabinets where there had been a dresser. Desk where there had been a bed. Glass teacup on the blotter, emptied of all but the wet leaves clinging to its bottom.

"They would have changed things," he told her. "After you left."

She stood with her hand on the back of the desk chair, her wrist bent with her weight, her eyes showing the despair he'd feared.

Inside his coat pocket, his fingernails dug at his palm.

"Did you think you could come back?" he asked her. "Mama, is that what you want? To come back here?"

Her eyes told him.

"You can't," he said. "Even if you want to. Even if you want to so badly that all your hair turns black again. Even if you lie in bed for a year. You can't."

Slowly, carefully, walking both hands down to the arm of the chair, she lowered herself into it. "Why did I ever leave?"

"You got better," he told her.

But she only said, again, "Why did I leave?" and he could see in her face that she meant not what had allowed her to, but what had forced her to, what had pulled her back out of the safety of this place where she had once lived.

He took his fist out of his pocket, held it in his other. "Us," he told her. "Mama, you left for us."

Behind her was the desk, and behind the desk, the window. Its blinds were drawn. The only light in the room came from above, down through the ceiling, down through the pane of glass, faintly shaking to the rhythm of the hail.

HEAVEN'S BREAST

And the hail spilled down, a ceaseless clattering of pearls stripped off a broken string wrapped round and round the welkin neck, each one a whisper through the clouds, a multitude of last prayers mouthed, until the final stone slipped off the necklace end and down the breast of heaven and left the clouds all hushed. Such a heavy bank of them up there, thick, dark, unblown by any breeze. It covered all the city, the lake, the sea of glass. Above it, the sky grew dim, the stars swarmed, the mirrors rose.

But below, no one could see them. That night the city was be-dimmed nearly to darkness again, the zerkala mere inklings, more felt than visible, as if—like the frogs who used their over-melatonined glow of belly skin as an insect lure; like the evergreens that, burned by unsensed winter, resprouted side-buds—the denizens of Petroplavilsk had grown another sense innate as knowing when someone's eyes were turned on them. And that morning the sun stayed just as hid. The sky's blanket smothered it. All day the world seemed unable to climb out of the grayness preceding dawn. Out in the Oranzheria, the workers mumbled gratitude for the respite, rolled down their sleeves, splashed faces in irrigation water that already felt a little cooler. Even the crops sensed the shift, their leaves a little stiffer, their stalks enlivened with a freshness plants used to feel at the end of night. But by afternoon, their rustling seemed restive. The workers felt the cooling prickle their necks. Through its glass skin the Oranzheria slowly leaked its heat, the hail from the day before melting into a pool one centimeter deep and five thousand hectares wide, floating up in the sky, and beneath it the world was murky as the underwater world it had become, and no sun evaporated the pool, and that evening the sleet began to fall. It sheeted down in one incessant torrent, switching all night between a storm of ice and a flood of rain, and by the morning the collection tanks were creaking at capacity, the water ducts were overspilling, the gutters between the panels of glass mucked motionless with slush. Through it all, the glass clearers moved with plastic-edged shovels and rubber-tipped scrapers and wide push brooms, thousands of them side by side in lines like the peasant harvesters who, sickles synchronized, once filled fields centuries ago. But as fast as they cleared it, the sleet filled in their tracks.

And that was how it was till night. The shift changed, the weather kept on. The clouds remained. Above them, the mirrors ran their tracks through the stars, and the stars shone as they ever showed, and the new moon looked down with its dark face on the impenetrable blanket of clouds, and the next day it was the same. That switch, the zerkala shift didn't go home. Some went down from the glass to do the jobs they had been hired for, and some of the incoming workers went up to help those who had labored twelve hours trying to keep the ceiling clear, who stayed up there now to work a thirteenth, a fourteenth, on into the day. Up on the glass it was cold and wet, slippery work. Some of the laborers twisted ankles, slammed down on elbows, sprained wrists. With sleeves soaked, chests splashed, they worked on, even as their heads grew foggy, their eyes began to ache, their joints whispered through their marrow warnings of coming colds. Down below the glass, in the dimness that had persisted now for days, in the chill slowly seeping in to replace the leached-out warmth, the laborers heard harbingers of a different sort. They came in a language only the plants and animals seemed to understand: the long leaves of the mammoth corn began to curl; the wheat to slump, whole fields synchronized in the slow-motion act of falling over; seedlings in the midst of sprouting stopped, stayed half-hidden in soil cracks, paused like small animals trying to sense if it was safe to come out. The actual animals seemed to say no. The laborers could hear it in the sound of summer suddenly dwindling off: the crickets that sawed beneath the glass all year ceased. What the grown fields lost in sound, the new-plowed soil made up in movement: it writhed with all the worms that usually stayed buried beneath the sun-heated crust, that only came up after irrigation, but now rose out of the earth all at once. The birds that should have fallen upon them were too frenzied to notice, or at least to land: in the last hours they had decided—warblers, wagtails, whaups, all the ones that used to migrate and no longer did—that the time had come to start again, and from all across the thousands of hectares they came, flying south, a second cloud even more roiling than the sleet-shedding bank above, seething southward into the southern edge of the glass. There, the translucent wall shook with their thudding, the din of their panicked calls, the bodies piling up. All day the laborers worked in a frenzy near that of the birds, piling all the added jobs onto the ones they were meant to do, doing all their crack-voiced foremen told them to, and all the while struggling, even more than with the work, to keep an unfamiliar foreboding at bay.

Another shift switch, but there was no one to switch out. The Consortium sent word into the city. All those who could came: anyone who had worked on the glass before, who had been injured, who had been let go, some who had never even glimpsed the Oranzheria until that evening, teenagers cutting out early from school, dockworkers in the middle of sleep between their shifts, shop owners shutting their doors, people too old to go out in such weather. They flooded in under the glass or scrambled on top, joined the workers who had already been there a day and a night and a day and more, trying to outlast the clouds.

Towards dawn the sleet finally stopped. The laborers on the roof were too tired to cheer. They stood still, shovels and scrapers in their hands, looking up at the sky. Now they could hear the sounds going on in the world beneath their feet: the shouts of the foremen, the roar of the added machines; some felt the glass shiver at the thudding of the birds.

And as the clouds cleared the cold came. The youngest workers felt their smooth faces tauten, a chill on the surface of their eyes that they had never felt before, and remembered back to a winter when they were fourteen or thirteen or twelve and thought *every few years it must happen like this*. Most of the men and women with parents old enough to tell them stories of a cold snap come half a century before—Kosygin in the Kremlin, the Americans on the moon—felt their nostrils sting and their mustaches sharpen to pins and the small crackling whenever they blinked, and started to get scared. Those old enough to remember that day in 1969 themselves, when in a few short hours the tail end of fall pitched straight into a chasm of midwinter cold, dropped their tools, found the nearest hatch, got the hell off the glass.

The teenagers were right: every few years a cold front sprang on some fall night, drove the thermometer down fast enough to freeze drunks stumbling home after dark. And once a decade it even happened during the day. But only every half-century or so did the mercury plummet like this, like a nail slammed down by a hammer blow, so low that drivers, getting out to check unwilling engines, froze their hands to the metal fast as hood ornaments; one had lost three fingers trying to tear free; others didn't and died with faces frozen to the grille. Geese fell from the sky, so frozen by the time they hit the ground that their legs simply shattered, small black icicles tipped with frozen bulbs of red, skittering down the frost-white streets. The lake ice set so fast that fishing nets froze halfway hauled up, water captured midseethe, carved by the last churns of fish. Some hundred boats were stranded. Half their crews died before they could think what to do, the other half set their crafts on fire. They stood around them close as they dared, the backs of their heads, necks, calves, freezing anyway. Some of the boats burned hot enough they melted through and sank. Some just burned out. A wide flat plain of ice, and way out on it all those scattered fires burning, and sometimes a tiny dark figure running for the shore, running, running, until it went still.

Of course, those were just stories. That's what the managers and foremen shouted at the old people as they climbed off the glass and down into the warmer air inside the Oranzheria. In there, the ground crews didn't know how cold it was getting outside. They had begun to celebrate. The ones who had just joined up that night were first, followed by the ones who had been working for almost thirty hours, who took with them the rest. Men kissing women workers; women dragging them to dance; others just collapsing, flopping down, splayed, as if to make a thousand angel shapes out of the soft plowed dirt.

The ground-level managers tried to get them back to work, but even some of the foremen shouted that their crews deserved a few minutes' rest. And that was before the workers from up on the glass started pouring down. The glass-level managers had passed out vodka to their foremen for keeping their teams' bellies warm, and when the sleet had stopped and clouds had started breaking, some of the foremen had unscrewed the tops, handed their bottles around. Some of the crews had refused to give them back, and the foremen who had hung on to theirs were mobbed by men and women half-dead with exhaustion and fevered with relief. For a few moments the ground seemed a mirror of what was happening above—two festivals wild with the same roistering crowd—and then the word went around atop the glass, the stories the old people knew, and suddenly it seemed even colder, and they broke into a stampede for the ladders and stairs and any way down. And as they poured in off the glass, unzipping parkas, flinging off hats, diving in to join the thousands below, the two plains of people met with a sound louder than all the rumbles of all the machines, their voices filling the Oranzheria with a single roar.

That was what brought Dima to a stop. Through the quiet of the buffering woods—no traffic, still trees, Dima standing in the middle of the street—the noise from up ahead surged like floodwater down the funnel of the road. A riot? Some kind of mob? He wondered, again, whether he should have come at all.

That morning he had woken to a pounding on his apartment door: Gennady bringing him the news; he was going to try to drive out to the Oranzheria, did Dima want to come along? *Just for the night,* the man had said. *They're desperate. They'll take anyone.* Dima shook his head, told him thanks, meant to shut the door. But he couldn't. When was the last time someone had visited him? When was the last time he had visited someone? Gennady stood peering at him, atwitch with urgency, shaking his car keys in his hand. *Do you want to come in?* Dima asked. The jangling stopped. The man stared. Then turned and was gone, his footsteps fading.

Back inside, Dima pulled an unrolled carpet open a crack. Outside the window, it was still strangely nightlike, dark as he had seen it since the mirrors had gone up. The sleet still hammered at the pane. His own voice said it then—*Just for the night*—and even as he shook his head, his mind was calculating the pay for one twelve-hour shift. He let the rug slap closed, went back to his room, got back in bed. *They'll take anyone.* If he worked one night would they offer to keep him on? Would they let him work in his brother's section? Eat his lunch in Yarik's office? Would Yarik sometimes bring his tea out to sit in the grass with him? He tried to sleep.

Sometime later the battering at the windows stopped. Through the small holes in the kovyor, a faint gray light spiked across the room, landed on his blanket and seemed to go right through, to touch his skin like the tips of icicles. His face felt just as cold. Shucking the blanket, he rose into a wall of frigid air. He could not see through the window; it was opaque with ice. He thought of Gennady's hand, shaking—*they're desperate*—the man standing in the hallway in the middle of the night, about to drive out in the middle of a storm. Everyone who worked on the Oranzheria, Dima realized, must have gone out there, too. Everyone. *Rattle, rattle, rattle,* went the keys.

He dressed in every warm thing he had: two pairs of long underwear, two of wool socks, a pair of wool army pants, and then a second pair, a turtleneck shirt, a high-collared sweater, and a low collared one on top of that. His legs rubbed at each other when he shambled to his bed, yanked all the blankets off, and dragged them into his mother's room. He lay them over the pile already on her sleeping lump. Then he went out to the foyer to get her a hat. On his way back, he heard the rattling again, louder, closer: there at his feet, Ivan's box shook. He crouched down. Inside: a pile of gold feathers shivering. He put on his mother's *shapka*, grabbed her heavy coat off its hook, and carried it and the box back to her room. She slept on, even as he nestled the fur hat over her head, as he opened her drawer and took out her sweaters, even as he wrestled them one after the other onto the bird, and stuffed the bird back in the box, and draped the coat over it, and went out and shut the door.

In the hallway, he struggled into his old Oranzheria rain-suit. The waterproof pants barely fit over his padded legs, the windproof jacket over his long wool coat. He wrapped a scarf around his neck and zipped the jacket up and wrapped another over his face and shoved a wool hat down on his head, added a second, lifted his hard hat off the hook it hung on, took the utility goggles out from under it, put those on, too. He had just sat down to pull on his boots when he thought he heard his mother. He stilled, listened. Nothing. Nor from outside: no bus rumble, no clatter of trams, not even the sound of a single car. He sat there thinking. Then he got up, grabbed his rucksack, threw his boots in, zipped it shut, and stepped to the hook beside the hard hat. There, his old ice skates dangled by their laces. He slid them off.

That dawn, he skated the streets of the city, their slush-stuccoed macadam frozen to a glaze, the avenues and boulevards become canals, their icy backs beginning to reflect the brightening of the sky. Through the thinning clouds the last of the mirrors glowed like ship lights in a fog. He passed parked cars hunkered under shells of ice; a square-nosed little Lada stranded in the street, its cab light on and door open and driver disappeared; a gas tanker jackknifed across the road. He swooped around it. In the middle of the avenues, trolleys sat their tracks, some with their windows still aglow, too opaque with ice to see anything but the stillness inside. The tracks were varnished with flash-frozen sleet, the wires above them glassy, sagging; some had snapped, and around the city their sparking lit up pieces of Petroplavilsk like signal flares. He skated north, the rough ice rattling his shins, his spine shaking, but the speed smoothing it out as he hurtled towards the edge of town, a dark bundled shape, scarf whipping behind him with his wind.

Now, stopped, his breath steaming from his wool-wrapped mouth, he stood watching the clouds clear over the Oranzheria. They were dark and thick as a forest floating above where one once stood, heavy as if filled with the souls of all the woods sawed down to make way for the glass, the barns razed, the bulldozed izbas, the dust risen up from all their falling, boiling away, blowing westward, as if in that direction their passage to heaven lay, and beneath them the glass reflected the boiling back, blanched with the brightening sky, the city's second horizon thickened with ice so it seemed the two halves of the world had slipped a little farther apart. He unzipped his rucksack, switched his skates for boots. And maybe it was the slowness of his feet, their drag on his speed-accustomed bones, the coming down of his muscles from their flirtation with flight. It might have been the thunder of all the voices trapped inside the glass, the way it burst upon him when he entered the Oranzheria. The heat of them, the thousands of bodies, his face beading with sudden sweat. Maybe it was their milling, the whole crowd riled, the riling building towards a burst, the chants of *No! No!*, yelling he caught coming through it in shards: *Go up? Shovel clear? In cold like this? In just our coats?* Or maybe it was simply the bodies of the birds, that his first thought was of all the meat, that he should stuff his pockets full; or that his second was of Ivan swaddled in his mother's sweaters, buried beneath her coat; or that his third was this: he wished one of those glass-smacking birds had managed to crash through, that others had followed, all along the half a hundred kilometers of the southward wall, first cracks and chips and a few shards falling and then the whole thing bursting, a thousand birds of every color exploding outward, their wings flashing in first sunlight, all around them flecks of glass flickering through the air.

Because the sun was up. All along the eastern horizon it had split the clouds. From inside the Oranzheria the ceiling was wavery beneath its coat of roseatted ice, and as the color filtered down it dissipated like blood in water, blushing the tops of the walls, the whites on the still-circling birds, barely a breath of pink on the rungs of the winding stairs, dissolved to nothing by the time it reached the throng in tumult below, reached Dima's face tilted up and gazing. He climbed into it, out of the noise, out of the anger, the redness rising on him as he rose towards the glass.

At first the quieting was so slight that those who stood around the ones gone silent didn't even notice. But gradually others went silent, too. The ones still shouting heard their own voices in their ears, and paused. A lull. Strange quietude. Here, a man with his neck craned back, easing a hard hat from his head, his Adam's apple shifting. Here, a woman, her eyes rolled upward, lips drifting apart. A manager unbuttoning the collar at his throat. A cluster of foremen pointing. A thousand faces peering up.

Up there, on the ice-sheened surface of the glass, someone was skating. They could see the dark lines his blades made. Two pen tips inscribing long arcs in the ceiling, curves and curls and loops, as if some giant of the old fables—some Koshchei or Norka—had reached down to scrawl his sign into the man-made sky. It was a rippled sky now, warped as old window glass, and the ice on it obscured the clouds into just the idea of clouds, shifting and floating, more color than shape, and through them floated the dark shape of the skater. At times the sunlight hit his tracks and they flared brilliant behind him. At times it hit him and he lit up fulvous, his clothes turned tawny, the fuzz of his wool scarf and hat seeming for a moment to glow. There he swirls, catching the sun's gold, the lines of his skates unfurling around him like the long sickle feathers of some fairy-tale bird.

What must it have been like to clamber up and join him? What must it have felt like to rush for the stairs, to pound up them with all the pounding feet of all the others, to push open the ceiling hatches and burst up into the cold and light in such a gusting of steam? And to watch the others bursting up all over the glass, a plain of geysers as far as you could see? To feel the ceiling shake with all their weight? To launch into a slide, boot soles slipping, arms flung out, face red with whooping? What must it have looked like to the managers below? Were they furious or scared? Did a shiver run through them as they stood in the darkling shade of the roiling shadows thrown down by all those madly cavorting souls?

One whole sector went. Simply caved in. There were the frolicking revelers, the jubilant crowd, the swirl in its center that all at once stopped. A first few gone still. And the stillness spreading to those around them, struck faces passing mute understanding, rippling fear, a wave of horror that in one panicked rush came crashing down on the surface of the great glass sea. There came a crack like bedrock splitting in a quake. Then the screams.

Watching at home on their televisions, or on the screens in the displays at the Universitetsky Rynok, standing frozen on the street, staring through first-floor windows at strangers' TVs, the people of Petroplavilsk heard the reporter say *Oh no*. A news station had sent a helicopter over the scene just as the glass collapsed, and all that day they showed the video: the stampeding thousands, the darkness blooming in their midst, sudden as a sinkhole, guttling them in, and then the whole surface going down. *No*, the reporter said, *no!*

Another station got footage from the ground—jags of glass jutting through bodies like monstrous teeth—and they played it over and over the next day and the next. But what most people watched had come earlier, captured in a shaking frame by one of the first who had climbed up: the fuming hatch, obscuring steam, a flash of metal, first glimpse of the skater on the glass, a gliding apparition so wrapped in layers and smothered in scarves and masked by goggles that it looked almost inhuman—except for its motion; there was something familiar in its ebulient glascading, in the near-weightlessness of its shape swooping by, that for those few minutes seemed to embody all that people felt they had lost.

That was what most people watched—leaning together over tables at supper, or alone in apartments silent but for the scrape of skates— and that was what everyone else blamed for what happened next.

The cold spike stabbed short and fast, left Petroplavilsk laid out under ice, palsied by downed power lines, but by the following day the weather had withdrawn, fast as it came, the city waking to a frigidity no worse than the common rawness of early winter. The sun returned, the streets were cleared, the buses began to run. And yet the laborers on the Oranzheria did not go back to work. The strike started with barely a hundred, a small crowd lining the road up to the greenhouse entrance, all stirred by something they couldn't fully explain, didn't understand any more than this: they didn't want to go back in.

Some were still wearing bandages, others knew ones who had died, all had witnessed the crawling injured, helped drag out the too badly crushed, been given, on the day of the collapse, the rest of the day off. Buried in bed for more straight sleep than they had had in weeks, or curled beneath blankets with their wives, nothing more pressing than how to keep their children entertained, something had seeped into their bones: memories of a time when there had been two days off in a row, two again a week later; a time when there were only a bare few things to eat but their families had spent hours, whole evenings, cooking together, eating together late into the night; a time when apartments were crowded and cramped but all the doors were open to all the other apartments' open doors; when there was always someone visiting or inviting a visitor in; when there were no ready-made cakes in the corner stores, but if you smelled a baking *kulich,* you knew that each family in every apartment on that floor would come together that night, sharing small slices, drinking tea from the samovar until one in the morning, or two, or three. . . .

And all along the southern wall of glass, the laborers inside paused, their shovels stuck in the heaps of dead birds. The workers on top of the Oranzheria quit the repairs they had begun, came to the edge instead, looked down. Some raised their hands in solidarity, some shouted calls of support; one reached up and—Did he know what he was doing? Was he only preparing to go back to work?—slipped his safety goggles on and pressed them to his face. Outside the Oranzheria, one of the strikers did the same. For a moment, the two looked at each other through their goggles and the looks on their faces said that if they hadn't known what they were doing, they knew it now. One by one, the others up on the glass began lowering goggles over their eyes while, on the ground, as if in a reflection, worker after worker did the same. Outside, all in the crowd who had brought goggles put them on, the gathering thickening with those fresh off the buses, growing with others leaving the Oranzheria, workers leaking out like heat drawn to cold, until, by evening, the throng outside was over a thousand strong.

By the next day, it had tripled. They gathered down by the lake, overflowing the statue's square, flooding out onto the esplanade, filling Kuibysheva Prospect, a legion of laborers bundled in winter parkas and knit hats, long wool coats and huge fur shapkas. The few who still owned ice skates hung them around their necks, blades flashing at their chests. Nearly everyone was wrapped in a scarf. And all who had a pair of safety goggles wore them; some brought a second pair for wives or children or strangers: thousands of be-goggled faces moving en masse up Onezhskoi Flotili Street towards the erstwhile parade grounds of Space Regata Square.

The goateed, stone-browed statue had long since been torn down. But even had it been there, there was no leader to scramble up the revolutionary's back, cling to his pate, cry out above the crowd. Instead, the square reverberated with cacophonous voices in disarray. Over by the locked post office doors some stood atop the mail collection boxes, others clinging to the flagpole, a mob below shouting for better safety procedures, more time off. Amassed across the Kosha Bridge, another cluster bellowed about overtime pay. In the center

of the crowd, around the bronze model of a space mirror that had
replaced the disgraced Vladimir, the Communists gathered, chests stiff
with medals, Red Army hats on their heads, a knot of old pensioners
half-smothered in the moth-eaten, water-stained banner they unfurled.
Power to the proletariat! they shouted, and shook the crimson cloth.
Strength in our collective struggle! They raised it above their heads.
Until a rabble of shaved-skulled goons waded in with boots and bottles
and roars for a return of the tsar. Above it all the loudspeakers mounted
on onetime lampposts blared out a voice boomed from some cavernous
chest: *The day has come! The day we've chosen! The day we choose
to take back time!* Each phrase followed by another voice howling
affirmation: *Fuck yes!* Or *Fucking right!* Or *Fucking zerkala!* The big
voice bellowed: *What we must do! What we* will *do!* And between
the shouted slogans there thundered down long disquisitions on the
senselessness of work, and between the disquisitions the lamppost
speakers played a crackly recording:

> *I was once there: I drank of mead;*
> *I saw the green oak by the sea;*
> *I sat beneath it, while the cat,*
> *that learned cat, told me his tales . . .*

Someone had hacked the advertising screens that flickered from rooftops around the square, and in the place of glossy lips and silvery
sedans there now loomed the image of a bearded man: perched on
the plinth of Peter the Great, or flat on a rooftop pointing a pistol at
the sky, or dancing across the Oranzheria on skates.

Among the multitudes below, the wondering ran like a thread
through all the strike's disparate swatches—the slight reciter's frame,
the skater's thick-bundled body, the black beard that might be hidden
beneath the scarf, the eyes behind the shooter's goggles, whether the
goggles were even the same—all waiting to see if someone would step
forward, pick up the needle, draw tight the stitches, knot the thread.

But no one watched for him here, in the lobby of the old train station, standing in the ticket line, no goggles or scarf of padding beneath

his coat, just his fingers worrying his knuckles, his teeth chewing at the beard hairs below his lip, his blue eyes trying to catch the cashier's glance. On her window, a posting declared her break times, and as the clock ticked towards the next, the line began to thin—the customers behind him breaking away first, and then the ones in front—and re-make itself before another window where another sheet signaled a new cashier would soon sit down. He stood in the ghost of the line, still the same half-dozen steps back, nobody before him but the last customer complaining at the window, nobody behind him but the people giv-ing him stares as they passed by. From outside, down Space Regata Prospect, the scending din of the demonstrations pressed through the lobby's walls, pulsed in the air.

And then the customer was done and there was nothing but the ticket window glass between Dima and his sister-in-law. For a moment, Zinaida's stare contained the shock of all that had happened since she'd last seen him. Then he stepped forward, and her face recovered the blank bored annoyance that was the mien of her profession. She looked away, pointed to the work-break sign, scribbled at some last bit of business, gathered up her papers, and left. He stared at the empty window. Around him people had begun to whisper. The roar of the distant protests washed up against their sound. In the slot where money and tickets were exchanged she'd left a scrap of paper. He turned it over. *Track 1, go right, last door.*

Near the end of the platform, Zinaida was waiting, her blond hair and her uniform and a cigarette's smoke lit up in the half-open door. He'd never seen her smoke and thought the cigarette was to make her look like any cashier on break, but once she'd waved him inside and shut the door to the dim hallway she brought it to her lips and took a draw.

"Is he OK?" Dima said.

The smoke she exhaled shook.

"Was he hurt?"

And she reached out and pressed her palm against his cheek. "We didn't know what to think," she said.

301

"Was he there?" he asked her. "The collapse? Zina, was Yarik—"

"I came by the apartment," she told him. "After I saw the news. We didn't know, we didn't have any way of knowing, we couldn't tell if you were still up there when . . ."

"He came, too?"

She took her hand away.

"To Mama's apartment?"

"Dima."

"Tell him—"

"Dima. You can't go around like this."

"Like what?"

She swept the cigarette between them, as if to indicate all of him.

"I didn't do it," he told her.

"But it was you? Up there?"

"I didn't—"

"I know," she said. "But they want you to do something now."

"Who?"

And she swept the cigarette at the shut door, the outside, as if to indicate everyone else. "Haven't you watched the news?"

He had tried. After he'd made it home, made sure his mother was OK, he'd gone straight to Gennady's apartment, banged on the door. Through it, he could barely hear the breathy reports from the scene of the collapse, even kneeling with his ear to the crack above the floor, couldn't make out any word of his brother. He'd run back downstairs, out onto the street, into a blini shop filled with the blare of its TV, but the reporters gave no names, and when people had begun to stare, he had left, gone to Yarik's building, stood in the stairwell, torn between worry about what might have happened to his brother beneath the broken glass and what might happen if he broke his promise and went up.

"Where is he?" Dima asked Zinaida now.

She ashed her cigarette. "Follow me," she said.

But the bathroom she led him into was empty and cramped, a single stall. She told him to stay, went out, shut the door. He listened to the sounds of her disappearing down the hall. The one window had been painted opaque and the room was dim. He left the light off. When she came back, she slapped it on. She was carrying a janitor's bucket. Inside it, a large bottle of laundry detergent. In her other hand, one of bleach. While she pulled on a pair of rubber gloves she explained to him what they were going to do. Then she shut her eyes, and Dima knew she was explaining it to God, or asking him if it was right, and when she opened them they held a certainty as if she had heard back.

He watched her mix the soap and bleach into a thick goop in the bottom of the bucket. "Can I see him?" Dima asked.

"Close your eyes," she said.

"Can I—"

"And your mouth."

Sitting on the toilet lid, his eyes shut, breathing through his nose, he felt her massage the mixture over his head. Her fingers, inside the rubber of the gloves, felt strange, good. She worked the bleach into each long strand, each clod of curl at his neck, the unwashed tangles clumped over his scalp, and when she moved in front of him, as she pulled the paste through his greasy bangs, it occurred to him that she hadn't touched him this much in all the past year. No one had. Except, maybe, his mother. And, one night last summer, the fleeting pressure of another's hand on his chest, a few warm breaths that had brushed his neck. A tingling. A prickling over his scalp. The strange scraping of the comb's teeth as she dragged it through his hair. Slowly she worked his tangles loose. How close her body was to his. He could feel her warmth. His sister-in-law. He missed his niece, his nephew. He wondered if this was what his brother felt beneath his wife's touch, this soothing calm, these fingertips on his skin, the heat of her on his face.

GOOD PEOPLE

This was not how Yarik had imagined flying. He'd always thought the first time he left the ground his fingers would be entwined with Zina's, that he would feel her slight squeeze. On their first plane trip the family would take up a row, Timosha between the two of them, Polya traded back and forth on their laps. They had even begun to save up sick days for it: a week's vacation a year from now. To the Black Sea. They had found a resort in Sochi. It had its own beach with lounge chairs and palm trees; he and Zina had leaned close to the computer screen, seen the mountains rising up behind the high-rise hotel. Another night, Zina on his lap while the two of them reread every page of the site, they had discovered the palm trees were fake. Who cared? They were palm trees. *With plastic coconuts,* Zina said, and pretended to drop one on his head. *Bonk!* she said. Timosha heard their laughing. They hoisted him up to see. He didn't seem to care about the palm trees, but when he heard they'd fly there in a plane he went completely still. His eyes locked on the wall somewhere above the computer screen. Yarik bent over him, gave his head a shake, said, *Breathe, Timosha, breathe.* And, as if bursting with air, the boy had leapt off Yarik's lap, gone racing around the room, arms stiff wings, lips revving wet burbling, as if he thought airplanes moved by passing gas. That was how it had been the past month. To the Black Sea. If Yarik thought of it like that it seemed like a command, something simply bound to happen.

Now he knew it wouldn't. Up in the cockpit, the pilot was talking to him, explaining the controls while they waited to take off. Yarik nodded. It was a four-seater, not counting the cockpit—the upholstery leather, the little bar stocked with labels Yarik could never afford, the carpet stamped with the logo of the Consortium—but the two of them were the only ones in the plane.

He looked out his window as they started to roll. It was a small airport—not like the one in St. Petersburg that he and Zina and the kids would have taken the sleeper train to—and he watched the other small planes. They seemed somehow less capable of bringing four human beings up into the air. He told himself that made no sense—how much heavier were those giant jets?—and then he thought, *Four people?* and there was his family in the other three seats, and he quit looking out the window and took a drink. It was whiskey, or basically whiskey, the pilot had said. Yarik had sounded out the American words on the label: *Buffalo Trace* and *Bourbon* and *Kentucky*. He shook the glass to make the ice clink, but the engines were suddenly too loud, the earth tearing by beneath him, the seat back pushing at his shoulders, the ground blurring into something less solid, and then it wasn't.

The air took over, the plane lurched, as if grabbed beneath its wings and lifted—and the one thing he'd least expected hit him: a sense of having felt that before. On his wrist the clamp of his uncle's huge calloused hand, the yank on the pit of his arm, his bare feet banging at the dirt as he ran around and around and then his heels lifting, his toes scraping, his body flying up. He could see Dyadya Avya leaning back, shirt off, belly huge, the bulging tendons of his thick neck, crimson face laughing. He could hear the laugh. He could hear his own, his brother's beside him. Around their uncle they had flown, Dyadya Avya turning circles fast, holding each of them in a fist, crying out,

305

I am your magic carpet and I will take you wherever you want to go! They would shout, *To the sun's sister!* or, *To the witch's hut!* and when they hit on one he liked he would open his hands and let them fly. Jouncing and skidding in the grass, they'd crash together, rolling, coming to rest in a heap, their uncle dropping to the ground beside them, starting, through his gusts of breath, to tell them a tale: *There once was a merchant who had two sons, and each night before they fell asleep he bade them to remember their dreams . . .*

When Yarik opened his eyes, the earth was far below. He took another drink, checked his seat belt. The roar of the engine, the shaking plane. They had taken off pointed north, beyond the Oranzheria, where old forests and a few struggling farms still remained, and he could see they were circling around now towards the south and the lake and somewhere beyond it the Volga and beyond that he didn't want to think. Below them there stretched the great glass sea. It collared the city on every side except Otseva's and it was so vast it had become a twin to the lake, a matching geographical wonder, glistening in the sun. Amid the two, Petroplavilsk looked small and dark as an arrow hole poked through the gleaming steel of some Rus knight's burnished shield. But there was a real hole now: the tiny shadow of the plane slipped across the glass towards it—a jagged crater that had opened in the Oranzheria's skin.

For the past three days he'd been out there, struggling to keep his crew together, to convince them to stay on the job, filling in whenever another walked off, wearing the same clothes, eating in the cafeteria trailers, collapsing on the couch outside his office any few minutes he could find to nod off. And every time he shut his eyes he saw his brother: Dima from below, all skate-blades and billowing coat; Dima with his scarf-wrapped beard and goggled eyes; Dima in the Web video someone had spliced together with the one from before. Thank God it was so hard to see his brother's face.

The plane was somewhere over Lake Otseva: the boats, the surface stirred around them as they unfurled their nets, a flock of seagulls swirling, white specks tiny as spilled salt. Along its shores, the forests

306

were a map of how many seasons the land had lived beneath the mirrors' light: the dead woods closest to the city giving way to evergreens malformed by winterburn, then broad-leafed canopies brown with undropped leaves, until, beyond the border of the artificial light, the forest floor reclaimed its natural calico of freshly fallen reds and golds. But his eyes were drawn back to the brown, to one small flame of color blazing there. Somehow, in all the land the zerkala had claimed, a single birch survived. He'd heard the rumors: that out of all the millions there might be one or two, aberrant among their species, born unable to sense the length of the night, the shortening days, that had adapted solely to reading warm and cold, that through this glitch in their genes had managed to even thrive. Far below, the ground around the birch was a lone burst of brightness, a patch of new-shed yellow leaves, surrounded by a sea of browned and rotting canopies.

He watched it out his window, leaning close, until it was gone. He wondered how far out lay Nizhi. If they were going to fly over it. If he would even know it if they did. He still had never seen more than that one distant glimpse, his brother beside him on the skiff, so long ago. But he thought he would feel it. He watched the water, the dark green islands slipping by, and waited for the pull. Surely he would be able to make out that huge wooden church, the surrounding walls of the pogost. Remembering his uncle's tales, he almost expected to see chimney smoke, tiny black flecks of monks moving in the fields.

He wondered how long ago it had been abandoned—the lures of life on the mainland, the church embraced again—how long ago the ferry had made its last journey out from Petroplavilsk. That was a trip he would have liked to take. That was what people used to mean when they said the word, when a vacation meant crowding onto a packed deck for a half-day's drift down the lake to see the loggers' festival; when a trip meant a railway carriage packed with bunk beds, bustling with passengers unrolling mattresses, flapping out sheets, calling for tea, slapping by in flip-flops and sweat suits and scents of sausage, and he and Dima sharing a top berth so near the ceiling they couldn't sit, so narrow they barely fit lying side by side for hours, gazing out at the world flicking by; a time when just *that* would have been trip enough to make them happy—their parents, Dima, him. For nearly nothing they had gone away—to a spa village, a summer festival—at least a month of every year.

Had he ever played that flying carpet game with Timofei? When he got home, he was going to take his son out to the playground, he was going to . . . With his lips he made the sound Timofei made when he was being a jet taking off. Then he thought, *If* he got home, and stopped.

The whiskey, or bourbon, or whatever it was, had blanched, the ice cubes all melted into it. He set it down on the empty seat next to him, leaned back. But his eyes refused to shut.

"Good people are kind and merciful," Bazarov said, taking out the gun, "but they rarely succeed in life. It's bad people who succeed, and they are rarely kind and merciful." His eyes creased a little; he showed his teeth. "Chernitsky said that." Flipping the pistol so he held it by the muzzle, he handed it across the seat to Yarik. "These people you're going to meet," he said, "are very successful people."

They were on a wide highway, heading into Moscow. Half an hour earlier, Bazarov had picked him up at the airport in a black Mercedes—in *two* black Mercedes: a tint-windowed SUV idling heavily and, in front of it, a sedan with silver piping that flashed bright as the oligarch's eyes when he opened the door, stepped out, pulled Yarik into a handshake. It had been raining; the driver had held an umbrella big enough to cover them both. Now the man was doing his other job, tearing past traffic already faster than Yarik had ever seen, slewing into spaces that seemed to open only once they were already in them, the SUV bulling along behind.

Yarik felt a swerve pull at all the soft parts of him, belly to throat to cheeks. Somehow, Bazarov's hand stayed unswayed where he held it out, the pistol butt jutting dark against the dark leather of the seat, the crosshatches rubbed bright: an automatic, Yarik could guess that much, some small deadly thing well used.

"Or maybe," Bazarov said, "you'd rather use the one you brought?" His eyes creased a little more; he tipped his head towards the satchel at Yarik's feet.

Yarik had bought the bag secondhand just for the trip. In it, at the bottom, beneath his clothes, a black dress sock stretched around the shape of his uncle's ancient gun. Now, hands rustling in the bottom of the bag, he tried to peel the sock up the handle, shove it over the trigger and off before Bazarov could see the foolish disguise. But his fingers had gone weak. At the edge of his eye he saw the billionaire shift the short-barreled pistol to his other hand, its butt back in his grip.

"What are you doing in there?"

Yarik pulled his own gun out. The sock still bulged over the chamber, the barrel stiff inside it, the toe dangling over the tip.

"When I said *protection* . . ." Laughing, Bazarov reached over, tugged the sock off the gun, tied a knot in the open end, and dangled it between them, an exaggerated look of disgust on his face. Then he dropped it to the floor. Merriness in his cheeks and eyes, he tugged the revolver from Yarik's hand.

"According to Korotya," he said, turning the old Nagant over to appraise it, "that was the problem with Chernitsky. He thought too much about life." He set the other pistol in his lap, unlocked the revolver's chamber, spun the cylinder with his thumb. "Korotya used to work for Chernitsky. Back before Chernitsky's armored car blew up like a Chechen in the metro. His driver . . ." Bazarov leaned forward and with the pistol barrel flicked his driver's ear. "Hey, Tolya, what happened to Chernitsky's driver?"

"Which piece of him?" Tolya said, and the two men were laughing.

"Of course"—Bazarov cut his chuckle short—"Chernitsky lived. But his business started to die. Korotya swears he had nothing to do with the exploding car. The damage to Chernitsky's business, on the other hand. . . . When President Slatkin decided to destroy the man, who do you think was whispering in his ear?" Bazarov popped the pistol's cylinder open, pointed the Nagant at the roof of the car, jiggled it. The bullets dropped like berries into his palm. "By then," he said, "Korotya was working for Yegupov. Yegupov might be there today, but I doubt it. He won't want to be around Shulgin, Shulgin's guards. Last time his men ran into Shulgin's men"—he held his hand full of bullets out to Yarik— "Yegupov had to buy more men." He shook his hand. "You don't want them?"

One by one, Yarik transferred the bullets to his own palm.

"People say Shulgin was there himself," Bazarov went on, "that he went around to those of Yegupov's men who were only wounded, right after, with a gun like this"—he tapped the automatic still sitting in his lap—"shooting them in the head and saying, 'One million roubles, one million roubles' each time he did it." Grinning, he turned his hand over, dumped the last bullet in Yarik's palm with the others. "That's how much an employer owes a bodyguard's family if the guard dies." He grinned wider. "Yegupov was pretty pissed after that."

"Because he owed so much?" Yarik asked.

Bazarov barked a laugh. "Because it was so *little*. Because it was done just for the insult. Three million roubles?" He shook the empty gun in his hand so his sleeve slipped down his wrist to show his watch. "That's not even enough to buy this. Shulgin might as well have raped Yegupov's wife, then filched her earrings." He reached to a button in the seatback before him. "So, at the meeting? Probably not Yegupov. But definitely Shulgin."

Out from the back of the seat, a drawer slid silently open. It was full of small boxes—bullets, Yarik realized, all different kinds—and while Bazarov searched through them with his free hand ("Where did you get this antique? Out of the grave of some tsar's guard?"), Yarik tried to think of where to put the bullets in his palm so, if he had a moment away, he might slip them back into the gun.

But Bazarov had found the box he wanted. "I'm out of black powder and musket balls," he said, "but these thirty-twos should work." With the new bullets, he reloaded the revolver's chamber, one by one.

Yarik tried to see on the side of the box, or on the open top, or anywhere any indication that they might be blanks.

"Talietzin, Vashchenko, Solovyov," Bazarov said, slipping a bullet in with each word, "they'll all be there. The others will probably send someone in their stead." He slapped the chamber shut, locked it. "The only one who might come unarmed is Gauk," he said. "And he has something a lot more powerful than this." He held the gun, handle first, out to Yarik.

Yarik dumped the bullets from his right hand into his left, took the revolver.

"Of all of us, Gauk is the one closest to the minister of the interior. He has a little laminated card, a dark red little plastic card that happens to have on it the signature of the minister."

As far as Yarik could tell, the gun felt the same. He told himself that was a good thing.

"A signature," Bazarov said, "that means the cops don't even have the right to stop him, let alone search him."

Unless, Yarik realized, the difference in weight between cartridges filled only with powder and those with lead wouldn't be enough for him to feel it.

"It means that he or his men can do anything, to anyone, and all he has to do is show that card and the police will nod and bow and back away. Now *that*," Bazarov said, "cost him more than my watch." With his chin, Bazarov indicated Yarik's hand full of bullets. "You bringing those to the meeting like that?" He grinned. "That's what I call a power handshake."

Yarik opened the chest pocket of his shirt and spilled the bullets in. When he looked back up at Bazarov, the man's smile was gone.

"You think I'd give you dummies?" Bazarov said.

"No," Yarik told him.

"Yes you do." He reached into the seatback drawer, took out the box, handed it to Yarik. "Do you know what those are?"

"I'm sorry—"

"Stress relievers. Hollow tips. They explode on impact. These people here today, they're not people you want to put a little hole in. If you shoot them in the arm, you better take it off." Bazarov reached out and patted Yarik's shoulder. "See?" he said. "A little less reason to worry."

Yarik nodded. He stared ahead at the traffic giving way before them. The driver was cutting things so close that any second one of the side mirrors would burst, come crashing up against the window. "These people," he asked, "they're members of the board?"

"The board?" Bazarov shook his head. "No, no. These, my trusty Cossack, are the people who make the decisions that the members of the board pretend to make. These are the people who have the money, who own the businesses that are the partners in the Consortium. Which is why they care about the Oranzheria. Which is why they're here. Because for these people, Yaroslav Lvovich, business is their life. Life *is* business. And sometimes in life we have to make decisions in private, decisions that would be difficult for people in public—say, members of a board—to make."

Each time the driver accelerated, Yarik could feel the hard lumps of the bullets push a little against his skin. "What about me?" he asked.

"You?"

"What do they expect me to do?"

"They don't expect you to do anything. They don't even know you're coming. That's why you're here. That's why—" He put his hand on his chest, then slipped it inside his suit jacket, excused himself, took out a phone.

Yarik was glad to look out the window for a while. He hadn't been to Moscow since he and Dima were small, and it seemed a wholly different city now. The golden domes still shone against the slate gray sky, the viridescent rooftops slanting sharply down from needle tops of towers, the old buildings with their white filigree and fading pastel facades, the slabs of pale concrete that smothered swaths of the city, rows of windows amassed like the battalions that had shaken Red Square on May Day parades. There was even Red Square, the clifflike rufous brick, the gold tower clock, the crimson stars on the spires. But across from it was a blurred plastic banner stretched long as the Kremlin's walls, high as the crenellations, a garish sales pitch beside the ancient stones. Billboards had shot up everywhere, faces florid with maquillage, soft-lit cars with their chrome agleam, frenetic video screens stamped into the still sky. To the city's south skyscrapers loomed, gleaming glass and steel in place of Stalin's ornate wedding cakes. Passing parks, he glimpsed flashes of eye-level billboards lining the paths, people careening by them on roller blades, skateboards, in suits and ties and flesh-flashing skirts, so many, so much time and money, as if somehow in the short span from his childhood to now Moscow had molted all it was—stolid, serious, stern—and wriggled out into a slick new sheen of everything opposite.

They were racing along the river's southern bank, down a narrow street fishboned with vehicles driven onto the curb and left, when Tolya slowed, said, "Hold on, we're parking," and slammed onto the sidewalk, too. The SUV pulled up next to them, rolled its wide tires over the curb. Its doors slapped open, spilled men: suits, sunglasses, heads swiveling as they hit the ground. One went into the street, another came close beside the sedan, the other two made their way forward with hands free at their sides and cautious lifts of their chins, as if acknowledging a greeting from someone ahead. Yarik tried to see, but as he leaned towards the window, a finger tapped his shoulder. He jerked around.

Bazarov's eyes seemed grayer than Yarik remembered them, no tinge of color at all. But they were crinkling at the corners.

"Is this where we meet?" Yarik asked him.

The man only motioned for him to come close. "Look." Bazarov pointed. In the middle of the river stood the tallest statue Yarik had ever seen, a tower built out of some fable dream—swells of a metal sea lifting a life-size galleon dwarfed by a titan astride its deck, feet planted, chest out, one hand gripping a giant captain's wheel, the other thrusting forth a scroll the size of the car they sat in—and Yarik asked, "Are the others here already?"

"I think he looks a little like me." Bazarov's laugh was short and tight. "The hair," he said, brushing his own back with his hand. There was something awkward in the movement. Then an SUV was pulling in front of their view; it rocked onto the curb across the street, followed by another, followed by a sedan.

313

"It was meant to be Christopher Columbus," Bazarov told Yarik. "Meant to stand in some country over there. Mexico? Canada? Maybe even America." The car doors burst open. "But they thought it was too ugly." The same stiff laugh. The same kinds of men in the same kinds of suits spilling out of the cars. "So we took it. Called it Peter the Great. Got it for a steal."

The wind came up off the river, blew open the men's coats; Yarik could see the butts of their guns.

"We Russians"—Bazarov tapped his temple—"have always had a head for business." He looked at Yarik, their faces close. Slowly, he reached out, poked a finger at Yarik's chest, jiggled the bullets in his pocket. They clinked around.

"I like to hear your heart," Bazarov said, and this time his smile seemed real. "But maybe it's not the best place to keep bullets." Spreading his fingers on Yarik's chest, he puffed his lips into a soft "Boom."

One by one, his fingers shaking, Yarik took the bullets out. And when he had them in his hand again, Bazarov opened the seatback drawer, motioned for him to dump them in. While he did, the man slid his own pistol into a holster beneath his arm. Peeling Yarik's fingers off the Nagant's handle, he reached behind Yarik, his arms slipping inside Yarik's jacket, pressing against his sides, and wedged the revolver into the pants' waist at Yarik's back.

"It's good manners," Bazarov said, "to keep your weapons out of sight." His hands patted Yarik's sides. And, for a moment, held on. "It's OK to be scared," he said. "We're all scared, all the time, we bad people." He smiled, and it was real, and it was also tight and thin. "Maybe Chernitsky was right. Being bad is what makes us successful in life. But being scared is what keeps us living." He patted Yarik's sides once more, then drew his hands away, put on his sunglasses, and reached for the door. "Or not," he said, and stepped out.

They met in the sculpture park behind the New Tretyakov, the museum's gray marble even more ashen in the rain, the square-edged columns and stark walls blurry behind the stockade of black iron spikes that enclosed the park. Beyond the fence, Moscow roared and pounded. Inside, bare-branched birch trees rattled at the rain, dark firs dripped a drumbeat on the cobblestones, the grass was smothered in old leaves murmuring. All throughout the park, the statues stood in their stillness. Once loomed above city squares, once peered down at thundering parades, once glowered over an entire empire, now pastured here: Dzerzhinsky, Brezhnev, Stalin, Lenin; it was a rest home for giants brought low, stone idols toppled, bronze bodies hauled off in ropes.

The park had been cleared out, sealed off. There were just the old statues and those the country's new sculptors had made—figures that seemed cast out of the very emotions the old Soviet ones refused to show—and, walking between them all, in dark suits and overcoats swishing beneath black umbrellas, the businessmen.

In his secondhand suit and stained blue parka, Yarik felt sure he would draw everyone's eyes, but when he chanced a look he found no one seemed to notice him at all. For most of the meeting they barely glanced his way, barely seemed to know that he was there. They had all converged upon an open-sided tent set up between two enourmous sculptures: on one side a red CCCP-stamped banner unfurled beneath two huge steel globes, on the other a mesh of rusted rebar holding hundreds of stone severed heads. Between them, beneath the tent, the men sat at a table. Around the sides, their guards stood out of the rain, a wall of black suits shaking out umbrellas.

Yarik stood with them. They didn't talk to him. Every now and then a couple leaned together in whispered conversation, but mostly they just watched—their bosses, each other—and the rain drummed and dripped, and Yarik strained to hear what the men in the middle said. What little he could make out he mostly didn't understand— convertible preferreds and xenocurencies and premoney valuation— but he put together that they were talking about the collapse, the strike. He had not known there were plans for Oranzherias in other cities, that in some places glass had already gone up: Syktyvkar at the edge of the Urals, Salekhard on the Gulf of Ob, Nizhnevartovsk in the Siberian lowlands, Lensk way over towards the Asian Coast—all across the country, all built by the Consortium, all funded by the men who were here. They talked of what they'd been able to keep out of the papers, off TV, what had leaked through on radios or computer screens or just by word of mouth. They spoke of foreign investors growing anxious, funds curtailed, any expansion of the original Oranzheria put on hold until Petroplavilsk was brought back under control. Most of it was said to Bazarov, or at him, or between the others about him, and he leaned into it all, gesturing across the table, running his hands through his hair, his laugh loud and his voice loud and everything about him tight. To Yarik, it all seemed beyond his ken—a world of such a different scale that the markings he lived by had no bearing—and he had begun to wonder if the meeting would end and Bazarov would walk him back to the car and put him back on the plane and return him to his life at home as if from a dream, had begun to think he'd been brought soley to make him see how small his dreams were—his hopes, his plans—when he heard his name.

No, they were speaking of his brother. Bazarov turned in his seat and let his face wilt—away from the others for a moment, the man's eyelids drooped, his cheeks slacked, the weight of his chin seemed to pull apart his mouth—and then it all firmed up again and he thrust out a hand, beckoned Yarik *come*.

Now they were all looking at him. His legs felt as if they had forgotten how to walk. But they got him there. He stood just behind Bazarov, feeling the bulge at his back as if the stares of all the body-guards behind him were pushing at the pistol, and not caring, because the stares of the men sitting at the table in front of him had gone right through and were pushing at his heart.

"This is Yaroslav Lvovich," Bazarov told them, "Zhuvov's brother." He glanced at Yarik, winked. "His twin."

"So?" one of the men said.

"So he's also a manager on the north-northeast sector of the P-vilsk Oranzheria."

"And?" one of the men said.

"Can he do anything?" another said.

"I don't know," Bazarov said.

316

"Why the hell did you bring him then?"

And Bazarov turned again to Yarik, raised his brow. "Can you do anything?" he asked. "About your brother? These gentlemen want to know if you can help us . . ."

"Get rid of him."

Yarik wasn't sure if they meant him or Dima, but he knew that, either way, he was not going to say anything. He was not going to move his hands, or his face, or anything, and he was not going to speak.

The rain pelted the tent. Something touched his shoulder. He looked down to see Bazarov's hand. The man slid his arm behind Yarik's back—Yarik felt the movement in the guards, their hands easing towards their own jacket flaps—and then Bazarov's forearm was pressing the pistol into Yarik's spine, the man's hand around his waist. He gave Yarik a slight squeeze, left his hand resting there.

"Why did I bring him?" Bazarov said to the men at the table. "Because I wanted you to see his face. Because it's the face of the man you're talking about. A man. A human being. His brother. I brought him because you're talking about killing—murdering: that, after all, is the word for it—his brother. Not some strange figure on a video. But this man's twin. Look into his eyes. Those"—Bazarov's free hand pointed at Yarik's face—"are the eyes of the man you want to murder. I brought him because if you do what you're talking about doing, I want those eyes to look forever on your souls."

Through the rain, Yarik could just make out the hiss of the traffic along the wet roads. The men at the table were so still that the breeze blowing the smoke from their cigarettes seemed intrusive. On his hip, Yarik felt Bazarov's finger twitch.

And then they were all laughing. Bazarov's hand was gone from Yarik's waist. The She Bear sat there beaming. His laugh was louder than all of theirs. The table shook with it, one man's belly pressed against the edge, jerking it up and down, another laughing out his nostrils like a sneeze, some wiping their eyes, one flapping his cigarette back and forth before his face.

The table stilled.

317

"Well," someone said.

And, as if he had cleared the air to start over again, Bazarov began: "Now . . ."

Across the table, a man held up his hand and stopped him. He wore a dark gray suit that made his face look pink beneath a bald pate that was almost crimson. His eyes were a deep, soft brown. They looked at Yarik. "You don't look like you think that was funny." The man cocked his head, as if he expected Yarik to answer. Then went on. "Either you don't have much of a sense of humor or your don't have much in the way of manners or"—he turned both his palms up—"you've got something serious that you want tell us."

Yarik tried to make his mind work, his mouth say something, but he could see Bazarov's blond hair in front of him, the stillness of the head not looking at him, not saying anything, and all he could think was that if Bazarov so much as moved he would hit him. The brown eyes held on him—never hardening, never rushing him—and looking back into them, Yarik tried to think of what he could say that would keep them from turning away, that would be the thing he had been brought all this way to speak, but there was only one thought that his mind seemed able to make, and so he said it.

"I'll do anything," he told the man. The man's eyes held. "I'll do anything if you don't hurt him. Anything. Whatever you want. I'll do anything."

The man looked down. "That is serious," he said, and folded his hands, and looked back up. "But not very helpful."

The eyes of the other men turned away from Yarik, found their hands, their cigarettes, Bazarov, and with each pair that Yarik felt leave him he felt something else fill in, felt it as clear as the tie around his throat, growing tighter with each look lost, as if someone was pulling the thin end in a fist—the knowledge that if he let this pass, did nothing, it would be the same as standing on the riverbank, watching his brother beaten, except worse—and then his arm was twisting behind his back, his hand shoving at his jacket, his fingers closed around the gun, and it wouldn't come out; it wouldn't move; his hand was stuck; he couldn't move his arm.

The scraping back of chair legs: stopped.

The rattling of the table: slowing.

Four walls of men around him, guns drawn: waiting.

Someone's chair thumped over in the leaves. Half the men at the table had stood up from it. All the bodyguards' guns were sighted on him, a line of small black holes perforating the world in front of him, and the same on his sides, and behind.

"Whoa," someone said. Bazarov. The voice close to his ear. When he turned to look, the man was standing tight up next to him. He was gripping Yarik's wrist. "I'm going to let go," he said, "and you're going to lift your hands very slowly above your head."

"OK." Yarik's voice came out so softly he wasn't sure he'd said it.

Then his hands were up above him and the pistol was slipping from his waistband and he felt the cold air find the sweat where it had pressed, and Bazarov, holding the gun up, laughed. "'OK,' he says." Bazarov smiled at them all. "Just like that." He turned his smile to the surrounding wall of guards, to all the muzzles of all their guns suspended a second away from slaughter, to the men still sitting at the table, sure to be hit in the potential fuselade, to the ones who had stood up, as if that could have saved them. Holding the gun out, he waited for one of his own guards to come and take it, and then, his hand relieved, clapped Yarik on the shoulder. "OK?" Bazarov smiled at the oligarchs again. "OK?" None of the men who had stood up sat back down. None of the men who were sitting stood up. "No?" Bazarov said. "Then let me make it OK."

And, his hands still held above him, the place where the gun had been growing warm again with sweat, Yarik listened to Bazarov explain to them why it would make things worse if they hurt Dima. How it would only rally the strikers. "Look at what just the mention of it did to him," he said, and Yarik, feeling his shoulders begin to burn, watched the men all look, as if Bazarov had put him on display. "You want a city full of *that*?" Bazarov asked them. He told them Dima would only stir The Dachas up, and he told them the solution had nothing to do with Dima at all, and by the time that Yarik's arms were shaking and

319

he didn't think he could hold them above him any longer, Bazarov was explaining to the men what the solution was.

You can't scare them back to work, he said. You can't force them. They'd be as useless and bitter as in Soviet days. "What we need," Bazarov said, "is a workforce as productive as in the States. Which, in the first years of the Oranzheria, we had. How do we get *those* workers back? That's what we need to be asking. How do we make them *want* to be back. *Believe* in why they're back. That's why American workers are so productive: they believe in the work. In what it will bring them. And that, my friends, isn't something you can force. Not any more than America could force a market economy on the USSR. Not until the people wanted it. That's why it has nothing to do with getting rid of some fool in a video. And everything to do with getting rid of everything else. You take away what they have, gentlemen, and before long they will remember how much they wanted it. They will need it back. They will choose to come back to work. They will choose to work even harder. Luckily"—reaching up, he slowly guided Yarik's hands to a rest on top of Yarik's head—"you have me." He grinned. "And I have a way to speed that choice up."

"What did you tell them?"

Bazarov looked up from the thin ruby drink he was pouring. "That you almost got half of the richest men in Moscow killed today." He filled Yarik's glass, started to pour his own. "Then I told them that I was taking you to supper, anyway. And that we would be delighted if any of them cared to join us." He set the bottle down, made an exaggerated show of looking to his left, his right, of giving Yarik a puzzled face. "I don't know"—he shrugged—"maybe it was something you did?"

Yarik tried not to smile, but he could tell from the way Bazarov's eyes lit up another notch that his face had showed it anyway. That was how it had been the last few hours. He had gone from fury to gratitude and didn't understand it, didn't understand the feeling that had flooded over him when the man's hand had eased his own hands onto his own head, pressed protectively on top of his knuckles, the almost childlike wish that they would stay there just like that, didn't understand why he had reached for the gun in the first place, what he had thought that could fix. After Bazarov had ordered Yarik be brought back to the sedan, in the hour he'd been sequestered in the backseat, his emotions had come unfastened from his thoughts: love for his brother; fury at him; confusion about what his role had been, about how—even if—he had been used; missing his children; longing for his wife; thrilled by being here, in Moscow, sitting on soft leather looking out a tinted window at the surface of a river alive with rain. All he'd understood then was that he owed it all—that he would see his children again, his wife, that he had a brother still—to Baz.

Now, sitting across from his boss in the restaurant Baz had taken him to, Yarik watched a trio of waiters lay dishes on the table: olives and pickles and cucumbers sliced thin as parchment; tiny eggs sprinkled with saffron; a flower of golden pastries ringed around a crimson dipping sauce; a pyramid of rice bejeweled with semolinas; heat-wizened pepper skins stuffed with meat; bread strewn with blackened sesames, steamy with the scent of butter. It all smelled of butter. And mint and lamb and fennel and cinnamon. And over everything the chef had scattered gems: some sort of small crimson fruit seed, bright as a rain of rubies showered all across the table.

Taking in the spread, raising the glass the billionaire had filled, Yarik said the only thing he could: "Thank you." He used the formal word— "*blagodaryu*"—and looked the man in the eyes, and added, "Baz."

There came the crow's feet wrinkling. "It's nothing," Bazarov said. "What would my mother think if I put you back on the plane without even filling your belly?"

"I don't mean for the meal."

The wrinkles deepened. Bazarov lifted his glass. "To life," he said.

The drink tasted like some fruit Yarik had never had and he took a second sip before he set it down. "Not just for my life," he said. "But for my brother's."

Bazarov tore a hunk from the loaf, swiped at a plate of earth-colored paste, spoke through his chewing: "Well, I guess I'm not Chernitsky. I don't believe anybody is truly good or bad. It's the things that we do that are good or bad. And we all do both. The key"—he cleaned his fingers with his napkin—"is knowing when to do which."

"You've done a lot of good things for me," Yarik said. He had finished half his glass already, but he took another sip.

"You like it?" Bazarov asked.

"And I don't think there's even any vodka in it."

"No, no alcohol."

"What is it?"

"Pomegranate." Bazarov reached into a dish on the table, plucked one of the scattered rubies, held it out in his fingers. Yarik took it—in the light of the table lamp the fruit was translucent, luminous as a tiny incandescent bulb—and slipped it between his lips. "Not bad, huh?"

He nodded, chewing, reached to a dish and picked out another.

"Careful," Bazarov plucked one for himself, "the seeds can hurt your teeth." He popped it in his mouth, chewed, said, "Hm," as if appreciating the taste anew again. Then he asked Yarik, "Do you want to know the truth?"

Yarik let the pomegranate seed sit against his teeth.

"You asked, before, what my business partners wanted you to do." Bazarov reached for a stuffed pepper, grinned, said, "Not, I assure you, what you did," and stuffed the whole thing in his mouth.

Swallowing the seed, Yarik watched the man chew, waited.

"The truth," Bazarov said, when he'd finally gotten the pepper down, "is that I didn't bring you here to *do* anything. I brought you here to watch. Did you?"

"Watch?"

"Watch." Bazarov stared at Yarik staring at him. "What did you see?"

"Under the tent?"

"If I was watching"—Bazarov shrugged—"that's probably where I would look."

"I don't know what you want me—"

"I want to know what you saw. Who you saw."

"I don't know who was who," Yarik said. "I don't remember their names. I don't know—"

"Whose names?"

"Them."

"Them?"

"The businessmen."

"You saw businessmen?"

"Yes."

"And?"

"I don't know," Yarik said. "I saw their bodyguards—"

"And?"

"And you."

Bazarov sat back. "Me?" he said. He plucked a dumpling off a plate, dipped it in a purple sauce, and asked, "What was I doing?"

Yarik picked his napkin off his lap. He held it in his hands. "Why are you asking me this?"

"Yaroslav Lvovich," Bazarov said, "do I not have the right to ask you a simple question?"

"Mr. Bazarov—"

"Baz."

"Baz—"

"Do I not have the right to ask you any fucking thing I want?"

Yarik stopped twisting at the napkin. He put it down on the table. "I already thanked you for protecting my brother. I thought I already—"

"Oh!" Bazarov cut him off. "*That's* what I was doing. I was protecting your brother."

"And me," Yarik said.

"*And* you." He shook his head, as if at the wonder of it. "I bet that wasn't easy. Did it look easy?"

"No."

"I bet," Bazarov said, "there were times it wasn't even easy to tell that that's what I was doing. I bet there were times when you couldn't even tell if I was doing something good or something bad. From your viewpoint," he said, "from what you saw, did it look like I was doing something good or bad?"

"Good," Yarik said.

"That's what it looked like?"

"No."

"But?"

"It was good."

"For who?"

"Me," Yarik said. "And my brother."

"Huh," Bazarov said. "Now why would I do that?"

"Because," Yarik said, "you know when it's the right time to do a good thing."

Bazarov grinned, lifted his shoulders a little. "Or a bad one," he said and, turning towards the waiters emerging from the kitchen, "ah, here comes the main course."

He winked when he said it. And all the while that the waiters laid out the dishes, the baked lamb and grilled fish, ground spices and hot fat and the sweet sharp smell of onions fried, Yarik didn't once look down at the table. He kept his eyes on the man across from him. The man who, when the waiters were gone again, leaned in a little closer, nothing playful about his face at all.

"Cossack," Bazarov said, "I have something good that you can do for me." He selected a skewer and clinked the metal tip on Yarik's plate and with his knife started sliding pieces of charred sturgeon off. "This strike won't last long," he said. "In a few weeks those people will flood back to work. They'll ask for *more* hours. The Oranzheria will be repaired. Its expansion will begin again. And with the other potential build-sites watching from all across the country, I'll push it outward at twice the pace. Let those other cities drool. Let their mayors beg for us to set up for them that kind of revenue. Let the investors break down the goddamn doors." He popped off the last piece of sturgeon. "I won't let anything get in the way of that." He set the skewer aside and dipped a ladle into a yellow stew, dished out on Yarik's plate onions and tomatoes, lamb on the bone. He made a small sound in his nose, shook his head a little. "I didn't mean to say *those people*," he told Yarik. "I'm sorry." He looked up through the steam rising off the stew. "They're your people, of course. You're still one of them. After all, that's the whole point of the publicity campaign. Except, the *other* point is that you're rising above them, out of them. That must be a tricky place to inhabit." He lowered the ladle towards Yarik's plate. "You aren't going to eat?"

Yarik picked up his fork, his knife. Across the table, Bazarov filled his own plate.

"As you've probably guessed," Bazarov said, "I've known your history from the start. Just as, from the start, we've both known another history: that of the land on which the Oranzheria is built. A history in which a small minority of former kolkhozniki have tried to play too big a roll. In Turgenev's words, 'The Russian peasant will have God himself for breakfast.'" He tore a turnover in half, bits of meat and onion spilling out. "In my words"—he put one half on Yarik's plate—"those are some seriously stubborn sonsofbitches. And for too long they've kept out of my hands a swatch of land, not huge, but smack in the way of . . ." He wiped his fingers on his napkin, grinned at Yarik. "But now you're starting to understand what I need you to do." He took a bite of the sturgeon, hummed with pleasure. "You look skeptical." He pointed with his fork. "Try more of the fish." He laughed. "You're thinking, why can't I just leave that little swatch alone. Could I not still have my fairly luxurious car? Could I not still fly a friend to Moscow for a day just to take him out to supper? Could I not eat a delicious *shashlik* of sturgeon every meal, if I wanted, and I might, because you have to admit this is really fucking good? But you already know the answer. Because I'm a successful person, and nobody becomes successful thinking like that.

"Maybe, though, you're thinking I could just build the Oranzheria right over it. Leave a little preserve. A kind of game park for old stubborn kolkhozniki. Maybe it could even be a tourist draw. Like one of those nostalgic outdoor museums, an ode to the old days, a real Russian mir with real Russian . . ." And with a shout he broke out into the old folk song—"*Kalinka, kalinka, kalinka moya, v'sadu yagoda malinka, malinka moya!*"—blasting at the top of his voice so everyone in the restaurant turned to look. "In the middle of the glass." He sat chuckling, shaking his head. "Frozen like some bug in amber." Lifting the bottle of pomegranate drink, he tipped it towards Yarik's glass, saw Yarik hadn't touched it, poured his own full. "Aside from the obvious impracticalities," he said, "ask yourself this: what kind of message would that send to the other farmers farther north whose land I haven't yet bought? Or to the ones outside Nizhnevartovsk and Salekhard and Lensk? Because I assure you, there are stubborn old sonsofabitches everywhere. But mostly," he said, "what kind of a lesson would that be for the next generation, the people who are going to build this country up or let it sink, keep it on the track that we—me, the men you saw today—started it on twenty years ago, or twist it back towards the past, what kind of lesson would that be to the keepers of the flame, the ones who are like I was when I was starting out, the people, Yaroslav Lvovich, like you." He took another bite of fish, paused midchew. "Oh," he said, through his mouthful, "which reminds me," and he turned and lifted a hand. The maître d' looked up like he'd been waiting for just that motion. Bazarov nodded to him. The man disappeared.

While Yarik watched him go, Bazarov lifted a tureen of plum-colored sauce and leaned over the table and poured a stream of it over Yarik's fish. "Try it with this." He put the tureen down with a clank. "At least eat a few bites. You're being rude."

But by the time Yarik had picked his knife and fork back up, the maître d' had reappeared. In his wake one of Bazarov's black-suited men carried a leather bag as old and worn as it was strange: two twin pouches covered in heavy flaps, bound by a band slung over the man's shoulder, one knocking at his chest, the other at his back. From one pouch a long hole-punched strip dangled like a belt, from the other, the buckle. The man stopped. The buckle clanked against the table-top. Tooled into the leather of the bag closest to him, Yarik saw four words, two he recognized—UNITED STATES—and two he didn't—POSTAL

SERVICE. Then the man shrugged the thing off his shoulder, deposited it in Yarik's lap, and left.

"Open it," Bazarov said, as if it were wrapped in a bow.

But Yarik just sat there, the heavy weight on his legs, the smell of old leather mixing with the scents of the food. "How much is it?" he said.

"Open it." This time it wasn't a request.

Inside there must have been enough to pay off the families of four or five dead guards, maybe enough to buy the restaurant they were sitting in. He shut the flap.

"The sturgeon," Bazarov said, and when he saw that Yarik couldn't eat it with the bag piled on his lap, got up and came around the table and, setting the bag on the chair between them, leaned down, took Yarik's fork and knife, started cutting up his fish. He cut it into bite-size pieces, talking close in Yarik's ear. "Next time, when all this is over, and you've done your good thing for me, we'll eat something even better than this. Just wait till your first taste of roast boar. Wait till you pick your bullet out and put it on your plate." Yarik could hear the smile in his voice.

"Do you remember," Bazarov said, "a while ago, back when we were first getting to know each other, we discussed the idea of opportunity. Seeing it. Taking it."

Yarik didn't shake his head, or nod, or anything.

"Friedman," Bazarov prompted. "Khodorkovsky."

"I remember."

"You remember Mizin? Yuri Mizin? No?" Yarik felt the warm breath of the word on the side of his face. "No one does." Bazarov paused in his cutting. "Though back in '92? Privatization? The state handing out shares to the old Soviet directors, workers . . . It was Mizin who saw how to take it: the geologias in the north where big gas was trying to expand, the shares held by the workers there. Goes up, tries to gain their trust, get them to vote the Red Direktors out, his directors in, and he might have, too, if he hadn't found he *liked* the people so damn much." With the knife he scraped a chunk of fish off of the fork. "Because when sweet talking wasn't enough, when he

327

would have had to push a little harder—cut someone up, break some-one's hand—he balked. Couldn't do it. So?" Bazarov set the fork and knife down with a clank. "The Red Direktors stayed on, the geologias stuck in their Soviet ways, outdated, corrupt, until they folded, and the workers lost their jobs, and a year later the second most common cause of death was drunkards freezing on the streets. The first most common was starvation. Suicide?" He picked the fork back up. "It barely came in third. And what about Mizin?" He shrugged. "Who cares?" Bazarov speared a piece of fish and held the fork for Yarik to take it. "He's not even why I'm telling you this now."

He left Yarik holding the fork and went back around the table and pulled out his chair. "I'm more interested," he said, sitting, "in what you think." He opened his palms. "What do you think? Was what Mizin did a good thing or a bad thing? Was what seemed a good thing a good thing in the end? Or would more good have come from the thing that might have seemed at first to be bad? What do you think, Cossack?"

One by one Yarik speared pieces of food, the tines scraping against the plate, until his fork was stacked thick. Then he set it down. "How much is in there?" he said.

Bazarov smiled. "In that bag?"

"Is there enough to buy Kartashkin's farm?"

"No," he said, his laugh a quiet accompaniment to the small smile. "That's only half of what the stubborn sonofabitch thinks he's going to get for it. And he's probably right. Which is why, even if he demands twenty million roubles from you, you're going to say OK. And he's going to trust you. Because you'll have a quarter of it in cash. And a letter from me promising the other three-quarters as soon as he sells the land to you. And you sign it over to me."

"Why a quarter?"

"Because," Bazarov said, "that's what's in one of those pouches. The other is filled with another five million roubles for you." He raised his hand, signaled in the air for the check. "Of course," he said, "that's only if you decide you want to do it." He tongued at something in his mouth, then opened his jaws as wide as he could and, lips stretched, teeth showing, dug with his fingers at whatever was stuck. When he got it, he yanked it out and wiped it on his napkin and told Yarik there were other solutions, of course, that he could always use on the farmers who were holding out, the sort of tactics Mizin hadn't had the stomach for, the sort of thing the businessmen they met with that afternoon had been talking about. After all, he said, Yarik and he both knew that half of what he'd spouted back there in that tent had been bullshit. There were plenty of things, he said, that the Consortium could do to Dima, and plenty of ways to do them, that would bring the workers back to the Oranzheria just as fast. "Eat up," he said. "We have to get you back on the plane."

But Yarik couldn't touch the fork. All across the table, the meat had gone lukewarm, the grease congealed, the smells settled into the cloth like mold. In his stomach he could feel everything he'd eaten sitting there, could taste it on the lining of his throat, and looking across the table at Bazarov, at his sated eyes and full cheeks and small dark slick of something stuck in the hairs of his goatee, all he could think was how hungry his brother must be.

PROPAGANDA OF THE DEED

He seemed to have rusted all around his face. His hair had turned an iron orange, stiff and brittle as the bristles of a neglected wire brush. Zinaida had done his beard, too, and, with the streaks of black she hadn't reached, his cheeks and chin looked like corroded metal scraps, his eyebrows—bleach applied by her mascara brush—like bent nails discarded to the weather.

His mother's eyes had widened at the sight, gone sad. "What happened?" she'd whispered, as if only some terrible loss could have turned his hair like that. The Golden Phoenix froze, head cocked, glaring like it had met its match at last, then launched itself at him, beating its russet wings against his head, his beard, his face. And when, after too many days hunkered inside—the protests a distant clangor still going on, the last of the bread peeled of its mold, dipped in the last of the oil—he at last went out onto the street it was true that other people's faces turned to his. But it was also true that, after a glance, they turned away again.

The city was full of faces that looked more like his. There: his old visage plastered to telephone poles, sooty mustache sticking out from the scarf over his mouth. There: posted on the sides of bus stops, black curls beneath a thick knit hat, goggles obscuring his eyes. Some bore slogans about the "sky-skater of Petroplavilsk." Some urged, *Remember!* Some had been spray-painted across Consortium ads, his likeness stenciled beside Slava's. All day Dima wandered among them both: the echoes of his brother, the immitations of himself.

At Peter the Great Square a man climbed the plinth, a pretender in a coat and hat like his, black beard and safety goggles, crying out over the crowd. For a long time, Dima listened. Gradually, he began to understand. This false twin was shouting out a story, the story of *him*—or at least what the immitator imagined that to be.

They stood on statues scattered around the city. In Kirov and Ilyinsky squares, alongside Maria Bochkaryova brandishing her sword, seated on the bronze back of General Kutuzov's wild-eyed horse. Some claimed he was a Lap come south from Finland; some insisted he had lived all his life in Petroplavilsk; some told of a boy born to Pakhomova and Gorshkov, love child of the golden ice-dancing team. He was the son of a literature professor, a steelworker, a ballerina forced to sell her body on the streets, even of Boris Bazarov himself, The She Bear's cub come back to haunt him. To remind them. To stir Petroplavilsk to life. Because his father had beaten him with a bear's claw, his mother had starved on her meager pension, the Oranzheria leveling crews had destroyed their home. They had dug up his sister's grave. His son had worked too many trawler shifts, fallen asleep, off the side of the ship, was ground up in the propellers, scattered across the lake. His brother was that fucking Slava. Which was how he could afford the helicopter that dropped him on the Oranzheria that dawn. The dawn he plummeted out of the clouds, parachute on his back, ice skates glinting. The dawn he was delivered by a flock of geese. Shaped like a golden eagle, he soared in; in the form of a hawk, he dove; it was a heron from the lake that settled onto the surface of the great glass sea and became a man.

Stanislav. Rodion. Vadim. For the first few days, an argument raged among the impersonators until, inevitably, they began to coalesce around the only name there ever really was, the same that all their antecedent fable makers, all the way back to old Kievan Rus, had come to call the heroes of their tales: Ivan. Ivan the Tsarevich. Vanya the Mare's Son. Ivanushka the Fool.

One day, long after the sun had set and the zerkala had risen in its place, when he had come again to the statue by the lake and was listening to another black-bearded tale teller recount another Ivanushka yarn, he saw his brother. Standing in the crowd. On the opposite side of the square. He had wrapped a scarf around his chin and mouth, sunglasses covered his eyes. Of course, Yarik, too, would have had to hide his doppelgängered face. His brother's breath leaked through the knit of the scarf: faint puffs of steam. As if on its own, Dima's breath settled into synch. Watching each distant wisp dissolve, he wondered how it was for Yarik always among effigies of *his* brother, surrounded by the guerrilla videos that still sprang up on advertising screens, having to hear impersonators tell him over and over the tale of his own twin.

"And so," the one up on the statue was saying, "Ivanushka went to his second brother. And he saw how much gold he had dug out of his hill. And he went to his third brother. And he—"

"Wrong!"

The shout was so loud the impersonator stopped. The crowd: a hundred heads turning. Were they looking at Yarik? Had his brother called that out?

And, before Dima could think, he had done it: "Wrong!" Now the faces turned to him. "He had only one brother!" Dima shouted, his stare on Yarik. "They were twins!" On Yarik straining to see him. "Dmitry." Yarik turning. "And Yaroslav." His brother disappearing into the crowd. And Dima could hear the whispering, the eyes picking at his face, painting his beard, could sense the movement of all the others, faint as the pull of gravity when a train begins to roll. Except he was still. And everything else had begun to come at him. The police must have sensed it, too. They shoved their way closer through the crowd, clearing a path through the surging throng, and Dima was about to turn, to struggle out, break into a run, when something hard jabbed into his back.

"This time," a voice said in his ear, "we know you know what this fucking is."

They smuggled him out through the crowd, Volodya using his bulk like a screen, Fedya using his forehead as a distraction (a crack against whoever's brow was in butting distance, a wail, the shave-skulled man sprinting away from the police); and through it all he followed the black buzzed back of Vika's head as she pulled him behind her by a fistful of his beard.

Twenty minutes later she had still not let go. Rejoined by the others, they had headed along the back alleys of Petroplavilsk, wound up at an old stuccoed building, where they stopped. It was on the far side of the city from where Dima lived, and he hadn't been there since he was a kid, but he recognized it right away: the old Pioneer Palace. Last time he'd been inside, it had still been The Past Life, the place teeming with children come after school, ringing with the shouts of komsomol sitters, the laughter of Young Pioneers.

For how long now had it been boarded up? Vika didn't know. But she knew a cellar door through which they could get in. Following her past room after room, he saw tables still spread with chessboards, model airplanes spinning slowly from their ceiling strings, easels standing still, as if soon the painters' club would be coming back, as if the building might burst again into the sounds of his childhood. But there was just the echoes of their footsteps, Vika's voice telling him how she'd been squatting there since, in solidarity with the strikers, she'd quit her job taking tickets on the tram. He could still hear her from summer—*If you were working* and *We never would have met*—and he wondered if she'd spent any of her newfound free time looking for him. Or if she'd been too angry. Her fist in his beard, the jerk in her hips: he seemed it now. Though, in front of him, beneath the fuzz of her hair, the skin bunched at the base of her skull looked so soft. He had not remembered that, had not remembered how the fine hairs below it whisped to a point at the nape of her neck. Her scent: the fungal fresh and bitter smoky whole of it, unlike anything in his life since that day in summer.

Lost in it, he let her lead him down the hall into a room that must have once been used by the ceramics club. Volodya shut the door. Vika let go his beard. Fedya backed him up until his legs hit the hard edge of a potter's wheel. The three of them stood, watching him. Rubbing his face where the hairs had been tugged, he watched them back.

"Our esteemed balladeer." Volodya opened his hands, palms up, as if presenting Dima.

"Ivanushka," Vika said, her voice all smirk.

"The Fool," Fedya added.

"Friend," Volodya went on, "was it something we did?" He rubbed his greasy beard as if in sympathy with Dima's sore skin. "How many restive nights have I lain awake face-to-face with that conjecture? Aggrieved by indigestion. Worrying myself thin." He lifted his arm; his sweater sleeve jiggled with a flap of armpit flesh. "Was it something about Yura?"

Next to him, Fedya turned ventriloquist, thrust a puppet hand into the fat man's pit, said, "Wash me!"

Volodya sniffed himself. "Surely, it's not *that* bad."

"I didn't think—" Dima began.

But Volodya cut him off. "And what of Fedya? Did you think of him? Lying up on the roof, shooting his pistol all alone?"

"Fuck this," Fedya said. He stepped away from the circle. "He didn't think of anyone but him-fucking-self. I have to piss."

"You fill it," Vika told the harelipped man, "you empty it." And, standing behind Dima, she reached around his head, to where he was rubbing at his chin, covered his hand with hers. His fingers froze. Hers kept rubbing. With tenderness? Or something too hard for that? "What did you think?" Her hand moved slowly up his cheek. "That we would see your new hair?" Her fingers brushed his sideburn. "And mistake you for a fox?"

Hearing the others laugh, Dima jerked his face away. But her fingers had slid up to hover over the very top of his hair, and it was as if around his head the air itself had suddenly grown stiff.

"We should cut his scalp off," Fedya said. "Sell it to some Moscow wife for a scarf." He was standing over by a counter, his back to the circle, his legs just far enough apart that Dima could see the bottom of the jar he held. It sloshed a dark yellow. The bright sound of a steady burble.

"No, my urinating friend," the fat man said, speaking to Fedya, but gazing at Dima. "His head is far more valuable than that." Volodya nodded thoughtfully. "We could learn from him. I think"—his eyebrows lifted—"I already have. All those fitful hours lying awake in bed, I never saw it. Till now. He was simply putting into practice the philosophy we all espouse."

"Spit on that," Fedya said.

"No," Volodya said, "think on it: there we were working away towards our revolution, and all the while he was doing nothing, avoiding even the action inherent in seeing us, simply waiting. For the right moment. Weren't you?" he asked Dima. "For the moment when doing what you wanted—simply ascending the Oranzheria provisioned with a pair of ice skates—would accomplish more than all our work."

Shaking his head, Dima tried to ignore the feeling of his hair brushing back and forth beneath Vika's still floating fingers. "No," he said, "I never meant to do anything. I never even wanted to be in your video."

"And yet," Vika's voice came from somewhere behind him, "you couldn't help yourself."

"Any more," Volodya said, "than you can now."

In the quiet, there was just the burble of Fedya's still-flowing stream.

"What do you mean?" Dima asked.

And Fedya broke the quiet with a sudden, "Fuck!"

"I told you," Vika scolded the pisser. "How fucking big is your bladder?"

"Bigger than this fucking jar."

For a moment, they all listened to the tinkling. Then Vika said something to Volodya, who crossed to the sink, dug in a cabinet, came up with an empty jar. Fedya's free hand flailed for it, had it. They all

335

watched him make the switch, heard him sigh. The full jar thunked onto the counter. The high-pitched tinkle resumed.

"That," Volodya said, coming back, "is what I'm talking about." His whole face seemed lit with pleasure at the thought. "If that was you—"

"If he was me?" Fedya asked.

"No," Volodya said. "If he was your . . ." His hand circled, as if trying with the gesture to conjure for them the word.

"If you," Vika told Dima, "were Fedya's cock."

Volodya's hand stopped. His massive shoulders gave a little shrug. "Then—"

"Then," Fedya said, zipping up, "we'd have to get you a bigger suit."

"A suit?" Dima asked.

"Then," Volodya continued, "the first jar would be full."

"What jar?" Dima said.

"Your deed," Volodya told him. "You skating on the Oranzheria. The Collapse. If that is the jar, then it's full of the result."

"My deed is the jar?"

"The strike," Fedya guessed, "is the result?"

"The protests," Volodya explained, "have stalled. Hit their peak. The inspiration of your deed has filled the jar—"

"Wait," Fedya said, "I thought his deed *was* the jar?"

Volodya shushed him with an open hand. "Your deed," he went on, "has filled as much as it can hold."

"So what you're saying," Fedya cut in, "is the fucker's pissed out. His bladder isn't as big as mine."

"No," Volodya corrected him. "His bladder is immense. Bottomless. More full of piss than ever before."

"OK," Fedya said. "So, if the jar is the deed—"

"Then"—Volodya cut him off—"now is the time for another jar."

"Now," Fedya said, "is the fucking time to act."

Dima stared at them. He had no idea what they were talking about. But he was sure he didn't want any part of whatever it was. "Look . . ." he started.

But Vika's hand was covering his mouth. Her other hand pressed at the back of his head. "If he's Fedya's cock," she said, "then what happens if I go like this?" And all at once she rubbed her hands up and down, fast, one through the bush of his beard from chin to nose, the other from his pate to the curled pelt of his neck, down and up, rubbing, laughing, the others laughing, too. "A third jar!" Vika shouted.

And Dima knew it didn't matter what she might once have felt; it had turned into this. "Ey!" Twisting his head, trying to jerk his shoulders away, he wrenched loose, grabbed her hands, held them still. "Ey!" This time his voice was loud enough to quiet them. "And what if I don't want to act? What if I don't want to *do* anything? What if I don't want anything to do with you?"

He had meant them. But had he felt her flinch? When he looked at her he couldn't tell whether it was from anger or hurt.

"Then why," Vika said, no hint of either in her smile, "are you holding my hands?"

He let them go. Her smile: it scared him how fast he could feel her pull inside him. "Whatever it is," he said, "I don't want to do it."

"You?" Volodya came closer. "Who's talking about you?" And nose to nose with Dima now, he grinned. "We're talking about your brother."

On Dima's shoulders, the fat man's hands seemed to contain his entire weight. Slowly, Dima let them press him down till he was sitting on the smooth stone of the potter's wheel. Volodya's face sank with his, the man's massive legs somehow bending to a squat. Around Dima, the others did the same, like three campers crouched around a fire. And telling him of their plan, their faces were no less lit. This was the moment they'd been waiting for, why they'd made the video, what they'd meant when they said they were going to *do* something.

Dima remembered—how they would break into the headquarters, the control room, *redirect the sonsofbitches,* turn the mirrors off, *all of them, all at once, one giant wink*—and as they spoke, each reaching out to turn him towards them, as the wheel slid beneath him and his eyes tried to focus on each face, he felt again a little of what had come over him on the roof—distant echoes of explosions in his chest, *paf, paf, paf, and that is going to be some serious propaganda by the deed*—until, by the time they were laying out how they would get him in, how they would help him out again, he had to shut his eyes. They turned him and talked and turned him until he began to feel as if they had filled him a second time with their hallucinogenic drink.

He told them to stop. He told them: even if it could be done he didn't want to do it. He told them why.

And, holding him still, Vika said, "Oh, because things are going so well with your brother right now?"

They had been following Slava, told Dima they'd seen him boating with the billionaire, getting on The She Bear's private plane, wearing a suit. The Consortium, they were sure, was planning something big. Some new venture? Some event meant to crack the protests, increase their dominance yet again? The only thing they knew was that Dima's brother was part of it. And that they had to do *their* something first.

Hearing them talk of Yarik—in suits, in Moscow, in meetings with the man who'd taken away their uncle's land, their lives together, the way they once would have never thought to hide such a thing from one another—sitting in the old ceramics room in the old Pioneer Palace where he and his brother had once played, Dima felt smaller than he had even then, as if, were he to wander back to that time, he would be one of the youngest there, the seven- or six- or five-year-olds set on the rug to hear the stories, that even then he would have been eclipsed, impuissant, that never before in his life had he been so powerless.

Gradually he began to listen more carefully to what they said. How the only way to bring his brother back was to shake the city back to its senses, the only way that they could turn the country towards what they had always wanted, reclaim what had been taken from the people by the capitalists of the New Russia, by the Communists before them, by the autocrats before that, all the way back to the age of the miri. Back when each world was its own few versts, owned by people who owned themselves, their work, their play, their time. A time, they said, that would come next. The time, they told him, that he would start.

Vika had lit a fire in the kiln. Volodya had run a piece of string along his arms, his back, his waist, his inseam. Fedya had taken the pistol. Together, the two men had gone out to get him a suit.

She'd left the kiln door open; he could feel the heat on his bare skin. Take your shirt off, Vika had told him before she'd begun to dye his hair. She used the same black dye she used for her own, and it struck Dima as somehow significant to learn her real hair was a color he couldn't guess, that she changed it to make it the same as his. The black that his had been. That she was dying his again. She wore no gloves, simply let her hands get stained, too, and he could feel the skin of her fingertips slipping over the skin of his scalp, and that was how the whole thing was, so different from how it had been when Zinaida had done the same, as if, then, trying to understand how it felt to be his brother, he had been unable to shed some impermeable shield. Which was gone now. Vika straddled him while she worked, the weight of her skinny legs so slight, his own thighs so thinned; even that seemed right, as if their bodies had been matched to let each sense the other's bones. He could sense, too, her fingers slipping behind his ears, her body leaning forward, muscles shifting atop the muscles of his legs, the safety pins that ran up her chest brushing the tip of his nose, her belt buckle caught for a second in the curled hairs of his belly—every touch she made was alive with intent.

Then her dye-black fingers were in his beard. They inched into the rusty tangles, tugged a little, tilted his face up.

It was the first time in his near-forty years that he'd been kissed. Not the brush of his mother's or his sister-in-law's lips, but kissed. He had no idea that lips could be so soft. He had no idea a tongue could be so alive. He had no idea the breath released from someone else's lungs would be such a different substance when unmixed with any outside air. He took it in.

When she was done, she pulled away, smiled down into his face, said, "So that's what it's like while you still have this crazy beard." Then, without moving from his lap, she reached to the sink. It was piled with toiletries that seemed dumped from an upturned purse, but the scissors were large enough she found them by feel, so rusted that as she snipped through his tangled beard they squeaked. She seemed to get a kick out of the noise. Soon she was making it, too. Squeak, squeak, with each snip, until the hedge of hair was gone. Then, with a thunk, she put the scissors back, picked up a bar of soap, dunked it in a bucket full of filthy-looking water, and, still sitting on his lap, scrubbed Dima's face into a cloud of charcoal foam. Which she proceeded to shave off. She didn't seem to notice when the razor nicked him. She didn't seem to care that the grayed soap, the cold water, dripped onto her as much as him. She didn't even wipe his face before she kissed him. "And that," she said, "is what it's like without it."

"Which is better?" he asked.

She shrugged. Then scooped a wet clump of beard hair off their laps and, holding handfuls to her cheeks, said, "You tell me," and kissed him again.

In the center of the Oranzheria, at the edge of the woods that ran along the access line, they stood listening to the whisper of the others' rail-boards disappearing down the tracks. Dima in his newly stolen suit beneath his old overcoat, his throat squeezed by a tie, his shaved chin cold, his shorn head strangely light beneath the knit of his same old hat. Beside him: Vika in her wig. A severe jaw-length wedge, it was black to match her brows. Her lipstick was the brightest thing in the shadows of the trees. She was bundled in the same man's coat she'd worn since autumn; once inside the Oranzheria, she'd shuck it, Dima would strip away his winter wear, they would cross the fields to the old sanitarium, enter it as Slava and his wife.

Under the drifting man-made moons the top of the Oranzheria gleamed like a frozen sheet of lightning laid flat. As far as Dima could see to either side, the wide glass wall facing the access line was fogged with steam. Through it, Dima could make out the silhouettes of the strike breakers, whispy and wraithlike farther out in the fields, the shapes of heavy equipment lumbering and indistinct as deep-sea beasts. Between the clouded wall and where he stood with Vika beneath the trees, the earth was made of all the things the clearing crews had

340

shoved outside the glass, the remains of old izbas, residue of villages, all grown over, filled in, a rutty landscape of scattered mounds.

They made their way onto it, into the mirror-light, eyes squinting, hunting the wall of steam for the nearest portal through which they'd enter, arm in arm. The ground was all holes hidden by shadows or shadows shaped like holes, and unaccustomed to her heels, Vika stumbled, snagged Dima's coat sleeve, slipped her hand a little early around his arm. Beneath her fingers his bicep seemed more part of him; he was aware of the way it hardened when she gripped, waited through the relaxing of her fingers for the moment when she might tighten again.

Part of him was just as eager to get inside the Oranzheria, dump the bulky coat that bunched between them, sense her through nothing but his jacket sleeve; to feel again the way she'd looked at him when he'd tried on the suit, her teasing whistle belied by the glimmer of her eyes; to see her shift again into the woman who, mince-stepping through the wave-and-smile of a politician's wife, had made him laugh, who, in her slim-fitted dress, had made him swallow. But the rest of him was scared. In there, he would have to be the politician, the salesman, Slava. In a suit and tie amid the farm fields? He'd been sent out to bolster the strike breakers' morale. And how to get from there to headquarters? On the bus beside workers from whose ranks he'd risen, or some manager's sedan they would flag down, or maybe they'd even comandeer a dump truck; a photo shoot, he'd tell the driver, just like Volodya, back in the woods, had told him. Back in the woods it had all seemed a whole lot better. Now, with each step nearer to the vast glass wall, it seemed a little worse.

Still, catching sight of the portal, what could he do but tilt his cold chin towards it, touch her fingers on his arm, tell her, "There's the door."

Then it was gone. The Oranzheria was gone. So was she.

So were the zerkala.

Dima stood in the sudden darkness, utterly still, staring up.

"What the fuck," he heard her say.

Up there, the blackness was so deep Dima could feel his pupils open for it, feel it flood his eyes, a pool of night. Strewn with stars.

341

The Great Bear. The Hydra. The Milky Way. The whole universe of them that he hadn't seen in years.

"What the *fuck,*" she said again.

In the dark, even the forest behind him sounded different, as if the wind in the trees was the woods' own exhalation of breath. From within the Oranzheria, behind its blacked-out wall, came the thickening quiet of the machines shutting down. Each vanished engine left another hole until all the darkness in front of Dima seemed shot through with the same silent shock. And then the crescendo of voices swelling to fill it.

Beside him, he could hear Vika rustling. Something heavy and soft dropped to the ground. The strange intimacy in listening blind, trying to read her sounds: a faint clicking, tiny metal tings, the whisper of cloth on skin—and then he knew it. As if struck clear, his eyes began to make her out. Paleness by paleness, her form emerged: she was standing next to him naked. Then she let out a whoop, and was off.

Beneath the moon's bare sliver she gamboled across the overgrown junk mounds, reveling in the wash of darkness as if it were a cleansing rain, leaping and whirling, a ghostly dervish loosed upon the night. In the starlight he could see her breath. Beyond her, blips had begun to glow behind the blacked-out Oranzheria wall. The workers' head-lamps: a thousand fireflies floating in the fog of the glass. And atop it, as far as Dima could see, they blinked on, too, clear and bright as a distant city aglister with its lights, the way Petroplavilsk had once looked from out in the farmland at night.

Now he could hardly see it. Looking left down the chute of dark-ness that was the access line, towards where he knew Petroplavilsk must be, he caught a dim flush—the fog lights of the trams and cars, the few lamps people still kept in their homes. And from there a far-off murmur, less sound than a sense of emanating panic.

Then she was there. Close, shivering, pulling at his coat. "Let me in," she said, her voice shuddering, pressing herself to him. He wrapped her in the wool flaps. She was so thin he could have rebuttoned his coat around them both, up the line of her back, but he simply held it shut, his arms around her. He could feel how cold her skin was through his suit, her legs clamped against his, her quivering ribs, the jut of her nipples just beneath his chest.

"What do you think happened?" he said.

They stared up, as if expecting any moment the mirrors to flash back on.

"Maybe the Consortium found out," she said. "Decided to preempt our plan."

"Why?"

"To deny us the moment."

"And now?" He pulled the coat closer around her. "What do we do now?" He waited for her to look back at him. And when she didn't, he said, "We weren't really going to be able to, were we?" Her eyes found his. "Did you even really know," he said, "where the control room was?"

"We could have found it."

"And then?"

There was the glint of her smile. "What does it matter now?" she said. "What we do, what we might have . . ." A shiver shook her body and her hands rose from beneath his coat, found his jaw, tilted his face back. "It *is*." He could feel her voice on his throat. "Someone already *did*." She leaned against his chest. "Dima"—he could feel his name in the movement of her cheek—"it's done."

He let his own cheek lower to a rest on the top of her head. A surprise to feel, instead of the fuzz of her shorn scalp, the long hair of the wig. And strange to sense their breathing slip into synch, her body swelling and ebbing alongside his. He imagined her mushroom tattoo riding the rise and fall of her belly. He could almost feel the touch of it. He watched all the lights moving in the Oranzheria's mist.

"Come," she said, and he thought, *Where?* but she was only pulling him down. They crouched together, a mound made of them, covered by his coat. "My calves were cold," she told him.

Her shiver, his heat: maybe it was his imagination, but it seemed to him the wall of glass was already losing a little of its fog. In there the lights moved with an urgency that made the night around the two of them all the more still. "What do you think they'll do?" he whispered.

She looked behind her at the workers, too. "That," she said, "is what *we* do. Now that the deed—"

"The propaganda."

She nodded. "That's what we start tomorrow. Tonight. . ." His coat shifted with her turning back and he tried to catch her gaze, but it went past him, lost in the blackness of the woods behind. When her voice came again—"I wish we had firecrackers"—it sounded young as a girl's. Or simply happy. He swore he could see the brightness in her eyes when they turned to him. "We should make a fire."

He hated to shake his head: they'd be seen; someone would come.

But she was looking back at the woods. "In a month then," she said. "On Korochun. If it's still dark, we should go and . . ." She trailed off.

If it's still dark.

Dima rested his cheek against the softness of her wig again. "When we were kids," he told her, "we used to go with our uncle, out to the graveyard and light the fires to keep the dead warm. Dyadya Avya would kill a chicken. We'd roast it on a spit, and for each bite we took we'd toss some skin or bones or even meat down on the grave to keep him fed. When we were older, my brother and I used to bring whatever we could catch—a rabbit, a squirrel—and do the same."

Her head shifted beneath his cheek, but she didn't look away from the woods.

She said, "After my parents left, I made the fire with friends. We'd do it on the Kosha Road, just outside the city, at the crossroads with the old highway. When a car would come we'd hoot and howl and throw burning sticks at it. Sometimes, we'd line up between the fire and some truck's headlights and dance the khorovod."

He nodded. "We danced it, too. Did you used to tell the story? The old tired sun that shuts its eyes just for a second, lets night creep up and kill it?" He could see Dyadya Avya's face bright with firelight, the sounds the old man made to dramatize night's dark knife cutting out the flaming heart, the moaning of the dying sun shifting seamlessly into the crying of the newborn one: from winter's womb it would come, return in spring aflame with vengeance, spend all summer hunting down the night.

"Sure," she said. And he could feel her smile. "But mostly we just went off into the woods and fucked."

Then her head was out from beneath his cheek. A strange sensation, her breath on his chin, as if his skin, covered so long by his beard, was learning again how to feel.

"But look!" she said.

The words were a puff of warm breath, and he jerked a little, peered at her.

"But look!" she said again.

Her face was turned to him, waiting for something, and he whispered, "At what?" In the faint moonlight, he couldn't quite tell if her eyes rolled.

"The door," she said. "It's open?" She paused, waited. And then: "A footstep?"

He smiled. "A nimble footstep!" he said. "You've memorized it?"

Her laugh was the first nervousness from her he'd ever heard. "Are you kidding?" Her hands lay flat against his chest. She pressed them there a little more firmly. "But you have."

The Khazar khan, Ratmir. Ruslan's rival. Asleep inside a castle, lured there by a keep-full of maidens. "'And through a silvery ray of moonlight,'" Dima said, "'a girl darts. Now's the time for dreams to spread their wings and fly!'"

"Really?" Vika said, all mock surprise, and, inside his coat, leaned into him.

"'Wake up,'" he went on. "'This is your night of nights!'"

"'Uh-huh,'" she said.

"'Yes, wake up—don't waste precious moments!'" He couldn't make out the sound she made through the sound of his own swallowing. But he felt her shake her head. She had placed her ear in the space between his neck and chest, as if trying to hear the vibrations of his throat: "'The covers slid from off the bed; damp forelocks fringed his

345

flaming temples.'" Her lips were on his throat. "'The girl stood over him in silence . . .'"

Vika opened her mouth and closed her lips around his Adam's apple. When she spoke he could feel the flutter of her tongue against it. "Go on," she said.

"'And on the bed where the khan lay . . .'"

"You skipped ahead," she told his skin.

"I know," he said.

"Good," her tongue told him.

"'She leant one knee . . .'"

"Like this?" Vika said, and she was on her knees between his bent ones.

"'She breathed a sigh . . .'" He could feel her breath on the soft skin beneath his jaw. "'. . . then bent her head down to him . . .'" Her hands slid up his chest, cupped his face, drew his own head down. "'. . . trembling and unsteady . . .'"

"And?" her lips said.

"'And with . . .'" He paused.

"With?" she said.

"'. . . with a mute and hungry kiss . . .'" Her lips were almost touching, tracing the movement of his own. "'. . . she cut his dream short—'" And he couldn't keep from smiling at the stanza's last two words: "'Lucky man!'"

He felt her smile with him. "I'll say," she said.

But did she? She was kissing him so hard he was sure no sound could have escaped.

"I don't know about you," she said, her tongue writing the words on his, "but I can't remember the last time I fucked someone beneath the stars."

And he would have reached down, stopped her hands, but they were inside his coat, and his were outside, holding her, and when she slid her fingers between his legs, feeling him, he didn't know what to do. Half his body tried to hunch away, and the other half of him turned it into an arc down to her, and he told himself it was to press her still, but her lips were pressing back on his and it was as if the pressure was released in the stroking of her hand, and for a moment he let her. Then he pulled his face away. He tried to focus on the stars.

"'The valley around here was lonely,'" he said. "'Secluded and engulfed in shade. Stillness . . .'" He reached down and held her arm. "'Stillness.'" And she was, her hand, the whole of her, watching him. "'Stillness had seemingly held sway there since the inception of the world.'" Still looking up at the stars, he asked her if she remembered that part of the poem.

"No," she said.

"It's the part where Ruslan finds the Khazar khan again. Finds Ratmir has given up the warrior life to live in that little cottage, by the river, fishing, happy."

He didn't know where her hands were, except that they were no longer touching him. "And?" she said.

He met her eyes. Crouching there, watching the faint hint of her face in the darkness of his coat, he told her how that part of the poem was what he thought of when he thought of the old miri. Of the dream of an age of new ones. "When we were young," he told her. "In our twenties. My brother and me. We lived like that. We had . . . we *have* a dream. A farm. Our uncle's old—"

"And me?" she said. "What do I have to do with any of this?"

"It's just—"

"I don't. What does *this* have to do with—"

"Vika."

"It doesn't." Her hands reached up out of the coat's collar between their necks. "Ivanushka," she said, and grabbed the lobes of his ears. She shook them, just hard enough to jerk his head. "Ivanushka the Fool. This isn't like that. This isn't anything like that."

"I know," he said.

And she flattened her hands against his temples, squeezed. "There's room in here," she said, "to want more than one thing."

Between her palms he shook his head. "No," he said. "Don't you see? That's what's happened to everything. Everyone wants too much, everything becomes nothing." It was as if the word knocked loose her hands. "What you want to have, what you want to *get,* you lose your focus and you lose everything. That's *why* the miri worked. They were small. They were focused. They—"

"Look at me." Her eyes pulled at him as strongly as if she had bent his face down with her hands. "I am focused," she said. "I'm focused on you. Now. Half an hour ago, I was focused on getting into the headquarters. Tomorrow, I'll be focused on something else. I can want to get fucked-up with my friends, and I can want to shake up this fucking world, and I can want to take off my clothes and dance under the stars, and I can want to fuck you here, tonight. And," she said, "I can want to fuck someone else tomorrow."

Yes, he thought, and that was why the dream she had—she and Volodya and Fedya and those before them, all the way back to Bakunin and before that—*that* was why it had never happened. Why it never would. Her eyes looked so large in the moonlight. He thought, looking into them, that they seemed the eyes of a child. That she wanted the way a child wanted. The way he might have when he was very small, before his father fell through the ice, and his mother was sent away, and his uncle lost his world, and he had begun to lose his brother. Because she was wrong: there wasn't room for more than one thing. Life knew when you were losing focus, or looking away, or simply for a moment shutting your eyes, and that was when it crept in and with its dark knife cut out your heart.

She was talking again about Korochun. How when she was a girl they had done things they never would have on any other night, and he stopped her.

"My papa," he said.

She waited.

"My papa was the one in the grave. We were ten."

She went so still she might not have been there, might have some-how slipped out from his coat—and then she moved and he was sure she was going to. But when she stood she pulled him up with her. Her hands were on his lapels, then working at the knot in his tie, got it lose, slid it off of his neck, and she undid the top button of his shirt and then the next and all the way down until she had untucked it and the warmth off the front of her was filling the space in front of him. Then she reached up. He felt it in the rising of her breasts against his skin. He waited for her hands to touch his face. They didn't. Instead, they went to her own, slid under her wig.

When she had slipped it from her head, she reached over and did the same with his hat. With one hand, she settled his hat on her. With the other, she placed the wig over his head. The machines had started up in the Oranzheria again. He listened to the glass-muffled din. He watched her watching him. She had begun to shake her head.

"Nope," she said. "No, it's no use. You still don't look like me." Then she leaned in and kissed him. When she was done, she backed away, broke his arms apart, was out. "Maybe you're right," she told him. "Maybe, for you, you're right."

There was the pale barely visible shape of her while she searched for her clothes, and then her dress was over her head and there was just the paleness of her legs and arms and neck, and then she must have slipped into her coat: there remained only a suggestion of her face. And then she turned and that vanished, too.

Revisitation

Up there, slipping between the last faint suspiration of the world and the breathless infinitude of space, the mirrors had all, one after the other, ten, then twenty, then half a hundred, then the rest, simply shifted their wings. A tiny movement. The glassy fields of quilted Kevlar twitched. And were still again, the zerkala again tracing their paths through the exosphere, their captured light cast down in the same beams that for years now had been strung like lambent threads from the mirrors to the earth.

But not to Petroplavilsk. The circle of luminescence swelled outward, yawned a hole, a ring around the empty center it used to light. Now it lit new land. Fir trees stiffened their branches. Spruce needles reached out, antennae feeling the effulgence. Whole forests of white birch trunks glowed. All around them, the circle's edge coruscated above new borderland fens. Night animals—raccoons and polecats and Ural owls—that had retreated from the ever-spreading light now fled the new refracted ring, back towards the darkness that had fallen inside it. Over the Oranzheria they flew, and across the lake, clouds

350

of nightjars and bewildered bats, came loping down the access line, stumbling along Otseva's boggy shores, returning in a horde. With them came humans, too. Villagers unable to sleep, farmers distraught at livestock gone half-mad, loggers and fishermen and old hermits who had lived all their lives far back in the woods and now came doddering out, confounded by what the world had done.

In Petroplavilsk, the people watched them come, watched the white hares and stoats and arctic fox streak across the snow, apparitions from an earlier age when it wasn't strange for animals to change the color of their coats, remembered a time before the zerkala, realized how much the mirrors had changed them. They called it The Revisitation, and they meant the returning animals and the refugees and the reemergence of poverty and the coming of the dark, but mostly they meant the way it stirred inside them a reconsideration of their own lives. These were the days of first true snow. The darkening of skies, the blanketing of roads. The sun hardly showed. Each morning it rose a little later, each evening set a little earlier, lighting the city for less and less of each spin of the earth, and soon there would be hardly any light at all.

Before, at night, the mirrors' beams would help to melt the snow. Now it piled up, no lamps to guide the snowblowers, no headlights on the plows. Without the Consortium, there was no money for new streetlights, the city spending all it had to keep government buildings from going dark, portable lights along the two most vital boulevards, no other way to get anywhere, except by foot.

People came out with flashlights, would have brought snow shovels, too, but who, for years now, had shoveled their own snow? So worn out from work, who wouldn't pay a company with armies of snowblowers to roar it clear in minutes? No one could now. Now they turned flashlights off when the moon came out, worried about the cost of replacing batteries, wished they had saved more. They canceled their satellite TV, took away their children's phones, stopped buying anything but food. On the shelves the delicacies went unpurchased—sundried tomatoes, gourmet coffee, purple-veined radicchios big as hearts and

351

starting to brown—and then went for the same prices as the cans of fish, ordinary cabbage, and then were gone, the rest going. And when even the pickles and potatoes stopped selling, families skipping meals to make it through the month, people started to panic.

But, above, the stars were beautiful.

Small groups of men and women walked beneath them in the streets, flashlights flaring on at sounds in the dark—a snarl, a hiss, something crying out—beams catching eyes bright as bursts from the muzzle of a gun. Sometimes it was. Along what streets the police could drive, they used their flashers for light, and on the others they went by foot, big flashlights burning batteries, said they would continue until their paychecks stopped. Crime came back to Petroplavilsk. Fear with it. People stayed in, hunkered around what few lamps they had, the TV showing clips of their darkened city, news anchors hinting it was their own fault, politicians hedging about when they might step in to help. Everyone knew they wouldn't. Everyone worried how long it would go on. If they had to be out on the street at night, they gathered in groups, hurried past the crude snow shelters the refugees constructed, igloos trembling with the glow of the fires inside, or gone dark and still, worrying the people passing even more.

It didn't take long for the worry to turn to anger, for the anger to get organized. Crowds began to gather wherever the Consortium had put pictures of its spokesman up, men and women clustering beneath the billboards on Chernishevskogo Avenue, collecting around the edges of Space Regata Square, shouting at the strikers still gathered in the middle and shouting back. Some had joined the strikers in anger at the shutdown of the Oranzheria, the billionaire's stone-hearted redirection of the mirrors. But each day more of the strikers left, crossed the cobblestones into the growing mass of those who catcalled and cursed, who wanted their lives to go back to how they were, who wanted work.

But out at the Oranzheria it was quiet. No chain saws roared, no backhoes groaned, no bulldozers knocked anything down, no tractors plowed, no harvesters cut fields, nobody called to anybody on the glass, or beneath it. It was a sea becalmed. The only ones who still had jobs were the guards. Stationed along the Oranzheria's edges, they faced those out of work, the ones that came each day, bundled in hats and coats, hands in their pockets, simply standing, silent, waiting. Behind the guards, through the glass, they could see the fields inside. Each day the plants were a little more dead.

At home, in the dark, Dima would sit with his mother on their square of cardboard beside the hissing heater, forks scraping at a barely visible pan. A bag heavy with wet potato skins, an onion from which to carve away the rot: in fish tin oil he'd fry whatever he'd found, popping and crackling over the balcony fire. He'd struck lucky with a sack full of sunflower seeds, and each night he put his mother to work splitting their shells—it was the kind of task he'd learned could keep her at peace for hours, the way her sewing had before he'd taken away her machine—and when he fried the seeds up with the rest they could elevate the dish to edible, even, on lunchless days when they were hungry enough, to good.

These nights, he left the bird unhooded. He left the kovyor-curtains up. Sometimes, before he went to bed, he would stand against the edge of his brother's old cot, hands spread on the empty mattress, staring out at the city. The dark sky and the dark buildings and all the scattered squares of lamplit windows: it looked almost how he remembered Petroplavilsk from when he was a child. Then he would wonder where among those lights his brother was. At home, with Zinaida, in bed? Curled on his son's cot, having read Timofei to sleep? Pacing the apartment with Polina bawling in his arms? Or was he still at work, still awake, trying to keep the Oranzheria safe, to keep his job, to keep things ready in case someday the zerkala came back? Unless he knew they wouldn't. Or knew exactly when they would. Unless he wasn't even nearby at all, was in Moscow, or even farther south, vacationing with his son and daughter and wife. Standing at the window, Dima would think about how any of it could be true and he wouldn't know, how Yarik could be as close as a five-minute tram ride or as distant as the sea and either way as far from him. *Choice*,

Yarik had once said, the choice he was making. But Dima had only ever wanted to keep the choices at bay. Once, they had just been two boys together in a boat. How still the stars above had seemed! How the skiff had rocked beneath them, as if held in place. But now he knew it wasn't. Eventually the tide would have taken it, the current would have pushed it to some shore. Even if the search boat hadn't found them. Even if his brother hadn't stood up, so desperate to be taken aboard. All that he would think about. And then he would go to sleep and dream of Vika.

He hadn't seen her, hadn't heard from her since the night the mirrors disappeared. At first, he'd worried it was too dangerous for him to venture out, that the anger over the city's plight would turn towards the myth that had been made of him. For three whole days he stayed inside, the food dwindling, his mother berating him for shirking work, even the rooster leveling at him a look of disgust, while over and over he tried to clear his mind of her, and couldn't. Then, one dawn, he snuck out onto the snow-deep streets and found the posters with his face were all torn down, the statues in all the squares abandoned, the only finger pointing at his shorn face and close-cut hair the one on the heavy hand of the bronze tsar alone again down by the lake. Above Space Regata Square, the screens that had been hacked were back to watches, perfumes, Slava asking those below, *What next?* Once, standing at the edge of the roiling crowd, he thought he saw her amid the pandemonium. Once, he thought he heard her shout. One day, at last, he went to look for her in the old Pioneer House.

The cellar hatch had been locked shut. In the front, a sign was nailed to the double doors—a stick figure in the crosshairs of an X beneath the words KEEP OUT—bright as if painted that morning just for him. Someone had nailed wood scraps over the windows; he went from one to the next, pressing an eye to the cracks, peering in. In the ceramics room the sink was empty, the counter bare, her pallet gone from the floor. Even the potter's wheels had been stolen or sold. Through a pine-knot hole, he looked in at another stark room: model rockets and planes still hanging from the ceiling, dangling motionless, fighter jets and helicopters and something that looked like the giant hull of some sort of flying boat. Yarik would know what it was. He would know which of the rockets had launched Gagarin into space, which capsule had held the dogs. *This one,* he had said so long ago, showing Dima his sketchbook for the cosmonauts' club he'd joined, *is going to take men to Mars. These are the landing pads. And these are the thrusters.* And *this* was something else he would invent, and *that* was the Martian station he would design. And this was how one day they would be able to live. And Dima could still remember looking at his brother's careful scratches, wondering, *Why?*

Why had he never asked? Why had he never allowed himself to wonder further? Had they always been so different, ever truly wanted the same thing? Had he simply wanted it so much he'd refused to see the signs his brother hadn't? Maybe *that* had been his choice. Made so many times, so long ago, by such a small boy squeezing his eyes shut in that floodlit boat, and again in the darkness of that hidden warren, and again in the shaking dom cultura hall, again and again and maybe wrong.

That afternoon he took apart his brother's bed. He lay the narrow mattress against the wall, tipped the metal frame, unscrewed the legs. He carried it through the living room he had long ago stripped bare, and into the elevator, and out to the Universitetsky Rynok, where he sold it. And that night, he lay awake in his cot, staring at the space where all his life the other cot had been. The room seemed not just emptier, but quieter.

The valley hereabouts was lonely, secluded . . . Watching the pool of night where Yarik once had slept, Dima could see the river so remote it didn't have a name, the cottage silent on its bank, the current slipping through the rushes, the rustle of the breeze, the Khazar kahn out on his boat, setting his nets, singing as he rowed towards the shore.

> *And from the cottage there ran out*
> *a pretty lass: her graceful figure,*
> *her hair, left simple and unbraided,*
> *her smiling lips, her gentle eyes,*
> *her bosom, her bare shoulders.*

Nothing like her. Nothing but the bare shoulders. And yet it was as if he sat with Ruslan on that bank and at the same time watched himself step off that boat, and when the khan spoke it was both to him and, inside his head, sounded like his own voice.

And here I am, contented now,
a peaceable, obscure recluse,
in this remote spot here with you, dear,
with you, sweet friend, my life's bright . . .

That Korochun he lit a trash fire on the balcony. Nearly a month since the mirrors first disappeared, the longest night of all the year; by three it was already nearly dark. He cooked an early supper, ate with his mother by the flickering light, got her to bed and fed the rooster, and by six was standing in the near-black hallway putting on his coat. Lifting his old Oranzheria worker's headlamp off its hook, he replaced its long-dead batteries with the new ones he'd exchanged for the pillow from his brother's bed. He picked up the broken broom handle. And, for the first time since The Revisitation had begun, he went out into Petroplavilsk at night.

Avtovskaya Street was still unplowed. Cars, unmoved for a month, hunkered beneath drifts at its sides. In the moonlight, the ground was bright enough to see without his headlamp. Bright enough, too, to show the shapes that loped across the snow, the ghostly figures far ahead floating on what must have been skis. He could hear their susurration, the barking of dogs, sirens howling somewhere police cars could still reach. He kept his headlamp on. Walking in the middle of the street, where others had packed down a trail in the thigh-high snow, he passed the makeshift igloos the homeless had built, didn't look at them, didn't want his headlamp beam hitting their translucent walls. Sometimes they were silent, and sometimes there were faint voices, and always they stopped at the sound of his footsteps. What dogs came stalking he scattered with a cocked arm—they had grown to know a throwing motion—and set his beam back on the path, and went on.

356

The closer he got to the outskirts of the city the worse the path was, and by the time he reached the Kosha Road his legs were too tired to take advantage of the swath the plows had cleared. How weak he was. How much his muscles had atrophied in the last half-year. *Pick up your pace,* he told himself. I can't, his body answered. Once in a while, a bus would pass, rolling carefully behind fog lights so faint they barely yellowed the road. He would step aside, stand breathing hard, walk on in its fading red wake.

It was nearly two hours before he saw the moonlit Oranzheria float-ing out in the dark like an ice shelf at the edge of an arctic sea. And it was a half-hour more before he saw the fire. That was how he knew he'd reached the crossroads with the old highway. And it was how he knew, long before he was close enough to make her out, that he had found her. He was still too far away to see more than the shapes of people in the firelight, too far to shape words out of their singing, when, pausing to let some strength leak into his legs, he seemed suddenly transported close. For a moment, he didn't understand—the singing abruptly loud, right beside his ear—and then out of the corner of his eye he sensed some bulk, a man; he jerked back, stepped to the side, saw him: massive neck bent forward over massive shoulders hunched atop a massive torso—Volodya in his headlamp beam. The gastron-ist must have been drunk; he didn't seem to notice the light. His eyes were closed and he was singing while he peed.

How I love my dear brown cow,
And how I'll mow her stinging nettles!

He was peeing into the trees at the side of the road, and with each beat, he swung his stream against their trunks, back and forth, keeping in rhythm if not in tune with his distant friends.

Eat what you want, my dear brown cow!
Eat your fill, my dear brown cow!

Then all at once his eyes flew open, his neck swiveled, his face caught the light. He held a hand up to his eyes. "Who the fuck . . ."

"It's me," Dima said.

"Who the fuck is me?"

"Dima."

The piss started up again. It was loud hitting the snow. And without warning the fat man tilted back his head and bellowed at the top of his lungs, "It's Dima!" He grinned into the beam, and turned, and still zipping his fly lurched into a belly-swinging jog back towards the fire.

Dima followed at a walk, the whole way listening to Volodya shout his name. Soon the fat man was out of range of his headlamp. There was just the blackness and the fire and the singing and—*Dima! Dima! Dima!*—the slowly growing shapes of the others. Until another figure took shape in the faint far reaches of his beam. She grew brighter as she came. Then, halfway to him, stopped. Held out her arms. And fell backwards into the snow.

He was surprised to find his legs could hurry. And when he was standing over her, out of breath again, his headlamp carving a circle of light out of the dark around them, he was even more surprised to see her eyes stay squinted tightly closed. "Are you OK?" he asked. And she surprised him again with a snort, a rattling wheeze; she started to snore. He held his breath above her. She let hers out below. It clouded her face like smoke, and cleared, clouded and cleared.

Finally, she said, her eyes still squeezed shut, her voice tight with exasperation, "Oh, come on!"

He knew then what this was—her playacting the poem, Lyudmila out cold, the wizard's sleeping spell denying Ruslan the consummation of their wedding night—knew it but still felt foolish saying it aloud. "Vika?" he said instead. And then, again, a little louder. And finally gave in and whispered down at her still face, "Lyudmila?"

There was her bad-toothed smile. "Listen," she said. And, her eyes still closed, her lips the only thing moving in his beam, she showed him: "'The youthful prince's desire blazed on without fulfillment, tormenting him, a virgin ever—'"

"A *martyr*," he corrected.

"'But did he really just keep watch over his wife and find his satisfaction in thoughts of love?'" Her face mimed doubt. "'Without the deed?'" The doubt turned to disbelief. "'Subduing all his better instincts?'"

"His *lower* instincts," Dima said. And picked up where she'd left off: "'The monk who faithfully preserved the record of our famous knight and left it for posterity assures us firmly it is so.'"

"That sucks," she said.

And as he knelt into the snow beside her he watched her eyelids flutter. "Good thing," he said, "that it's just a poem."

Then they were open. Her eyes stared up at his face, straight into the light, her pupils growing smaller and smaller and staying on his. "Also"—she smiled—"that I'm no maiden." Her words were a cloud blown over his face, and breaking apart, and showing her eyes again. Still on him.

"Where did you go?" he asked her.

She reached up through his breath. He shut his eyes. But when he felt her hand it was on his headlamp. Slowly she tilted it, tugging his head, sweeping the beam down the length of her body, back up to her face. Her eyes. "I'm here," she said. And shut the lamp off. From the darkness, she asked him, "Are you?"

He nodded. Felt the motion move her hand. Then her fingers were gone from his forehead. Beneath him: the shadow of her shape slowly solidifying amid the moonlit snow. When she started to slip off his glove, he let her. His hand felt plunged into a hole cut in the frozen lake. Until she led his bare fingers into the unzipped collar of her coat, through the opening of her sweater, beneath the wool, onto her breast.

"And here," she said.

He could hear in her voice how cold his hand was, feel it in the shiver that shook her body, the pebble of her nipple under his palm. But she only reached for his other hand, stripped off its glove, guided it down towards her waist, buried it beneath the coat and sweater that covered her belly. Her gasp. His fingers spread over the shudder of it. The swell of her breath.

"And here."

He knelt, frozen, his arms out, hands motionless, his skin surrounded by her heat. Through her breast he could feel her heartbeat. Her navel: a warm well in the smooth stone of her belly. He tried to send his blood into his fingers, share his own warmth with her, but beneath him she was already unfastening the saftey pins from her fly, and he could feel his blood loosed all through him, racing.

Reaching down, she undid his pants. Her hands must have been as cold as his, but they felt burning. Her knuckles in the hair above his pelvis, her fingers finding him, the freezing air and—"Still?" she asked; "Here," he answered—he was in her.

So fast, such warmth. He stared at her beneath him—that she could be so deep, he so far in someone, her the one to take him there—tried to make out her eyes. "Here," he said again. And listened for her voice giving him the same word in return—*Zdyes,* she would say, and he would tell her, *Zdyes*—but her mouth stayed open in the moonlight, her eyes shut, her face full of such concentration she seemed already gone to another place.

Tempering

On the road out to the Oranzheria the plow had cleared a path no wider than itself, and as Yarik drove—an old diesel-breathed Mercedes he'd bought secondhand—the car parted the crowd like a blade through snow, the jobless stepping up onto the piled banks, down again as he passed by, rising and falling in waves. Until, up ahead at the crossroads, he saw a few former workers motioning for him to stop, beyond them, a barrier. He braked. Another time, he would have gotten out to help them move whatever was in the way. But not with a saddlebag of cash on the seat beside him, all those laid-off people massed around the windows. The ones in front were dragging apart a dead fire's remains. Long, blackened logs. Last night must have been Korochun. He wouldn't have thought anyone would light the crossroad bonfires anymore, feel the need to frighten spirits from claiming others' lives too early: it seemed so far removed from the real dangers of this world. He cleared the quiet with a gunning of his engine, waved thanks at the men, looked away as they called out for money, and, pushing forward, put the fire and its ghosts from his mind.

Ever since Moscow they had been haunting him: memories of his father, his uncle, the kolkhozniki he'd known as a boy, the old kulak he was going to have to see again. His brother, who, afterwards, he would have to face. The choice he would have to make. Though in the end it seemed to him the billionaire had left him none. Just a letter for Kartashkin, a contract, the cash.

Beneath the Oranzheria, the day went dim. Above, no one had cleared the snow. It smothered the glass, and under it the fields seemed to draw in, as if sliding back to the years before the mirrors, and Yarik slipped back even further: winter wakings, Dyadya Avya sleeping off a drunk, nothing but sunlight to rouse the boys; they pulled blankets over their heads, the morning seeping in as if through the canopy of a deep forest from one of their uncle's fairy tales. Here, harvesters slumped like giants slain; feller bunchers had suffered some warlock's curse, died off in herds, their steels jaws open wide with last breaths; everywhere the boom-arms of excavators were bent like broken dragons' necks, their shovels hanging loose as half-severed heads; the mage had found the trenchers, too: there they sat frozen still as all the rest.

Then he was through to the other side. He squinted into the brightness, the sun on the snow, the snow falling in sparkler bursts from spruce boughs, the Kosha River gleaming, frozen. But not solid, the way it had been on the city side of the glass. Here, the ice showed the wink of water, a rippling gap snaking down the middle of the river. Here was where the zerkala sent their light now.

He drove through a village, between the wooden houses with windows blocked by blankets newly nailed to sills, mattresses propped on their ends against the light, past the sense of people sleeping who had never slept through daylight before, bare winter trees that seemed somehow more alert, as if their sap had shot through them like adrenaline and they were stiffened, waiting, as he sped by.

Then he wasn't. He sat in the stopped car. All around spread winter fields the way fields had been before the Oranzheria—snow smothered, barren, white to make his eyes water—and before him there was only the curve of road disappearing into dark pines, and there was no reason for him to have stopped. He stared through the windshield, as if waiting for a reason to appear. Nothing but the squat, boxy bell tower rising over the distant pines, nothing but the distance and the road taking him towards it, and then he could hear it: the heavy, low clanging of the bells. Ten kilometers ahead lay the farm. Ten minutes more and he would reach it: the barns and paddocks, their uncle's soot-dark izba, that old kulak Kartashkin waiting in it for him.

The bell wasn't ringing—he could see the dark inside the tower, the lack of any movement, any glint—but he could hear it. He could hear the music, too: the gusli and balalaika, the fiddle slinging its tune above the trees, onto the road, at him. He could hear the people roar and clap. He could feel the rumbling: all the farm trucks coming from the villages around to pull up in the muddy lot beside the dom kultura.

But when he pulled into a swath shoved clear by a plow there was no one else there. Getting out into the cold, the air stinging his face, he could see that for a long time, now, no one had been in the dom kultura. The bell in the tower wasn't just still; it was gone. Zerkala light and gusts of wind had thinned the snow on the roof, and Yarik could see patches missing from its rusted tin. The sallow plaster was scrawled with graffiti, or crumbled off the brick walls. Most of the windowpanes were broken. The front door gaped.

The slam of his car door shutting startled something in the building. For a moment there was the lingering smack, the sounds of something banging inside; then it came flapping out of the dom kultura, gray and black feathers shining in the sun, and he wondered as it cawed off what there was left here for a crow to eat. Opening the car door again, he leaned in, lifted out the leather bag of roubles, grabbed Dyadya Avya's gun, shoved it with the money into the pouch. This time he closed the door quietly, used his hip to press it shut. His footsteps crunched through the snow. He was wearing heavy boots with his suit pants tucked in the tops, and a parka over his suit jacket, the fur-lined hood hanging down his back, the shouldered saddlebags tilting him with their weight. In the sunlight, his breath made puffs of steam.

Then he was inside, the creak of the boards beneath him. Something scrabbled on the wood, a brushing like swipes of a broom, a flurry of exhalations. Or wing flaps? As his eyes adjusted, he made them out: a few big shapes, their black heads and wings and legs disappeared into the dark, only their gray visible, less like crows than the headless bodies of birds floating, rustling, feeding on something. It was too dark to tell what. But he could smell it.

Once, it had smelled like life in there, the whole huge room full of people's breath, sweat, mud, spilled kvass, vodka, wafting through the windows with the scents of roasting meat, the piss stink of drunkards propping themselves against the buildingside, of the women crouched at the edge of the field. He could remember the smell of Zina the first time he had slept with her, the scent of him spread on her skin, her scent still sticky on his, when they had come back from the woods into the crowd, her astride his shoulders, wet and warm on the back of his neck, and him breathing her in. How light she had seemed when he had started to dance!

Now, the saddlebag of roubles was growing heavy. Beneath its weight he made his way towards the stage. Whoever played last had left their music stands: a few metal glints, a couple empty chairs. Deeper in the darkness of the room, the crows fluttered at his approach. He stopped. He let the saddlebags slide from his shoulder. Two heavy thuds to the ground and, before the leather strap could slap quietly after them, the birds were up. They clattered into the air, wings smacking wings. And Yarik dropped to a crouch. He flung out a leg. Slowly, kicking first one then the other, he began to dance. His winter boots banged at the floor, his suit jacket flapped inside his parka, the hood slapped over and over at his back. He crossed his arms in front of him and shut his eyes and thumped his heels against the boards, and the music stands behind him rattled with the shaking, his cheeks shaking, the skin below his jaw shaking, and the heat starting to cloud inside his coat, until his sweat was coming—he could feel it seep into his clothes, prickle his neck, his belly, his chest, and his lungs already sucking for breath, and his heart thudding loud as his boots—thump,

thump, thump—so he could feel it beneath his crossed arms, and he uncrossed them, and held them out, and opened his hands and, shaking with his kicks, shut his fingers as if grabbing on to hands holding his. *So simple,* he thought. And then his leg cramped and gave out and his other crumpled with it and he toppled onto his back.

Lying there, arms spread, legs spread, head cushioned by the crushed fur of his hood, he stared up at the shapes of the circling crows and thought, *You danced until you were tired and when you were tired you stopped and when you stopped you slept.* He shut his eyes. He was still breathing hard. The sweat on his face was already beginning to chill. Up above, the ceiling was dark, and the wingbeats of the crows went round and round and it seemed strange to him that they wouldn't caw, that there was just the sound of their panicked flight, their moving, moving, going nowhere. Had any of the choices he had made been right? To sell their father's boat. To marry. To have a kid, another. To work on the Oranzheria. To let his brother lead the kind of life he did. To leave his mother in Dima's care. To take the promotion. To take the money. All of it, from the first steps that started to separate him from his brother, to the last ones that had led him now to here: when he thought of it like that, the answer seemed clear. What right did he have to think the choices Dima had made were wrong? What right did he have to choose anything for Zina, for their kids? To make a choice now for them all? It seemed then that whatever he did it would be wrong. And yet here he was, ten kilometers away, ten minutes from what might be the biggest decision he would ever make. He opened his eyes, looked for the crows. Nothing. They must have found a hole, squeezed through one of the gaps in the roof, flown off. But then he saw something dark flit through the light, and another shape flapping and gone, and knew they were still up there, still circling.

"Go," he shouted into the darkness. "Get out of here!"

But the echo of his voice only brought with it the sound of their wingbeats falling back down on him again.

He spread his own arms and slid them, winglike, slowly up and down on the floor, up once and down once and his right hand hit the leather of the saddlebags. For one more flap his left arm worked on its own, and he thought, One more bad choice: why had he not emptied the pouch full of the cash Bazarov had given him to keep? Why had he been too afraid to leave it in the apartment, thought they wouldn't trust him at the bank if he walked in with stacks and stacks of bills? Now, he would have to lock it in the car—five million roubles spilled out, shoved beneath the seat—while he carried into the meeting the other pouch full, the money meant for Kartashkin. Something about the thought stopped his left hand flapping, sent his right searching for the buckle. He found it, flipped the pouch open, dug inside, grabbed a stack of roubles, drew it out. The revolver came, too, fell out with a clank. He lay with his neck swiveled, his cheekbone against the floor, staring down the length of his arm to the roubles in his fist, to his knuckles nearly brushing the old revolver. The last person to pull the trigger had been his uncle. He saw it again: Avya's face as he'd heard his nephews calling from the riverbank, the brothers splashing after him, their uncle turned, water swallowing his cheek, one eye above the surface, staring back. Yarik had thought the raw fear in that eye had been a pleading for them to save him, but he knew now that it was anger, anger that the old man had made his choice in life—three hammer clicks, four, five—and now, as the two of them rushed towards him, life was making him choose all over again. Yarik wondered, then, if their father had really fallen through the ice. No. Life gave you choices, and you made them. Chance, fate: they were no more real than the Chudo-Yudo. He wondered if that was why Dyadya Avya had told them the story of the devil snake, of their father's soul, wondered if their uncle had thought them too young to understand. Well, he wasn't young anymore. He thought how he was almost as old now as his father had been. And then he dropped the stack of roubles and his fingers closed around the grip of the gun.

His hand shook. The barrel rattled against the floor. He told himself it was just the awkwardness of the position, his arm stretched out, his wrist bent, his hand reaching, and then he laughed. He laughed at himself, at the idea that he would even think of doing it, laughed out loud, and the sound went up into the ceiling and brought down with its echo the panic it gave the crows, their wings whapping at the walls, the walls shedding dust, and in the sound of the dust tinkling to the floor he realized he wasn't laughing anymore. He thought how nice it would be not to have to make the decision ten kilometers away. He thought how nice it would be not to have to make any more decisions at all. In the end, Zina always told him, that was how it would be. Everything clear, nothing left in the dark. The eternal light. She said it would be everlasting as the flame that hung above the tabernacle to remind them of the unceasing presence of the Savior, the Light of the World. He thought he understood why his wife had such faith. Why she believed in heaven. He wished he did, too.

Maybe then he would have been able to lift the gun. Instead, he had to slide it on the floor until his arm was bent, his elbow stuck out from his side, the gun upside down, its barrel touching the side of his head. *If there's no such thing as chance,* he thought, *then what of Bazarov and his revolvers?* Maybe that day in Moscow the man had loaded one blank among the bullets; it would be just like him, the thrill he'd get knowing there was that little extra risk. He wondered if the game could be played with one chamber empty instead of one full. And, his finger touching the trigger, tentative as the nose of a dog brushing some stranger's knuckles, he knew, with a sense as deep as any animal's deepest sense, that all the chambers were full. He wondered if it would count as a game of chance simply due to the shakiness of his hand. Then he remembered the explosive tips.

How many times had Dyadya Avya pulled the trigger before the gun had finally gone off? Before Yarik, slipping down the muddy bank, splashing into the current, catching the hammer flash—*The gun!* Dima had shouted behind him—the flash again—*Get the gun!*—fought the weight of his boots, the shoving current, come so close to their uncle floating on his back—the hammer clacked—his eyes squeezed shut, his belly ballooned with the air in his lungs—clacked—so close Yarik had reached out, grabbed the barrel . . . The boom came so loud it stripped the sound from everything else. Ripped away even the feeling of Yarik's bruised fingers, his burned palm, the coldness of the water, the warm blood. It sprayed from the lung pierced in their uncle's chest, slicked Yarik's face, his arms, as he tried to smother the spume from the hole Avery Zhuvov had blown in his fast-sinking self.

Lying on his back, his own chest swollen with his own breath held, Yarik could feel it now: the slipperiness on his fingers, the bruise of his grip, that river's chill. He listened to the boom. Why did it seem so much louder than that one time, even longer ago, when he had fired the gun? In his own hands, it had gone off just as close, shot the same kind of bullet. Even the water beneath them, even his brother's voice shouting behind the blasts: it should have sounded the same. But in his memory the ones he'd fired from the rowboat when they were kids were so much smaller, quiet pops, pop, pop, pop . . . He let the pistol barrel fall from his temple. It thunked against the floor. Not just the same kind of bullet: they had been the very bullets their uncle had loaded in. He had not been trying to play with fate: years ago, their dyadya had loaded all seven chambers. He'd never used the gun since then, hadn't know the boys had taken it, wouldn't have thought to see if any bullets had been spent. What a shock it must have been to work up the nerve to pull the trigger only to hear it click. And to do it again, and again, each time thinking *this one must be the last*: how horrible. How horrible that on the last try it was. Horrible, Yarik thought, because it was such a small thing that made the difference: that night on the rowboat he had shot six shots.

When he drew in his breath, it was shaky with anger. How close he had come to making another. If he was so bad at choices, what had made him think that *that* one would have been right? How would it have helped anything, anyone? He imagined Zina having to identify his body—his *body*, not his face: the explosive tips would have left her nothing of that. Not even a body she could bury: the church wouldn't condone such a sin with a cemetery plot any more than it had for his uncle, his father. He imagined Dima hearing the news, then, and knew there would be no one to hear the news of what Dima would surely do to himself. And, seeing two new piles of stones beside the two ones overgrown, he thought of his mother, of her home, and Zina moved into it, Polina crawling the bare floor, his little boy the last man left, and his anger hit him so strong he didn't even know what it was or why until he had squeezed the trigger and the boom had blasted around the cavernous room and the echo was filtering down on him like the wing-brushed dust.

Except there was no dust falling. He lay on his back with his arm outstretched above him, the pistol pointing straight up at the roof. No tinkle of glass. No clatter of plaster blown loose and tumbling down. Surely an explosive-tipped bullet would have done some damage he could see or hear. But there were just the crows, cawing now, wild with frantic circling. He watched their shapes flit by the shards of light, watched until he could make out their full circles and the nose of the pistol circled with them and he followed one until his gun moved as if strung to the bird.

The boom again. Again, the jolt jerking his wrist. There flew the bird, circling just the same. And no sign of the bullet hitting anywhere.

"Sonofabitch," he said.

He pushed himself up, pointed the gun at the low wooden wall of the stage a few meters away and pulled the trigger again. There was the sound. And nothing else. The boards stared back at him, blank and unmarred as before.

"Sonofabitch," he said again, and fired two more shots, in fast succession, not aiming at anything, just shooting to hear the booms and feel the handle slam into his palm and clench his jaw and make himself watch the absence of any sign of anything fired at all.

"Explosive tips," he spat, smacked the lock off the chamber, jerked it open, was about to shake the casings into his palm, the last unfired blank. . . . But the gun had gone still in his hand. He held his hand still beneath it. He looked at the saddlebags on the floor. Next to the one full of the money meant for him, the stack he'd pulled out lay wrapped in its bands. Crouching down, he picked it up with his free hand, thumbed slowly through it. It all looked good. But there were a lot of other stacks. He flipped the pouch open again, and pulled out another one, and had flipped through it, and another, and a fourth, when it hit him. It was all there, and if it was all there, it was enough. It would be enough. He would make it enough. At the thought, he stood, took a few steps, sat down on the edge of the stage. As if they had been waiting for him to leave the center of the room, the crows came down in the corner farthest away, landing, their wings flapping noisily, their talons clacking at the floor. He watched them gather, dark shapes clustering, the flock growing as if out of the darkness of that corner. He still had the gun in his hand, the shells still in it, and as he watched the crows amass, he slapped the chamber shut. Maybe it was useless, he thought, maybe it was a dud, maybe it wouldn't do anything at all, but at least it was a bullet, the last one he had left.

At first, he thought Kartashkin's farm had been abandoned, too. The fields were stubbled with spindly knapweed spikes, cagongrass gone brittle and gray, tamarack bushes lifting hummocks of snow on their backs. In the pastures, the snow was unbroken and smooth as the fields should have been. Where were the cows? Not in the milking parlor; it was silent, doors shut, feed paddocks empty. Between it and Kartashkin's house stood the giant equipment shed where once the combine harvesters had been kept, the harrows and hay rakes with their curved metal teeth, the new Belarus tractors hosed down and gleaming. Now the inside gaped cavernous and empty.

At the turnoff to the house, Yarik stopped. The car idled. The driveway wasn't plowed. A slight depression in the snow, it led to the garage, a glassed-in porch, two stories of wide windows below a bright blue roof: it looked like one of the houses he'd seen in the new-built subdivisions outside of Moscow. Except there was no door on the garage, no car in it, the windows plywooded over, the porch wrapped in plastic, no smoke rising from the chimney. Instead, way in the distance a faint wisp unfurled above a smudge so far off no one but him, or Dima, or perhaps their mother if she could still remember, would have known what it was.

He parked in front of an old Ural dump truck turned snowplow, pulled his even older Mercedes up till its nose nearly touched the big metal blade. Behind the truck, a door split away from the farmhouse and a woman shoved her head out into the cold. She looked old as his mother, and she wore a sweater over a nightgown and track pants under it, and it took him a second to place her as Kartashkin's wife. It was the curls of her uncovered hair, the way she dangled her cigarette when she looked at him and said something. He couldn't hear over the engine any more than that it was a shout, and by the time he'd shut the engine off she had ducked back inside and closed the door behind her. But she hadn't been shouting to him: farther back in the yard, beside the privy, the door to the big shed where Dyadya Avya once kept his geese swung open as if knocked loose by the house door slapped shut. In it: Kartashkin, bundled in a coat, one hand pushing the door, the other holding a burst of colors blooming upward from his fist, riotous and shimmering in the light. Feathers. As the man stepped out, Yarik glimpsed inside: dim shapes moving, thin glints of cage bars. From in there, a rooster shrieked, another shot its call in answer, the whole shed exploded with the racket of the birds. Kartashkin closed the door on it and started for the house, the feathers shaking in his fist, walking carefully on the beaten path of snow and ice, looking at Yarik's car the whole time. When he got to the steps that led to the izba door, he took hold of the rail and stopped. His stare kept on. No raised palm, no call hello, just the impatience of his coat-wrapped body waiting there in the cold.

Inside, Yarik bent to shuck his boots, watched Kartashkin lower himself to a stool, ease out one creaky leg, call to his wife to tug off his own. She pulled out a chair at the table, motioned for Yarik to sit, said, "*Dobro pozhalovat*, Yaroslav Lvovich. It's been a long time."

It had. Sitting at the table, feeling the floorboards with his toes through the holes in the slippers she'd slid towards him with her own slippered foot, he took in the room. When he had lived there with Dima, it had all been one open space, but the Kartashkins had put up partitions that ran from the log walls to the whitewashed masonry stove in the center, each room warmed by a section of its heat-holding brick. The partitions had been wallpapered, and the log walls plastered over, and, at first, it must have hardly felt like an izba at all. But that must have been a while ago, back when they had begun to build the big new house they'd never finished; he remembered hearing that they had sold their place in town, were going to make do with Avyeri Zhuvov's old izba until their new home was done. When had that been? He couldn't remember, but he knew it must have been before the Oranzheria.

Through one open doorway he could see into what looked like a bedroom: a mattress big as the one he and Zinaida had just bought, smothered in a pampering of pillows, their cases worn, the edges split. Through another doorway: a mammoth television, its dead screen skewbald with mottled splotches. On top of it someone had placed an ironing board. From beyond, there came the chirrups of hatchlings: cages covered with once-bright towels faded almost free of the depictions dyed in their cloth: a dolphin, a starfish, two trunks of palm trees silhouetted by a sun.

When Mrs. Kartashkin brought Yarik his tea, the cup was monogrammed in silver: *LMK,* same as was stitched above the fraying edge of her robe. He pulled his glance from both: on her age-pilled sweater, he recognized the logo of some designer brand Zinaida had only recently been able to buy. But when the old kulak joined him at the table, he could not stop staring at Stepan Fyodorovich's face. They had called him that—*old kulak*—since long before he was old. Now he had grown into it. It wasn't the way his mouth had pinched, his skin sagged off his neck, not even anything contained in his eyes—his eyes were pit-hard and calculating as ever—but something inside the man, the life in him: it hung off his frame like the flesh left after a sudden loss of weight. Now that Kartashkin had taken off his coat, Yarik could see the old man was still in his pajamas. *SFK* over the heart. Half the buttons gone. Through the gaps, patches of gray hair curled.

He was glad he had worn his suit. The night before, he'd asked Zina to trim his hair. That morning, he had shaved, ironed his slacks, put on the new tie. The saddlebags had wrinkled his jacket—he had slid them off his shoulder when he'd come in, let them slump beside his boots—but they had left their leathery scent on him, and he was glad of that, too. The room stank of chicken feathers and bird scat and the smoke of the woodstove and of cigarettes. The old kulak drew on the one in his mouth, took out the stub, stuck it in a cake pan full of sand. The pan was already littered with a pack's worth of butts, and in between them the sand was stabbed with deep small holes, too small for cigarettes, as if someone had poked it with a knitting needle, over and over again. Next to it, on the table, a cigar box sat: gold-foil seal, some coat of arms stamped on top. Kartashkin lifted the lid. Inside: a pack of the same cheap Troikas that Yarik smoked. The old man dug a cigarette out, offered it. Yarik shook his head. While the man lit up, his wife bent before the masonry stove, pot holders in her hands, opened the iron door, drew out another cake pan, and taking off the table the one full of butts, slid the new one in front of her husband. It was full of sand, too. Yarik could feel the heat come off it. The woman watched Kartashkin as if she expected him to do something with what she'd brought, but he hadn't even seemed to notice. Smoke leaking out his nostrils, he stared past Yarik, at the floor, the leather bags.

"You want to know what's in the bags?" Yarik asked him.

Kartashkin tugged his gaze away. He had dumped his handful of feathers on the table when he'd sat down; now he reached to the pile. "I thought," he said, "you would come with your brother."

"He's at home."

The old man nodded, drew a feather out. It was viridescent, speckled with flecks of blue and brown, long as his forearm. "You live together?"

"Money," Yarik said.

"He told me . . ."

"In the bags."

". . . that when you had the money"—Kartashkin raised the feather over the cake pan—"you would come each with your half to buy it."

"That was almost a year ago," Yarik said, and watched the kulak stab the feather into the hot sand. "What are you doing?"

373

"Tempering," Kartashkin told him. He left the feather standing straight up in the pan and, searching through the pile for another, said, "Does he know you're here?"

Through the smoke the old man breathed out, Yarik could see his wife standing over the stove, picking the old butts out of the other pan.

Her husband's fingers picked through the feathers, drew another out. It was a rich purple deepening to black, a gleaming plume that swooped down in an arc so long it swished against the table. "I gave him one of these," Kartashkin said.

"A feather?"

The old man laughed. It was a phlegmy sound cut short by a cough. "The whole bird. He said he was going to give it to you as a gift."

"For my daughter."

"A daughter!" He turned his wrinkled neck till his cough-wet eyes caught his wife's. "Little Yarik has a daughter."

"How old?" she asked.

"For her first birthday," Yarik told them.

"That bird?" the woman said.

The old man was shaking his head. "He told me it was for you. A Golden Phoenix is not a gift for a little girl."

"I know," Yarik said. "I made him take it back."

"Back?" Kartashkin had stuck the feather in the sand, and he said the word with such force the black plume shivered from his breath. "He didn't bring it back."

"He kept it," Yarik said.

"I wouldn't have taken it back." Kartashkin sucked at his cigarette, fished out a third feather, jammed it in, too. "It was a gift."

Watching the old man hunt out a fourth, Yarik tried to glean from the word what it was that was really making him so mad.

"It was a gift," Kartashkin said again, "from *me*."

"My daughter—"

"Not to your daughter. To your *brother*."

"I'm sure—"

"Do you know how much a full-tailed Golden Phoenix is worth?"

THE GREAT GLASS SEA

"No," Yarik said.

"I could sell a bird like that—"

"But you didn't." This time Yarik cut the old man off. "You gave it to my brother as a bribe because you were hoping to get out of the contract you signed, because you were hoping to stab in the back the kolkhozniki . . ."

"What are you talking about?"

"My uncle . . ."

"I have a right—"

"You have a right to sell the land only to one of their sons. Or—because my uncle had no sons—to me."

There was the squeal of another stove door opening, and a flickering orange light flashed around the room. Kartashkin's wife tossed her handful of butts into the fire and shut the door again. At the table, the old man stuck one feather after another into the baking pan, stab, stab, stab, in quick succession, until the entire handful he'd brought in stood straight up in the hot sand, brilliant reds and golds and green-tinged blacks shivering between the men. When he was done, he pointed through the feathers, his finger jutting palely between the colors. "Where did you get them?"

"The bags? They're from America."

"They look like something your brother dug out of the trash."

"We're not talking about my brother," Yarik said.

"He said he had half."

Yarik reached out and, with the backs of his knuckles, pushed the cake pan aside. The metal burned, but he didn't take his hand away until the space between the two of them was clear again. "In those bags," he said, "is much more money than my brother could ever come up with. More than you could ever get from both of us combined."

Kartashkin finished his cigarette, stubbed it into an empty corner of sand. But instead of opening the cigar box for another, he reached past it and dragged across the table a knife. A pen knife, the blade folded away into the handle. "That's the problem," he said. "What you two could ever get could never be enough."

375

Yarik watched the old man open the blade, test it along the hairs of his forearm. "I said," Yarik told him, "that it was *more* than we could get."

The kulak pulled out of the cake pan the first feather he'd stuck in the sand. Its stalk had gone from the clearness of fingernails to clouded as bone. "But you also say that you have it." With the edge of the knife, Kartashkin began to scrape upwards along the opaque tube, millimeter by careful millimeter, stripping away the plume. "And," he said, "although I am impressed with your suit and your tie, although I can see that you cleaned yourself up meticulously to come and see me, I once was clean and meticulous and had money, too, and I can also see that your tie is too short, and that you don't know how to make a knot, and that your suit is old and worn-out, either by you or, more likely, by someone else before you even bought it, and I know that however much you've managed to get, it can't be enough." He had cleaned the quill smooth for a length as long as his long fingers, and he leaned forward now and blew the scrapings from the table. "Because," he said, "you might be one of the few who have the right to buy it, but I'm the only one who has the right to sell it." He held the feather as if it were a pen, moved it in the air a little, testing how it felt in his fingers. "I set the price."

Pressing the feather against the wood, so its arc bent away from the table, he angled the blade carefully against the bottom tip of the stem. Kartashkin had just begun to cut when Yarik shoved back his chair and rose, the table creaking beneath his hands, shaking as he left it. The old man lifted away the blade, steadying the feather as Yarik strode to the saddlebags, hauled them up, back to the table, heaved them on it and, yanking their buckles loose, turned them over and shook. The stacks of rubber-banded roubles tumbled out. They mounded in the middle of the table and filled it and mounded higher until Yarik had emptied every last note from both saddlebags, and then he dropped them, buckles clattering, and pushed out his chair again and sat.

"Ten million roubles," he said.

Kartashkin looked from the pile to Yarik. Then back down at the feather in his hand. With the tip of the knife, he began his careful cut again. Yarik stared at him, watched the old man make his cut and turn the feather and make a smaller cut from the other side, and the whole time he could feel Kartashkin's wife standing in the room staring, too.

"Stepan," she said.

The old kulak raised a hand to hush her. "This is the tricky part," he said. "You squeeze the tip like this and press it flat until you hear . . ." From the quill beneath his fingers there came a quiet crack. He held the tip up, as if for Yarik to see. "Just a small slit. Just enough to guide the ink . . ."

"Styopa," his wife said.

" . . . into the nib."

She took a step towards him, towards the table, and he whipped around. "Go outside," he told her.

"Styopushka . . ."

"Get your coat on and go outside."

"Styopushka, it's a lot of money."

"Go into the goddamn shed and feed the goddamn roosters and don't come back until I call you." He watched her until she was gone and then he put down the feather and he put down the knife and he looked at Yarik. "She's right," he said, "it is a lot of money. It's probably about as much as a reasonable man could expect in reasonable times."

"It's more," Yarik said.

"But let me ask you something. How long do you think a reasonable man would live like this?" He swept a hand at the room, the house. "How long, if he was sitting on land worth ten million roubles?"

"You couldn't—"

"And at my age?"

"You couldn't sell it until—"

"You think other sons of other kolkhozniki didn't try?"

"Not with ten million roubles."

"At my age!" Kartashkin said. "What in the world do you think I've been waiting for?"

Yarik reached down and lifted the saddlebags off the floor. He set the leather on his lap, opened a pouch, reached to the pile of money. The old man's hand was on the back of his before he'd closed his fingers around the first stack.

"Then let me ask you something else," Kartashkin said. "Do you think you and I are living in reasonable times?" His hand still gripping Yarik's, the old man stood. He tugged at Yarik's wrist. "Come," he said, let go, patted Yarik's knuckles once, and, in his unsteady gait, shuffled to the window.

The air in the room was so filled with smoke that, from a distance, the glass had looked fogged, but stepping beside Kartashkin, Yarik could see it was just old glass, wavery and flawed, but clear.

"Look," Kartashkin said, as if out there existed the answer to everything the old man had asked: the brown slush of the yard; the old woman in her coat and curled hair hauling a heavy bucket of feed; the privy with its dark ditch at the back; the vast white field marred by all the scrub; the lone blue roof and plywood windows out in the distance; the church spire and the chimneys of town beyond that. And just on the other side, just a little farther, the long slit in the sky: a strip unending from one edge of all that could be seen to the other. "Half a year ago," the old man said, "we couldn't even see it from here. Half a year before that, it seemed a rumor." He turned, his face close enough Yarik could smell the smoke on his breath. "How long do you think it will be before it reaches the village? How long after that before it gets here? That"—he jabbed a finger at the window, the tip pressed pale against the glass—"is what I'm waiting for. Because sooner or later that rich bastard is going to need this land. And if he needs it, he'll find a way to buy it, or his lawyers will, or whoever he hires to get around the rules that other people can't. I've set my price. And I'm sorry, Yaroslav Lvovich, but it's twice what you have there. Twenty million roubles. Unreasonable? To a man like you, maybe. Even standing here now, saying it, it sounds unreasonable to me. But to Boris Bazarov? It's nothing. If The She Bear wants it, he'll pay for it."

Yarik nodded. Then turned away from the window, went to the table, took a cigarette out of the cigar box. He struck a match. "Except," he said, "The She Bear doesn't want it."

From the window Kartashkin made a noise that Yarik couldn't tell for a cough or a laugh. "Except," the old man said, "he told me already that he does."

Yarik drew in, listened to the crackle from the cigarette's tip. Breathing out the smoke, he turned to Kartashkin. "How long ago did he tell you that?"

"Why even ask?"

Back at the window, Yarik spoke as close to the old man's face as the man had to him before. "Let me ask *you* something now," he said. "How much closer has the Oranzheria come in the past few weeks?" He let the smoke leak out on his words, cloud a little between them, and when he spoke again, his breath cleared it. "And while you're thinking about that," he said, "try to think of any time ever before, even one day since it first appeared, that you've seen its expansion stop." He held the glowing tip of the cigarette between them, shook it a little. "Why do I ask?" he said. "Why don't *you* ask *me* how I know that Mr. Bazarov isn't interested in your land anymore."

Kartashkin made the phlegmy sound again, but it came out quieter, and in the quiet after, Yarik could see that something different had entered the man's eyes. "Go ahead and finish the cigarette," Kartashkin told him, turning back to the table, "but, please, put your money away by the time you're done."

Yarik turned, too, shrugged, started doing exactly that.

The old man stood at the table's edge, watching him. He opened the cigar box and took out a cigarette and held it and didn't light it and said, "Why should I believe you know anything about it?"

"Because I work for him."

The phlegmy cough again. "Who doesn't?"

"Not for the Oranzheria," Yarik said. "For *him*." He paused in filling the saddlebags, looked at Kartashkin. "Don't act like you haven't seen the billboards. The ads on TV."

"We don't get TV," the old man told him.

"On the sides of the buses, then. Next? You've seen it. It's everywhere."

"So?" the old man said. "They paid you to be in their advertisements. Maybe they paid you ten million roubles. You still just—"

"You think they would pick just anyone to put up there? You think Mr. Bazarov wouldn't use someone he trusted?"

"They're just advertisements."

"They're me," Yarik said. "He trusts me."

"Well I don't," Kartashkin told him. "Everything is just talk."

"Just talk?" Yarik tossed one of the stacks of bills at the old man. It hit him in the chest, and Kartashkin fumbled to get a hand on it before it fell to the floor. "Is that just talk?" Yarik asked him. "Is this . . . look at . . . Now I want *you* to look at something." He reached inside his suit jacket, brought out the letter Bazarov had given him, lay it on the table next to the cash he hadn't repacked. Sticking his cigarette in his mouth, he unfolded it and smoothed it out and stood there with his hands still on it, while the old man shuffled forward and stooped over and read it. Yarik held it so that the pages behind the letter of introduction—the contract folded in with it—stayed pressed flat, held it just long enough that the old man could not help but make out the letterhead and the signature, the words *confidence* and *full power of attorney* and *emissary* and *on behalf of Boris Romanovich Bazarov* and when the old man was done, he folded it back up and slipped it back in his jacket pocket and took the cigarette out of his mouth. He said, "You know those men you talked about, the ones The She Bear hires to get around the rules that other people can't? You want to know what they look like? I'll tell you. They wear old suits and new ties and"—he flapped open his jacket just enough to show the butt of the gun jutting out of his pants' waist—"they walk around like that."

The cigarette was still unlit in the old man's hand. He made to take a drag, stopped just short of his mouth. "That money"—he gestured with a small tip of his head—"you said it was more than I could ever get from your brother and from you."

"Yes," Yarik said.

"Combined," the old man said.

"Yes."

"Then where did you get it?"

Yarik stood there smoking, silent.

"Whose," Kartashkin said, "is the rest?"

Yarik took another drag on his cigarette. Then another. Then he took the half-smoked thing out of his mouth and ground it out in the sand in the baking pan next to the feathers, and left if there, and said, "Whose do you think?"

The old kulak reached for the matches then, and for a moment held his hand over them, as if surprised to find the cigarette in its fingers, and then he simply put the unsmoked cigarette down beside the matches and left it there and said to Yarik, "I don't understand."

"I know," Yarik told him. "I've been trying to explain it to you."

"If it's Mr. Bazarov's money," the old man said, "I need to—"

"To what?"

"To call him."

Yarik tried to make the sound that came from him seem like something he'd meant to do instead of something his throat had done to him. "You think you can get through to him?"

"I'll try until I can."

"No," Yarik said.

"You take your money and let me call and come back—"

"You want to call? I'll call. I can get through. I'll call if you want, but you know that if you talk to him you say good-bye to this." He gestured at the money.

"Why?"

"Because it's his," Yarik said. "And I've told you: he doesn't want to spend it on your land. A month ago, maybe. A month ago, you might have sold it to the Consortium. You might have gotten your twenty million roubles. If they had found a way to get around the contract."

"You," the old man said. "You could have bought it for them, transferred—"

"But a month?" Yarik cut him off. "A month the way the world works now?" He shrugged. "You said it yourself: we don't live in reasonable times. Look at what's happened the last few weeks. Even without TV, you must have seen the papers. The collapse of the glass, the strike, the trouble the Oranzheria is in. Did you hear the rumors that the Consortium could go under? Have you seen all the crops dead beneath the glass? You must have read about the panic of the other business partners. It was all over the papers: they won't put money in. You know this. You *knew* it. So, why is it even a surprise to hear me tell it now? The expansion is over." He went back to the window, pointed where the old man had pointed before. "That's as far as it's going to go. You want to understand why I'm here? It's simple. Because I'm in a position to know all this before almost anyone else. Because I know that what this land was worth a month ago doesn't matter anymore. And a month from now, when everyone else knows? It will be worth so little even the sons of the other kolkhozniki will be able to buy it. And I don't want that, because I want it. For me. My brother. The memory of our Uncle Avya. Our father's grave. Which is why I'm offering even more than what the land is worth right now. That, Stepan Fyedorivich, is why I'm here."

The old man stood still as the feathers stuck in their sand, looking at their plumes. He reached out and brushed a palm slowly over the soft ends, brushed it back.

In the quiet, they could hear the old woman outside: her shouts and swears, her banging in the shed, the shrieks of the roosters muffled by the walls.

"Ever since they turned the zerkala's light on us," Kartashkin said, "the roosters have been crazy. At first, they crowed all day, all night. Now they don't at all. They don't seem to know what has happened to their world. Maybe they're just confused, or scared, but you can't go in there without them trying to tear you apart. You can't get close without boots and gloves." He stopped brushing the tips of the plumes. His hand hovered. He looked up at Yarik. "I heard all the night animals have gone to the city."

382

"It's dark there," Yarik told him. "They turned the mirrors away."

"I heard," the old man said. Steadying himself against the table, he shuffled to his chair, lowered himself into it.

Yarik sat back down across from him. The money between them, the feathers. He reached out and picked up the one that Kartashkin had been working on. "Dyadya," he said, addressing him out of respect, the way he used to years ago when he and Dima were still small and the old man wasn't yet old, "how much do you sell these quill pens for?"

Kartashkin shrugged; his eyes were on nothing, his thoughts not there.

"It can't be much," Yarik said. "And I don't know how much the birds out there are worth, but I know it can't be enough, you can't sell enough of them, not to live on for long."

"Why would they do that?" the old man said. "Why would they take the zerkala light from the city and put it out here?"

"They're desperate," Yarik told him.

"And what about us?" the old man said, his voice loud again. "*They're* desperate."

"That's what I'm saying."

"What about *us*?"

"It's all going to hell."

"Fuck," the old man said. He said it with such vehemence that Yarik jerked back, and Kartashkin said it again. "Fuck."

"Dyadya—"

"Fuck that."

"It's not so bad."

"Fuck it's not."

"If it's so bad," Yarik said, "what's all this?" He lifted one of the stacks of bills out of the pile that remained, let it fall back to the table with a quiet thump.

"Come back tomorrow," the old man said.

Yarik shook his head.

"Let me think about it," Kartashkin asked him.

"I won't have it tomorrow."

The old man looked at Yarik, and his eyes came back from wherever they'd been, and Yarik could see them starting to pinch down and grow hard again. "If it's his money," Kartashkin said, "then what are you willing to spend of yours?"

"Of mine?" Yarik said.

"Ten million roubles for the *land*," the man said. "But what about the house?"

"This dump?"

"And the barns," Kartashkin said. "And the new house."

"It's not even finished."

"The Consortium would just knock it all down. But you'll use it. How much is it worth to *you*?"

"I think," Yarik said, "I'm offering enough."

"Of *his* money."

"Of my risk."

"That's your decision," the old man said. "That's the choice you're making. It concerns you. I'm talking about my property, my houses, my barns."

"How much," Yarik said, "do you think they're worth?"

"A million and a half," the man said. He said it without even thinking, a number that had been in his head for a long while now.

And Yarik knew a little further and it would be done. He could feel the muscles in his back start to loosen with the thought, and he forced them tight again, forced his face still, thought of how much he could get by that afternoon—how much he had saved in his account, in his and Zinaida's joint one, what the largest amount was that he could lose. "I can pay you almost half of that," he told Kartashkin. From the way that the old man took that in and showed nothing in return, not even an attempt at faking indignation, not even a smirk, Yarik knew that Kartashkin was thinking the same thing he had a second ago. And as if that was enough, it was done. The old man's eyes lost their hardness. When he spoke, his voice was quiet, even soft.

"What are you going to do," the old kulak said, "when he finds out?"

384

"Like you said," Yarik told him, "that's my concern. You'll have the cash. It's right here. I can drive you into the city right now and we can go to a notary and write up the contract and you can take this home with you tonight."

The old man looked at him. Outside, the door to the shed smacked shut. Yarik glanced behind him out the window. Mrs. Kartashkin had overturned the empty feed bucket, set it down, and he watched her sit on it and wrap her arms around herself and watch him back through the window, waiting. Behind her, closer than he had remembered, he saw them: the two gray stones showing through the matching mounds of snow. When he looked again at her husband, the old man was still staring at him.

"You know what you're doing?" Kartashkin said. "You know we'll be gone by tonight?"

Yarik tried to smile and felt his lips stick. He knew he should tell the old man yes, should say something to make Kartashkin believe it, maybe lift the feather in his hand, make a quip—*we can even use one of your pens to sign it*—but his throat was closed, and all he could do was hold the quill, hold it there between them, trying not to let it shake.

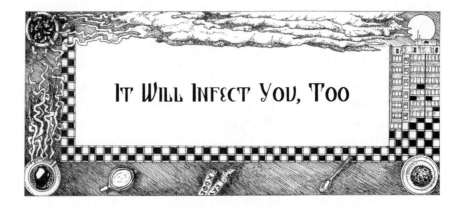

It Will Infect You, Too

Late last night, or early that morning, or whatever time it had been when Vika had wrapped her legs around him, pulled him in, they had lain in the snow not even long enough for the elbows of his jacket to get soaked, his knees to grow cold. She'd reached to his face, drawn it so close he couldn't help but shut his eyes, feel her breath on their lids, her lips at his ear ... Then it was over and she was sliding out from under him, pulling up her pants, starting to walk away. Looking up from the snow, his whole side suddenly wet and going cold, he had called after her, *What are you doing?* And turning, walking backwards, still away, she'd told him, *Proving it to you.* For another few steps, she kept her eyes on him, as if trying to make him remember what once before she'd tried to make him understand—how, right then, she could have been so focused on him; how, tomorrow, she'd be focused on something else—until, her back to him again, she'd disappeared into the blackness before the crossroads fire. That was when he'd shouted to her the address where he lived.

So when, that afternoon, an hour before sunset, someone knocked on the apartment door—the rapping on wood as startling as a phone pealing in the middle of the night—his first thought was her.

I can want . . . she had said, *and tomorrow I can want* . . . and last night, walking home alone under the stars again, he had understood. She could want him that night and want another the next because that was the way of lovers. Maybe with some it took a little longer, months or even years, but in the end each would leave, whether with their bodies or only in their hearts, all eventually in some way disappeared. Crossing back beneath the sparking tram lines, Dima had known a heart could make that choice. Because if the thing he'd felt for her hadn't been there before they'd met, then simply was, it could be let go again. And at home, in the bathroom, kneeling in the tub beneath a stream of steaming water, he had understood this, too: the thing they'd done, that he'd never done with anyone but her, was just another want, another desire pulling him another way, drawing him farther from the only one who could not leave, not in his heart, because no matter how the world tried to keep them apart theirs would always beat with the same blood.

The knocking, the knocking.

But when he opened the door, it was Zinaida. If she saw his surprise, she didn't show it. He looked to her side, behind her.

"He's not with me," she said.

Of course, Dima thought; Yarik would be at work. And, he realized, she should have been, too. "You're playing hooky?" His month-thick beard shifted with a nervous smile.

But instead of smiling back, her lips tightened. He had expected that, expected even the rebuke in her eyes. But he hadn't expected her to look scared.

He stepped back, motioned for her to come in.

She shook her head. Last light was sifting through the windows, and he knew what she was seeing behind him: the open refrigerator, its half-rotten food; the living room tracked with soot; his mother on the floor between a bowl of seeds and a mound of shells, her hands dipping in and out of a giant sack. He had tethered the rooster close enough to keep her company, and he could hear the bird squawk each time she slapped it away from the seeds.

Down the hall, the elevator door opened. Zinaida turned to nod at whoever was coming out. The man shot Dima a disgusted glare; the woman whispered to her husband. The clicks of a key turning a lock. The smack of the door shut behind them.

"How do you stand it?" There was the old kindness in her mouth, her eyes soft. "I don't think I could," she said, and her voice caught. She cleared it, called past him, into the room, "Hi, Galina."

"Good afternoon," his mother called back.

"How are you?" his sister-in-law asked.

And his mother: "We're very well, thank you."

"She doesn't know who I am," Zinaida whispered to Dima. "Does she?"

"If you came in . . ."

"No."

"Then . . . ?" He let the *why* hang, hoping she would reach for it.

But she only shook her head again. She told him she would pray for him, that she already did. He thought then that she would turn and go, but she just stood there and, instead, asked him if he prayed. When he said nothing back, she asked him what he would pray for if he did.

He knew he didn't have to tell her for her to know.

She shut her eyes. "Dima," she said. And her eyes flicked to the inside of the apartment. "Look at this. Look at you."

He touched his cheeks, as if suddenly aware of them. "I shaved."

"I see that. And then you grew it back."

"Please."

"Dima, you look thin," she told him, starting to turn. "Take care of yourself."

But he reached out and held her by the shoulder. "There's nothing wrong with me," he said. "I'm not sick. I'm not crazy."

"I never thought you were."

"It's not like just seeing me . . ."

"If you were . . ."

". . . is going to infect him."

". . . I would understand. I could accept it. Your mother couldn't help it," she said. "It was something her mind did *to* her. If it was that, Dmitry, I could forgive it. But it's not. All this"—she gestured at the apartment, at him, the movement of her arm shaking off his hand—"is an excuse. I've seen it before. Every time I bring donations to The Dachas. I used to think it was horrible what was done there, to those people. I used to think Yarik was right to give so much to keep you out."

"I told him he didn't—"

"You don't even know what he gave," she said. "What he's done for you."

"I never asked him for anything."

"You don't even know what you take." Her voice had risen. Somewhere down the hall a door opened, a woman called out for them to hush. When the door shut again, Zinaida's voice was quieter, and worse. "Don't you feel it?" she said. "Their scorn? Their disgust? No, more than that. They hate you, Dima. How can they not? When they see what's happening to this city, everything already lost, everyone so scared of what we're going to lose next, and they see you, what you've done to yourself, to Galina, your own mother, they see you like a warning of what's to come, and how can they not hate you, Dima, when they know none of this is being done *to* you. Not by the Consortium. Not by your brother. Not by me. Not by anyone. Not even your own mind. Not for any reason but that you *choose* it."

"But I'm not costing anybody anything," he said.

"Except your brother."

"Zinaida . . ."

"Have you ever thought, even for a second, of what you're costing him?"

"Zina," he said, "has something happened to Yarik?"

In the time it took the quiet of the hallway to absorb the echo of their voices, he watched the anger fade from her eyes, watched them fill instead with the worry he had seen when he'd first opened the door.

She must have seen something fill his face, too, because she stood there looking at it, and when she spoke her voice had lost its hardness. "Let me buy you a coffee," she said, her words almost too soft to hear. "Let me get you something to eat."

On the corner of Avtovskaya and Yremiva streets, in the place where a bare cafeteria once served blini and soups in Soviet days, an American-style café had opened up. It was the same chain as the half-dozen others that had appeared in Petroplavilsk, big windows plastered with bright posters advertising ever more elaborate ideas of coffee. Over the door, on one side, big brown letters spelled out КофЕ ХауЗ; on the other, in English, KOFE KHAUZ.

A month ago, it would have been crammed with people on break grabbing a jolt to get them through the hours to come, but now it was almost empty, almost no one able to afford the frothed foam, drizzles of chocolate.

When Zinaida asked him what he wanted, Dima asked her to choose for him. *Americano*, she told the girl behind the counter. All they had to eat were pastries he'd only ever seen in ads. She ordered him a blueberry muffin, then chose a small round table by the big plateglass windows. Outside, the sky was beginning to streak with pink. Soft jazz spilled from the speakers. On the table, an ashtray sat, filled with cigarette butts.

While she spoke, Zinaida watched his fingers picking through it. "We never had a lot of time together—you know that—but now we have almost none. And when we do . . ." Dima stopped digging, looked at her. "He's not like he used to be," she said. "He hardly ever plays with the kids. And after they're asleep, *he* goes to sleep. Or tries."

The waitress put a cup in front of Dima. In the middle of the table, she set the plate with the muffin, and a pitcher of milk and, instead of a bowl of sugar cubes that he could hold between his teeth, some packets printed with the logo of the café. Then she reached to clear the sooty cigarette ends Dima had gathered on the table. Guarding them with his hand, he told the waitress thanks. She gave him the look his neighbors gave him, whittled to a point he could feel prick his skin.

When she was gone, Zinaida pushed the plate towards him. "Eat," she said. She reached to the muffin, tore off a small chunk. "This is all I want."

He brushed his hands of the cigarette ash, tore off a bit as small as she had. It was sweet and soft in a way that he thought at first was strange, almost troubling—before he realized it was just fresh. He tried to chew it slowly, tried not to let her see how much he wanted to grab the thing off the plate and cram it whole into his mouth.

"He eats twice as much as he used to," she said. "But he's always hungry. Every day, he's more and more nervous."

"About what?"

She looked out the window at the people hurrying along paths in the snow, rushing for home, urgent as if a blizzard threatened. But the sky was clear, its roseatted streaks deepening to crimson, the blue beginning to darken towards dusk. "Last night," she said, "when he came home and took off his coat and sat down to eat, he reached behind him and pulled out that old pistol of your uncle's, just set it on the table and picked up his fork. He wouldn't tell me why he'd been carrying it. And today, when I went to the bank . . ." She reached to the muffin, took another bite, rolled it into a ball between her fingertips. "Everything we'd saved is gone."

Dima stopped chewing. "Where?"

"He left for work before I was awake. I tried calling him. He won't answer." She dropped the marble of muffin onto the table, let it sit. "I found someone to swap shifts with me, went to his sector. But he wasn't there."

"So you came to me?"

"Nobody there knew where he was."

"Maybe he's there now?"

"I'll go back." She looked out the window again. The clouds were leaching their color into the sky, the emptiness around them darker.

391

"When I woke up this morning," she said, "he'd left his plate half-full on the table, his potatoes cold. The pistol was gone."

Dima sat with the piece of muffin in his motionless fingers, his untouched coffee a still black pool in the cup. "What can I do?"

She looked at him. "Nothing."

"I need to do—"

"Please," she said, a panic in her voice so clear it quieted him. "Anything you do will only make it worse."

"We don't even know what *it* is."

"You will make it worse, Dima," she said. "I know that. I thought maybe he might have come to you, maybe I shouldn't have, I shouldn't have said anything, but I know now the best thing you can do is stay away. Please."

"Zinaida."

"And take care of your mother," she told him. She put her hands on the table, then, as if she meant to push back her chair, stood. But she stayed there, sitting, and said, "That's the other reason I had to come to you."

Dima placed the bit of muffin on the edge of the plate.

"The envelope," she said. "Each month."

"You know about it?"

"It's what he was going to set aside for me."

He reached inside his coat.

"Spending money," she said.

From the chest pocket of his shirt he drew a matchbook out.

"But how could I? How could we? When we knew you needed . . ."

He shook his head.

"Your mother, then." And watching his other hand hunt the ashtray for a butt, she brought up her purse. "We couldn't." Rummaged in it. "But now"—she lifted out a pack of cigarettes—"we have to." Passing it across the table, she told him, "At least this month. Next. Dima, I know how much you must rely on it, your mother, I know that without it . . ."

He reached over, stilled her hand. Softly squeezing her fingers around the pack, he told her it was OK. "I don't rely on it," he said. "I've hardly even used it. It's all right, Zina. We'll be all right."

For a moment, her hand stayed under his, and in the twilight coming through the window, in the warm glow that fell on them from the studio lamp that had been set up in the corner, they might have looked like lovers come to some quiet decision about their lives. Then her hand slipped out from under his, and she took the cigarettes back, back all the way until she was holding them against her chest, and she said, "You haven't been using it?"

"Only a little," he assured her. "The rest—"

"What have you been doing with it?"

He drew his own hand back. "Saving it," he said, and watched her mouth grow hard again.

"For what?" she asked, and before he could answer, "Why was she sitting in the dark?"

His fingers went to the table, searched blindly for the stub of a cigarette to hold.

"Galina," she said. "Your mother. Why was—"

"It wasn't dark."

"Why hadn't you turned on any lights?"

He found a butt and picked it up and sat there, picking the paper tube apart.

"Dima," she said, "the refrigerator door was open."

"That's OK," he said.

"Why?" she demanded.

"Because," he told her, "it's not using electricity."

"Why?" she said again.

"We don't need it."

She shut her eyes and pinched the bridge of her nose and she said, "Don't let me get mad." She said it again, and a third time, and then her eyes snapped open and she tore her hand away and her voice was rising even as she spoke: "You mean to tell me that all this time in your mother's apartment . . ."

"Not all this—"

". . . you've been taking the money we gave you to take care of her—"

"I didn't take it," he said. "I've been saving it."

"In the name of God, Dmitry," she said, "what were you saving it for?"

"The farm."

Her hands hit the table with a smack. The coffee cup shook, the spoon on its saucer rattled off, all around them people looked, and she didn't seem to notice. "*This*," she said. "This is why you make it worse. Because this plagues him. It plagues *me*. His yearning, his hopeless plans to buy it. Every time you try to call, every time his son's face reminds him of you, it gets worse, and worse, and the worst thing, the thing you cost him, Dmitry, is that it's a yearning for the impossible."

He had picked the cigarette almost entirely apart. His fingers kept working. "He's trying to buy it?"

"And you say it's not infectious. Look at you. You're stricken with it. With some idea of the past. Of a Past Life everyone else knows was worse, everyone else is afraid we will return to. That's the only thing crazy about you, Dmitry. Your refusal to see the reality of how the world is, instead of how you think it used to be."

"It was," he said. "It can be."

"Stop," she told him. "Please, stop. Why can't you stop wanting more than what everyone else wants? You're not just stuck in the past, you *want* to be stuck. You want to stay there. As if you alone don't have to grow up."

"Did you check for him out at the farm?" he said. "Yarik—"

"Yarik is more than just your brother," she told him. "He doesn't only love you. You aren't the only person he can love. You know what Father Antipov told me? Months ago at liturgy? He told me to be careful, he told me that the way you are—this unreasonable clinging to the past, this inability to share your brother's love, he said you were stunted, he said to be careful with my children—"

"Zinaida," Dima whispered, his hands finally still. "You don't believe that."

"I believe," she said, "that you might infect them, too."

Slowly, his hands bunched into fists, tobacco flecks falling to the table from his fingers. He watched them fall. "Just tell me," he said, quietly, evenly, "please, tell me if you checked out at the farm."

"How would I get out there?" she said. "When was the last time you were?"

"Zina, how much did he take?"

She hushed him then—*Shh*—and with both hands reached across the table. "He's not out there."

"How much was in that account?"

And she held his fists in her hands and hushed him again.

"Aren't you afraid to touch me?" he said.

"Shh," she said, "shh. I'm afraid for him." Outside, it was dark. The street was empty. "I don't know where he is." She closed her eyes.

He could see she was praying. And, looking at her—leaning across the table, holding his hands—he watched the slight shivering of her shut eyelids, the quaking skin, and thought how fragile it seemed, how, beneath the makeup she had armored it with, it must be as thin as his.

SHOT NUMBER SEVEN

Fingers locked together, knuckles a seam along the top of his head, arms up and elbows out and the nose of a gun in the small of his back: this was not how Yarik had hoped to face his boss. One bodyguard walked him in while a second held the door. Behind him, Yarik could sense people watching from the atrium of the old sanitarium where his mother had once been held. Then the door shut. The guard who had closed it stepped forward, spoke—*unannounced* and *into your office* and *armed*—but Yarik was barely aware of what the man was saying; all his attention was on Bazarov.

His boss was barefooted. He stood with his toes half-buried in the carpet's soft pile, his metallic black suit jacket still buttoned at the waist, bolo tie clasped to his throat by a silver-set stone. That the formality was unbroken even by his bare feet seemed only to strengthen the seriousness of his face.

Bazarov had been talking into an earpiece when they came in; now he pushed the boom away from his mouth, took the thing off, set it on the table. The room was so quiet Yarik could hear the person on the other end of the line still yammering: a pinched vibration of a voice.

The guard who had been talking stepped forward, put Dyadya Avya's revolver on the table, too, slid it closer to his boss. It spun, came to a stop with its barrel against the earpiece. Whoever was on the other end shut up.

Bazarov looked at the gun, looked at Yarik, told the two guards to go.

The earpiece made a noise like a voice asking a question.

"I said leave him here," Bazarov told the men, "and leave the gun, and get out."

When they were gone, Bazarov reached to the table and turned the earpiece off. Then he picked up the pistol. He unlocked the chamber and clicked it slowly through seven slots, the six empty ones and the one still filled, and pushed it shut again and looked at Yarik. He raised his eyebrows. He made his mouth into a picture of shock.

How stupid to bring the gun. Last night, after all the papers had been signed, after Kartashkin had taken the cash and returned to the izba to get his wife and pack to go, after Yarik had gone back as near to home as the plowing allowed, after he had walked to the apartment block where five stories up his own wife sat waiting, he'd veered away from the stairwell door and walked out into the playground and, ducking inside the rocket ship, hanging by his arms from the bars, thought about what Bazarov had told him that day in Moscow sitting in his armored car. He had tried to come up with a way of getting bullets for the gun. If it had been a rifle, he might have been able to find a shop in the morning; if it had been registered, they might have sold him some, but it was a pistol and illegal to own and the only way would be to flash enough roubles on the street. He had hung there, feeling his weight pull at his elbows, his knuckles, let his body sway. He had looked up through the bars, scanned the lit windows for his home, found it, let go. He didn't want to live his life scared. He didn't want his children to, his wife. He didn't want to be one of those people. The kind who would go down near the dockyards where the lowlife lived, who would buy bullets off someone as likely to put one in him, who would be the kind of person to load the gun and carry it into the billionaire's office. . . . He couldn't do it. He would bring the gun in as it was, he'd decided, not as a weapon, but as evidence: how Bazarov had betrayed their trust first. Yet here he was, hands on his head, empty saddlebags over his shoulder, his heart pumping blood as if he had already been opened up.

He watched the revolver in Bazarov's hands. With his thumb, the man gave the chamber a whirl. "You lied to me," Yarik said. The click, click of it turning over, stopping. "You said they were explosive tips."

Bazarov looked at the gun as if it had just been handed to him. "You didn't fire them all," he said. "Maybe one is." And, setting the gun back on the table, he flicked its butt to make the whole thing spin. "Look at you." He showed a hint of the old grin. "Wearing those bags. Wearing that *face*." And the grin busted loose. "You look less like a cowboy than the horse."

Unclasping his fingers, Yarik lowered his hands, the leather strap shifting on his shoulder. "I'm bringing them back."

"I told you," Bazarov said, "they're yours."

"I don't want them."

At that, the man turned his knuckles on the table. And began to knock a quick, galloping rhythm against the wood.

"I only wanted what was mine," Yarik said. It was an imitation of hoofbeats, he realized, mockery to accompany the smile Bazarov turned on him, and he hauled the saddlebags off and threw them down. They hit the table in a clattering slap, sent the gun skidding, almost bashed the man's hands, and, watching Bazarov jerk his fists away, Yarik told him, "And so I took it."

Bazarov shook out his fingers. "That was very dramatic," he said. "I feel . . ." He scrunched his toes in the carpet, looked down at his feet. "Maybe I should put on my boots. I think it would help me get into character." His shoulders hitched a little. "Here," he said, "let me try." And looking straight into Yarik's face, his smile died. His eyes hardened. He said, all hints of humor gone from his voice, "You took the cash?"

"No. The cash I gave to Kartashkin."

"OK."

"All of it.

"Five million rubles?"

"Ten. My share, too."

"Why would you do that?"

"In exchange for the land."

"Exchange?"

"Bought," Yarik told him. "I bought the land." He could see Bazarov's eyes beginning to crinkle. "For myself. I bought the land for myself."

"Oh," Bazarov said. It was a small sound that told Yarik nothing, made with a movement of lips so small it that showed nothing, either. "He sold it to you for that little?"

"I own it," Yarik said. "We signed the documents. Had them notarized."

"Oh," Bazarov said again. He shook his head. "You *are* a cowboy."

"I did what you taught me to do. What Slava would have done."

The man's smile was small and brief and held nothing in it of a smile at all. "Well," he said, "welcome to the Wild West."

"I saw an opportunity—"

"And you grabbed it." Bazarov lifted his palms. "But why?"

"You were the one who told me playing it safe was the most dangerous thing to do."

"True." And in his smile this time there was a little bit of pleasure. "But this is pretty dangerous, too." He held his hands forward, as if presenting Yarik to Yarik. "Why are you here?"

"Good people don't succeed," Yarik said. "Right? It's bad people—"

"I told you," Bazarov said, "there are no bad people. Just good people who do bad things." He reached over to one of the saddlebags, lifted a flap, glanced in. "What do you think you've done, Yaroslav Lvovich? A good thing or a bad?"

"That depends for who," Yarik said.

"For you," Bazarov told him. "Oh, you definitely got a good price," he admitted. "Unless . . ." And he dropped the flap back closed, came close to Yarik. In his bare feet, he was a little shorter. "What else did I tell you about success?"

That close, Yarik could see that his eyes, above the tie clasp, were tinged with turquoise.

"Half of success is lying to people," Bazarov prompted. Then reached out with a finger and made as if to tap Yarik on the forehead. Yarik jerked away. "The other half," Bazarov told him, "is knowing to whom you don't." He brought his finger back to his own forehead, tapped it on his own brow. "Remember Chernitsky? With his armored car and his— What's the best way to put this? Ubiquitous?—his ubiquitous driver." He looked like he would smile, and then like he would suppress it, and then it got the best of him and he mimicked a little explosion with his hands. "That guy," he said, "got around everywhere." He shook his head at himself, and when he looked up again, his smile was gone. "You didn't believe," he said, "that a squirmy sonofabitch like Korotya had the balls to do that, did you?" He stepped to the table, turned his back, undid the latches of a briefcase, took something out. When he turned to Yarik again, he was holding a small red rectangle of gleaming plastic. "Here." Bazarov tilted the card so the glare slid off. He stepped close again. Yarik glanced away from the man's face long enough to see the face in miniature, laminated over, and some words, someone's signature scrawled. When he looked back at Bazarov, the man was watching him. "You think Gauk's the only one who knows the minister of the interior?"

Yarik tried not to look away, and then he tried to find the card to hold his gaze, but Bazarov had slipped it into his breast pocket, his hand over his chest; he gave the place over his heart a pat. "Coward-ice," Bazarov said, "is the most terrible of vices."

The man's hand patted out three beats. Four.

"That's from Bulgakov," Yarik told him. "And I'm not scared." As soon as he'd said it, he wished he hadn't. When he looked up, the man's face was grim.

"I bet your wife would be," the man said. "I bet she is right now."

Yarik could feel the blood throbbing through the bruise in his back where the guard had shoved the pistol.

"I know she's religious," Bazarov went on, "so we can hope that gives her some peace. But your son? Surely, little Timosha is too young to have that kind of faith. Surely, you've thought about that. And has your daughter spoken her first words yet? No? If she could, what do you think she would say to you?"

He left Yarik standing there, walked around to the other side of the table. It was long and narrow, flanked with leather chairs. Bazarov waved a hand at them. Yarik stayed standing. Across the table, his boss stopped, tipped his face to the ceiling, neck muscles straining as it bent back, throat stretching, until all Yarik could see was the bottom of his jaw, the blond goatee.

"The Afterlife," the jaw said, the goatee twitching. "I don't believe in it. Too much like The Past Life. Everyone equally happy, every need equally fulfilled. Except, of course, for a few lucky ones who happen to sit a little closer to God."

The ceiling up there was made of glass and Yarik knew that somewhere above were the night and the stars, but the lights in the room were too bright: he could only see the reflected table, his own face looking up, and then the top of Bazarov's head as the man went back to looking at him.

"Sit down," Bazarov said. And when Yarik still stayed standing, the oligarch pulled out a chair for himself and sat. "Heaven's for the kind of people," he said, "who would have been Communists if they weren't suicide bombers. People who don't have second thoughts. People I've never wanted to know. The way I wanted to know you."

Under the man's stare, Yarik's legs began to feel stiff, his whole body exposed and awkward, and when Bazarov said it again—"Sit down"—he did.

"Here's another lesson for you," Bazarov continued. "We come to know who people are by watching what makes them scared. How they let it drive what they do. If they let it push them. Or what they do in order to push it away. That's the beautiful thing about using a pistol to hunt boar. You get to see your partner's fear up close. How he overcomes it. You see it in yourself. What a shame we never did that, huh?" He smiled across the table at Yarik. "Of course, I guess I'm getting to see it now. Yaroslav Lvovich, I know you think you're doing the right thing. Taking this chance, coming straight at me. But the only one who charges straight ahead, who has no second thoughts, Yarik, is the boar. Don't be the boar, my friend. I'm sure he's very brave. But in the end he squeals like hell."

How, Yarik wondered, had he ever thought of this man as a friend? Was this friendship in the billionaire's world? A series of tests? Even if they had hunted together it would have been nothing more than another test he had to pass. The man had never truly believed in him. The way a friend would, the way his mother had wanted to, the way he hoped his wife did, knew his brother always had. Looking across the table, Yarik understood then that in this world he had stepped into no one else ever would. From here on out he would have to watch every movement everyone made around him the way that Bazarov, over the briefcase and the saddlebags and the earpiece and the gun, was watching his. And when the man leaned forward and started to reach, Yarik jerked so fast he half-fell from his chair, his hand shooting out, onto the pistol, grabbing it to him.

Bazarov stayed midlean, hand still hovering. And in that moment Yarik thought he saw a ripple of doubt, a glimpse of fear. Before it was washed away in Bazarov's laughing. He laughed loud, one hand still held out, the other on the table, laughed hard enough to make the table shake. When at last he could get the words out, Bazarov said, "I thought you told me they were all blanks?" Then, continuing his reach, past the place where the gun had been, he took up the earpiece.

He sat back, put it on, pressed the button on the side of the mike. "Yes," he said, "get me the control room, please. Thank you, Masha." He winked across the table at Yarik, leaned back in his chair till it creaked. He rocked a couple times, creaking. "Hello, it's me. Yes." He said a string of numbers and then, "That's right," and "Do you think I give a fuck about them?" And listening to him tell whoever was on the other end how bad it would be if he had to walk over and write the order out, catching a couple names he remembered from the men that day in Moscow, listening to the billionaire say "What *isn't* on my head?" Yarik understood the enormity of it all—the Consortium and the zerkala and the Oranzheria—in a way he never had till then, not the scale of the thing, not its mass, but its weight, the weight of responsibility for the thousands who worked beneath it, on it, the hundreds who had invested fortunes in it, and, heaviest of all, the gaze of whoever must be watching Bazarov from above. Because, he knew, suddenly, that there was someone—with more money, or more power, or simply in a position so high up he could press his weight down even on a man like Bazarov. He knew that for every story the billionaire had told of things that had been done to others, there must be one about the things that others had done to him.

"When am I *not* sure?" Bazarov said and, reaching to his earpiece, pushed the button, tossed the thing onto the table. His eyes held on Yarik. In them, there was the other thing about that weight: the strength it must take to hold up under it.

"You want to know the other half of success?" Bazarov said. "Who it is you shouldn't lie to?" His bare heels shoved on the carpet, his chair scooted backwards, hit the wall. "You want to know who you shouldn't fuck around with?" He reached up to a bank of switches. And in one swipe of his hand knocked all the lights off.

Blackness. The sound of his feet, the wheels of the chair returning. The table shaking with his thump. Then nothing. Yarik sat in the dark, listening. Nothing but the sound of his own breathing. And, if he listened past it: Bazarov's. Gradually, as his eyes adjusted, he began to make out the shape of the figure sitting across from him, its neck craned back, face tilted to the ceiling glass again. He could swear he saw, as if reflecting the light of the stars, a ghostly sliver of wet white gleam: the man's teeth.

Looking away, Yarik tilted his own head back. It *was* the light of the stars; they were up there by the trillions. And he realized that, in this past mirrorless month, his children must have seen them for the first time. It pained him that Timosha had said nothing of it to him, that, if Polya had whooped a first word at the sight, he hadn't been there to hear. He promised himself then that if they ever got to the Black Sea he would take them out to the beach at night and lie with them on the sand—Zina and his daughter and his son—and simply gaze up. The way he hadn't since he was young, since before he was married, when he and Dima used to bed down for the night in a field or pasture or wherever their ride had let them off between the city and the farm.

Gradually he became aware that he couldn't hear Bazarov's breathing anymore. Holding his own breath, he thought he heard an intake—then nothing. He breathed again, and heard, from across the table, the breathing begin again, too. Only when he sped his own up, and Bazarov's matched it, did he realize the man was trying to keep in synch. He stopped, exhaled one long hard breath. And when it petered out there was just Bazarov's long own dissolving into laughter. For a moment, the sound filled the darkness. Then the darkness was gone.

It was as if a searchlight blasted the room. Yarik shut his eyes. Opened them again. The stars were gone, too. Instead: their dim doppelgängers returned, drifting in their man-made constellation as they washed the night out of the sky. The light they sent down lit the table, pulled the carpet from the dark, showed the gun glinting in Yarik's hand, and Bazarov, sitting there, staring at him.

From the hallway, behind the door, came muffled sounds of celebratory shouts.

"No," Bazarov said, "if you're going to try to betray someone, you probably don't want to chose the guy with his hands on the controls of the fucking sun."

Yarik had forgotten how different the light of the zerkala was. Eyes still adjusting to it, he told the man, "You know, I get to see it, too. The boar hunt. You." In that second, Bazarov's face looked blown out with brightness and shadow, the blond of his goatee and hair almost white. "When were you supposed to switch the mirrors back?" Yarik asked him. "How much too soon did you do it just now? Who were you supposed to check with first? Whose hands are on you?"

Bazarov leaned forward across the table. A low long sigh. As if he had been storing air in his lungs ever since they'd met and now was at last letting it out. "Do you remember," he said, "the first question I ever asked you?"

"Yes," Yarik told him. "But this isn't about what I want. It's about what I have. What you *don't* have your hands on. What whoever has their hands on you wants."

Bazarov stayed with his weight on his forearms. "What makes you think they can't just take it? These hands you talk about." He closed his into fists. "Just squeeze it out of you, and take it, and throw what's left of you away."

Yarik pushed his chair back. "Me?" he said. "I know they could do that to me. But to your spokesman? The face of your entire publicity campaign? The person people see when they see the word *Next?* People who you spent so much time and money to convince? To convince that they're following in his footsteps? In mine?" He stood up. "Slava?" he said. "Him I think it would be very hard to throw away."

"What *do* you want?" Bazarov asked.

"Or his family," Yarik said.

His weight still on his elbows, still leaning forward, Bazarov lifted his hands off the table, turned up his palms. "Yaroslav Lvovich, how can I give you what you want if you don't tell me?"

"I want my family safe," Yarik said, "and my job secure, and my roll as spokesman continued, and my promotions in the company guaranteed."

"But you already had all that," Bazarov said.

"And," Yarik told him, "I want the rest of the money."

Looking down at the man's face turned up to him, Yarik thought he saw the flicker of a smile. "Cossack," Bazarov said.

"The other ten million," Yarik told him.

"Cowboy."

"All of what the farm is worth." And there was no question now: the man was grinning. "What," Yarik said, "you were going to pay Kartashkin from the start." The sound Bazarov made was like a snore cut short. "What you were going to pay to buy it from him." Again, the sound, drawn out longer. "Except," Yarik told him, "now you're

405

buying it from me." And the man's mouth gaped, his cheeks caved, his nose sucked the air: a long rattling snort. Yarik stared at him. The billionaire's eyes were rolled up to look back at him, and his entire face was stretched with the effort of his snorting, and then it was gone, slipped out of sight below the table, and in the second it took Yarik to realize the man was coming for him, to put together the clattering of table and chairs with the body rushing beneath them, he raised the gun. But when Bazarov burst out and saw it—saw Yarik backing up, the gun leveled at his boss—the man didn't stop, didn't leap for the pistol, didn't quit snorting. Instead he threw himself at a scrambling crawl across the carpet, lunging after Yarik's legs.

"Am I the boar?" Bazarov shouted, and Yarik stepped back, nearly stumbling, away from him, and he shouted again, "Am I the boar?"

Then he was there, on Yarik's legs, arms locked around them, and Yarik lifted the gun higher and told himself *hit him*, crack him over the skull with the iron barrel, *hit him*, knock him out, but Bazarov was down there snuffling, his long hair flying, his face burrowing into Yarik's shins, and Yarik could feel the beard scraping back and forth on his pants, the wet mouth—Was he trying to bite him?—and he kicked, backed away, tried to shake the man off, but still couldn't bring himself to club him. Then, with a slam of shoulders against his legs, arms yanking at his calves, Yarik's feet were off the carpet, and he was falling, and it was too late.

By the time he hit the floor, Bazarov was over him. Bucking, trying to shove with his legs, wrench loose his wrists, Yarik knew he had never felt the man's full strength. His legs were pinned. He couldn't move his arms. Above him: Bazarov, breathing hard, his hair falling crazily around his face, his mouth wet and teeth glistening and goatee dark with spit. He expected to hear Bazarov's laugh, to look up and see The She Bear grinning down. But what he saw instead made him stop struggling. The man's eyes were sad. They were filled with something that might have been regret, or hurt, or even the pain of some great loss, but wasn't; was something else—disappointment? a dead hope?—pressing down on Yarik with the sudden terrible fullness of all the man's weight.

A CLATTERING OF STONES

Dima was eating supper when the zerkala returned. He sat with his fork frozen in the pot, his breath caught, his body gone still in the sudden light blown through the windows, shocking and bright as a skyful of full moons risen all at once. Beneath the kovyor-curtains he'd left rolled up the new near-day spilled in, spread over his mother's startled face. Out from its box, the unhooded rooster came, stood ruffling its feathers, began a slow stalk towards the balcony door. His mother struggled up, crept after it across the room. They both came to a stop silhouetted against the brightness outside, the bird all twitchy steps and head jerks, his mother motionless, her hands splayed out on the glass, her wild hair a fog around her head.

Out there, people had started cheering. From the apartment above: a thudding like someone jumping up and down. The hallway had begun to fill with whooping and laughter, the babble of TVs cranked up, all flooding in fast beneath the door to where Dima sat with his fork in his hand, listening. Then he set the fork down. It clinked against the pot. And he rose and went to the window and undid one clamp, undid the other, let the rug unfurl. He went to the next window and did the same. Over by the balcony door, the rooster began to crow.

Even after he had reblinkered it with the hood, convinced his mother to go to bed, crawled into bed himself, he couldn't sleep. Downstairs, Gennady was throwing a party. Music throbbing, people shouting. The same in the streets, even on rooftops. There were explosions. Fireworks? Gunfire? Dima lay in the dark, beneath the blankets, eyes open, his whole body awake, as if waiting for a sign, as if the zerkala's return might hold in it some hint of what was happening with his brother.

In the morning it was there: an envelope slid beneath the hallway door. It looked just like the ones that had appeared once a month in the mailbox stamped with his mother's name, except this one was hand scrawled with his.

> *Bratishka, forgive me. This isn't forever. But please listen to me now. You must be careful. You must not go where there aren't people around. Stay home as much as you can. Do not go back to the Oranzheria, Dima. Or the farm. For me, please, OK? I'm sorry I can't say why. I'm sorry for everything.*
>
> *—Yarik*

Years from now, when people talked of The Revisitation, they would recall almost everything about the weeks in which it began, and almost nothing of the days in which it ended. The dark left, the long-dusk returned, the wild animals fled for the wilds again, the refugees went back with them. The strike was forgotten. Workers were rehired. New ones, too. The Oranzheria needed repair—the crater in its roof rebuilt, its vast fields replowed and planted—and the great glass sea needed new shores, its edges expanded, its surface spreading faster and farther than ever before. The Consortium needed as many people as Petroplavilsk could give it. And in the months and years that would come after, what the people would remember, more than anything else, was how much they needed all that the Consortium had brought.

A few days after the Oranzheria reopened, all those who'd clamored for it to close were rounded up, packed into The Dachas, guarded by new hires who would ensure the gates stayed shut. Why he wasn't dragged off, too, Dima didn't know. At first, he thought that that was what his brother's message meant. He waited at home for the thuds of police boots coming up the stairs, for another knock at the apartment door. And when the raids that swept the city seemed over, he opened the door himself, went down the stairs. A glaring white mid-January morning. He took the reinstated tram out to the train station and walked between the long rows of abandoned railcars out back until he reached the beginning of the access line. For most of the day he searched the snowy woods for any sign of rail-boards stashed, kicked and dug at any clump of drift-smothered brush that seemed to strike his memory, until by the time the late sunlight sliced through the boughs, the forest floor around him looked like a scene of battle, the snow cratered and churned as if a band of others had struggled there. But there was only him, standing thigh-deep in the wrecked whiteness, knowing that, in the end, the main thing she had proved was that, in the beginning, he had been right: there was a finite amount of room in life; to let her in, he'd let a little of his brother out. He'd looked away. He'd let night sneak upon him, and he could feel the edge of the knife against his heart. He pulled it out and held his flesh closed again, pressing together the meat of his chest in the hope it might knit shut.

And in the nights he slept as he had slept before, the artificial light outside his window threaded through the holes in the kovyor, fine strings spun faint and colorless out of the mirrors' caromming, drifting lucent through the darkness of his room, sewn to the feather-filled duvet, to his bare shoulder, to the Adam's apple in his arched neck, to the eyelashes of his closed lids. Until, in the mornings, the sun plucked the pale strands away, and strung its fire in their place, and, as if his eyelid skin had grown to know the two kinds of light, his eyes blinked open. In the summer, he had awoken after a few hours; now, in winter's depth, he slept half the day.

Below on the street, the traffic mumbled as ceaselessly as every hour. The dogs, once more unmoored from the turning of the earth, barked their same sleepless barks. The steam pipes hissed with heat. Dima would draw on his robe and shuffle through the near blackness of the near empty living room, until he reached the balcony doors and, groaning as he bent, lifted the bottom edge of the kovyor and rolled it up. The blast of sunlight built him as it built the room: his thick socks, red as if knit of blood; his bird leg shins; grease slicks in the nap of his wine-colored robe; behind him, the box his mother had made for Ivan catching fire, the only piece of furniture left.

Inside, on its pillow bed, the hooded rooster always hunched, still as if sleeping. But, at his footsteps, it would jerk its head, flap a wing, wamble out to the end of the rope tied to its knotty gray leg, and stand there, facing him through the felt. On its back, its golden feathers shone smooth as water washing over a sunlit rock, its long black tail shimmering with a hidden green discovered by the sun. He would reach out and trace the length of one almost endless plume, let his hand float over the feathers, bury his fingers in its chest until he felt its heat, and hold them there, and talk to it.

"Poor Ivan," he would say, "what do you have to show for it all?"

Or, he would ask, "What will you make today? Some shit? A new feather? Will you add another millimeter to your tail?"

Or simply, "What use are you?" He would smile, poke a finger at its puffed chest. Its bullish neck would twitch. It would try to peck him through the felt.

"Oh," he would say, and, trapping its legs in a fist, pull it to him, press it to his chest. He would rock it a little. He would sing, low and quiet:

The night has gone
And with her taken the darkness
Papa has come
And rolled up all the rugs
Wake, wake.

Sometimes he would stop before the verse was done, sure someone was listening. But when he looked around, the living room was empty. The windows above his balcony showed no shape leaning out. He was sure, then, that the rooster in his arms was watching. Somehow, through its hood, it was peering at him while he sang.

Opening the glass doors, he would set it on a rail, the bird's tail feathers unspooling to the balcony floor. He would untie the cinch around its neck, draw off Dyadya Avya's old felt hat. In the instant after, he would try to catch Ivan's eye. But it would have locked onto the sun. The flesh around its socket lit bright red, nubby as pig leather, each tiny bulge stubbled with a tiny barb, as if the quills of feathers grew backwards out through its skin. In the golden light the curved membrane twitched, glistening. The pupil, a dark tunnel shrinking so quickly that soon it would be gone.

And then the rooster would lift its neck and crow out its morning-cracking call. Dima would shut his eyes and listen. He would feel the woodstove heat on the side of his face, hear the crackling of new logs thrown on. The air smelled of eggs still warm from the hen, the sour breeze of his brother's yawn. How good the first hot sip of tea felt on his throat.

He would swallow, open his eyes. On each balcony each flower pot displayed the same bright bloom. The Landscape Replacement Crew had come again, exchanged the potted plants that had failed to blossom for plastic ones that came prepetaled. Sunflowers. Single stalks whose small yellow heads now sat beneath caps of crusted snow. He would watch the cold breeze shake them, the only movement on all the floors of all the balconies. But for him. Making the trash fire, settling the kettle on the grill, he would go in to wake his mother.

One morning he woke to a clattering on his bedroom window glass instead. The room was still dim, the threads of light untinted by the sun. He lifted his watchface into one of them: a quarter past ten, almost an hour after he had awoke the morning before. When the clattering—it sounded, he realized, with a jerk, like pebbles thrown—struck the glass again, he rose and went to the window and rolled the kovyor up. New snow. The first since the mirrors had returned. It was still falling, the sky still thick with it, the daylight dimmed. Below his window: footprints. A man's boots? A woman's shoes? He followed them to the street, where they were lost in the crowd of others.

When it happened again, a few weeks later, he checked the time—half till eleven—and, throwing the duvet off, stumbled to the window, got the kovyor up enough to duck his head beneath. No figure running, no eyes peering up. And in the emptiness below it occurred to him that whoever it was wouldn't have been able to run off that fast. They were somewhere close. He scanned the sidewalks. It was not snowing yet—no way to tell fresh footprints from the mess of ones already made that week—but the sky was just as dark with all it would soon throw down.

The third time—awoken from late sleep again—he scanned the parked cars instead, their wet roofs, winter-grimed glass, searching for one with its tailpipe smoking. There were two: a small rust-stained Lada and an old sky blue Mercedes Benz.

The fourth time, he leapt from his bed at the first knocking of the stones, flapped the kovyor open, saw the blue door smacking shut. Out on the balcony, he rushed to the railing, peered down: the Mercedes's window was open, a dark jacketed elbow resting on the sill. He watched it for a while—the elbow never moving, no face peering out—and then went to the rooster and took its felt hood off. It crowed. Before he went inside, he checked the street again. The window was up. When he came back with the kettle, the car was gone.

After that, he woke each morning thinking that he'd heard the pebbles, but the sun was in the strings of light and his watch read the normal time for him to rise, and he knew he hadn't. Until, almost a week later, he woke with the clattering still in the air. Before his eyes were fully open, he was out of bed and at the window, looking down at a figure in a fur hat, a fluttering coat, skidding and slipping away. Even before the man yanked open the door to the sky blue car, Dima knew he had thrown the rocks. And even before then, he was sure it was his brother. But by the time he got downstairs and out to the street, there was just the empty space between two parked cars, the tire tracks broken through the roadside drift, the faint shadow of the Mercedes already disappearing beneath the falling snow.

That night, the Shopsins either weren't home or wouldn't come to their door. He went out to the sidewalk, pleaded, tugged on sleeves, finally found someone who let him use their mobile phone. Standing in the cold, beneath their impatient stare, he waited for someone to pick up. When his brother's voice answered, he spoke right over the hello: "I know it's you, Yarik!" But his brother only carried on. For a moment, Dima stared, perplexed, into the face of the phone's owner staring back, and then the answering message was done and Dima said his brother's name to the machine, asked it, "Why are you throwing rocks at my window? Why?"

"That's enough," the phone's owner told him.

But Dima only raised his voice. "Come up," he said over the other man. "Come up."

It was into the second half of winter, more than a month since the last time he had seen the car, and there was a meter of new snow on the ground, his underclothes damp with sweat from pushing through it, his pants dark with slush, his jacket wet, and all of him cold, the day Dima came home to the apartment and found the heat turned off. He didn't even realize how cold it was inside until he hung his jacket above the heater, stripped off his pants and shirt and lay them over it, and the back of his hand touched the metal and wasn't burned. Then, standing in the hallway in his underwear and bare feet, it hit him. His jaw started shaking, as if the bone had realized it, too.

"Mama?" he said through shivering lips.

She wasn't on her mattress where he'd left her that morning. It had become hard for her to move around—she needed a doorknob or chair arm to cling to—and he had moved her bed to the living room, set it near the bathroom door, brought her a piece of plastic piping for a cane. It was missing, too. He called louder.

"Good evening, lyubimy!" she called back.

Her voice came from inside her bedroom, and grabbing his bathrobe and socks off the floor, he crossed the living room and went in.

She was sitting on the dark patch of old carpeting where her bed frame had been. Her back was to him, and, standing on one foot, putting on a sock, he said, "Good evening, Mama." Her head swiveled. "Aren't you going to ask me how work was?"

"You don't work," she said.

His fingers froze. And, before she turned back to whatever was in her hands, he saw it: the lucidity in her eyes, the sudden presence of the mother he remembered.

All around her was mounded everything he hadn't sold: her meager jewelry, the dresses and shoes and hats she'd never wear again, the boxes that stored the artifacts of her life, all left untouched by him, now strewn across the floor. She had separated it into piles, islands of clothes, trinkets, toiletries, each item tagged with a torn piece of paper. Her sewing box lay on its side, drawers spilling a hundred colors of thread, a cloud of pinheads shimmering above their cushion set beside her.

"Are you OK?" he said to her back. She was wearing what he'd dressed her in that morning—her threadbare nightgown, wool socks and slippers, the kosinka that always bound her hair—nothing more. "Mama, aren't you cold?"

She stayed bent over whatever was in her lap. Going to her, he crouched before a pile, picked up a low-heeled shoe. A pin had been pushed through the black leather where the bridge of the foot would be. The scrap of paper it held in place proclaimed, in her unsteady letters, ZINAIDA. He set it down, picked up a knit hat. YARIK, the pinned tag said. There was a half-used jar of face cream. SELL, she'd written on it. He picked through half the things in the pile—TIMYA on a Young Pioneer scarf; POLYA on a tangle of hair ties; DIMA on a leather wallet, the pin bent as she had shoved it through—and, in another pile, he sifted among old reading glasses; a chewed tobacco pipe; the first tiny pair of ice skates that he and Yarik had shared. He crouched behind his mother, put his chin on her shoulder, looked down at what she was holding. A sheaf of papers, holes punched along one edge, bound together by a brittle strip of leather. The ink had browned, but the drawing was exactly as Dima remembered: the rowboat with its prow leaping over a curl of wave, the oar a tiny stick floating away, almost into the stars that his own fingers had scattered across the top of the page. Below them, two boys huddled in the boat, wrapped in each other's arms. A child's unsteady script: *Now that they had stopped rowing they were starting to get very cold.* He could not remember whether he or Yarik had written the words, but he remembered the two of them reading it aloud together to their mother that long-ago day in the sanitarium.

Now, he asked her, quietly, which pile the book belonged in. Her eyes stayed on the page. He tried to ease it from her fingers, but they gripped tighter.

"Is there a pile for each of us?" he asked.

She held on, her hands shaking.

"Is there one for me?"

She nodded.

"Does this go there?"

"No," she said.

"I'd like it," he told her.

"No," she said again. And when she turned her eyes on him, he could see the clarity was still there. He could see her trying to fight whatever was trying to take it from her, the way she had in the week after his father, her husband, had died, and he sat with his chest pressed to her shoulder, a nine-year-old boy looking at his mother with her gone-white hair, her determined eyes, her lips trembling when she spoke: "It's for Yarik."

"Why?"

"For Yarik."

He nodded. "OK," he said. "Do you want me to put it in his pile?"

It was one of the worst things that he had seen: his mother, so there just a second ago, beginning to leave. He almost put his hand over her eyes to keep from having to watch the confusion come back in.

"What pile?" she said.

Just as, all those years ago, in that week before the men from the sanitarium had come to take her from her sons, she had lost the battle, too.

415

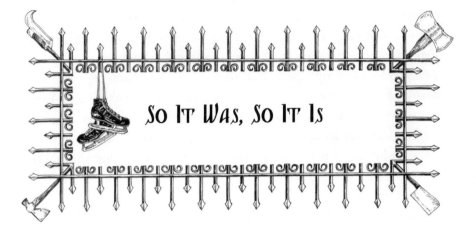

So It Was, So It Is

The children were running around the old grade school, past the dun brick, the slatey window glass, circling the building in single file, tramping a ring in the snow. The path they beat was dark and gray as the sky above, and watching them from behind the wrought iron fence, the old pair of ice skates hung around his neck, Dima felt again the burning freeze: six years old, and he and Yarik doing the same—the screwed-down stare at the back of the boy in front, the mittened hands rubbing at ears turned to icicles, the shouts of the gymnastics coach, *Take those hands down!*—though thirty years ago the song had been a different one.

"Russia, our beloved country!" the children sang now.

"United and mighty, our Soviet land!" they had sung then.

And, too, they had run it—his and Yarik's entire class—in their bare feet.

That first winter at school, each time the gymnastics coach made his whistle shriek, they had dropped to the ground, lain rocking on

416

their backs, feet clamped in their hands, howls mixing with the white-breathed agony of all the other kids.

Look, Yarik had later showed their father, *they're bleeding.*

What if our toes fall off? Dima had said.

And their father, knocking that past night's tobacco from his pipe, had bent to peer at their feet, the flame from his match so close to their soles they could feel its heat.

Your toes won't fall off, he told them.

How do you know? Dima said.

Because—he shook out the match—*I'm going to teach you how to keep them on.*

He told them to lie down on their backs, and, grunting exaggerated puffs, laughing through the smoke in his mouth, he hauled them by their arms and legs into the position he wanted. They lay there feet to feet. *This is how your dyadya and I would do it,* he said, *every time the gym coach blew for the break* and they had let him arrange them the rest of the way, his calloused fingers on Dima's ankles as he dragged him into his brother, his big hands lifting Yarik's small ones as he made room for the one's feet to wedge into the other's underarms. When he was done, they lay with their toes in each other's pits, their arms pressed tight to the sides of each other's legs.

The armpits, their father said, crouched at the middle of their single tangled shape, *are the warmest part of the body. Except*—he grinned—*for the crotch.* And with the bowl of his pipe he rapped each one a quick knock there. Over them, he stood, his face scrimmed by pipe smoke, watching them squirm with laughter and pain.

All that winter, every time the gymnastics coach blew his whistle, they would drop to the snow and scoot into the shape their father showed them, lying still, squeezing, amid the wild writhing of the other kids. And all that summer they worked at Dyadya Avya's barefoot, building a layer of calluses opaque and hard as the trimmings carved off the milk cows' hooves, so that by winter they could run all ten circles around the grade school without ever having to stop.

417

Until the winter they turned nine, when the boys from the grade below came running, shouting from too far away to be understood, their billows of breath like some signal the brothers couldn't read. Dima and Yarik were halfway through their laps when the boys burst into them, blood in their cheeks, their eyes alight with news.

They ran barefoot all the way to the lake, their feet crunching snow, slapping the ice alongside trolley tracks, the frozen surface of Otseva. Out there: a huddle of men. Dark shapes against the brightness, more hurrying from the shore. The ever-gusting wind had blown the glassy surface clear and on it stood a hundred oystercatchers, red-beaked and black, and they rose in waves around the running boys. Wingbeats, caws. The men seemed to part as easily, the first not knowing who was pushing through, the next gone still at the sight of them, a last few hands grasping for their arms, their jacket collars, anything to grab them by and hold. They fought the grips, silent, struggling, until they saw him. So close they could almost have touched his face with their outstretched fingers, if it hadn't been under so much ice. His black hair a floating blur beneath the surface, the black strip of his mustache—it had always smelled of pipe smoke, been warm with breath, tickled their cheeks—shifting with the current down there like something alive.

Coming through the crowd: a man in a hard hat, gloves gripping a long black pole, its iron tip wedge-shaped as a serpent's head. Behind him: the open ice of the lake, and three more men crossing it at a strange and shuffling run. Between two a ladder rattled. The third carried a heavy maul.

By the time they dragged the body out, Dima could feel the ice like spikes through the soles of his feet. They stabbed up through his ankles and split his shins and pierced his knees. Still he stood, barefoot, watching his brother tear free of his jacket, run to their father, grab a frozen hand, shove the stiff fingers beneath his armpit, call for Dima to take the other. And fighting their father's cold wet coat, pushing his own fingers into the crevice between arm and chest, he'd felt the hardness of the skin in that hollow where his father's limb joined his father's body, the utter absence of heat.

418

Plenty of room for dreams and for life
The coming years promise to us.
Allegiance to our Motherland gives us strength.
So it was, so it is, and so it will always be.

The last words submerged beneath gasping breath, the slowing shrush of boots in snow, and then the children stopped, and there was Timofei standing bent over his knees, coughing. A few kids around him collapsed into the drifts. The gymnastics coach kicked snow onto their faces, started to herd them all inside.

Dima looked for something to throw at the child. He was standing behind a wrought iron fence, far enough away he would have to shout to be heard. Between the fence and the street, around his boots, food wrappers were strewn among cups and straws. A single red glove, wet to the color of old blood, spread like a hand emerging from the sooty bank. Around it: brown glass bottles barely visible beneath the snow. Around them a bright scattering of metal caps. Quickly, he pried four out.

The first one didn't come close enough to even make Timofei look. The second hit him in the cheek. The boy jerked, slapped a mitten to his face. Dima gave a quick wave, the skates clanking. The boy said something he couldn't hear. Gloved fingers flapping at his palm, Dima urged him closer. The boy shook his head. Dima put his whole arm into beckoning. But Timofei just shook his head again, turned, started for the steps that led to the building's door.

"Timosha!" Dima unlooped the laces from around his neck, dangled the skates from his glove extended over the fence towards his brother's son. Timofei paused. He was the only child still outside and while he stood there the school door shut. Through it came the muffled bellows of the gymnastics coach. "Timosha!" Dima called again.

Slowly, head bent, eyes down, as if approaching an unsafe dog, the boy came. Behind Dima, a trolley clattered by. The snow in that far edge of the schoolyard was deep; it piled at the boy's knees and sloughed away and Timofei neared slowly, as if pushing through sand.

419

He stopped close enough that Dima could see the weight on his nephew, the small boy bent over his chest like an old man. It made the skates feel heavy, too. He drew them back, hung them again around his neck.

"Timosha," he said, "it's me. Your dyadya."

The boy's eyes stayed on the snow where his legs were buried. "I'm not supposed to see you."

Behind Dima, in the street, cars passed in steady shushing waves. "You mean you can't even look at me?"

"Mama said if I see you, just act like I didn't."

Dima leaned his chest against the fence, his arms over it, the blade of a skate knocking at a bar with a quiet clank. "Well," he said, "I bet you're allowed to see *this*." He held his arm out towards the boy. Between his gloved thumb and forefinger was a third bottle cap. When the boy looked up, Dima waggled it so it winked in the gray light. Then, with a flick of his thumb, he sent the cap arcing into the air. It spun, high above his head, and he opened his jaw wide as he could and leaned over the fence and caught the falling bottle cap in his mouth. With a chomping sound, he shut his lips around it. He made them big while he pretended to chew. Then he squatted down to the boy's height, bent his neck back so the ribbing of his throat showed through his beard. Beneath the skin, he knew the bulge of his Adam's apple would be huge.

"Come here," he croaked.

From the other side of the fence: silence.

"Touch it," he croaked.

With his face to the sky, he listened to the boy's first hesitant step. When he could feel Timofei was close enough, Dima put his own finger on his Adam's apple and croaked, again, "Touch it. Take off your mitten and touch it." A faint spot of pressure joined the one from his own finger. He took his finger away. The boy's stayed.

"Should I swallow it?" he croaked. He could feel, easily as if it had been Yarik, when his nephew nodded. "I can't see you," he croaked. "You have to tell me."

"Swallow it," Timofei said.

And with a gulp, he jerked his head back upright, his Adam's apple disappearing. The boy's finger stayed on his throat. He felt the other tiny fingers join it, until Timofei's whole hand was searching his neck through the tangle of his beard.

"I ate it." Dima watched the boy's eyes go from big to huge. He opened his mouth, showed the gaping emptiness.

"It will *kill* you," the boy whispered.

"No," Dima said.

"Yes, you'll *die*." He sounded more in awe of the idea than scared by it.

Dima laughed. "You think?"

The boy nodded, very seriously. His eyes had not yet left Dima's throat.

"Then I better get it out again," Dima said and, standing up, made with his lips a bubbling imitation of a fart.

The boy jerked back. And in the second before his nephew's shock shifted to laughter, Dima shook his left leg, shook it harder, shook out of his pants a bottle cap that plunked into the snow.

It seemed such a long time since he had heard a child laugh. Covering his own smile, he slipped the bottle cap out from under his tongue, told the boy, "I have something I want to give you."

He watched Timofei's eyes flick to the ice skates around his neck. "Do you have your rucksack inside?" Dima said. The boy nodded. "It's very important that you put this in it." And, reaching into his coat, he drew from the inside pocket a sheaf of papers rolled around its leather-stitched spine. "It's for your father." He held it through the fence. He could see the disappointment in the boy's eyes. "And for you, too," he said. "But the note in it"—Dima tapped a paper clip with his thumb—"is for him. Timosha, will you give it to him for me?"

The boy didn't take it. Instead, Timofei said, "Are those your skates?"

Dima nodded.

"No they're not," the boy said.

"Timofei," Dima said, "please take this for me. Please put it in your rucksack and give it to your father."

"They're too small," the boy said.

Dima lowered himself again to a squat. "Of course they are." Through the fence, he smiled at his nephew. "That's why I'm giving them to you."

The boy beamed so broadly Dima could hear his teeth chattering.

"Now take this," Dima told him, "and put it in your rucksack." He watched to make sure the boy slipped the book safely inside his jacket. But starting to lift the skates off of his neck, Dima stopped. He could see how it would be: Timofei running back to the school, him watching until his nephew disappeared inside, and by the time Dima might see him again—maybe before the winter's end, maybe not for another year—his brother's son would already be a different boy. He left the laces where they were. Instead of handing them through the fence, he reached out with his empty glove and ruffled Timofei's head. "Go inside," he said. "Get warm. And when school is over, don't follow your friends to the gym, OK? Run here right away, without anyone else, straight back to this fence, and I'll take you to the lake. I'll tie these on your feet. I'll show you how to use them."

That afternoon, he reached across the fence, gripped Timofei under his arms, and, struggling with what should have been an easy weight, lifted him over the wrought iron spikes. Setting the boy down on the sidewalk, the ache leaking out of his atrophied shoulders, Dima bent his legs, put his hands on his knees. "Climb on," he said.

They went like that, the boy riding the man's back, down Antonova Street towards Lake Otseva. The sky was still as dark, as gray, but the slab of it had slid a little off the horizon, and there a bright strip attested to the nearness of the sun. Every now and then, Dima would shrug his shoulders, hefting the weight of the boy's thighs on his forearms, leaning into the press of the arms around his neck.

"You're bony," Timofei said.

"You're chubby," Dima told him.

"You're smelly," Timofei said.

"Oh yeah? What do I smell like?"

"My papa," the boy said.

At Dima's chest, the small skates clacked.

"You smell like Papa after he comes home from work."

Dima nodded. "Well," he said, "you know your father and I—"

"Like Papa," the boy cut him off, "but a whole lot worse."

Down by the lake they passed beneath the statue and Timofei reached up, as if to grab the brass tsar's finger, but he could not, and they went on out, over the guardrail, onto rocks half-covered in snow, and, Dima carefully shuffling forward, made their way onto the ice. All along the shore, old pleasure boats were sealed in, forgotten speedboats marooned in frozen water, abandoned sailboats with their hulls holding high banks of windblown snow. They looked like the gargantuan bodies of some ancient beasts cut down by giants, their bare masts jutting into the sky like great spears that had slain them. Way out, over the vast expanse of white, the island hovered, faint as a cloud, almost invisible in the middle of the lake, a place where the spear-throwers might have dwelled.

Holding Timofei's hand in his, Dima led the boy out to the spot on the ice where he used to skate when he'd been his nephew's age. Together, they brushed at the snow with their boots, clearing away a small circle, the two of them the only things moving on the lake. Above, jaegers rode the breeze, the most distant mere sharp-winged shapes cutting across the low strip of last light. As they widened their circle of ice, the man and boy passed before it, too, silhouetted by that crack between the horizon and the clouds, coming into the sun and circling back to cutout shapes again and circling again into the light.

When they had cleared enough, Dima took the rucksack off Timofei's back. He loosened the straps, was about to slide his own arms through, when Timofei said, "Wait." The boy opened it, dug inside, took out a small package of *sukhariki* crackers sealed in cellophane. "They'll make you strong," his nephew told him. Dima could feel his throat swallow his smile. "Let's save them for after," Dima said, and

423

they sat on the ice while he removed the boy's boots and laced the skates onto his feet. Then he helped Timofei stand. His hands around the boy's waist, he walked with him, each small slide of his boot soles matching each small slide of the blades.

After a while, Dima was only holding his hand, standing in the middle of the circle, like a trainer with a horse, their arms the tether, and a while after that the boy was skating one length and then the other, unsteadily and slowly with Dima shuffling along beside. By the time the sun's color had deepened towards orange, Timofei was skating on his own. By the time it had gone red, he was going so fast he could have broken something when he fell.

Before the boy even hit the ice, Dima was running after him. Timofei landed all sprawled out, but by the time Dima got to him he had curled up on himself, a dark still lump. At first, he hoped that the red on his nephew's face was just tears and snow caught by the setting sun, but as soon as he was bent low he knew it was blood.

"You're OK," he said, scooping the boy in his arms. "Are you OK, Timosha?"

As if the ice against his face had sealed all sound inside him, the moment Dima lifted the boy his wailing came. It blew over the frozen lake. Sitting, Dima pulled his nephew to his chest, wiped at his face, asked over and over, "Where does it hurt?" The boy shook his head and wailed, and Dima shucked his gloves, lifted Timofei's lips, felt his teeth. He wasn't missing any. All the blood was coming from his nose. Dima wrapped the boy in his arms then and let him wail. It was only when he realized that his nephew, held over his shoulder, was broadcasting his pain towards the shore, the city, that he turned him to face the darkening lake, set him on his lap.

"Timosha," Dima said, "it's a bloody nose. Only a bloody nose." He stole a glance over his shoulder at the shore—just the tsar's brass back—and leaning his face close to the crying child's, asked, "What do you want me to do?" The boy bawled on. "Do you want me to take you home?" The boy shook his head, flinging drops of blood. "Do you want to skate some more?" More droplets flung. "I know,"

Dima said. "I know. Do you want me to read you a book?" The head shaking, twice as violent; the wailing turned up a notch. "It's what I gave you to give to your father, Timosha." The wailing kept on, but this time the head stayed still. "Don't you want to know what it is?" Just a little, the head nodded. "Your father and I wrote it," Dima told him. "When we were very young, barely older than you." Timofei had gone quiet. He tilted his face up to look back at Dima.

"Good," Dima said. "Hold your face up just like that. And with your hand"—he took Timofei's hand, the mitten still on, in his bare one—"squeeze the tip of your nose like this. Good, Timosha. Stay just like that, and the blood will stop, and I'll get the story out of your rucksack, OK?"

Face to the sky, blood half-hidden by the mitten at his nose, Timofei nodded.

They sat facing the last of the sun, the nephew cradled in his uncle's chest, the uncle holding the loose-bound papers before them both. Dima had put his gloves back on and his fingers were thick and cumbersome.

Once upon a time . . . In the low light, the cold stinging his eyes, he could hardly read his childhood scrawl. But the words had lodged in him long ago and he read as if reading from the memory inside instead of from the page.

"Once upon a time there were two brothers. They were twins. They lived on a farm. But not with their papa or their mama. With their uncle. His name was Avery Leonidovich Zhuvov. He was very funny and told good stories. Almost as good as this."

Timofei made a pinched noise through his nose that sounded like "No."

"What?" Dima asked.

From beneath his mitten, the boy said, "Start at the beginning."

"That is the beginning. Once upon a time . . ."

"No," the boy said again, and with his free mitten pushed at the page opened over Dima's left hand, the back of the cover. There, he had clipped the note to Yarik.

425

"That's for your father," Dima told the boy. "Remember I asked you—"

"But you said you were going to read what you gave me to give to Papa."

"I meant the book."

The boy pulled away from Dima's chest, leaned over, sounded out the first word. "Dear," he said, very slowly, and a drop of blood dripped off his face and spotted the first page. He didn't seem to notice, only sounded out the next word: "Yarik."

Dima pulled him back so he would not bleed more.

"That's my papa's name," Timofei told him.

"Yes."

"I can read it." Timofei struggled against Dima's hand, got free long enough to read aloud "I am" and start sounding the next word before Dima pulled him back again and told him, "OK, OK. We don't have time, Timosha. I'll read it, and then the book, and then we'll go home, yes?"

He could feel the back of the boy's head nod against his chest.

"Dear Yarik," he read. "Mama wanted you to have this. Last night I didn't know why, but now I do. Do you remember how you would start to say an idea and I would finish it? Or I would start and you would finish. 'Into the lake,' I said. 'Where they drowned,' you said."

Dima's face felt too stiff with the cold to get any more words out. He cupped a glove to his mouth, blew into the leather. When the boy looked up at him, he nodded and took his hand away again.

"I am worried about Mama," he read on. "I try to help her, but I think I am failing. I think she needs your help. You know what I am saying. If I come back one night and she is not there I will know you understand. I will miss her. But I will be grateful to you, big brother. Yesterday, the building turned off the heat."

Dima coughed to free the air from his throat. The sun was almost down. He dipped his head until his face was against the top of his nephew's head, and said with his lips in the wool of the boy's hat, "That's it."

"What's that." Timofei pointed again with his mittened hand.

"That's just my name."

"No it's not."

Dima nodded his face against the wool. "It says, 'Your little brother.'"

"OK," the boy said. "Now let's read the book."

By the time he was halfway through, the sun had gone and the zerkala had come up. They were barely bright enough to read by. He had just reached the point where the brothers lost their oars, when he heard shouting from the shore. He turned. Back there, three men were climbing over the guardrail between the statue park and the rocks that edged the lake.

"How?" Timofei, in his lap, said. "*How* did they loose the oars?"

Behind the men, behind the rail: a car. It was the shape of the cars the city's policemen drove, it was a police car—on its hood he could see the flashers—and he almost let go of the book.

"How—" Timofei started.

But Dima had looked down at the boy and seen the blood dried dark on his face and said, "Oh no."

Then he was scrambling up, saying, "Stand, stand," trying to steady Timfoei on his skates with one hand while, with the other, he shoved the storybook in the rucksack.

The men were close enough now that he could hear their words slapped across the ice at him, hitting like pucks—*don't* and *boy* and *move* and *drop*—and he let go of Timofei and felt the air waver behind him where he knew the boy was and reached out again and pulled his nephew tight. The men were in uniform. Two ran with a hand on their sides, like men with cramps, or men who had hurt a hip, or men who carried guns. The third carried a long stick in his fist. He was the faster one. There were the boy's words mixed in now, too—*who* and *who* and *who*—and Dima's words back—*OK, OK*—and Dima tightened his arm around Timofei's shoulders and stooped to grasp the bag and all the while shouted at the men things that came out—*uncle* and *nephew* and *skating* and *my brother*—and when he straightened up, the rucksack hanging from his free hand, he rose right into what felt like a hammer smashing the side of his head.

427

The second blow felt like the stick it was. It hit his stomach and his eyes saw it leave his body, saw the policeman's boots stepping back on the ice, and his mind shot the thought through his head *thank god it's just a stick* and then it hammered down against his skull again. There was a sudden wind on his face. There was the sound of Timofei screaming. There was a slab of rock, large as the lake, dropping from the sky, falling so fast all he could do was clench his teeth against it before it smashed full on into his chin.

Once upon a time there were two brothers. They were twins.

A double-headed axe.

They lived on a farm.

A single-bladed hatchet.

But not with their papa or their mama.

The cleaver Dyadya Avya used to crack the backs of the chickens and cut them into quarters.

With their uncle. His name was Avery Leonidovich Zhuvov. He was very funny and told good stories.

That long-handled brush hook with its wide blade shining flat and straight before the sudden vicious curve at the end.

Stories almost as good as this.

That night, the night that their uncle had told them how their father died, that night while Dyadya Avya slept on the floor by the big woodstove, the empty bottle clutched like a kitten to his chest, that night they had lain on the straw, each boy pressed to one side of the dog, the dog breathing, its breath smelling of its organs, of the blood that their brushing had drawn from its gums, the crack beneath the stove door flickering with just enough firelight to find the boys in the blackness of the hut, that night they had decided to gather the tools they would need for killing.

One by one, week after week, they snuck them from the house or from the barns, brought them across the fields into the forest. They did it at night—carrying them through the birch woods, the white trunks long stripes of moonlight, the blades in their hands like chips of stars—while Dyadya Avya slept. And when he found his cleaver missing, his sickle gone, after a fit of furious searching, their uncle would stop, his belly heaving, and curse at the ceiling, as if to shame the heavens into giving back his tools. But they were no more above the roof than beyond the clouds. If God had had a hand in it, it was only in the perfect place that He'd afforded the brothers to hide them.

They would crawl inside the buried banya, nestle a jar of sinkers in the leaves that lined the earthen floor, or add a blacksmith's mallet to the pile of weapons they had stored, and sit, knees drawn up against the cold, shoulders hunched beneath the carved-out ceiling, hair catching in the roots, and talk of what they might use for a lure.

It could not be just a piece of meat, they knew. It had to be a soul.

Eyes slowly adjusting to the dark, chests to air thick with the ancient scent of mushrooms grown and died and decomposed above their heads, they debated where in a body the soul could be found. The lungs that allowed an animal to breathe? But then it would escape on every exhale. The brain? But then how could a headless hen still scramble feverish with life? They thought for a while that it might reside in the eyes. But they had seen their father's blue, blue irises, his black, black pupils, staring back at them up through the ice. The heart: no one had reached down his throat, no one had cut into his chest, no one had sawn through his breastbone, wrenched it open, no one had seen whether or not their father had still had his heart.

In the threshing barn, hanging on ropes from the rafters, were all the parts of the hog their uncle had slaughtered and smoked that fall: hams, ribs, shoulders, hocks, all wrapped in muslin and frozen hard. The liver their uncle always cooked up fresh. The head he boiled into cakes of gelatin and brain. But there was a bag that hung by itself that held the ears, the snout, the cheek meat, and, somewhere among all the smaller parts, a rock hard heart.

But it's frozen, Dima said.

They debated whether or not the soul could be killed by cold. Or if it would slip out before the temperature got too low. Dyadya Avya had told them it was the part that God chose to bring up to Him, so they were sure it would not be stupid enough to let the heart's walls

429

freeze it in. Besides, even if the cold was of no concern to it, it would have surely left for heaven by now.

It leaves right after something dies, Yarik said.

It leaves before, Dima said.

It can't, Yarik said, *you can't live without it.*

See? Dima said, as if that proved his point.

That was when they decided the soul was smart enough to know when the body was wounded too gravely to go on, smart enough to flee before it got trapped inside. Unless something snuck up and killed the body while the soul was unawares, caged it in there until it could be devoured still alive. And when did it come down from heaven? When did it enter the heart? At birth? No: they had seen the belly of a pregnant rabbit cut open to show the lingering life of her brood inside. They had seen in their breakfast the spots of blood in the yolk, even, once, the beginnings of a beak.

They left while Dyadya Avya was in his deafness of midday drunk, napping on the pallet upon the stove. They hitched the mule to his cart. They loaded the cart with their arsenal of blades and bludgeons. They took the jars and the eggs. They took the live goose, a hood on its head. Dima had it tight beneath an arm, one hand squeezing shut its beak, his other hauling him up onto the cart, when Yarik suddenly jumped down, ran back to the house, disappeared, and a minute later came back out holding something that gleamed: Dyadya Avya's ancient revolver, gripped in his two small hands. Climbing up beside Dima, Yarik's eyes had shown how scared he was by what he'd done. His mouth had shown how set he was on doing it. Towards the mule's ears he made a click. They drove down to Otseva's shore. They loaded up a little rowboat they found tied to the dock. They slipped the knot. And rowed together out towards Nizhi, into the lake, to hunt for the Chudo-Yudo.

"Until it came up," one of them said, "and crushed the boat."

"And they drowned," the other said.

"Or it ate them."

"Or anyway—"

"Dima."

430

His face was numb. All but his ear.

Or anyway.

His ear was burning with cold.

"Dima!"

Swooping away from his eye, carved in the ice: a long thin cut, smooth line arcing on the lake, the lake blurry with snow. The moonlight—no the sunlight—shone through the splinters of ice that the blade of the skate had lifted. Then something steamed between the groove and his eye and when he blinked the bottom of his eye had filled with red. No: the ice, filled with red. He watched the skate's track turn color, the blood running along it, away from him, so fast, as if it meant to draw its line all the way across Otseva to the opposite shore. And then it stopped. Pooled against a thick black wall. The sole of a boot. The light of the mirrors: gone. His brother's voice: "Dima."

Even without it, he would have known the grip of his hands, known him by the way he hauled Dima up to a sit and crouched beside him on the ice and cradled Dima's head against his chest, his hand patting harder and harder at his brother's cheek.

"Yarik," Dima said.

"Oh God," his brother said. "What those fuckers did to your face."

"*Your* face," Dima said and, through the numbness, tried to smile.

He didn't know whether the smile made it, but the pain came through like a nail. When he shouted, the nail drove the rest of the way in. Through the pain, he knew his brother was saying something, knew he could have even understood it if he could have thought about anything but the pain.

Then his brother was standing behind Dima, his hands beneath Dima's arms, gripping the sides of his chest, dragging him slowly backwards, and it was almost worth it. The lake slid away: the clearing he and Timofei had made growing, the vast white plain of all the rest shrinking, the island of Nizhi too far to make out in the reflected light. His brother's gusty breathing came from somewhere above his head. His brother's hands slipped and gripped again. He tightened the insides of his arms around them, trying to keep them warm.

431

Night Known

From the end of the 6:00 P.M. news to the beginning of the eleven o'clock edition playing now on the waiting room TV, Yarik had sat in a hard plastic chair or paced the wide linoleum squares and fought the urge to leave. When he had first left Dima with the doctors and gone back down the hall, he'd thought the glances the nurses gave him were merely the usual thing—*Isn't that the guy from the Oranzheria ads?*—had expected one to approach—*Mr. Next?*—the way people did on the street. But in the waiting room the whispers had been unfriendly, something unsettling about the stares, and then he'd seen the report he'd missed on the earlier hour's news and known he'd had it wrong: the only reason they were talking about him was what was being said about his brother.

And now, there was Dima, on the arm of an orderly, being walked into the room. All eyes turned. Yarik's, too. And the thought that he was joining them, another spectator taking in the sight of his brother's face, made him look away.

He'd spent the past hours thinking of what he would say, but when he stepped forward to ease his brother from the orderly's arm, it was

Dima who spoke, mouthed a word so garbled only Yarik could have understood. "Bratan." And, through the Novocain that numbed his jaw, working with his swollen lips: "You look good."

The starch in his collar, the tie loosened around his neck, the new winter jacket with the Consortium logo on its chest: right then he would have ripped it all away. But watching Dima's smile—a little saliva slipped from the corner of his mouth, his eyes trying not to show the pain the analgesic was already letting through—how could he not smile back? "You don't," Yarik said. As much for himself as to steady his brother, he put his arm around Dima's back. A murmur rippled through the gawkers. *Good,* Yarik thought, *let them doubt what they'd been told.* He gave his brother's shoulder a gentle pat. "Come on," he said. He'd been holding Dima's rucksack by a strap, and he saw Dima watching it, made out his brother's slurred, "Where's Timofei?"

"Home," Yarik told him.

"We were only—"

"It's late." Yarik heaved the bag to his shoulder, felt his neck muscles tense. "Let's get you there, too."

But, helping his brother down the corridor, feeling Dima's unsteadiness beneath his arm, he knew it was too late. He'd waited too long.

A day after he'd confronted Bazarov, after the man had called his guards back in and given Yarik back his gun—*One last lesson: load it yourself*—and had him escorted outside again, on the first full evening reillumined by the zerkala, Yarik had returned from work, stepped into the stairwell, shut the building's door behind him, and heard a voice say *Slava.* When he turned, a thin figure waited there, half-hidden by shadows, half by a hood, barely discernible but for her hands, her face. *You even answer to it,* she said. And he could just make out a smirk. He'd thought she was a stalker, someone after a snapshot or an autograph, but when he'd asked her what she wanted she'd spoken his brother's name. She'd come, she told him, because she knew it might be the last day she could. Because, with her last hours of freedom, she wanted to do something good. For Dima. *Who are you?* Yarik had asked. *I'm the one,* she'd said, *who he might love if he didn't already love you.* While she'd talked he had gradually been able to make her out. Her fingers working over a sliver of something metal, snapping it open and shut while she spoke of how close she feared his brother was to coming undone, how she'd seen others so troubled they needed The Dachas' walls around them to keep the rest of the world at bay, the way, she said, that Dima needed him. *You,* she said, shoving her hood back. *Not Slava.* The anger showing in her face. *Someone who could be the twin your brother talks so much about. Because this*—she stepped close, snagged his tie, slapped it back against his chest—*isn't him.* Watching her face soften, the fury fade from her black eyes, he'd listened to her try to paint a picture of the life she seemed to believe that he and Dima could still lead. But beneath the smoke of her cigarette breath he'd sensed her desperate need to believe in it herself, and it had been that—the knowledge that he no longer did, the hole he could feel where once he'd needed to believe in it, too—that, when she'd said the words *good brother,* had made them hurt so much.

Now, outside the hospital, in the perpetual sidewalk crush, all he could do was try to help his stitched-up brother make it through the harried crowd. "Excuse me," Yarik said, over and over, "I'm sorry," and, pushing aside those who paused to peer at their faces, "please."

When they got to his car, Dima stopped. In the light from the zerkala the sky blue of the Mercedes looked almost gray. "When did you get it?" his brother asked.

But Yarik was already walking around the other side, opening the door, sliding, for a second, out of sight. Stuffing the rucksack in the passenger footwell, he glanced up at the window: Dima's bloodstained coat, the face hidden by the car's roof, the stab of shame that Yarik felt at being glad for that. He leaned the rest of the way across the seat, lifted the lock.

When the engine rumbled alive on the first crank of the key his brother raised his eyebrows, as if impressed. But Yarik caught his wince; even that small movement must have hurt. And when Dima reached to his forehead, as if unsure what his fingers would find, Yarik reached over, too, flipped the visor down. The small dim mirror shook.

434

Watching Dima see his own face in it, Yarik made himself look, too: a split in one eyebrow taped together, the forehead purpled close to the skin, blood crusted at his temple, in his beard, a patch, mustache to jaw, shorn clear for the gauze. Which was what the doctor had told him: eleven stitches in the chin, a few more in his torn lip, five above the left eye. His brother's nose would just from now on be a flattened nose.

"I didn't mean for them to hurt you," Yarik said and began backing out. "When Timosha's principal called Zina, and Zina didn't know where he was, she called the police. Told them Timosha was missing. I knew it was you."

"You knew?"

"I called them. Told the dispatcher I thought Timofei was with you. But when I called again she said someone else had called in a sighting. At least she told me you were on the lake." And, yes, he knew. He knew that when he'd told her it must be Dima she hadn't just called the police. Or the ones in the squad car had made a call of their own. How could he have believed that anything with which he'd threatened Bazarov would keep his brother safe? They would simply bring Slava down in the same way, tie him to some disgrace, drop him from their campaign. And once he had been replaced? "Dima . . ." he said, and told himself he'd tell his brother all of it now, everything, he had to, and the car hit a stretch of potholes and he peered out the windshield as if he could see them before they were already under the wheels, and told himself *tell him*, but when the road smoothed out again, he only said, "I got there as fast as I could."

"How did you know?" Dima asked. "When you first heard Timofei was missing. How did you know it was me?"

Yarik pulled close behind the car in front of them, pushed the heel of his hand against the horn. When he let go, let the blare blow away again, Dima's question only seemed to sit louder in the quiet. He looked at his brother. "The way we always do," he said. Then he shifted, gunned the engine, pulled around the car into the oncoming lane. The rucksack slid against Dima's shins, and Yarik glanced at it, at his brother, back at the road. "Timofei gave me your letter," he

435

said. He could feel Dima watching him. He kept his eyes ahead. "I'll take Mama." There was the whir of the tires on the frozen asphalt. "How is she?"

"OK," Dima said. "Confused."

"Is she eating enough?"

"No."

"Are you?"

But Dima was staring ahead, as if at the blinking yellow signal of a trolley coming towards them on the tracks between the lanes. "Yarik," he said, "what's going on?" On the avenue a stoplight turned: a spot of red, the brake lights of cars. "Where did you go that night Zinaida was so worried?"

Yarik brought the car to a stop. "I don't know what you mean."

"She came to the apartment. Bought me coffee. She said you'd left early that morning."

"What morning don't I—"

"She said you'd taken Dyadya Avya's gun." Across the intersection, the tram was waiting, too, its signal flashing. "That was the night you left me that note," Dima said. "Why? What was going on?"

The light changed; Yarik pulled right, caught his brother looking at the turn signal ticking in the dash, then back at the road they'd left behind, heard Dima blow a small laugh from his nose. "When you said get me home, too, I thought you meant . . ." The rest was lost in his brother's throat.

"Dima"—Yarik's own voice softened—"who would take care of Mama tonight?"

"We could take her together to your home."

"No." The word came out harder than he'd meant it. "We couldn't."

"I thought you said once you had the job, once things were settled—"

"What's settled?"

"You said you'd get a car."

"I got it three months ago, Dima."

"You said you'd tell them to fuck off."

436

"Don't you think," Yarik said, "that if it changed anything, any fucking thing, it would have changed it three months ago? Do you have any idea what I risked when I stopped those cops? What a risk I'm taking now? Waiting for you in the hospital? Driving you to your apartment? Dropping you off?"

"You took the risk all the time," Dima said. "In the mornings, when you threw rocks at my window."

"Gravel."

"When you sat down there in this car."

"A few pebbles."

"Why?"

"You were sleeping late."

"So?"

"I had to get to work."

"Then—"

"I had to get to work and I didn't want to go without hearing the rooster, all right?"

"I don't understand."

"There's nothing to understand! I wanted to hear your rooster. You're my brother and I wanted to hear your fucking rooster, one fucking rooster, crow in the fucking morning again."

They sat in the sound of the snow and ice beneath the wheels, the rattling of the car over the cracked road, the ceaseless shush of the heat breathing out of the dash.

"He crows every morning," Dima finally said. "You could just come and hear him. It doesn't have to be so complicated. Why does it have to be—"

They braked, jerked forward, sat in the middle of the road. In the rearview mirror: the fog lights of cars coming close fast.

"You want to know why?" Yarik said. "I'll show you."

And he turned, sharp, onto a side street, and sharp again onto another avenue, driving too fast, out towards the city's edge, until they were rushing past the shops cropping up before the bigger out-lying stores, and he didn't slow until he hit the strip where they sold electronics, the wide windows displaying sound systems and washing machines and computers and TVs, and they stopped.

A wall of televisions turned to the street, stacked tight as tiles. The Mercedes idled before them. Peering past his brother, Yarik stared through the the plate glass, scanning the bank of TVs, searching all those boxes of color and light.

"I don't know why I thought it would still be playing," he said. And, when Dima asked him what, "You. On the news. The old clips, you on the roof, the stuff of you skating on the Oranzheria."

"Again?"

"And what someone shot tonight. You, all bloody."

"Why—"

"Timosha, with his bloody face. Me dragging you off the ice. 'Bringing you to justice,' the reporter said. The police . . . You don't want to know what the police said." Behind Dima, the jittery images shook the screens.

"Why would they have said anything?"

"Because they were told to," Yarik said. "They were *paid* to. You're right, Dima, it's not that complicated. But it is hard."

With all the garish TV screens backlighting his head, his brother's face seemed almost too dim to see. But Yarik knew his own was lit, that Dima must be watching all the changing colors on his face. He tried to keep his jaw still, his mouth steady. But he knew that Dima felt it. Knew it from the softness in Dima's voice when he said, "It didn't used to be. It doesn't have to be."

Behind his brother the televisions seemed to shake. "But it is," Yarik said, and in the wavering of his own voice knew that the shaking wasn't the TVs.

"Who says so?" Dima asked, barely whispering. "Who paid them? Bratan? Who's doing this to you?" Reaching across the shift, he touched Yarik's leg so lightly his fingers hardly released their weight.

But Yarik jerked his leg away. He sat there, feeling Dima's gaze on him, gazing past through the glass at the TVs. Some of them were on ads. One, he knew, would be the Consortium's. There it was, the last few seconds: him in a suit and tie stepping out of his office, down from the trailer into a hard-hat crew, slapping their backs, returning their smiles as he got into a sedan—new, black; it had been one of Bazarov's—and the camera closed in on one of the laborers watching. It was him, looking as he had a year ago. The old him lifted a hand and the camera cut again to the man in the suit, sliding into the leather interior, lifting a hand back, as if to say so long. But before the car drove off, before the camera showed the crowd of working men again, before the one word caption he knew would come, Yarik told Dima: "Him."

Dima turned then, as if to try to see what his brother was looking at, on which TV, but by then Yarik had stopped watching the screen. He was staring, instead, at the wide window hazed over with mirror-light, and in it, their own reflections, their two ghostly faces peering back.

At first, he hadn't believed her—this stairwell woman claiming to have been his brother's lover—and then he didn't want to: the way she'd told him how Dima had stopped her straying hands by speaking of his love for Yarik. *Why do you think,* she'd said, *he chose that poem?* And how had he never seen it till then: two souls joined only to be torn apart, one taken captive by a wizard, within a strange world's walls, the other seeking nothing but to bring his lost half back. Though in the end it was his very need to not believe—in the idea of her with Dima, of Dima wanting to be with anyone but him—that had trapped him with the truth: the bond between them that had so skewed his twin still lay buried inside him, too. If he had made a different choice, chosen the same as Dima, allowed them to live out their lives alone with each other, simply two brothers together, he might have been as happy, just in a different way. A way that might—he shut his eyes to it, shook his head, shoved down the gas, turned back—have been a better life.

The rest of the way they drove in silence, as if each was waiting for something to happen before they reached their mother's apartment block. Then they were there. Yarik pulled to the side of the street. He let the motor idle. He knew that if he looked at Dima he wouldn't be able to tell him to go.

439

"Did you read it?" Dima said.

"Your letter?"

"The book."

"Why?"

"I gave Timofei—"

"Why did you give me that?"

"I thought maybe you'd remember . . ."

"I remember," Yarik said. "But I'm not Mama. The situation . . ." He reached down and pulled up the parking break and sat back against his seat, sat there with both hands on the steering wheel. "It's different, Dima. Then it was about Mama. This was never about me, or you. It was always the situation. And the situation hasn't changed."

"So change it."

"What did you think? That I would read a storybook we made when we were kids and give up my job and sell my apartment and move with you out to Dyadya Avya's and bring Zinaida and Polina and Timofei and Mama out there and . . ."

"Yes."

"And what? We would all farm?"

"Yes," Dima said. "That's what I thought."

"We won't." It was as if by saying the words he'd broken something open inside him, loosed an occlusion in his veins, released his blood, and his grip eased on the steering wheel, his head lay back against the seat, and he said it again: "We won't."

"Maybe not now," Dima said. "But someday . . ."

And Yarik could see he'd broken something in Dima, too. "Bratishka," he said, he could only hope that whatever had become ruined inside his brother would wash away with it, "when was the last time you were out at Dyadya Avya's?"

"You told me not to go."

Go, Yarik thought. *Go and see it and bleed it all out.*

"Maybe now," Dima said, "now that you have a car. Maybe we can go together for a day—"

"No," Yarik told him. "Not for a day. Not ever." He reached to his brother then, just wanting to touch him, somewhere, as if his fingers might find the break, stanch the flow, for a moment. "Bratishka," he said, "can't you see that we were never really going to?"

But before his fingertips could brush Dima's face, Dima's fingers had clamped around his, squeezing them tight in a fist.

They sat there, the two of them in the idling car, and someone driving by, glancing through the window, might have thought they were holding hands. A first few flakes of snow landed on the windshield.

"You're wrong," Dima said. "You're wrong about that, just like you're wrong about the situation. It *is* about us."

"No," Yarik said. "No, Dima, it's the situation *I'm* in. It's *my* situation. And it isn't going to change."

It was a wet snow, and the flakes became wet blurs on the windshield, and where enough had landed some had begun to stick.

"You know it has to," Dima said. "It has to, Yarik. Because when I open the door and go upstairs and you disappear again, it will have changed. A little more. A little worse. And you will have been the one to change it." He stopped, and Yarik could see him wait for the ache in his jaw and chin to begin to subside, and then, as if Dima meant to shoot it through his face again, he said, "You always could change it. Just like you always could have chosen to save the money, to go to Dyadya Avya's with me."

"Please," Yarik said.

"You could have chosen me."

Yarik reached up with his free hand then, and cupped it around Dima's, and pulled until he had pried open his brother's fist. He drew his bruised fingers to him. "Please," he said. "Take your rucksack and open the door . . ."

"But the situation," Dima said, "it did. Because you're wrong about that, too, Yarik. It's *our* situation. It's the situation *we're* in. It has become *us.*" He opened the door and stood up out of the car into the snow. He held the door by its cold edge. He began to close it.

"Wait." Yarik sat holding his fingers in his hand as if they hurt, but there was no anger in him, not even any strength, just the same stripped-down sorrow he had felt when he'd first seen Dima come out into the waiting room. Except this time he made himself look Dima in the face. "Take the rucksack," he told him.

Dima glanced down at it. The fabric around the zipper at the top was stained with blood, sagged into a hollow. He didn't touch it.

There was the sound of the engine idling, the faint smell of the exhaust, the snow beginning to cling to Dima's hair, his bandages, a few flakes drifting into the car. "Take the rucksack, Dima," Yarik said, again. He shut his eyes. "Please, take it and go."

"Look at me," Dima told him.

But Yarik only squeezed his eyes more tightly shut. "Go," he said. "Go far away. You're not safe here. You're not safe anywhere in Petroplavilsk. Or anywhere near the Oranzheria. Or near me." Behind his shut lids his eyes were shaking. "Bratishka," he said, "take the rucksack and go far away from me."

He heard his brother reach down, take hold of a strap, lift the bag out of the car. At the sound, Yarik opened his eyes. He reached for the door handle. Dima held on to its edge. His brother stood there with it open and the snow falling all around him and said, "No. I won't. I won't because I know how you knew it was me when you heard the police were looking. I know because, no matter what you tell me, or won't, I knew you were in trouble that night you took the gun. And even if I can't see you, even if I can't talk to you, I won't live somewhere so far away that I can't even feel you anymore."

For a moment, Yarik sat leaning across the empty seat, towards Dima holding the open door, the snow swirling in and blurring his eyes, looking out at his brother's blurring ones. Then he shut his own. And when he opened them again, he could see Dima's face so clearly. The stitches must have pulled, or the crusted blood must have softened from the flakes, because the snow that had settled in his brother's beard had turned a watery red.

442

Dima watched the taillights go, small red spots in the gauzy air. On his cold face, the stitches burned. In his mouth, his pulse pounded at his gums. He could hear it in the hammering beneath the cotton where his lower front teeth used to be. No: the sound was too erratic, sharp. He listened through the pain, through the snowfall and the traffic, to a distant tapping like fingernails drumming glass.

Inside the building's lobby, the sound was gone. He felt too weak for the stairs, got himself to the elevator, the button pressed, stayed on his feet while the cables moaned. Inside the lift there was just the throbbing of all the parts of his face that hurt. And then the door opened and he was in the hallway, and there was that hammering again.

At the apartment door it was twice as loud, as if his mother were still up inside, still had her sewing machine, was trying to stitch shut the holes in the tops of the cans he brought home. He opened the door and stepped into the sound. The apartment felt different. Not just the noise, not just the rugs still clamped above the windows, but something in the air itself that made night known. The deeper cold, the murmur of the TV show that leaked down through the ceiling, the sense of his mother asleep in the stillness of the room: it sent over him a faint breath of peace, that the world was bigger than anything man could send into the sky, that night was something more than just a rhythm in the lives of people, darkness or light. It made even the clacking seem small.

And when he came into the living room and saw what was making the noise, he almost laughed. Out on the balcony, Ivan was banging his beak against the glass. The dark shape of a rooster silhouetted against the dimly glowing world framed in the doors. While Dima watched, Ivan exploded in a furious ridding of snow, tail feathers whipping, wings jerking out, comb slapping madly back and forth, and when he was done, he went utterly still. Watched Dima. Then started banging on the glass again.

Dima glanced at his mother's mattress by the bathroom door, the duvet a quiet pile. He set the rucksack down and, creeping towards the balcony, shook his head at himself: as if his footsteps were going to wake his mother over the racket of the bird. Ivan's hood was still off. Maybe, Dima thought, the bird was going mad with wanting dark. Or it was simply unfed and throwing a tantrum. Sliding open the door, he blocked the bird with his legs as it tried to rush inside. "What's with you?" he said. "I know you've been hungry before."

The rooster batted at him with its wings. It began running circles in the snow. The flakes felt good on his face when they first landed, soft and cool, and then they melted and were just cold, and he thought he understood—its box inside, its bunched blankets—and he wanted, then, his own bed, too. Squatting down, he spread the hood, clamped the bird between his thighs, dropped the felt over it, tied it on. The bird kept struggling. "What happened?" he said to it, the way his mother would when he was a child and came to her crying. With his palm he held its head from beating at the glass; with his other hand he stroked its back. "What happened?"

In the quiet after his voice, the words came back at him. He stood, the rooster in his arms, its talons scrabbling at the air. All its movement made the inside more still. He peered through the glass. The rooster had freed a wing. It was whapping at his chest. He set the bird down in the snow. He opened the door and went inside and shut the door behind him. "Mama?" he whispered.

Halfway across the room he smelled the urine. He didn't have to crouch to the duvet and work his hands through it and pull it away and touch the sheets beneath to know she was not there, but he did. And he didn't have to step to the open bathroom door, or stand in it, or look down, just as his hand didn't need to search for the wall switch, or his eyes to wait for a light to come on that he knew wouldn't, didn't need to do any of that to know she was in there. His hand stopped rattling the switch. His eyes relented.

She was lying on the floor. Her feet were swaddled in thick wool socks and her legs were wrapped in wool tights and above them her nightgown had fallen upwards so it showed her wool-covered knees, her thighs. Beneath her, the floor was wet. When he crouched he could feel its coldness on his shin, his knee, and he grabbed her nightgown and

444

pulled her away from the toilet where her head lay buried in shadow. He crawled over her to reach her face. He held it. It was cold, too. On her cheeks, his hands shook. Shook her skin. Looking at it shake was bad and he yanked his hands away. Looking at it still was worse. He said her name, what her name was to him. In the last reaches of the window light, it was too dark to see if the wetness was just urine or also blood and, crouched over her, patting at her hair, around her skull, down her neck, finding the wetness on the nightgown by her belly and squeezing it and slapping his hands onto the tiles and sliding them back and forth in the wetness there, he still couldn't tell, and he shoved himself up off the floor and ran to the kitchen for the flashlight.

In the brightness of its beam she looked almost alive. Her long white hair was gathered into all its fullness at the back of her head, her eyes were closed as if in mere weariness, her mouth slightly open, as if he had just put her to bed and she was simply whispering to him good night. The yellow of her bathrobe looked yellower in the light, almost warm. Beneath it she had put on a sweater. Around her neck she had wrapped a knit scarf. Her hands were mittened. And he thought, *She must have been so cold.*

Then he shut the flashlight off. He walked out of the bathroom. He walked all the way to the balcony door and he stood with his back to it, looking across the dim, still apartment to the dark doorway where she lay, and he could feel the thudding of the bird's hooded head against the backs of his calves, and when he slid down and sat, he could feel the banging against his spine, the taps going all the way through his body to drum at his chest, and he leaned into them and put his face in his hands and cried.

That night he cleaned her. Twice, running the water in the bath, he held his hand beneath it to make sure it wasn't too warm or too cold, and then he realized what he was doing and simply sat on the edge of the tub and let it run. When he shut it off there was just the beat of the bird's hood against the glass again.

He had set the flashlight on the tank of the toilet, standing on its end, and, in the weakened light the ceiling reflected back, he pulled off her mittens. The way her gold wedding band shone it looked warmer than her finger, but they were both cold. He left the band on, crouched at her feet, pulled off her socks. On each foot, she had worn another sock beneath the first. When he saw that, he gripped his bandaged face and squeezed until the pain was so bad he stopped thinking about it, and then bent to her feet again and pulled off the second pair. He stripped her tights down her legs. Beneath them, she had put on a pair of long underwear. He took that off, too.

Her nightgown wouldn't come over her head. She had gone too stiff to get it off her arms. He went into the living room, and there was the quiet clack of her sewing box opening and the louder clack of it shutting and he came back with the scissors shaped like a heron. The metal of the handle-wings was freezing on his fingers. With the long sharp beak he cut her nightgown off. He cut her sweater off. He cut away the long underwear beneath. When he slid the lower blade under the front of her bra, he felt as if he were cutting through her breastbone and he looked away when he snipped. When he looked back, her breasts were hanging loose and large and with a heaviness that seemed it must have hurt such shriveled, wrinkled skin. He touched one of her nipples, drew his fingers back. He wished he could remember what it was like to be held by her. This time he touched the center of her chest. He pressed his whole palm to her, and pressed his weight against his palm, and knelt like that, his fingers spread over her old skin, her skin spread against the boniness of her chest, touching.

Eventually, he rose. He turned her over. He pushed her to the wall and, with the dry parts of her clothes, mopped up the last of her urine. Then he rolled her onto her belly and, dipping a dishrag into the bathwater, washed her skin.

When he had put her on her back again, and washed her front, he stood. She lay there naked, damp. Behind her head, the hairpin shone, hair still wrapped around it, a few loose strands wet. The thumping from the balcony door had stopped. He bent down again and lifted her head off the floor and pulled the hairpin out. It rustled strangely, as if her hair were made of paper. And when he reached behind her head and with his fingers began to draw her hair out of its twist, he felt it: it was paper. He worked it free: a torn strip, faint blue lines, wide-ruled like the papers he had used in elementary school, pierced on either end where the pin had gone through. One side was blank. On the other, in her old and shaky scrawl, she had written the word AVYA.

He looked at the paper in his hands for a long time. Then he folded it and put it in his pocket and finished working his fingers through her hair. When he was done, it was all spread out, a wide white fan of it. It was so long. It reached to her fingertips, covered her breasts, her belly, all the way to her thighs. He looked at it for longer than he had looked at the paper, and then he looked at her old face framed in all her old hair. He tried to see it as his father must have once. Then he took the scissors and, slowly, carefully, cut it all off.

A few strands at a time. The small beak opening, shutting. The tresses falling thick and soft. And when he was done he raked it all up with his fingers. He gathered it in his arms. He held his mother's hair to his chest and put his face into it and breathed.

Later, Dima stood in the nearly empty living room, in the nearly silent apartment, watching the strips of light cast by the windows. They were brightening, their glow becoming stronger, their outlines sharper, as if a full moon had broken out from behind the clouds.

On the balcony, it was no longer snowing. Through holes in the sky first one zerkalo and then another showed. In their light, Dima stood looking down at the world below, the white bandages on his brow and chin almost glowing, a few long strands of white hair stuck to his clothes almost glowing, the snow on the railing where his hands had not sunken through it. Down there, the world was filled with all its ceaseless movement: the night workers working, the day sleepers out on the streets, the trams clacking and clacking along their tracks. Beside him, in the glowing snow, the rooster stood perched on the rail, motionless beneath its dark felt hood. Dima reached over, untied the leather strip, and took the hood off. The Golden Phoenix shook its head, its comb flapping, the feathers of its neck shimmering in the

447

mirror-light like flecks of mica. Its red chest heaved. It took a step, long black tail brushing the snow on the balcony's floor. Then it looked up at the sky and crowed.

Across the alleyway, window lights went on. Shapes appeared in the glass. People called out, shouted. Balcony doors slammed, and others opened, and voices were hurled at him, and someone threw something that clanged off the guardrail, and it went on like that, until, sometime later, Dima finally turned and opened his own balcony door, and closed himself back inside.

In there, he could hear Gennady shouting up through the floor. He could feel the thumps of the broom handle that beat against his ceiling below. It followed his footsteps while he walked, as if the man could hear the creaks of his steps and was tracing his route one story down. When Dima got to the rucksack he stopped. The bag sat there, jouncing slightly, the broom handle beneath going boom boom boom.

Bending, he found the zipper tab with his fingers. It was shaking with each knock on the floor, too gunked up with dried blood to make a sound. He gripped it and unzipped the bag, the zipper as quiet, the blood in its teeth as thick. When he let go of the tab, it fell as silently. When he stood up and the bag fell to rest on his pant legs, it sat there shaking just the same. Shake, shake, shake, it went against his shins. Gennady was shouting something with each bang of the handle. Dima couldn't hear what it was. For a moment, he couldn't hear anything— not the rooster, not the pounding. He could only feel the shaking of the bag, could only see the money spilling out from inside.

AT SHORE'S EDGE

"It's too much," Dima told him.

"I know," Yarik said.

"It's much more than I'd saved."

Yarik looked like he was going to say something, but his eyes began to fill, and he shrugged his shoulders, reached to the heat on the dash, turned it up.

They were riding in the cab of a company truck, a pickup Yarik had borrowed to take their mother's body out, and they wound along the old Kosha Road, the river meandering on its ancient course, and every time they went around a curve the coffin slid in the back and knocked against the plastic liner of the bed.

Ever since they had entered the Oranzheria, they had driven in a dimness that didn't deepen, and didn't brighten, but remained the same tenebrous light. Above them, on the glass, lay a thick field of snow, as if the clouds had been pounded into a layer of felt. All around them: the green fields of corn, new shoots of wheat, the barley beginning to bend with the weight of its seeds.

449

"You know what I wish?" Dima said. "That Dyadya Avya was still alive. He would have liked to see her buried there. He would have liked to see us burying her. He would have liked to tell it afterwards." The air Yarik had turned up was blowing on Dima's face, and he could feel his sweat coming. He looked for the crank to roll his window down. There were just buttons. He pressed one. The door locked. He looked at Yarik and he said, "And when the snow stopped . . ." He waited. He said, "And the Oranzheria was still covered . . ." After a moment, he went on, "They drove together . . ." and he reached out and pushed the vent so the air was directed at Yarik. "Beyond the great glass sea . . ." He stared at his brother. Yarik stared at the road. The road rumbled away beneath them. Finally, Dima said, "To the farm."

He found the button for the window. It opened a crack. The noise of the men and machines working the fields came in and the wind came in and Dima said, "That's how he would have begun the ending." And when Yarik didn't even look at him, he said, louder, over the wind, "That's how Dyadya Avya would have begun the ending."

"To what?" Yarik said. He sat behind the wheel in the suit he had put on that morning to go to work, the tie he had been knotting in the hallway mirror when Dima had knocked at the apartment door. Zina was out, driving Timofei to school, dropping Polya at the day care center, and Yarik had laced his boots, pulled on his gloves, wrapped a scarf around his neck and, thinking of the state his brother was in, of what he knew Dima now would surely see, of what the Oranzheria security might do, of the way even Bazarov had paused simply at the sight of the gun, he had slipped the small revolver between his pants waist and his back. He could feel it there now, just one more thing he'd kept secret from his brother, and he knew that, for him, the ending had already come and gone.

"Yarik," Dima said, across from him in the cab, "I want you to know that last night, when I found the money—as soon as I saw it—I knew you weren't giving it to me so I could buy the farm for us. Not for us to farm together. But for me. I knew that, Yarik. I know. I understand." He spoke slowly, and carefully, trying to move his split mouth, his bruised jaw, as little as possible, and his voice came out too thin to fight the noise of the rushing air. He slid the window shut again. In the quiet, he said, "But I hope that, maybe in a month, on Defender of the Fatherland Day, you might come out with Zinaida and Polya and Timosha, and we'll go fishing with them on the Kosha. And maybe, next Victory Day, you'll drive out in your new car on your own and spend the day with me in the fields." With each word, the ache spread further into the muscles of his face, and he paused to let it drain back out until it was back to just the dull pain that was there like part of his skin, and when it was he said, "And at the end of the day maybe we can go into the birch woods. Maybe we can find the old banya and all the mushrooms growing over it. We might sometimes pick them together there for a while. That's all I want, Yarik. That's it. A small wish." And he held up his hand to show how small with his fingers. Then, looking at his brother through the gap between his thumb and his forefinger, he said, trying to put into his voice the smile it hurt too much to make, "But compared to your head, it's so damn big." He reached out as if to shrink the space compared to Yarik's head, and his fingers brushed Yarik's cheek. His brother looked at him.

"You know what I wish?" Yarik said. "I wish Mama was still alive, too."

Ahead, there was a crack in the ceiling, a gap between two panes where too little adhesive had been laid in: a thin strip of water sheeted between, splattering in a straight line right across the road, and through it the other side was all ablur. They hit it and it drummed from the hood to the windshield and on the cab over their heads and the coffin and the tailgate, and then they were through, and it was quiet again, and the road was the road going through the fields again and the windshield was wet with the wind blowing the rivulets, and Dima said, "Yarik, why did you go to Moscow?"

Yarik stared at the rivulets until they were just a few long upward-streaking trickles, and it was as if he were looking from high above at the landscape of winding, forking rivers, and beyond it was the real river and the vast cropland all around, and he heard his brother say something about Bazarov. For how long? Dima was asking.

A bus came and passed and went towards the way from which they'd come, and Yarik drove through the cloud of its dust, and the dust turned the rivulets brown and the world a map of dry creekbeds on the windshield glass. Beyond them, in the distance ahead, Yarik could just make out the shape of a bridge. He knew Dima would be seeing it, too. He looked over at his brother. Dima didn't look back; he was staring through the windshield. And, watching him, watching the slow affliction of his face, Yarik told him about the first meeting and the day out on the lake and the promotions and what had happened in Moscow. "Why do you think they put me in those ads?" he said. "How else could I have made the policemen stop? They would have kept on, Dima, they would have . . ."

But Dima wasn't listening. He was staring at the bridge. He knew the slightly arching back, knew the slope of the bank beneath, but he was telling himself it could not be the bridge over the Kosha where he and Yarik used to fish. It could not because where was the old stage road, the hay barns, the garage with its steel sheds full of farm machinery to be repaired? Why was there still the glass? How could they have driven long enough—they couldn't have; it was too fast—and that glass still be blocking out the sky above. It couldn't be because it was the Oranzheria, here, above them, and there ahead, and as far as he could see. And when they passed the two huge stumps at the side of the road, the place where the roadbank was broken, as if to lead to an old road that had, somehow, disappeared whole beneath the black soil of the new-plowed field, his hand grabbed at his face. It covered his mouth, his chin, and the throb went up into his teeth as if he was biting the pain out of his fingers.

They passed the bridge. It was the bridge.

And up ahead a streak of sunlight sliced down over the fields. Another: sudden brightness cutting through the dusky blue beneath the ceiling of snow. Another, another. Somewhere here lay the souls of a hundred thousand birches. The bones of the old house, the old barns: all buried now. Somewhere beneath that flat and endless simultaneity of all the mass cultivated fields was a place where once a patch of color had glowed amidst dark woods, a mound of collapsed logs and earth and roots dense and tangled and impenetrable as the muscles of a heart.

And their uncle's body? Their father's?

The truck stopped. The engine died.

From above them they could hear the steady scrape of the shovelers. Through the windshield they could see the glass panes coming clear. The snow disappeared in strips behind the rubber-tipped shovels of the workers who pushed them, and in the clear strips there walked the black boot soles of the men, and there were thousands of them. Where they cleared the sky there was the deep blue of late afternoon. In the silence between the brothers there was the creaks and sloshing of the shoved snow emptied through the release chutes into the colliquation tanks. The light hit it as it fell: brief avalanches, mirages of waterfalls, coming one after the other all over the landscape in small moments of thunder, flashing over the cisterns and gone, and flashing over another and gone, and another.

Then Dima was out in it. He stood beside the truck, the door hanging open, the dirt road in front of him, and across it, where Dyadya Avya's farm had been, the endless yellow of the wide rapeseed fields. The driver's side door opened; he heard it smack shut.

"Dima," Yarik said.

Dima's fist shot out, slammed against the fender of the truck. "Why?"

"Bratishka."

"Why didn't you tell me?"

"You must have known."

"How could you let them buy it?" He swung his glare on his brother. "When you knew, you *knew*, Yarik . . ."

"I didn't let them buy it."

" . . . you knew that I had enough to buy at least *some*. When you"—his fist shook between them—"you had enough to buy all of it. Why—"

"I did. I did buy all of it."

453

Dima started to speak again, but the sound died in his throat and there was just his fist shaking against his brother's chest, and his eyes with the question shaking in them.

"Where do you think," Yarik said, "all that money came from?"

"Why did you give it to me?"

"It was yours. It was half. Half of what I got for us when I sold the land to him. He was going to get it anyway, Dima. I just got it first so we would get *something,* we would have something of what Dyadya Avya left, something of what was ours."

"Ours?"

"Put your fist down."

Instead, Dima's other came up. He stood there with both fists against Yarik's chest, the knuckles touching, the hands shaking. "*Ours,*" he said. "Not yours."

"If you hit me, bratets, I swear I will hit you back."

Slowly, Dima lifted his fists away. He brought them together to his face, and clenching them in front of his mouth, he looked at the fields, tried to remember where the old izba had been, to see any sign of the chimney or the foundation or the gate, and there was nothing, and he said, "Why did you even bring me here?"

"You asked to come here."

"To bury Mama."

"To show you," Yarik shouted. "To show you what the real world is. Mama wanted me to have our book? You think she wanted it to wake me up?"

"Yarik, where did they bury—"

"I'm awake, Dima! I live awake."

"Where can we bury her now?"

"You live in a fucking dream."

"At least—"

"We'll bury her in the cemetery."

"At least, if I live in a dream . . ."

"Where people bury people."

". . . it's *my* dream."

454

"Your dream," Yarik said, "is what killed her."

It felt to Dima like his fist must have hit the truck again, but in the second afterward he watched his brother's face whipping back to him, and then his own eyesight whipped around, a crack of pain ripping up his jaw into the socket of his eye.

"You had half the money," Yarik shouted at him. "You had that much! And she was freezing! She was starving! And she blamed me! Me! She had to. Who else was going to take care of her? You? When did she ever expect anything of you? Why did I? Get up," Yarik said. "Get up and get the fuck back in the truck."

Above him, Dima could see the men gathered, looking down at where he lay, shovels in their hands, pools melting in the sunshine around their boots. The sun came down on his face and warmed it and he felt like he could lie there forever, like the men would stay forever leaned over, still, looking at him, and if they would just stop and stay there, and the sun would stay as it was, and he could stay in it . . . But there was the sound of his brother's boots on the dirt road. The driver's side door opened and smacked shut. The truck engine shook awake. He heard the passenger side door open.

"Bratets," Yarik said, and in his voice there was a pain as if each word was stitched to his throat and each utterance yanked them out one by one. "You think this is about Mama. You think it's about us. It's not. It never has been. It has always, always, always been about *you*. Your selfishness. Your jealousy. Because I married? Because I had a child? Because I refuse to cling to some fairy-tale time of our lives? Because when I go swimming in the lake it's Timosha's feet on my shoulders, my son's fingers that I feel tap the top of my head, not my brother's, not *yours*. Jealous of a *child*. Of a six-year-old. That's what this is about, Dima. The fact that every morning I wake up beside my wife and you wish it was still you."

"No," Dima started to say, "all I wanted . . ."

". . . is for me," Yarik finished for him, "to wish it, too. But I don't. I don't even *wish* it. Can't you see that? If I wished it I would have kept the land. But I didn't want that. I don't. I don't want my dream to be my own, Dima. What I want is for it to be real." There was the chiming of the open passenger door. "Come on," Yarik said through it. "Get in."

Slowly, Dima rose. The men above him seemed to back away straight up, as if they thought he would rise through the glass and into them. His brother was saying, "I didn't make the deal just for the money, Dima. I made it for *that*. To keep it safe, all of it, work and life and my family and you. But now you know—we both know—that it's not. You're not. Dima . . ."

But Dima was walking past the open door. He went around the truck to the tailgate, opened it, let it bang down. Through the rear windshield, he could see his brother, neck twisted, staring at him, saying something. Reaching in, Dima found the handle of the shovel. He dragged the metal head out along the plastic bed.

"Where are you going to dig?" his brother said from inside the cab. "Where would you bury her?"

And then Dima pulled the shovel back like a logger about to swing an axe, and his brother stopped talking, and a second later there was the crash. He slammed the shovel head into the rear taillight. He brought it back and slammed it again.

When his brother's shouting came at him—"You think I wouldn't have had them move Dyadya Avya?"—it was louder—"Papa?"—nothing between it and him but the air, and he spun and saw his brother stop at the sight of the shovel raised and, without taking his eyes off Yarik, he pulled back and slammed the metal into the side of the tuck. It buckled in. He slammed it again. And, his brother a still shape standing, watching, the men above standing as still, watching, the sun flinging off the shovel blade and up at the glass and over his brother and down to dissipate into the fields, he made his way around the truck, smashing the fenders and the side-view mirror and the grille and the glass, until he was back where he had started. Everything was silent. Above the truck the crowd on the cleared patch of glass had grown, and all except off in the distance the scraping had stopped, the snowfalls in the ditches had ceased, the fields were quiet.

The whole time, Yarik had stood in the shovel's gusts, the flashes off its blade, stood still, watching. But when Dima began climbing into the bed of the truck, he moved. Stepping close, he shot out an arm, tried to grab whatever he could of Dima, saw the shovel head glint, the glint rushing at him. Then he was ducking, low, half-fallen into a crouch, one hand on the ground, the other on the tailgate, the blade ripping by above his head with an air-slicing whoosh that filled his ears, until another sound smashed down and knocked it away: metal slamming wood, wood cracking, the shovel crashing, the pine lid shattering. It was as if, instead of the shovel, the sound had hit him. For a second, his hearing left, his sight bleached, the world slipped his hold. And when it came back he was standing behind the tailgate pointing a pistol at his brother.

He must have said something. Or Dima simply felt it. The last crack of the wood hung in the air, dwindled away, was lost in the sounds of distant snow swept down. Dima stood above the caved coffin, shards scattered around the truckbed, the shovel still in his hands, his hands still. Above them: the slight shifting of the workers' boots, all their soles on the glass, a smothered thunder. From the truck's cab the door chime tolled, over and over, like some paltry imitation of church bells. And on his brother's face, Yarik saw a thing that drained the life out of his own: Dima looking back at him as if he didn't know who his brother was.

Yarik's throat wouldn't work. The muscles of his hand were failing, too, the gun too heavy; it would have dropped if Dima hadn't reached out and taken it. It was as if the weight came off his throat. "It's not loaded," Yarik said. "They're blanks." And then his words were rushing out: "Dima, there's one left, but it's a blank, believe me, I wouldn't . . ."

But Dima's eyes were fixed on their uncle's old revolver in his hand. "Try it," Yarik was saying, "you'll see," and Dima let the shovel drop out of his other. He held the gun in both. "Believe me," Yarik was saying, and the handle fit Dima's palm just as it had his brother's, as it had Dyadya Avya's, their hands shaped by tools, by blood . . .

The blast tore between them, smothered Yarik's voice, filled his ears, loud as two shots, as three, and as the sound scattered and fell away he could hear breaking through it, slowly finding his ears, the tinkling. It came distant and accruing as bird chatter at dawn, and then he was seeing it: the glittering air, the tiny shards sparkling through the light, the chips of glass hitting the truck cab, the bed, the coffin, ricocheting and rattling like hail. All over the road, in the ditches at its edge, pieces of the exploded pane lay scattered. He could feel them in his hair, stinging his face, could see them on his brother's, and he saw again Bazarov's eyes as the man had watched him from across the table—the glimmer of fear, the sneaking smile—and when Dima turned away, when he set down the gun, when he picked up the shovel, when he broke the coffin open and hauled their mother out, Yarik let him.

She was still wrapped in the blanket Dima had bound her in, and as he heaved her up, her cut strands of long white hair fell out over the black liner of the truck. She had lost her stiffness, begun to smell. The blanket was soaked heavy. Dima tried to get her over his shoulder without letting go of the shovel, felt his brother watch him fail at it, take a step as if to stop him, and, holding to the shovel with his other hand, Dima simply dragged her out. The chips of glass fallen onto her through the broken pine lid fell off, clattering, as he pulled. At the edge of the truckbed he climbed down and lay the shovel on top of her body and, gripping just above where her ankles would be, backed up until she hovered between him and the truck end, her shoulders and head on the bed, and then, as her shoulders dropped and her neck bent and her head was about to smack into the ground, his brother was there, holding her. Slowly, Yarik lowered her until her top half was resting on the dirt, the shovel still resting on her, her blanket-wrapped legs still under Dima's arm. For a moment, the blanket was touched by them both, their mother's body stretched out between their hands. Then Yarik let go and, walking backwards, dragging her, Dima made his way across the road.

The workers followed him above, flowing around the hole in the glass, moving in their fur-hooded parkas like a slowly blown cloud.

And the black shapes of their boot soles were like flocks of geese flying beneath it, and their steps were like wing flaps. Occasionally, in
the sun, one of their shovels gleamed.

Down there, Dima hauled his mother's body in its heavy wrappings
of wool. It left a wet dark trail in the dirt of the road. Then he was
crossing the overflow ditch, and the water was splashing around him
in the light, and the blanket came out dripping. The flowers of the
rapeseed plants shook as he entered them, bright yellow in the sun
and deep yellow in the shadows of the men who stood above. The
field was mottled with all their shade, and Dima moved in and out
of it, a row of bent plants shaking in his wake. When he stopped, the
men above him stopped. The shadows held. He lay the bundle down
in the yellow rapeseed flowers, and with the blade of the shovel began
to cut at their roots.

He had dug away the first black layer of topsoil, a rough rectangle
of dirt, when, across the field, back on the road, the company truck
began to move. Even from above, the workmen could see how bashed
in it was, how smashed the windshield, the missing side-view mirrors,
the way it made a slow turn, forward and back and forward and back,
between the edges of the road, until it was facing the way from which
it had come. They watched it go. The dust hung in the air where it
had been, and thinned, and was gone, too. Then, as if they had been
waiting for a sign, the men themselves began to disperse, some scraping with their shovels at the last of the snow, some following with
the wide brooms. Only a few lingered on, their heads bent over the
glass, watching the figure down below: the sway and flap of the coat
around his legs, the sparks of sweat and shards of glass flung from his
tangled hair and beard, his thin arms driving the shovel blade over
and over—flash and gone, flash and gone—into the dark hole slowly
opening before him.

Tonight he will go down to the lake. The sky will be dark and murky as
a river, the zerkala glinting in it like the Chudo-Yudo's eyes on its two
dozen heads. How huge the arm of the great bronze tsar beneath them.

How small the shape that passes beneath its outstretched finger. How still the masts of the leisure boats. There, caught in the ice, a rowboat lies, its old wood white as some calcified fossil, extinct amphibian, gunwales for bones, hull for its shell, the two oars jutting out like frozen limbs. He wanders past it through the snow. In the place where he had cleared it the day before, the new snow is a slight depression. In the mirror-light it lifts before his boots: puffs of glow. Over on the industrial docks, the winter crews are repairing the summer ships, their headlamps small pinpricks of brightness, warm-seeming the way lamps used to seem on the streets in the hour between daylight and dark. But they are only headlamps. The rest of the light will stay like it is for the rest of the night.

Soon he will be far enough from them that they will seem part of the world of the shore, and he will seem part of the world of the lake. He trudges through the snow, over the ice, his long wool coat dragging at the drifts where the wind has lifted them like waves. His back is bulged with his rucksack. His rucksack is bulged with something tied to it. The rope dangles down—long, thin, black—into the snow. And when he reaches the wide open windswept plain where the gusts have cleared it of all but ice, and the ice is all a reflection of the sky, and he is a dark shape amid the countless gleams of the mirrors above and below, the rope seems to move. The rucksack shivers. For a moment, small black wings sprout from his back, flap at the air, and fold away again.

THE SOUND OF THE CLOUDS

The ice had broken on the lake, and there remained only a thin crack-ing ring of it breaking up along the shore, and it was spring, when Yarik went out to Nizhi to see his brother. He caught a ride on one of the smaller fishing boats, paid the captain to take him out. The big trawlers were at work, and above them the flocks of jaegers and oystercatchers and gulls followed in dark swirls, as if caught in nets cast into the sky. Standing at the gunwale, out of the way of the mill-ing crew, he could almost feel on his palms the rough wet rope two dockside crewmen were drawing out of the water; there was the strain in his shoulders, pulling the heavy net; Dima's grunts beside him. . . . A tug at his mouth; he pressed his lips together, stilled it. Staring out at the waves, he tried to press the rest still, too: the rocking under him, the heartbeat pulsing in his fingertips. How long had it been since he'd been this far out in the lake? Never on his own. Around him the water was wide as a second sky. He looked away from it, up: his own boat's own small cloud of birds. Where, once, there had been stars. Flickering with the barks of a distant dog. On that long

461

gone night when his brother, lying beside him in the rowboat bottom, had let out one quiet bark of his own. *Gav!* Through his smile, Yarik had sent up a yip to join the sound. Together, quietly, they'd said *Gav! Gav! Gav!* up at the stars. He could still feel it. He could still hear his brother's whisper, a while later: *I'm glad that there were two of them together.* They had been studying the pre-Sputnik days in school—Cosmonaut Dezik, Cosmonaut Tsygan, first dogs to reach suborbital space, first living breath heard back on earth by mission control—and that night they had wondered: when the panting had paused was it the companions catching their breath at the sight of the moon rolling around the earth? When the world outside the capsule went up in flames, was the whimpering from fear, or pain, or were they simply trying to tell each other *I'm here?*

By his sides, Yarik's hands had clenched. He stretched them open. The birds circled above. The cold wind came on. He zipped his jacket up. And, gripping the gunwale, tried to press the pulsing from his fingers. His hands, motionless, doing nothing. He looked up—all around him the fishermen were in their churn of work—and let go his grip and walked off the deck into the cabin.

Where he stayed until the boat stopped. He had unlatched his case and taken a folder out and sat hunched over it, trying to read, trying not to think about his brother, about what his brother would think of all that had happened in the months since he had disappeared—their mother's body reinterred in the cemetery of the Alexandro-Nevsky church, the apartment where she'd raised them sold to the Shopsins for little more than Gennady's good will, the way Yarik needed allies, now that his office was four doors down from Bazarov's, now that The She Bear kept him close in all ways but the one that had once mattered, the cub who'd acted out become a colleague now whose worth was soley in how much he could increase that of the Consoritum—and, shutting his eyes to the words that swayed with the rolling of the boat, Yarik did not see the island rise out of the lake like the back of some pelagic beast, nor the winter chapel shape itself out of the shadows of the clouds, nor the bell tower, nor the dock.

So when the captain called to him down the steps and he shut his case and gathered his gift in his other arm and climbed up onto the deck, he was not prepared for how huge the church was. As boys, they had studied the monks from centuries ago, the way they'd felled the pines, brought them on barges across the lake, each log and plank and sliver of wood scribe-fitted, round-notched, dovetailed, not a nail, not a pin, not a single piece of metal in the entire thing, each tiny shingle hand-hewn from an aspen's heart, cut like lace, all fifty thousand of them covering all thirty swooping domes. He'd known the numbers. But not how the shingles would shimmer in the sun, flickering like ghosts of the leaves of the aspens they had come from. Not how the domes would crowd each other, tight as a phalanx of geese, an entire V-shaped flock bursting upwards towards the sky.

He sat in the skiff, facing the crewman the captain had promised to send back before dark, watching the island draw near. On his lap, he held the gift he'd brought. The plastic covering the wicker basket crackled in the wind. He bent his head around it, thought he saw someone running out of the aspen woods—but it was only a caught piece of cloth, flapping. He thought he saw the shape of a thin man in a distant field—but it didn't move, and didn't move, and was a post. The oars splashed, the boat creaked. He listened to the rower's breath, his chest too tight around his own.

They pulled up beside the only part of the dock that hadn't fallen in, and the crewman held the boat steady while Yarik heaved up onto the canted boards, and then the man passed him the basket and his briefcase, and was rowing away.

The wind tugged at Yarik's hair. His jacket puffed, snapped. There were no boot prints in the mud along the shore, no muddy footprints on the old wood, either. Something about that made him need to swallow and something about the stillness of the island made him unable to. These things moved: reeds, grass, a few small specks of birds, flecks of straw lifted off a long-rotted haystack, the broad wooden sails of a far-off windmill turning slowly. He watched for a long time waiting to see anything else.

The pogost—the church, the bell tower, all that was inside the enclosure of the walls—was hidden by the bulwarks that surrounded it. They were high stone walls made higher by logs built on top, then covered with a shingled roof that ran the entire length of the stockade. But he could tell there was no chimney smoke, could see the broken glass in some of the windows, the lack in all of them of any shape stirring. Amid all that stillness he made himself move, walked off the dock, carried his briefcase and his basket through the wind and up the overgrown path towards the huge high cross that stood above the open gate.

Mud, wood, walls, windows. All the round stones of the enclosure. Standing inside it, he wondered what had happened to all the monks. If they had all left long ago, or if some had stayed, and if any who had had lived, and if they had, where were they? If there had just been one he would have gone to him, and spoken quietly, slowly, in case it had been a very long time since anyone had spoken on the island at all, and he would have asked, *Have you seen a man? Did he come out here in winter? Did he look like me?*

The only people there were in the graves. A sparse crop of wooden crosses in the overgrown field in the shadow of the smaller church. Each marker was as tall as his chest and roofed in a small peak of boards, and all of them were weathered gray and splintery and half-hidden in the brittle stalks of last summer's dead grass. He walked through it, feeling it scratch his hands, snap wind-whipped at his legs, looking for a cross of still-raw wood, a grave that was newly dug. But who would have dug it?

He set his briefcase and the basket down. For a moment, he stood in the high grass and the strong wind, still as if he had been planted there and would stay until he weathered and grayed, too. Then he began to run. He ran across the churchyard into the smaller winter chapel and shoved open the door and ran inside and his footsteps echoed as he tore around the dark of the room, and he ran out again and across the yard again and into the giant summer church and the cavernous wood-smelling world of the place and shouted at the broken candles and the

464

window light streaming over them and the icons peering back from the walls, shouted his brother's name, and he ran out and across the yard and into the bell tower and up through the close air that seemed as if it had hidden inside the deep well of the stairs for longer than he had breathed air at all, and when he reached the top he rose into the cold fresh wind again and the thin strings tied to the end of the ropes fell over his face, light and drifting as an infant's fingers. He grabbed them in his fists. He wrapped them around his knuckles. He hauled down.

The sound of the clanging hit him as if the brass bells themselves had dropped. So loud, so close by his ears. He threw his weight into the ropes and slammed the knockers against the bells again. And then they were moving him, dragging his arms up and down, his weight caught in a dance with their weight, and lifting, falling, rocking back and forth, he watched the country that spread out from far below to far away. The scattered roofs of houses that had once belonged to peasants. The hayfields scrubby with saplings. The faint strip that ran through the high grass, connecting distant house to distant house, that must, once upon a time, have been a road. The bell clangs were coming further and further apart, his body slowing in their ropes, when he saw the dark square of a field. Nearly black newly turned soil. And standing in the middle of it: a dog. The sound came to him through his still ringing ears: high, wind-borne barking. The bells clanged, and slowed, and some stopped, and the others stopped, and he hung there in the ropes, in the quiet, listening. He thought he heard a whistle. He thought he heard the faintest hint of a man's far-off voice. But when he saw the dog cross the field into the grass and saw the grass moving ahead of it, and ahead of the grass the shape of a man walking, he knew it was his brother.

They met on the phantom road halfway between the windmill and the pogost. The dog got to Yarik first, and he stopped to let it sniff at his legs and stood there watching Dima come. He wore a tunic down to his knees, some griseous sailcloth stained in patches and streaks. Over it: the same winter coat he had worn for years, the down coming out of splits in the chest and sleeves. Along the thin trail of trampled grass he walked in bare feet. And as he neared, Yarik could see what had become of his face: his black beard hung in matted tangles down to his collarbones, hid entirely his mouth, bushed out around his shrunken cheeks, below his cracked brown skin, his eyes blue as their eyes had always been.

They stood looking at each other, the dog between their legs, its huff of breath, its tail slapping. The wind tugged their hair, dragged at their coats. Dima's beard moved around his mouth as if he might speak, but he didn't. His hands hung in front of him, fingers working over each other, dirty. For a moment, Yarik wondered if his brother had gone mad. And the thought came to him that Dima had been going mad for a long time, and that he loved him and didn't care. Watching his brother's eyes, he felt his own begin to well. He looked down at the basket in his hand, held it out. He could feel his own mouth trying to shape the words that would be right and knew it was doing the same silent thing that Dima's was inside his beard.

Finally, he said, "Happy birthday, bratishka."

Dima took the basket then. And Yarik watched his brother peer through at all the jars and tins, the small boxes in their cellophane, the shrink-wrapped sausages and cheese nestled in the artificial straw, and then Dima was squatting on the ground, tearing the plastic open. The wind took it from his hands and blew it away—a shed skin crackling—and his hands roamed all the things inside, each box, each jar. Until he opened one. He dug two fingers in and lifted them gloppy with purple to his mouth, and squatted there with his eyes shut and his fingers buried in his wind-whipped beard, and beneath it his whole face gone still.

"I thought," Yarik said, and waited for his brother to finish it for him. But Dima only drew his fingers out, sucked first one then the other, and Yarik went on: "I thought maybe I'd find you dead."

His brother's eyes—such pleasure in them, such joyful gleam—looked up at him. "Happy birthday, bratan," Dima said.

When they hugged, Yarik could feel the jar still in his brother's hand, its glass curve pushing against the bone of his shoulder; he could feel his brother's ribs, his breastbone, the tunic's rough cloth, the scratchy mossiness of the beard against his own cheek. His brother's neck smelled so sharp it stung his nostrils. He breathed in. And into the warm and filthy skin he said, "I thought maybe the Chudo-Yudo got you."

Into Yarik's neck, his beard brushing against Yarik's skin, Dima said, "Don't you remember? He only eats the soul."

It was as if once his brother's lips had made words again they could not stop. The whole walk back to his house Dima chattered, hands raking through his beard, throwing themselves into gestures, trying to get the most out of each word he spoke. Yarik followed him along the faint path, wondering, Did he talk to the dog? Aloud to himself? Watching Dima's hands flap about, Yarik tried to listen as intensely as his brother spoke.

But as Dima talked of the fields he'd planted, Yarik, turning to look where his brother pointed, could only hear how Dima's voice mixed with the rustling grasses, the soft flapping of his frock. In the house yard, he knew Dima was telling him of how he'd fixed the fences, the wild cattle that he'd tamed again, the fowl he had trapped in the woods, but the words dropped in and out of the lowing blown over from the near pasture, the clanking of something stirred beneath the roof of a livestock shelter lined with hay, the clucking of hidden chickens, the breeze over woven mats on the threshing barn floor.

In there, through the open door, he could see a grain sack leaning against the wall. Slung over it: a flail, bent at the hinge that joined the handle to the club, the wood studded with knots, the handle carved with figures Yarik could not make out. While his brother talked to him of all the tools he'd found, the few he'd made, Yarik went from peg to peg touching them—the long-tined potato fork, a beet shovel's iron-slotted spoonhead, a turnip chopper propped on its crossed blade—all of them whittled with simple patterns, hints of shapes worn down by how many hands, until he came to a measuring bucket overturned on a bare patch of pounded dirt. Its curved panels were made of wood warped beneath water, held together with iron strips, growth rings swirling on its sides. But it was the carving that held his eyes—a childish attempt at long-legged birds frozen midflight—the fact that it was half-finished, that the whittled wood was raw and bright and

467

still ungrayed, that on the dirt beside the bucket the curls and slivers that had been carved off still lay. While his brother talked, he watched them come alive in some faint wind, heard it find the pitchfork tines, the teeth of the hay rake, listened to it whistling through.

Inside the house, Yarik heard how Dima had found the izba half-fallen in, how he'd used an old metal pipe as a chimney for the stove. But he didn't catch how Dima had gotten the pipe, or if it was really warm enough—these sooty walls, that cracked stove, those ancient blankets and seed-sack pillow and the heat of his lone body—to live in all through the freezing winter. Though Dima was talking about the cows, the straw around the edges of the room where they had slept last night, and Yarik saw the hens nestled in a corner, heard the rustling of their feathers, the lowing of cattle beyond the walls, a deep and ceaseless hushing that might have been the swaying of the aspen trees, or the brushing of the lake against the shore, or the sound of the clouds drifting across the sky. The longer he listened, the more he was sure that's what it was. He recognized their sound from the echo of sometime long ago when he had lived a life that let him hear it. His brother's voice, then, seemed simply part of a world that had been left alone to drift. He stood there, listening.

Dima's hand touched his shoulder. "Yarik," his brother was saying.

"Yes?" Yarik could tell from his brother's smile that Dima had asked him a question. "What?"

"Do you want to see it?"

When he reached the top of the hill, Dima turned so he was facing Yarik, still climbing, and pushed aside the tall grass and sat. Behind Dima, on what must have been the island's highest point, Yarik could see the windmill turn against the darkening sky. As he climbed, he watched its sails spinning slowly behind his brother sitting still. By the time he reached Dima and turned and sat beside him, he was breathing hard.

Somewhere behind the thickness of cloud the sun was going down. And south of there the sky was dim. And beneath it the lake was a harbinger of how much dimmer yet the sky would become. Between them was a thin dark strip of land. The southern shore. A distant hint of a place Yarik had never seen before, so far across the water it seemed almost a different world.

They watched it. The dark shapes of the ships passed back and forth out on the lake, and the pale spot in the sky slid down, and the wind grew slowly stronger, and slowly the creaking of the windmill behind them sped up, and the first fog lights of the ships blinked on, and they passed back and forth out on the lake, and the brothers sat there for a long time.

Somewhere below, a rooster crowed. Listening to the sound, Yarik thought he could feel on the back of his neck the glow of the mirrors beginning to rise behind them. He wondered if they had reached all the way to here, if his brother was subsisting on what few crops could grow without a stretch of dark. The woods below looked as woods should, the spruce boughs heavy and full, white birches budding with vernal green. If the zerkala had come, this was their first year. Next year, the birches would be gone. The year after that, the hemlocks, too. He shut his eyes. And saw, instead, the single birch he had once glimpsed from up in the sky, that spot of yellow surrounded by all the brown rest, and as he watched he saw its offspring slowly spread, imagined the entire island covered with them, a world of silver trunks, golden leaves.

There: the rooster's call again. He opened his eyes, looked at his brother. "Ivan?"

Dima shook his head. "Soon as it was warm enough," he said, "he wandered off." His mouth kept moving after the word, a small shifting beneath his beard. "Sometimes, I think I see him. A black arc out of the grass. A little gold in the woods. But he never could crow as long as that." It went on and on and before it was done another had begun. "The monks' long crowers," Dima told him. "They must have let them go, too." And he smiled. "Maybe Ivan learned from them."

Long drawn-out throaty calls coming from the forest spread below, from somewhere beneath the canopy catching the first light cast by the first mirror risen, joined by another, and another, and they listened to their sound and watched the lake drawn back by the zerkala from the darkness it had nearly reached and Yarik said, "Do you remember why Ivan Popolyov went out to kill the Chudo-Yudo? Why he went in the first place?"

"Because," Dima said, "the Chudo-Yudo had cast a spell on the land."

"And it was all darkness," Yarik said.

"All the time."

"And he wanted to bring back the light."

Hidden by his beard and covered by the wind, Dima did something Yarik could feel was almost a laugh.

"Maybe," Dima said, "the Chudo-Yudo swallowed our hook. He might have choked on it." He raised his eyebrows at Yarik, almost a smile. "Maybe we killed him after all."

"No," Yarik said, surprised by the loudness of his voice, the insistence in it when it said, again, "no." And he could hear again, the way he had said it that night on the rowboat so long ago—*No!*—not when he had felt the oar slip from his hands, or heard it splash into the water, watched it slip away on the waves, but when he had turned and seen his brother lifting his own oar out of the lock, seen Dima—ten years old and watching Yarik's face—throw his own oar purposefully away. He did not think that until now he had ever understood why.

He reached out and put his arm around his brother's thin shoulders. Dima drew up his knees, pulled the hem of his frock over them. It was getting colder. Watching the fog lights of the boats, Yarik thought he saw one coming slowly towards the island. He wished it wouldn't. He wished it would turn around and go back without him. He would stay there on that hill, under the darkness of the clouds, the wind growing into a night wind the way it had for all of time before the mirrors and would for all of time after them, he wished he could stay there, stopped, still as a hand on a wound-out clock, listening to the roosters crow, watching the lights fill the lake like a memory of stars, feeling Dima's shoulder filling the warm hollow between his arm and his chest. He wished that, wished it forever, and wishing it he tried to surround his brother with as much of himself as he could.

Acknowledgments

When I was a teenager I lived for a while as an exchange student in the Soviet Union. My experiences there set me on the path towards the writing of this book. So I owe thanks, first, to the Tarasov family, who took me into their home back then. And second, to Raisa and Oleg Kuznetsov, who did the same, two decades later, when I returned. While in Russia, Ludmila Chernova, Jesse Loeb, Julia Ioffe, and many others helped me understand the ways in which the country had changed. None of which I would have come to know if not for the ways my high school Russian teacher, Jude Wobst, helped change me long ago.

This novel, too, changed greatly over the course of its life. It found its shape due in large part to hard work and huge help from my agent, PJ Mark, who sustains me with his good judgment and generous friendship, and my dear and dedicated editor, Elisabeth Schmitz, who, along with Katie Raissian and Shelly Perron, gave this book the kind of attention most writers can only dream of. I am so lucky to work with such a team.

Josh McCall gave me extensive and thoughtful notes that improved the earlier manuscript immeasurably. As did my friends and first readers Mike Harvkey, Elliott Holt, Robin Kirman, Irina Reyn, Suzanne Rivecca, Jen Sheffield, and Laura van den Berg.

Their support is evidence of one of the great joys of writing a book like this: discovering, over and over, how giving of their time good people can be. This novel, in particular, required that I ask much of many. Dr. Helen Michaels, Dr. Michael Geusz, Dr. George W. Keitt Jr., and Florian Sicks helped me understand the details of photoperiodism in plants and animals. Dr. Ann Martin, Sarah Scoles, and Chelsea Cook did the same for the physics surrounding the space mirrors. I had help in translating the Russian from Peter Blackstock, Dr. Natasha Simes, Nikita Nelin, and Jude Wobst (no doubt dismayed at how much her former student has forgotten).

I got a lot out of a great many books, too, chief among them *At Day's Close: Night in Times Past,* by A. Roger Ekirch; *Why Work? Arguments for a Leisure Society*, edited by Vernon Richards; *Sale of the Century,* by Chrystia Freeland; *Labour and Leisure in the Soviet Union*, by William Moskoff; *The Overworked American: The Unexpected Decline of Leisure,* by Juliet B. Schor; and *Russian Fairy Tales,* compiled by Aleksandr Afanasev. Although the snippets of Pushkin's *Ruslan and Lyudmila* are my own interpretations, they were cobbled together from various translations, most notably Roger Clarke's. This book benefited from the generosity of institutions, too: the MacDowell Colony, the James Merrill House, and Virginia Center for the Creative Arts all gave me the gift of time and space. As did my ever-supportive friends Ken Banta and Tony Powe.

But no one has given me more than my family: my parents, who believe in me no matter what; my grandmother, who gives me strength; my brother, who has been my rock since the beginning; my sister-in-law, whose brilliance never ceases to expand my mind. I am, always and forever, most grateful to them. And to Jen, whose fierce heart braced me through the writing of this book, and whose wisdom helped make it better, and who I love.

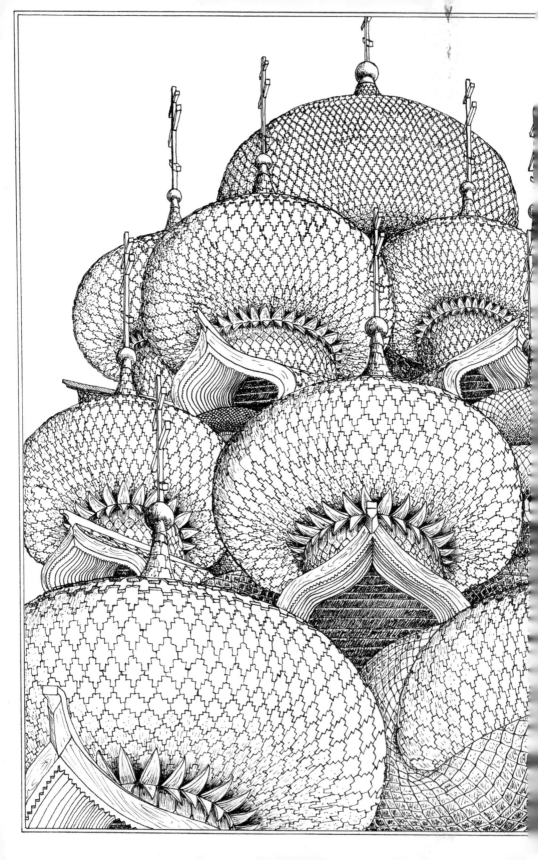